Forest of Hearts

FOREST OF HEARTS

M. A. KUZNIAR

SIMON & SCHUSTER

London   New York   Amsterdam/Antwerp
Sydney/Melbourne   Toronto   New Delhi

First published in Great Britain in 2025 by Simon & Schuster UK Ltd

Text copyright © 2025 M. A. Kuzniar

This book is copyright under the Berne Convention.
No reproduction without permission. All rights reserved.

The right of M. A. Kuzniar to be identified as the author of this work has been asserted by her in accordance with sections 77 and 78 of the Copyright, Designs and Patents Act, 1988.

1 3 5 7 9 10 8 6 4 2

Simon & Schuster UK Ltd, 1st Floor
222 Gray's Inn Road, London WC1X 8HB

For more than 100 years, Simon & Schuster has championed authors and the stories they create. By respecting the copyright of an author's intellectual property, you enable Simon & Schuster and the author to continue publishing exceptional books for years to come. We thank you for supporting the author's copyright by purchasing an authorized edition of this book. No amount of this book may be reproduced or stored in any format, nor may it be uploaded to any website, database, language-learning model, or other repository, retrieval, or artificial intelligence system without express permission. All rights reserved. Inquiries may be directed to Simon & Schuster, 222 Gray's Inn Road, London WC1X 8HB or RightsMailbox@simonandschuster.co.uk

www.simonandschuster.co.uk
www.simonandschuster.com.au
www.simonandschuster.co.in

Simon & Schuster Australia, Sydney
Simon & Schuster India, New Delhi

The authorised representative in the EEA is Simon & Schuster Netherlands BV, Herculesplein 96, 3584 AA Utrecht, Netherlands. info@simonandschuster.nl A CIP catalogue record for this book is available from the British Library.

HB ISBN: 978-1-3985-3408-7
PB ISBN: 978-1-3985-3410-0
eBook ISBN: 978-1-3985-3411-7
eAudio ISBN: 978-1-3985-34124

This book is a work of fiction. Names, characters, places and incidents are either the product of the author's imagination or are used fictitiously. Any resemblance to actual people living or dead, events or locales is entirely coincidental.

Typeset in the UK by Sorrel Packham

Printed and Bound in the UK using
100% Renewable Electricity at CPI Group (UK) Ltd

For my mum, Irena Kuzniar,
for bringing me up with love and stories,
especially our favourite 'banialuki'.

PART ONE
The Cottage

*There was nothing to do but silently
wait for the danger to pass, praying to the
old gods that I would not hear the scrape of
claws on my roof, the rattle of my door handle,
a fingernail sliding between my wooden
shutters to open them from the outside.*

CHAPTER ONE

I hated the taste of human hearts.

Rich and meaty, they sang with all the bitterness of their unspent years. Preparing them was a bloody affair that stained my hands and fingernails, leaving them reeking of iron and salt.

The heart I held now was still warm. Humming an old folksong, I pared thin slivers and set them aside. Pastry was neatly laid out inside a pie dish with the rest of filling already assembled; herbs and vegetables, accompanied by a rich tomato sauce that had been simmering since morning, with a generous glug of a dark red wine I hoped would disguise the flavour of the heart. Make me forget that it had not long been plucked from a man's chest.

I used to believe that my heart was a home for all of my hopes and dreams, but now I knew the truth; it was just meat. Pushing them off the chopping board, I slid the slivers into the pie with the same knife I'd used to steal the heart; sharp enough to slide through skin like butter, strong enough to part a ribcage. Before I lost my nerve, I capped the pie with a pastry lid and shoved it inside the stove. Only then did I slump against the countertop and take a slug of that blood-red wine. It burned a path down my core. Soon, the pie would golden and I would be forced to eat every single bite, but until then I could pretend otherwise. Pretend that I had carved out this lonely life in the last pocket of magic in Stary Bór, the oldest forest in Mazrovia, because I was suited to a solitary existence amid the bloodthirsty trees and lost spirits and the owls that watched every step I took outside. Not because I had been cursed by the Queen of Mazrovia. My own mother.

Seven hearts was the price of reclaiming my queendom.

The pie in the stove contained number six.

The sun set as I scrubbed the blood from my hands until the water ran clear. This deep in the forest, night fell like a shroud, filled with the kind of creatures who prowled beneath a moonless sky. Casting a wary glance out the window, I hurried to light candles until my cottage glowed with buttery light, offsetting the near-black wooden walls. The lower half was one room, warmed by the large stove, scented with thyme and rosemary drying in bunches along the windows. I closed and locked the shutters, one by one, sprinkling salt and dried lavender from my apron pocket over the windowsills and doorways, sealing each threshold with protection, lest something evil tried to steal inside.

While the pie cooked, I straightened the two chairs around the table, tidied the military maps and papers spilling onto the floor from the threadbare settee, and fed another log to the fire. It crackled and spat at me. It was never wise to signpost the location of your fragile existence this deep in the forest; it was hungry and I was not the only one living here who feasted on human meat. But flames were necessary for my secret, which I kept buried beneath their ashes and embers.

A sudden pain shot through my ribs.

'Not now,' I groaned, clenching my side and hoping it would subside, that it had just been a warning pain. I was not so lucky. It seized my body like I'd been caught in a hunting trap, making my vision flicker in and out. Struggling to draw a breath against the all-consuming pain, I staggered up the wooden stairs that led to my tiny bedroom clinging on like an afterthought. Pushing through the thick door that stuck on its hinges every winter, I stumbled over to my bed. There, I collapsed.

My bed was beneath the steep eaves, where a single window peered out at the wych elms hemming me in. Their branches rested on the slanted roof, scrabbling against it with gnarled fingers as if they were trying to claw their way inside. Taking deep, slow breaths, I curled up like a crescent moon until the pain passed.

Outside, the forest fell still. Silent. Too silent. Stary Bór rustled and snarled without pause until something truly dangerous wandered by, then everything held its breath to avoid attention. With my mother's curse waging war on my body, I was defenceless. Gritting my teeth, I reached out to bolt the shutters on the single window upstairs. There was nothing to do but silently wait for the danger to pass, praying to the old gods that I would not hear the scrape of claws on my roof, the rattle of my door handle, a fingernail sliding between my wooden shutters to open them from the outside. I swallowed the searing pain down, hoping that I had not drawn the eye of the forest demon, said to be descended from the god of the underworld, Weles, himself, ancient and terrible enough to cleave your mind with fear. But fear was an old ally of mine. Even back in the castle, it had been my bedfellow. Teaching me to keep my blades sharp and my wits sharper. Giving me the strength to battle the curse that lurked in my veins.

The pain vanished as quickly as it had appeared. Rising to my feet, I swept aside the curtain that shielded the single mirror I permitted inside the cottage. One quick look couldn't hurt.

When my mother had cursed me, for a moment I thought I'd glimpsed a flash of hurt in her silver eyes, but her stare had been iron, hard and imperious, simply reflecting my own pain back at me. The betrayal had been as cutting as an execution. A final severing between the queen and her sole heir. Mother and daughter. Myself and the only home I had ever known.

'Seven human hearts will be the price of your return,' my mother had hissed as she'd cursed me and stridden away. These would have been her final words, a parting horror, had I not called out after her, forcing her to turn on her heel and face the daughter she had cursed one last time: *'I'll fight this; I won't let you be the death of me.'*

My dearest companion and closest friend, Katia, had helped me flee the castle as the curse flooded through me, the banishment taking immediate effect. While I'd wheezed for air, my heart squeezed as if it were being held in a fist, she'd wrapped my greatest secret in cloth and bundled it into a knapsack with supplies before dragging me through the secret passages and dispatching me in the direction of Stary Bór. Journeying through night and day and night again, I eventually stumbled upon an abandoned cottage, nestled in a tangle of wych elms, that I laid claim to.

I spent my first winter shivering in the cottage, refusing to kill anyone. I couldn't stomach killing a bird nor skinning a rabbit – how could I ever steal a human life? But winter stayed long past its welcome, its frost creeping inside the cottage, turning my breath white and my fingers unfeeling. By the time the thaw came, my meals had stretched thinner and thinner, until I might have been glad of a heart to thicken my meagre stews. I stayed strong, believing I had survived the worst of my banishment. Until the day I awoke to a terrible, twisting pain, deep within my chest. Convinced that death was reaching its shadowed hand towards me, I'd ripped my dress open before the mirror. I'd been marked by the curse: a root was growing through my chest, the thin line of bark visible through my milky skin. A rising sense of horror engulfed me as a single leaf sprouted from the skin along my collarbone. Perhaps this was a fate worse than death. Trying to pull out the leaf had drawn blood; these strange markings were part of me now. It was as if I had swallowed the forest and it was taking root in me.

It became suddenly clear that this curse was no mere banishment; no ploy to keep me away from the castle. It was a death sentence.

For the first time, the thought of killing crossed my mind, but I refused to sacrifice innocents; instead I would sharpen my knives for the person who had cursed me. But even if I could have returned home, killing my mother would not end this curse; as a child I'd read in her secret journals that no curse she cast would end in the event of her death.

I surrendered.

I found five different people daring their luck in the forest that first summer. Five hearts that I'd devoured, making me a murderess five times over in a birth of blood and bone.

When winter had once more grasped the forest in its frozen fist, my firewood was stacked high, cupboards groaning with everything I'd set aside for the grimmest of seasons. Yet not a soul ventured into my part of the forest and so it was not long before I grew a second root, this one stretching down my left shoulder and into my arm.

Come spring, I hunted deeper and farther than before, until I came across a woodsman chopping trees. It was his heart baking in the stove now.

Now, unlacing the armoured corset I wore at all times, made of stiff black leather and veined with metal from the Iron Sea, I bared my chest to the mirror. I bore three roots. Dark scars that creaked inside me, stiff and sore. A painful reminder that my time was running out: I'd made myself a murderer, but I was still one body away from breaking my curse. Anger, remorse and guilt blossomed as I traced my roots with my fingertips. Snapping the curtain back over the mirror, I crept downstairs. The forest was beginning to resume its normal rhythm; the tap of branches on my roof, wind gusting through the leaves, the plaintive howl of prey meeting predator.

I'd just returned to my kitchen and taken the pie out of the stove when I heard it.

A hoarse scream.

Grabbing my still-bloodied knife, I ripped off my apron and dashed to the back door, sliding the peephole open to survey the dark treeline outside. Nothing rustled in the foliage, no eyes glittered in the black night. A second scream sounded, weaker than the first, filled with pain and fear. Perhaps a person, caught in a hunting trap. Perhaps my seventh and final heart.

Silently unlocking my door, I slunk into the forest like a shadow.

CHAPTER TWO

Entering the treeline was like walking into battle.

It took a beat for my eyes to adjust; the canopy was too thick for a single shaft of moonlight to light my path. Tangled ferns and prowling tree roots threatened to trip me. I paid close attention to my footwork, which was every bit as important here as it was in a swordfight. An owl swivelled its head to stare at me, its eyes preternatural lanterns that sent a shiver down my back: just an owl or was something *else* looking out through those glowing eyes? From eavesdropping on the queen's meetings with castle intelligence, I knew my mother was not the only one with spies everywhere. The owl could be hers. Or it could belong to the forest demon, keeping watch on all who passed through his territory. I did not know which was worse.

I crept in the direction of the scream, my heart thundering.

'If you step into Stary Bór, it's kill or be killed,' Katia had whispered to me during our race through the secret passageways the last time I had seen her. Her brown eyes wide with warning, her knowledge of the forest greater than mine, thanks to her

upbringing in one of its neighbouring villages, rich in old folklore and superstition. *'The forest demon will know the moment you set foot in his territory. Find shelter and stay there. He is the only thing in this world the queen fears: she will not step into his forest. You'll be safe from her there.'* She'd left the rest of her warning unvoiced: that I might be safe from my mother in Stary Bór, but only if I could survive the forest itself.

The trees rustled hungrily as I passed, smelling the dried blood on my clothes.

Somewhere nearby, a stick snapped like a spine. I froze, tightening my grip on the knife, listening. A crunch of leaves, a whisper of wind and *there*. Ragged breathing. I tiptoed towards it, hoping against hope I wasn't walking into a trap; I was in no mood to meet the forest demon tonight.

Lying against a moss-coated rock, in the crevice where two oaks met, was a man, unconscious and bleeding.

He looked a few solstices older than my nineteen years and even through the darkness, I could see he was unbearably handsome, his jawline sharp and stubbled, hair tousled. Pity he was most likely dead already; a stopped heart wouldn't count towards my seven. My curse was too cruel for that.

As I bent over him to feel for a pulse, his eyes snapped open, startling me. 'Do *not* touch me.'

I sprang back, keeping my blade pointed towards him. 'I was checking if you were still alive. You're badly wounded.'

'Believe me, I'm aware,' he groaned, holding his side. His shirt was torn, the skin beneath it ripped through with tooth or claw. A black, woollen cloak spilled off his shoulders and his dark trousers were plastered against his legs, with something that could have been mud or blood. A carved dagger hilt peeked out from his waistband. I was willing to bet my last bottle of goat's milk that it bore the likeness of Dziewanna, goddess of hunting and wild animals, favoured among hunters. Only fools, hunters and woodcutters risked their lives by wandering into Stary Bór, and this stranger's broad shoulders and strong arms marked his as either huntsman or woodcutter. The dagger instead of an axe decided me. Huntsman.

'What attacked you?' I shifted into a defensive position, cursing my own recklessness for charging out here at night. I should have stayed in my cottage, in the warmth and light, feasting on my sixth heart before the curse continued to crawl eagerly through my veins. I was still shaken from the pain of growing another root.

The stranger grunted, trying and failing to sit up. 'It was too dark to see. Do you have to keep that thing pointed at me? I'm no threat to you.'

But I had not yet decided if I was going to be a threat to him. He could be my seventh heart. The key to uncursing me, ridding this pain I carried every day and leaving me free to plot my return to the castle. Realisation dawned on him, his gaze turning wary as he drank me in, from my snug leather leggings to the loose shirt I wore, hiding my armoured corset beneath, the knife in my hand, and up to my mass of raven-black hair pinned atop my head with a second, smaller knife.

I shivered under the directness of his gaze. With a jolt, I realised I was staring back at him and began speaking in a hurry. 'You're endangering us both,' I told him. 'The trees have already smelled your blood.' I nodded at the nearest oak. Its thorned roots had risen through the earth while we'd been talking and now they were slowly creeping along the moss, towards him. 'It won't be long until others come. And, believe me, you don't want to meet *them*.' I wasn't sure why I was still speaking, I should have already claimed his heart so that I could be free of this forest and its wicked ways. But I'd never taken a life like this before. This stranger was wounded, defenceless. Killing him felt like something the queen would do and that realisation was enough for me to sheath my blade. Sighing, I offered my hand instead.

His gaze was still locked on me. 'Why should I trust you?'

I arched my brows. 'Would you rather a death sentence?'

The first root reached him, its pointed tip burrowing into his thigh. He yelled out and I lunged for him, hauling him up and away from the danger. The oaks hissed, their roots contorting in anger, branches rattling. In the distance, a howl pierced the veil of night. The huntsman clenched his jaw as he battled the pain, breathing fast and tight. Even hunched to one side, he was tall; I barely reached his collarbone. 'Are you going to tell me your name?' he bit out, sweat beading along his forehead as he continued to hold onto one of my hands, stabilising himself.

'Not here,' I hissed, scanning the darkness. 'Anyone, any*thing* could hear.' It was one of the basic laws of the forest. 'Shouldn't a huntsman know that?'

His hand tightened on mine. My palm tingled and I hesitated, glancing back at him. He was evaluating me anew, his distrust tinged with curiosity.

'I never said I was a huntsman.'

A thorned root scuttled over my boot. Snapping to attention, I grabbed his arm, yanking him away. Another howl echoed through the trees, this time close enough to send a couple of smaller creatures skittering through the undergrowth. A raven cawed a warning. Swearing under my breath, I pulled his arm over my shoulders and began to walk him back to my cottage. My back ached from supporting his weight, my newest root straining against my skin. 'We need to see to your wounds,' I said between gritted teeth, ignoring the way we were pressed together, that this was possibly the worst idea I'd ever had, that my cottage held too many secrets that could be my undoing.

'Thank you,' he whispered softly.

I could always kill him later.

CHAPTER THREE

There was something inside my cottage.

The moment I unlocked the door, I smelled it. Heady and wild, it perfumed my cottage with wrongness. You didn't grow up with a witch for a mother without recognising the tang of magic in the air. However much she'd tried to hide it, I'd been a curious child, skulking through the castle to learn as much as I could without her knowing.

'Wait here.' I ducked under the huntsman's arm, propping him up against the wall.

'You shouldn't go in there alone.' His gaze was keen, alert, despite his blood loss. *Did he smell it, too?* If so, it wasn't too much of a surprise; Mazrovia was a queendom with a rich magical heritage: even if its citizens were turning against magic now, it was still baked into their bones.

'I've dealt with worse than whatever is inside there,' I told him as he lingered on my face, assessing me anew. Some back-up could be helpful but he was a stranger, injured. He was a liability. He waited outside.

Steeling myself, I drew my biggest knife and entered alone.

It was an effort not to run over to the hearth and check that the fire still concealed my secret. *Never rush into an attack if your defence is not rock-solid*, Pan Jedrick, my weapons master, and one of the people I missed most from the castle, used to lecture as he swiped at my boots with his staff, searching for weaknesses in my stance. Short and stocky, with a head as bald as the mountaintop on which he'd grown up, in the farthest western reaches of the queendom, his harsh accent echoed through my memories. *Or your last thought will be the worst kind of regret.* It was his knife I clenched now; its hilt embossed with the mountains and swollen moon of the Dragonspines, its blade able to cut through magic.

Keeping my back to the wall, I circled the lower floor, searching for the source of the magic that was burning my nostrils. When I drew near to the fire, I finally permitted myself a single, sweeping look. Relief flooded me; the hearth was undisturbed.

Something rushed along the kitchen floor.

I whirled round, trying to see where it was. *What* it was. 'Where are you hiding?' I raised my knife, creeping closer.

It flew out from beneath the cupboard and lunged under the stove. It was an unformed, shadowy mass with seeping tendrils of darkness. My hand shook as I swallowed my dread down. Showing fear was declaring weakness, and weakness was an invitation to be eaten. *Kill or be killed*, Katia had said. Eat or be eaten, more likely.

The heart I'd baked into a pie sat atop the stove: was that what this creature was after?

'Come out, come out,' I whispered, reaching up to pull my second knife from my hair. I would not lose my sixth heart.

Something grabbed my wrist from behind.

I span round, striking out with my first knife.

But the huntsman moved faster, seizing that wrist, too.

'Let me go,' I seethed, about to raise a knee to kick him where he'd fall to his knees, but he shook his head at me, a hint of a smirk on his lips.

'You don't want to do that,' he told me.

'Go to Nawia,' I growled, attempting to free myself so that I could dispatch him to the underworld myself. With a twist of my wrists, I tried snapping my arms down to free them, but the huntsman's grip was unyielding, his hands flexible and strong, easily resisting my efforts to break free from him. I frowned. How could he be stronger than me, injured as he was? Perhaps Pan Jedrick had always taken it easier on me than I'd believed.

His smirk grew, further enraging me. 'That's a domowik.' He nodded to the horrifying pool of shadows skulking under my stove.

I paused, lowering my knee and glancing at the shadows. One tendril was still visible, lying on my kitchen floor like a fat snake. 'You're lying,' I said flatly. 'Nobody's seen a domowik in years.' I ought to have known; the castle had once had hundreds of protective house spirits dwelling beneath its turrets, but they had all evaporated when the queen began her purge against magic a decade ago. I still remembered the one that slumbered under my bed when I was little; it used to steal my hairbrush to sleep with. 'And that looks nothing like a domowik. According to the stories,' I tacked on hastily. Not everyone was lucky enough to have had a house spirit and my true identity was a secret second only to the one I harboured in my fireplace.

'Nobody's seen a fully formed domowik in years,' the huntsman corrected me. 'This one seems to have been lucky enough to have survived the Purge, though it's in a weakened state. Still worth not angering it though. Give it a few saucers of milk and I'd wager it will start to recover its shape.'

'Fine,' I grumbled.

'If I let you go, are you still going to kick me?'

I levelled a glare at him. 'If you *don't* let me go, you're going to wish I'd only kicked you.'

He gave me a slow smile. 'Maybe I should keep holding on to you, then.'

My stomach tightened, my cheeks warming against my will. 'Try it and suffer.' I had never wanted to kick a man more. If he hadn't been injured . . . I resisted.

The huntsman slowly released my hands, watching me carefully. His eyes were a deep holly-green with flecks of gold that glinted in the lanternlight. My hair chose that moment to finish unknotting since I'd pulled the knife from it. It tumbled down around my shoulders, as wild and black as ebony.

The huntsman's eyes darkened. 'I was worried you were going to kill me earlier but, gods, it might just be worth it.'

Guilt snapped its jaws around me like a trap. My previous six victims' faces flashed through my mind in quick succession. It took everything in me not to glance at the pie sitting behind him, not to draw his attention to one of my secrets. 'If you thought I was going to kill you, why did you let me bring you here?'

He shrugged then winced, clamping a hand on his side as he suddenly remembered his wound. 'I wouldn't have survived much longer out there anyway,' he admitted. His shirt was stiff with blood, so much blood that I wondered how I hadn't smelled it when we'd walked back to my cottage together. I was covered in it, too. Bile rose in my throat, along with the memory of the last words I'd exchanged with my mother as her curse took root in me. *'I'll fight this,'* I'd called out after her, my heart already tightening as the banishment took effect. *'I won't let you be the death of me.'* A strange little look had flickered over her face as she'd glanced back at me. *'Darling Snow White, my purehearted girl, you do not have what it takes to fight this. You're not a monster.'*

I swallowed it all back down. So what if I'd become a monster? I was *alive*.

'I need to see to your wound – now.' With one boot, I kicked out at the nearest chair, spinning it round and pushing the huntsman down onto it. Unlike when he'd grabbed my wrists, he yielded easily. Almost . . . eagerly. 'Take your shirt off,' I ordered, lifting my box of healing supplies down from one of the kitchen shelves.

He grinned. 'Only if you ask nicely.'

Placing my hands on the armrests, I bent closer as he sucked in a breath. 'Would you prefer the cold embrace of death?' I whispered seductively, apparently unable to play nice. Gods, this stranger, this huntsman, had creeped under my skin.

His chuckle was deep, dark. Delicious. Unbuttoning his shirt with bloody fingers, he revealed his chest; taut with the definition I'd expect from a huntsman with his arrogant attitude, taking no heed of the danger before venturing into Stary Bór. I glanced away, pretending it had no effect on me. Then he hissed between his teeth. The torn rags of his shirt clung to his wound like moss to bark. Gently taking over, I peeled fabric from skin, revealing his shredded side. 'Whatever attacked you had no intention of killing you,' I told him, examining the claw marks. They were shallow, but the surrounding skin was swollen crimson red, coated with something that looked like sticky sap. Poison had clearly been secreted into his wound, and there was only one monster I knew that was capable of that.

'It must have been my lucky day,' he said dryly.

'You've been poisoned.' My chest tightened like I was growing another root. 'It was a bauk.' Fear seeped into my voice. 'They have dagger-sharp claws that release a slow-acting poison, but they're patient creatures. It'll wait until the poison takes hold before it returns. That way, it can take its time.' I'd never crossed paths with a bauk before, but Pani Agata, one of my tutors when

I was a child, had had me well versed with all the different kinds of creatures that prowled through Mazrovia, from Stary Bór to the Iron Sea to the Dragonspine Mountains, and every territory in between. Each bauk carried its own signature venom, a specific scent to enable tracking its prey.

And I'd dragged the huntsman through the forest to my cottage. Leaving a bloody trail right to my door. 'I'm a damned fool,' I muttered, twisting my hair back and shoving my smaller knife through it.

'It isn't a weakness to care for others,' the huntsman said softly.

'You would say that,' I pointed out. 'I'm going to die because of you.'

He looked at me, considering. 'I couldn't help noticing your growing patch outside.'

'I'm a keen gardener,' I snapped sarcastically.

'Are you?' His tone was knowing. 'Or are you a witch?'

An old memory rose, pulling me back to the age of seven. The age when a witch's heart ripened with magic, and the only time my mother had ever regarded me with something like hope. 'Let us see if you are truly my heir,' she had murmured, taking my hand and slitting a finger before I could pull it away. She'd squeezed seven droplets of blood into a bowl before conjuring an iridescent violet flame. Careful not to touch it with a single fingertip, she stared at the fire, at my blood. But I was staring back at the flames reflected in her eyes, along with something else: fear. When I was seven, I had not yet realised my mother was a witch, that she had been testing me for that inherited witchhood. But I did learn something else that day: my mother feared fire.

Later I discovered the truth: witch's blood burns. Mine did not.

'Believe me, I am no witch.' My laugh was sour. By the time I'd grown older and more curious, learned that my mother was a witch and that nobody knew outside her most trusted advisors, it had been too late, and she'd already begun her Purge.

Witches paid with blood for their magic. A tithe. But in Mazrovia, the land itself was soaked with old residual magic, enough to sustain the magical creatures that wandered through its forests and mountains and lakes. Until my mother decided that her own blood was not enough to pay for the kind of magic she wanted to use. Then, she started leaching it from her own queendom, forcing all magical creatures, like the domowik, to flee. Further and further, until they were stuck living in pockets of magic that the queen hadn't yet exploited for her own gain. Like Stary Bór.

Everyone outside the queen's circle of trust believed that she was simply banning magic under the laws of the new religion sweeping the queendom, which enforced all citizens to denounce the old gods, magic and witchery, and turn to the One True Path. I understood why my mother kept her witchblood secret; since the famine that had hounded Mazrovia decades ago, when neighbours and friends had turned on witches. Fear of another famine sent Mazrovians running into the arms of the True Path. That, too, I understood. I did *not* understand why my mother was its greatest advocate, using the religion to make sure she was the only one who could control magic. I guess power tasted sweet enough to disguise the hypocrisy. No matter, soon I would be rid of this abhorrent curse and the queendom would find somebody else to sit on its throne.

'Monkshood, laburnum, belladonna,' the huntsman recited. Well. Someone had a good memory. Along with sufficient knowledge to recognise the plants on sight, in the dark. He was not to be underestimated. 'You can't have grown them by accident. Not this deep in Stary Bór.' His breath was labouring now. 'You have a poison garden; you must know how to craft antidotes. Stop this poison surging through my veins and I swear I'll kill anything that comes sniffing at your door.'

Closing my eyes, I massaged my temples. This was considerable trouble for a stranger. But a poisoned heart was no use to me. When I opened my eyes, his stare was pinched with pain. 'I'm not making any promises,' I warned him. Relief flooded his face. Something within me ached with regret. In a bid for distraction, I rummaged through my healing supplies for a sterilising tonic. I may not have been a witch, but crafting a potion only required following a recipe, and I'd spent enough years hoping that my witchhood would still take hold, that I could be the daughter my mother had set her sights on, that I'd snuck into her private rooms and memorised her spell books. Those crisp pages of parchment promising a world of power, read like a fairy tale to one little girl who only wanted to be good enough for her mother.

Seven hearts was the cost of returning to the castle, but the queen's heart would be my eighth. For I did not forget my grudges. I nurtured them until they bloomed, as deadly as the glossy black berries of my belladonna plant.

'Swear that you will not lay a hand on me again,' I said.

'I swear it to the gods,' he said simply, sincerely.

'Good.'

'Unless you ask me,' he added.

I rolled my eyes. 'I'm going to clean your wound first—'

'Kazimierz – Kaz,' he said, his voice deep and even, giving his name weight. A significance that I didn't yet know. But I would find out. 'And you are?'

'Elka.'

He murmured my name under his breath. It sounded sweet on his tongue. I gathered myself together with a little jolt.

'This might sting a little, Kaz.'

CHAPTER FOUR

The huntsman slept in my bed.

After I'd cleaned his wound and packed it with antiseptic herbs and moss, I'd brewed a special tea to battle the poison taking hold over him, with willow bark to ease his pain and a pinch of lavender to guide him to sleep. With a prick of my thumb and a whisper, 'To the gods above and below, accept this tithe and let my will be done.' I stirred a droplet of blood into the steaming tea, watching it vanish like mist. Grinding my molars, I beseeched Dola, the goddess of fate, to let it work, to let my witchless blood be enough to pay the cost of the magic I was requesting. In Mazrovia, anyone could do simple magicwork if they paid the price, but only those with witchblood could effect real power. The gods listened to them, hungry for a taste of their blood.

Kaz had grown pale and lifeless as I'd helped him upstairs, falling into a deep, dreamless sleep the moment he'd laid down on my bed. His eyelashes were unfairly long and dark, making him look younger, more vulnerable. 'You better be worth all this trouble,' I sighed.

Now, padding down the stairs, I grabbed my bucket of well water, next to my unwashed dishes, and a lantern, eyeing my cold heart-pie with distaste and remorse, before slipping out into the darkness.

The domowik followed. When I shut the door behind me, it perched on the doorstep, a curious shadow watching me. Since the cottage was shuttered up tight, not a scrap of light shone through, and I was strangely touched that the domowik had braved the night with me. By lanternlight, I made out the dark wooden cottage, tangled in the mossy branches of the two wych elms it sat between, my little poison garden, and Kaz's blood dripping down the wall he'd leaned against earlier.

Leaving the lantern next to the domowik, I wet my cleaning rag in the bucket and started scrubbing. Freezing scarlet water trickled up my sleeve, making me shudder. 'Perun give me strength,' I muttered, invoking the god of thunder, chief of all gods, as the huntsman's poisoned blood marked me, too.

The forest was a dark maw, waiting to snap shut on its prey. It was thick with the scent of rich earth, of bark and moss and green things, with an underlying pungent tang. I'd become well used to its sounds and smells since I'd made the forest my home, but I was careful not to mistake feeling at home with feeling safe. The back of my neck prickled, like something was watching me from between the trees.

Moving swiftly, I dabbed my bloody cleaning cloth onto the trunk of an old oak a few paces away. Then the tree two paces beyond that, and so on, my heart beating harder with each step further into the black forest. Tree roots creaked underfoot, winding round the trunks of neighbouring trees like vines, craving a taste of the blood trail I was creating. Hardly daring to breathe, I wrung the cloth onto a fern, squeezing out the last bloody drops before hurling it as far away as possible.

Then I fled back to the safety of my cottage. When the bauk came tracking the scent of its poison, and it *would* come, hopefully it would follow my re-directed path, taking it back into the forest and leaving the cottage alone.

Pausing only to snatch up the lantern I'd left outside, I ran back through my front door. The domowik scurried along at my ankles; it seemed like it had been waiting on the threshold for my safe return. *What was happening?* I'd gone from living alone to saving a stranger, now sleeping in my bed, and letting a domowik camp out in my kitchen. Bolting the door shut, I scattered salt and lavender over it for luck.

Turning a critical eye over the rest of the cottage, I began tidying, hiding anything I didn't want Kaz to find. Buying myself some time before I confronted that pie sitting in my kitchen. As I swept military maps and charts out of view, stowing them beneath my clothes in my wooden chest, I felt eyes on my back. 'Fine.' I sighed, trudging over to the kitchen and retrieving my last bottle of goat's milk from a pail of icy stream water, kept on a slab of cold stone. Life in the cottage was more rustic than the castle, which was filled with modern comforts and luxuries fresh from the Amber City, but lately it had been getting harder and harder to miss it. In the castle, the beasts hid their teeth and claws behind politics and courtly machinations, but their bite was just as deadly.

'There you go.' I poured some milk into a saucer and set it on the floor. The domowik rushed over at once. 'I guess you still have a mouth after all,' I said, watching it suck up the milk, leaving the empty saucer rocking on the floor. 'I'm sorry about the Purge.' I refilled the saucer and sat on the floor beside the domowik. One shadowy tendril tilted my way. Listening. 'I'm glad you're not all gone,' I whispered, 'And I hope more of you are hiding out here, too.'

I wondered which part of Mazrovia the domowik had fled from; the land that my mother had plundered of magic was left scarred. Plants and trees grew slower, smaller. Crops failed. I had believed that all the protective house spirits had vanished once the magic was depleted from their homes, but it was cheering that they hadn't been killed off, only reduced to this formless shape as they searched for a new home.

'We're both far from home now,' I told the domowik, reaching for a fork and my heart-pie. With a deep, gathering breath, I speared the pastry with my fork and began to eat. It was cold. The meat – for I would continue to tell myself it was only meat, even as my stomach knew the difference and roiled like I was on board a merchant ship on the Iron Sea – was tough and slimy. It slipped down my throat in unpleasant chunks. I forced myself to finish every last bite. Until the single candle in the kitchen had burned low. Until the forest began its nightly howling. Until my legs had gone numb from sitting on the cold floor. The domowik stayed beside me the entire time. I gave it a chunk of my leftover pastry. 'Number six,' I said bleakly, staring at the empty dish.

I was feeding another log to the fire when it began.

It started with a gut-curdling snarl that sent ripples of fear down my spine. The bauk was hunting us. Sitting back on my knees, I scanned the lower floor of the cottage. All the windows were locked and shuttered, both doors bolted shut. Thick lines of salt marked each possible entrance.

A second, louder snarl sounded. My stomach twisted; that one was too close for comfort. My hand fell to the knife I wore at my hip as I waited for another sound, too afraid to move in case I signalled my position. Silently pleading that the bauk had taken my bait and ventured deeper into the forest, away from my crooked little cottage. A moment of silence passed. Then another, and another. Somewhere in the distance, an owl hooted, a nightjar sang, and the trees moaned in the wind.

Slowly, I stood. The floorboards let out a low groan, sending the domowik scurrying back under the stove. Smiling to myself at how jumpy it was, I rolled my neck, easing the stiffness that had set in while I'd crouched before the fire, prepared to defend the secret I'd hidden there with blood and blade. Now that the bauk had carried on its way, following my fake blood trail, I could focus on my next problems: what to do with the huntsman asleep in my bed, and where I was going to find my seventh heart.

Something smashed into the side of the cottage.

Smothering a scream, I unsheathed my knife, stumbling back to survey the damage. The windows were faceless eyes, the external shutters had held up from the bauk hurling itself into them. But they wouldn't hold for long. The creature howled outside. My blood turned to ice. Bauks were tracking beasts, hunters. Once they latched onto their poisoned victim's scent, nothing could stop them from devouring their prey. Nothing, save death.

I stood beside the fireplace, knife in hand. Waiting. I could hear the bauk through the wall, making strange huffing sounds.

It was *sniffing*.

A bolt of panic lanced straight through me – could it smell Kaz's blood on me? I'd scrubbed my hands and arms clean, but I'd been so confident in my plan to redirect the bauk that maybe I hadn't been as careful as I could have been. Lifting a shaking hand to glance at it under the firelight, I swallowed nervously. Blood had dried under my fingernails. The bauk threw itself at the shutters again. The entire cottage shook. It had targeted the closest window to me. I crept away, into the middle of the cottage, next to my little table and pair of chairs. There, I dipped a hand into a basket of dried herbs and salt, and crushed thyme and rosemary in my hands, attempting to disguise the scent of blood clinging to me.

It went quiet again.

This time, I was not so naïve to think that the bauk had left. I could still hear it sniffing outside the cottage.

The bauk lurched at the same shuttered window again. This time, it cracked, splintering straight down the centre like a rotten trunk splitting in two. Falling back into a defensive stance, I fought to keep my panic at bay as I waited for the bauk to jump at the cottage again. This time, it would make it straight through the window.

But I hadn't heard the bauk fall back to the forest floor. It was still breathing through the split in the shutters. As I stared at the black glass, at the wood that was slowly giving way on the other side, something moved through the crack in the shutters. An eyeball. The bauk had fixed one orange eye to the crack and was watching me.

Rooted to the spot, I stared back at the slit pupil, my palm wet on my hilt. Just as I was ordering myself to move, to open the window and stab the bauk in its eye, it pulled away. My lungs almost collapsed in relief. Until one of its claws punctured the wood, its hooked nail scoring the glass with a screech that made my skin crawl. Then a second claw, then a third.

It wasn't until it had dragged the first claw away that I realised: it was climbing up the outside of the cottage.

CHAPTER FIVE

I threw myself up the stairs, knife in hand.

Kaz was still asleep. The tea I'd brewed for a deep healing sleep had apparently been too effective and now I'd left him defenceless against the beast that would stop at nothing to devour him alive. Cursing my own stupidity, I stood at the foot of my bed like a sentry, determined to protect him; if he was going to die, then it would be by my hand alone. Twirling my knife from blade tip to hilt, I listened to the bauk's scraping claws as it climbed higher. And higher still. Until I heard the unmistakable sound of a heavy beast pulling itself up onto the eave that slanted over my bed.

It was on the roof.

I held my breath as it paused, sniffing. With the deep slant of the roof, the bauk was as close to me now as Kaz was, asleep on my bed. Its claws scrabbled for purchase on the wood right above my head. Sweat slid down my armoured corset as I stood there, half waiting for the bauk to crash through my roof and land on top of me. The roof was making an alarming creaking sound now, reminding me that I didn't know how well built it was or wasn't; I'd just moved in the day I found it and nobody else had come to claim it since.

As long as we remained still and silent as a corpse, perhaps—

Kaz's eyes snapped open.

Turning to look at me, he sat up and opened his mouth.

Before I could think, I silently vaulted onto the bed, pinning his hips down with my thighs and pressing my hand over his mouth. His green-gold eyes widened at me. I lifted my eyes to the ceiling and back onto his, watching the moment he realised that the bauk was on the roof, its claws clacking over the wood as it searched for a way in.

Kaz gave a sharp nod, then I felt him move beneath me. Face to face, with one hand on my knife, the other on his mouth, I watched as he slowly slipped a hand under my thighs. My breath caught.

Kaz slowly withdrew his dagger. His hunting blade. This close, I saw that it wasn't carved with a token of the hunting goddess, Dziewanna, but the face of a god I had no name for, their eyes deep and searching, able to see straight through my flesh and down to my bones, my soul, my marrow. Jagged lines surrounded their face like broken branches. A shiver stroked my spine. If this was just a likeness, I had no desire to meet the owner of those eyes.

The bauk suddenly shifted direction, building up speed as it crawled overhead. Kaz lurched up. Wrapping his arms round me, he lifted me up against his chest as he leaped off the bed, before setting me down on my feet, my thoughts whirling.

Kaz was still holding me tightly. His breath warmed my neck as he bent his head towards me, sending my imagination spinning wild and free. Then his mouth found my ear and my imagination ground to a halt. 'It's coming down the chimney,' he whispered.

Kaz ran downstairs without making a sound. I followed on his heels. Panic screamed down my veins; the bauk was headed straight for my secret. I had to reach it first, but when I got there, I didn't know what to do. Though Kaz was injured, he was still managing to move in ways which surprised and alarmed me, making it clear that he was a formidable force, which begged the question of how he had fallen victim to the bauk that was currently hunting him in the first place. He was a stranger with secrets of his own and I could not let him discover my secret at any cost. Guarding the fireplace would only signpost that I had something interesting to hide, and I did not know this man – I could not trust him – and I had a troubling suspicion that if we were pitted against each other, that would be a battle I would lose.

There was only one thing I could do.

Just as the bauk was crawling down the chimney, I ran towards the fire and looked up. A long muzzle, dripping with dark liquid, and a pair of slit pupils looked back. Shoving my fear down into a box and slamming the lid shut, I reached up into the chimney with both arms, and grabbed the bauk as it snarled, twisting and turning to try to fasten its jaw on me. Through the flash of the fire, I saw rows of long, jagged teeth and a coarse grey hide.

'Elka!' Kaz shouted. My eyes were stinging with smoke, the

fire starting to burn through my shirt, but I couldn't let the bauk, nor the huntsman see what was hiding in my fire. I would protect it even if it killed me. Yelling with effort, I pulled with everything I had, fur coming loose as the bauk writhed with fury. With another great heave, it lost its grip on the stone and fell down the chimney. Before it could land in the fire, I heaved it towards me, sending both of us careening onto the cottage floor.

Kaz grabbed my waist, yanking me up and away from the bauk. 'That was a *terrible* idea.'

'I'm not done yet,' I shot back, unsheathing two knives at once and circling the bauk.

It rolled onto its hind legs and stood, taller than a bear, its head stooped against the ceiling. It was a grey-furred beast with a long snout that enabled its incredible sense of smell and deadly claws, leaking venom. With a roar that shook the cottage, it sprang at me.

'Watch its claws,' Kaz yelled. 'They're venomous.'

'You don't say!' I ducked under one swiping claw, gashing the bauk's chest before ducking out of the way of the other claw. It roared again and I braced, waiting for it to charge again so that I could deliver a killing blow.

The bauk pivoted and went for Kaz instead.

I jumped onto my settee and launched myself onto the bauk's back. It didn't notice. It was still advancing on Kaz, its attention locked on its prey.

Kaz's lips curled into a malicious smile. One that promised

such violence and pain, I hesitated. Until I saw the first bloom of blood on the fresh shirt I'd given him.

'Perun give me strength,' I cursed before driving my knife between the bauk's shoulders with a sickening crunch.

Now it noticed me.

With an enraged howl, it whipped round, trying to shake me off. I wrapped my legs around it tighter, yanking my knife out to plunge it back in again. With both hands on the hilt, I swung my legs free, letting my body weight drag the knife down through the bauk until my feet hit the floor.

The bauk crashed down, glassy eyed and gutted.

Panting, I bent down to pull my knife free before I realised I was covered in dark, viscous blood. I looked like I'd been painted with the blood of my six victims, my inner darkness displayed, but Kaz didn't look away from me. He did not shy away from the monster that stood before him. My chest heaved with effort, my breaths fast and hard, and still he looked at me.

'There could be more,' he said eventually, sinking down onto the settee with a grimace. 'Too much blood has been spilled in your cottage for the forest not to take notice.'

Glancing around, I winced. The floorboards were soaked in blood, running down between the planks and into the waiting earth below. Morning wouldn't arrive for hours yet, but this couldn't wait. Dead bodies always attracted attention in Stary Bór, one of the reasons I'd never murdered anyone in my cottage before; the clean-up after preparing a heart for the stove took longer than the heart did to bake. Though this was different: I'd slain the bauk in self-defence. 'Killing is always more about the cleaning,' I complained without thinking.

Kaz tilted his head curiously. He was pale, sweat beading along the stubble of his upper lip, his breath too shallow for my liking. 'Go back upstairs,' I told him, 'You've overexerted yourself when your injury hasn't had time to heal; you need to rest. When I've got rid of this,' I jerked my head at the dead bauk. 'I'll bring you another brew to help. Your heart is working hard to rid your body of poison.'

With a nod, Kaz made to stand. He fell back onto the settee. Stepping around the bauk, I grasped his hands and pulled him up. He wobbled in place, looking down at me, my hands swallowed in his. They were too hot, feverish, giving me grave concern that I'd slain the bauk only for him to succumb to its poison. 'Sometimes I don't think I have a heart any more,' he whispered.

A lump lodged itself in my throat. 'Me neither.'

'Oh, no,' he tilted my chin up with one finger, searching my eyes intently. 'No, you have a heart. If you didn't, you never would have saved me.'

I sucked in a breath. Gods curse him, this huntsman was making it exquisitely difficult to consider stealing his heart. The way he looked at me . . . 'Twice,' I pointed out, not letting him see how his words had rattled me. How *he* rattled me, with his finger lingering just below my chin as if he couldn't bear to break that contact between us. I hadn't been touched with such simple affection since Piotr, the queen's guardsman who'd sneaked into my chamber every night in the long, hot summer before I fled the castle. And that had not felt like this.

'Twice,' he echoed, letting his hand fall from my face. 'I'll try not to require your services a third time.' He gave me a wan smile. I felt the loss of that touch in ways I didn't quite understand, and definitely must not think of again. I just missed simple human contact, that was all; since my curse I'd only laid hands on someone with violence. That was the only reason I was coming alight under Kaz's touch.

Then his eyes rolled back to their whites and he collapsed.

CHAPTER SIX

Kaz slumped against me. My battle rush had burned out, leaving me weak and aching, and I couldn't fight to hold him up for long. We slid onto the floor together, the huntsman falling across my legs, my hips. Sliding out from underneath him was no easy feat; Kaz was broad as well as tall and weighed as much as a giant boulder. Eventually, I managed it, propping Kaz up against the settee, his head lolled back onto the faded cushions. The domowik scuttled over, its tendrils flickering in distress. Lifting the back of my hand to his forehead, I cringed at the blazing heat emanating from him. 'He needs a stronger antidote,' I told the domowik. Somehow, I was glad I wasn't alone for this. 'Herbs won't do the trick any more.' It would have to be blood magic alone. In the end, it always came back to blood. This time, I squeezed half a cup of my own into a saucepan, warming it gently as I added milk and lavender to ease it down his throat, and whispered spellwork with a touch of despair. 'To the gods above and below, *please* accept this tithe and let my will be done. Save him.'

*

After I'd helped Kaz to my bed again, I shut my eyes and leaned against the stairs. My body was screaming in pain, battered and bruised from one of the hardest days of my life. From killing my sixth victim to rescuing Kaz, suffering the curse's wrath, then slaughtering a bauk to rescue Kaz again, this day had been one long bloodbath. The newest root within me was tight and rigid. When I slid my sleeve up, the skin was blister-red and sore. And now I had to drag the dead bauk out of my cottage and dump it far enough away in the pitch-black forest that I wouldn't attract any other deadly scavengers, before returning to scrub my floors clean. At this point, I would have taken Kaz's injury if it meant I could sleep.

Instead, I stumbled downstairs.

'Let's get rid of you, then,' I muttered when my feet hit the lower floor, forcing me to stand and confront the body of the bauk.

It wasn't there.

Now I was awake and alert. Grabbing my knife, I whirled round, looking for the beast's body. Nothing. My cottage was too small for anyone to hide in, let alone a hulking bauk that was larger than a bear. If I couldn't see it, then it wasn't here any more. But if it wasn't here, where in Nawia was it? Surely it couldn't still be alive; my blade had almost torn it in two, and I'd never read anything about bauks being able to recover themselves from such injuries. Or walk the earth, undead – it wasn't a strzyga. Oh gods, if it was still alive, if I had to fight that thing again, I didn't know how I would manage to kill it a second time.

Then I noticed the floor. 'What in the—' The wooden floorboards weren't just free of blood, they were shining. Buffed and polished. I gaped, mistrusting this vision. Maybe I'd hit my head when fighting because this could *not* be real.

The domowik shyly slithered around the settee, its shadow puddling together to stand in front of me, reaching up to my knees. 'Did you do this?' I gasped. It gave a gentle flicker. 'Thank you,' I told it, my voice wavering a little. *'Thank you.'* It flickered again, sidling a little closer. I glanced at the settee, looking plumper than I'd ever seen it, and the flames roaring in the fireplace. My secret was safe. And sleep was calling my name. Then I glanced back at the domowik, which was still standing in front of me, almost like it was expecting something.

'Do you want a biscuit?'

I awoke with a jolt, knife in hand, my heart hammering. Sitting up, I blinked at the stone walls surrounding me, until the last dregs of my dream misted away, leaving the dark wooden walls of my little cottage in their place. I was in the forest, not the castle. I'd been dreaming of riding again. It had been the one skill I had learned that hadn't been ordered by my mother. Perhaps that was why it was the only thing I'd done that had filled her eyes with fear as she watched me from the window of the highest turret. But, oh, how I had loved it. Migot was my favourite to ride. She was the biggest and the fastest. Well, second biggest. But not even Pani Smok, who'd taught me to ride, dared mount Ogień. Migot was powerful and sleek-muscled but tender-hearted, too. I was the only one she would lower herself to the grass for, as I struggled towards her under the heft of my leather saddle. On good nights, I dreamed of soaring over the ground with her. On the bad ones, I dreamed of the sound she'd made when my mother had had her killed.

Last night had been one of the bad ones. My stomach cramped. Grief, anger and my heart-pie dinner twisted my guts. Fumbling for lavender in my pocket, I pressed a sprig of it to my nose, inhaling deeply until my stomach settled and my mind cleared. *Kaz*. Had he survived? Springing to my feet, ignoring the way my body creaked and groaned in protest, I climbed upstairs.

The huntsman was abandoned in sleep. His defences down, his arms spread wide as he made himself at home in my bed, a lock of tawny hair fallen across his forehead. Gently, I tucked it back, letting my knuckles graze his face. He really was too handsome for his own good. And mine.

But his fever had passed.

Smiling in relief, I wandered back downstairs and worked on the fire. When it was roaring with heat, I opened the windows and shutters to let in the fresh dawn air. This morning, Stary Bór was its best, most deceptive self; nightjars were calling to each other, and the trees smelled like rain. A trail of chanterelles had cropped up overnight, so I grabbed a basket and popped outside to fill it. Until I spotted a lone tree root crawling over the moss in my direction and had to retreat in a hurry, leaving my basket half empty. After taking another quick peek at the huntsman slumbering in my bed, I paid a trip to the well just beyond my kitchen door for a bracing wash, ridding myself of the blood crusted in my hair and under my fingernails. The domowik came outside with me. It looked a bit plumper than the day before, so I fed it another couple of biscuits.

I was stirring a cauldron of soup over the kitchen hearth when Kaz finally sauntered downstairs, buttoning a clean white shirt over his freshly bandaged chest. One of mine. On me, it would disguise my armoured corset and root-hardened veins, reaching down to my knees. On him, it was tight. Tight enough to distract me into dropping my spoon in the cauldron. Cursing under my breath, I fished it out, forcing myself to stop staring. *Honestly*, it was like I'd never seen muscles on a man before. 'How did you sleep?' I asked casually. The domowik shuddered and I frowned at it, alarmed at the huffing noise it was making until I realised it was laughing at me. I threw another biscuit at it.

'Like the dead,' Kaz said, then grimaced. 'Only alive, thank the gods. And you?' Our eyes locked. I gripped my spoon harder, battling the way my stomach dipped and soared when he looked at me like that. Like I was every bit as delicious as the cakes I'd feasted on back in the castle. Like he wanted to devour me. 'Whatever you did worked; I lived to see another day.' His gaze flitted past me, to the kitchen window and the bluster that was setting in outside. The fragile dawn light had long since faded and I'd needed to shut the windows and light candles already. Another gloomy afternoon beneath the forest canopy. Soon, it would rain; the air was moss-thick with the scent of petrichor. 'How long did I sleep for?' Kaz rubbed his forehead with the back of his hand, making his hair fall further into disarray. I couldn't stop picturing the way he'd looked in my bed. Dishevelled and undone.

It was an effort not to let the spoon fall back into the soup. 'You needed it,' I told him weakly.

He swept into my kitchen nook, peering into the cauldron I stirred. 'That smells good.' He reached a finger in to taste it.

I swatted him away. 'I haven't finished yet. In the next few days I need to go to the nearest hamlet, Sanok, to pick up some things from their market since somebody's drunk the last of the milk.' I glanced at the domowik, who retreated sheepishly under the stove. I slid it another biscuit, still grateful beyond measure that it had cleaned the entire cottage for me. 'But that's half a day's walk and you're not strong enough to make it yet.'

Kaz leaned against the nearest countertop. 'If you'd planned to go today, you could leave me here.'

I pursed my lips. I didn't trust a stranger in my home, with my secret in the hearth, without me. And between saving his life three times in the space of a single day, we hadn't discussed how long he would be staying. 'No.'

'Oh, Elka, how much mischief do you think I can get up to by myself?' His mouth quirked. I couldn't stop wondering what he was thinking. Or how my name sounded in his mouth, his tongue curling over the 'L'.

I cleared my throat, turning my attention back to my cauldron. 'There's a storm coming, can't you feel it? The temperature's dropped.'

He shivered. 'Now that you mention it, it does feel like winter has returned.'

'We'll have to stay put and ride it out. I have plenty of firewood.' I didn't mention my dwindling pantry, but I'd made do with less.

The cottage glowed with candlelight, clouded with the scent of my wild garlic and leek soup, and the rye loaf I'd baked earlier, now resting on the side. It was quite the cosy, domestic scene if you ignored the stained pie dish, soaking away the last traces of human flesh. I poured a ladle of soup into a cracked bowl. 'Here, take this and sit next to the fire – you need to stay warm while you recover.'

Pouring another bowl for the domowik and sliding it under the stove, then a third for myself, I went and sat next to Kaz. Sharing the settee was strangely intimate and I found myself not knowing what to say. In my old life as a princess, I'd been tutored and coached, dressed and fussed over, but living in the castle had been more isolating than life in the forest. Katia had regaled me with stories of her romances with different girls in the Amber City, but I'd only had stolen kisses from some of the royal visitors from faraway lands, who were as restless as me, and that brief but intense summer with Piotr, the queen's guardsman with the sky-blue eyes and the impish dimples that had caught my eye. I'd never had a real conversation with someone who wasn't paid, never shared a meal with anyone simply for the pleasure of company. It didn't help that this huntsman looked like he'd escaped from the pages of one of the romance books Katia used to smuggle into the castle for me. Or that each time I caught a glimpse of those cheekbones, that jawline, I skipped a breath.

'How long have you lived in this cottage?' Kaz asked. 'Were you born here?'

'No, I'm from Wanda.' Wanda, the first queen of Mazrovia's name had jumped into my head first. Both the castle and the river winding through the Amber City were named for her. 'Have you heard of it?'

Kaz shook his head. Unsurprising, since I'd invented it on the spot. 'There's not much there,' I said honestly. 'It's just outside of the Amber City so most people don't bother stopping off there,' I finished, less honestly.

'So what brought you to Stary Bór, then? It's an unusual place to end up.'

I dipped a chunk of rye bread into my soup, buying time while I frantically threw a backstory together. Tangy and chewy, the bread tasted good. My best since I'd moved here and I sidled a glance at Kaz eating his, hoping he liked it, too. 'Bad break-up, needed some time to myself,' I told him. Light and breezy and simple. 'What about you – where are you from? Tell me about yourself.' Strange that I didn't already know these things yet I'd saved this stranger's life three times already. Stranger yet that he didn't feel much like a stranger any more either.

He spooned the rest of his soup into his mouth and set the bowl down on the floor before answering me. Almost like he too was playing for time. Curious. 'I was born on the edge of Stary Bór. I never knew my father; my mother raised me and my younger brother.' He smiled to himself. 'Filip was a pain in the ass, but you couldn't help but love him.'

'Was?' I softly echoed.

Kaz inclined his head. 'I lost them both. It's been just me for a long time now.'

I didn't know what to say to that. His loneliness ached through his voice, and for a moment, I wondered if Dola, fate herself, had brought us together so that we'd no longer be alone. I rested a hand on his arm, giving him silent comfort. He placed his hand over mine and the air crackled with the coming storm.

'I was a wild thing, though.' He smiled to himself, closing his eyes. Leaving me free to memorise every detail of his face. 'I spent my days running through the forest, learning it, the wiła and tree roots and songbirds and beasts and all. Which ones were friendly, which to avoid.' His eyes snapped open then, finding me. 'My mother hated me spending all my time in the forest but, to me, it was magic.'

'I can understand that,' I said softly, remembering the young girl I'd never lost, the one that had desperately pored over her mother's spell books, craving just a taste of that power for herself.

'I know you do.' He stared back at me, giving me the strangest feeling that he saw straight through me to my softest, vulnerable parts. Recognising me for exactly who I was and not who he wanted me to be. Clearing his throat, he forged on. 'When I lost my family and needed to make a living, it was inevitable that I'd turn to the forest. Being a huntsman, treading where others were too afraid to go.' He spread his hands. 'It paid well. Loneliness can be cutting, but it can be liberating, too.'

'I'd never thought of it like that before,' I admitted as he waited for me to share my story. 'My mother is still alive and it was always just the two of us.' In fact, I'd never known my father either. My mother had borne me young, before the age of twenty. She'd never mentioned who my father had been; I didn't even know his name. 'But we have a . . . complicated relationship.' I winced.

Kaz looked intrigued. 'Does she know you're here?' he asked.

I frowned to myself. 'Gods, I hope not.' He looked pensive, his face filled with questions I didn't want to answer. His flirtatious manner had melted away, and I wondered if it was the subject matter or if he was feeling rotten from the bauk's venom. 'You should probably rest,' I told him before he could voice any more questions.

He got to his feet with a groan. 'I should probably start heading home.'

'You can't,' I exclaimed, tugging his curiosity back onto me. My cheeks flushed warm. That blush was my second curse. 'It's not safe to travel through Stary Bór until you're healed. And with a storm on the horizon—'

Kaz gave me a faint smile. 'I've already intruded enough—'

'Nonsense.' I said firmly. 'We're two lonely people, who else are we going to spend time with?' It wasn't until I said it that I realised how much I wanted it to be true. I needed a seventh heart. I needed to kill the queen. What was I doing here with my head crammed full of this huntsman's cheekbones, soft, full lips, and thick arms that had felt far too good wrapped round me?

'I have friends,' Kaz pointed out, but the twitch of amusement in his mouth betrayed him.

'But they don't know what it's like, do they? To truly have nobody there for you in this world?'

Kaz's amusement extinguished and I could have cursed aloud. My mouth had a habit of running before my brain caught up with it. If I wasn't careful, by the time Kaz did leave, he'd be taking all of my secrets home with him. 'No, they don't.' He eyed me thoughtfully. 'You're one interesting person, Elka.'

He winced as he bent to pick up our crockery and return it to the kitchen. 'I wonder what other thoughts you've got tucked away in that head of yours.'

'Too many to count,' I said brightly, heading into the kitchen on his heels.

Later, when Kaz was dozing before the fire, I made him another tea. Last night's brew had been packed to the brim with good healing herbs, blood and magic to combat the poison crawling through his veins. Tonight's cup was laced with a pinch of dried, crushed belladonna berries. Not enough to taint his heart, should I still wish to steal it, just enough to rob him of a little strength. Living a lean life in the forest may have weakened me, but thanks to Pan Jedrick I was still a skilled fighter and, yesterday, Kaz had managed to overpower me, despite being wounded. It was troubling. I didn't want him to leave. But I didn't have to trust him, either. So long as he stayed with me, he would be fed a slow, steady slip of poison.

As he sipped it, I stared into the fire at my secret, sleeping beneath a blanket of flames. This was why I was poisoning Kaz: I had to defend my secret at all costs.

'Tell me a story.' Kaz's voice was a low rumble, echoing the thunder creeping over the horizon. The cottage was aglow with candlelight, the shutters the domowik had repaired bolted shut, and though the forest made itself heard, rustling and chittering and screeching around us, we couldn't see it. We could have been anywhere in the world. Or nowhere, two souls lost in a void.

'You need to sleep,' I told him.

'I'd sleep better if you gave me something sweet to think about.' His gaze lingered on my face until my cheeks flushed from the warmth of the fire and candles and those golden flecks in his eyes that looked like tiny burning stars. Thunder rolled, skulking closer.

'Once, before Queen Serce and her Purge, before the two queens and the great famine forty years ago, the queendom of Mazrovia had a different name. And it wasn't a queendom.'

Kaz groaned. 'That wasn't what I had in mind.'

'Well, it's all you're getting, so be quiet, unless you'd rather be left alone?'

Kaz fell silent. His eyes resting on me, still. If I didn't feel guilty for poisoning him, I was about to feel guilty for boring him to sleep, but I was tired too and there were things that needed to be done without Kaz's knowledge. So I plunged into retelling the origin myths of Mazrovia, intoning them the same way that Pani Agata had that had me dozing off in her class. 'One day, a great hunter king rode out over a vast land, filled with ancient forest, verdant valleys, plentiful rivers and lakes, and towering mountains. As he looked up, a white eagle soared above him and he called the land Gniezdno, after the creature's nest. He settled in his new land with his queen and soon they bore four sons. The queen told her king that he should carve the kingdom into four lorddoms, so that each son might inherit one. Then, through being good brothers to each other, Gniezdno would prosper from good trade and peace between the lorddoms. To Jaromir, ambitious and eager to explore, the Hunter King gave the Tundra, so that he might build merchant ships and trade across the Iron Sea. To Arron, timid and intelligent, he gave Mistpoint to build places of art and learning. To Vladislav, brave and resourceful, he gave the hostile Dragonspine Mountains. And, finally, to his strangest and least understood son, Dobrogost, he gave the most fearsome land of all; Stary Bór, an ancient forest even then, said to be the entrance to Nawia itself. But, like all brothers, the four lords fought and disagreed and Gniezdno was torn apart by greed and arrogance and war. Until Arron's daughter, Wanda, who was cleverer even than her father, reunited the four lands and seized the crown for herself, renaming Gniezdno as Mazrovia, the queen's land.'

Kaz gave a light snore.

Later that night, by the light of a single candle, burning low, I pulled out the maps and plans I'd stashed in my trunk and spread them out on the floor in front of the fire. Kaz had long since gone to bed.

He was the easiest path back to the Amber City and the old castle I had grown up in, Wanda's Castle. And he was deep in a sedated sleep. One that would make it oh so easy for me to steal upstairs and slit his throat before he'd even awoken. But now that I'd spent a day with the huntsman, every time I considered taking his heart, all I could think of was that flash of hurt and fear I'd seen in my victim's faces and how I couldn't bear the thought of watching that play through Kaz's holly-green eyes.

The first man I'd killed had been a thief. I'd been mushroom-picking on my way home from Sanok, the nearest hamlet, when I'd heard a young girl scream. Number One had come crashing through the undergrowth seconds later. It had been child's play to stretch out my leg and trip him. He'd fallen, shattering the glass bead necklace clenched in his fist. A chunk of hair was twined round its broken clasp, no doubt belonging to the owner of the scream. I'd thought about this moment a dozen times beforehand, preparing vials of numbing poison, planning my attack. But when it happened, it was fast and bloody and brutal and there had been no time for any of that, only desperation and a blade.

Shoving my guilt away, I looked over the plans of the castle. I methodically went through the main wings, the great hall, the throne room, the kitchens, the stables, the newer extensions, including the cavernous nursery that had been empty for years, and the riding grounds. Now that I had consumed my sixth heart, I needed to make a serious plan. Grabbing a pencil, I started mapping out all the secret passages I knew. How you could enter the dungeons from an old storm drain behind the stables. The hidden serving hallway that you could still run through, undetected, from the kitchens to the grand hall, and the tallest tower in the castle, inaccessible except to the queen. That, I circled, before sitting back on my heels and thinking hard, until my candle guttered and died.

CHAPTER SEVEN

The storm hit the forest like a runaway carriage. For four days and nights, it roared through the trees, rattled branches and sent waves of rain hurtling down like spears. Each time I dashed outside to the well, I was soaked to the marrow. Day was as dark as night, the storm an unending beast, thundering until it was impossible to sleep, but I didn't mind one bit. The cottage was warm, I managed to scrounge enough food together to make pierogi that fell apart in the pan and had Kaz laughing as he tried to scoop the filling back into the flat cases. 'I'll make them next time,' he told me, with a twinkle. 'Or maybe I'll just let you make them again since you need the practice,' he teased in a way that sent heat rushing to my cheeks. Not from embarrassment but from the way his words promised more time together, that he wasn't in a hurry to leave. I was starting to grow used to his company, our long conversations about all the places we wanted to see, the books we'd read and the music and paintings we loved. When I'd boasted that my geography of Mazrovia was exceptional, he'd tested me:

'Glenwich?'

'A kingdom in the south-east, across The Deep.'

'Narol?'

I hesitated. *Where in the gods was Narol?* Kaz's building triumph vexed me until I caught the glint in his eye. 'You made that up,' I accused, throwing cushions at him until he laughed and threw them back.

Things between us were easy, cosy, like I was just a girl talking to the boy I liked and nothing else mattered.

Until the storm entered the cottage.

Kaz bolted the shutters as night rolled over the treeline. I could smell the salt and crushed lavender he was trickling over the windowsills, and the rain that had fallen for five days straight, flooding the forest with weeds and mushrooms.

Chopping the last of my onions, carrots and cabbage for tonight's bigos, a hunters' stew, I trained my senses on Kaz, listening to each step he took across the creaking wooden floorboards. He was near healed. If I wanted to kill him, now would be the time; I would have my seventh heart. But something deep inside me was clinging on by its fingernails, and I knew I couldn't take a blade to him now.

When I glanced his way, he was standing by the fire.

I dropped my knife. I was scarcely aware of the domowik rushing to fling it away before it cut my foot. My heart dropped out of my chest, leaving me paralysed in place.

How had I not heard Kaz move to the fireplace?

His green eyes silently glinted with knowledge and, in his hands, rested my secret. Its familiar dark red glowed as bright as a lantern.

'Do you have any idea what it is? I found it in the cottage when I moved in,' I quickly lied, bending to retrieve my cooking knife from under the stove. Two eyes suddenly appeared, making me jump. The domowik was becoming more and more corporeal with each day that passed. It peered balefully back at me with wide black eyes and I swallowed nervously; why was it hiding? My head rushed as I stood. 'I've been using it as a heating stone for my bed. Well, the settee since you've been staying.' I clutched the knife hilt, gripping it hard to calm my shaking hand. Kaz held my heart in his hands, the one thing I had managed to claw back from the queen, the secret I would die to protect.

Kaz looked like a bolt of lightning, ready to strike. Reflex had me counting the other blades secreted about myself: hip, ankle, hair and a tiny needle-sharp dagger, the length of my finger, that was tucked in my armoured corset. 'Do not lie to me.' His voice was a low, dangerous rumble. Any hint of flirtation, of the cosiness of the past days long lost. Who was he really: the charmer or the threat? He'd told me he was from a nearby forest town and that he'd lost all of his family, but now I realised that those were cleverly worded evasions. Sentiments and feelings only. I knew almost nothing about who he really was or where he'd really come from – his fears and hopes and loyalties. 'Where did you get this from?' he demanded.

'I told you, I don't know.' I glared at him defiantly. It took every bit of self-control I had not to look at what he was holding, to snatch it from his hands. I'd thought that keeping it in the fire and making Kaz sleep upstairs in my bed was enough distance to prevent him from prying in my fireplace. I'd been a godscursed fool.

Kaz stalked towards me, making the words shrivel in my throat. He was too tall for this little crooked cottage. He was a hunter on the prowl. Pan Jedrick had taught me a thousand ways to wield my blades, but he'd never taught me how to separate swordplay from your own feelings or how to plunge a knife through the chest of the man you couldn't stop dreaming about. But I would not be his prey. I would be the monster he never saw coming.

My shields snapped up. 'This is a nice way to thank the person who saved you from a bauk, who cooked up the antidote to your poisoned wound.'

'Ah yes, my wound. Which you so expertly crafted that antidote for. Impressive.' A vein in his neck pulsed. I slid my knife into my apron pocket, within reach but careful not to invite violence into the conversation. 'Then again, it also gave you the perfect cover story. That I'm weak as I recover, as the last dregs of the bauk's poison works its way out. Not because you've been slipping belladonna into that restorative tea you've been brewing for me every day. I know you've been poisoning me.'

Kaz set my secret carefully down on the table.

My anxiety drummed as loud as the rain falling on the roof as I stared at it, weighing if I could reach it before Kaz could.

'You're a clever thing, aren't you?' Kaz stepped closer, looking down at me as he bent to whisper in my ear. 'But I'm cleverer.'

He wasn't. Faster than the thunder carving the sky in two, I seized his wrist and whipped it up behind his back, pinning it between his shoulder blades. 'Don't make the mistake that so many others have,' I snarled at him. 'Do not underestimate me.' I waited for him to whimper or plead, and when he did not, I tightened my hold on him, until his joint bulged, threatening to pop right out of his socket. He made no attempt to fight back; to my surprise, he was keeping his oath not to lay a hand on me. At least for now.

'Oh, I wouldn't dare underestimate you,' Kaz growled. 'No more than I would be stupid enough to believe your little story. You don't just find a dragon egg in your fire. Dragons haven't been seen for the past ten years. Not since they were the first to go in the Purge.'

My head roared. The domowik emerged from beneath the stove, waving its tendrils anxiously. I released Kaz, shoving him away as I drew my favourite knife.

Cleaved apart, we faced each other warily. My chest rose and fell as fast as his. I pointed my knife at him.

Kaz's eyes glittered with barely suppressed rage. 'Before the

Purge even had a name, Queen Serce executed the oldest and largest dragon, Migot, and hung her bones above the door of her new church in the Amber City. A symbol of all that she claimed the True Path had conquered.'

I cautiously lowered the point of my knife. His rage was not targeted at me. 'I don't need a history lesson,' I said through gritted teeth. I knew it all too well. Better than Kaz did. In the Dark Dragon Ages, hundreds of years ago, dragons had ruled the skies of Mazrovia, fearsome beasts that hunted humans, until Alvorian forces crossed the Iron Sea and began targeting the Dragon Heartlands, capturing young hatchlings to tame and stealing precious dragon eggs. Then Mazrovians began protecting their dragons, studying them and learning how to live alongside them. A large nursery was carved out in the castle itself, ensuring that hatchlings would be at the heart of the queendom, safe and protected. Treasured. Until the Purge. No dragons remained in Mazrovia now. Those graceful, ferocious, loyal creatures were all long gone, wiped out of existence by my own mother, who I would never forgive for such a crime. Even our flag, blood-red with a golden dragon flying across it, had been torn down, replaced with a white flag with a shining silver path running through the centre. But the dragon hangars remained: they were still one of the first things you saw on approach to the Amber City – cavernous shells, sitting empty next to the bristling military barracks.

'Then tell me how,' Kaz's voice trembled with suppressed

fury. 'How is it that you have a dragon egg sitting in your fireplace?'

'Why do you care?' I whispered.

Kaz reared back as if I'd stabbed him. 'I—' his throat bobbed up and down. The gold flecks in his eyes burned brighter in the candlelight. 'I've spent the last decade believing that they were all gone, that I'd never see another dragon again. If I'd have known—' his voice choked.

'All followers of the One True Path fear dragons. That's why they were the first to go in the Purge,' I said. That godscursed Purge. Whatever had triggered it was the thorn at the centre of my mother's life. If only she wasn't holding onto it tightly, a private wound I couldn't see, then I might begin to unpick the reason why she'd turned on her own queendom. She shut out the world that night before the Purge suddenly began, including me. Nine-year-old me couldn't understand why her own mother had stopped talking to her; it took years before I realised that the Purge hadn't been started to punish me. The queen was punishing us all.

Through my maelstrom of fear and rage, Kaz was silent. From his shock at discovering the dragon egg I'd kept hidden in my fireplace, he'd let the truth leak out, let the real Kaz surface, uncloaking his real identity underneath his carefully crafted mask.

Followers of the One True Path feared and loathed dragons, but Kaz was looking at that dragon egg the same way I looked at it. Like it was an unimaginable prize. Being a princess came with immense privilege, shielding me from the dangers of heresy. Kaz was not protected from that danger; he was treading a deadly path.

'You're a heretic,' I whispered, realising the truth. 'That's what you're doing this deep in the forest. You're not hunting, you're *hiding*.' This explained his wariness when we'd first met; he had feared I would discover his secret. And that was why he hadn't wanted to leave my cottage; when I'd encouraged him to stay, to heal, he hadn't protested. It was safe here, as far away from the True Path and their churches as you could get, unless you took the old, creaking reindeer-drawn sleighs up into the tundra of the frozen Witchlands.

'Perhaps.' Kaz stared me down. 'But I'm not the only one.'

He couldn't know. Could he? 'I don't know what you're talking about.'

'Really?' He walked over to the dragon egg and picked it back up. I tightened, tracking his every movement. 'Imagine my surprise when Princess Elka, the sole living heir to the throne of Mazrovia, stepped out of the forest to save me from a bauk.'

My breath hitched.

But he didn't know the rest of my story. Nights spent prowling through the forest, the taste of heartblood and wine on my tongue, blood caked under my fingernails, blood in my hair, water that kept running red, red, red.

'I had heard of you, you know.' Kaz's voice turned husky.

'They used to call you Smocza Księżniczka, the Dragon Princess. As brave as she was beautiful. I had no idea you would have an actual dragon's egg sitting in your fire.' He gazed at the egg as if it were treasure. Which it was; it was worth far more than its weight in gold on the illegal magic markets that veined through Mazrovia. And its weight was not inconsiderable.

'Why didn't you tell me you knew?'

He lifted a shoulder. 'I was waiting for the right moment.'

There had been a hundred right moments over the past week. I felt a fool for opening up about my past, my complicated relationship with my mother, when all along he had known I was talking about the queen. Omittance was a lie. But I had lied to him, poisoned him, as well. Gods, it was hard to know what to think. But while he was standing there, holding my egg, all I needed was to say whatever would get him to return it.

'Your secret is safe with me, princess.' Kaz raised the dragon egg. Its scaled shell, the darkest red-black, glimmered with a light of its own like a burning star. My fingers opened and closed, desperate to seize it back, but I was too scared to make any sudden movements. 'Both of your secrets,' Kaz continued. 'I won't betray you to the True Path or the queen and her Angels of Death. You know I'm a heretic. I'm in hiding, too.'

The Angels of Death terrified me more than Kaz holding my dragon egg. Cavalry in the Mazrovian army who wore black raven feather-wings on their armour and had their tongues cut out the day they joined the army. A painful symbol that they would never speak back to their queen, never disagree, only silently carry out her bidding. It was the Angels of Death who had executed the dragons and banished our resident dracologists, including Pani Smok, silver-haired, sharp-eyed and even sharper-tongued, who'd led the dragon breeding and training programmes in the Amber City, and been the one who'd seized me before I'd learned to walk and put me on the back of a dragon. With Pani Smok seated behind me, strapped into the huge leather saddles designed for riding dragons, I flew before I walked.

Something snapped inside me. 'Hand it to me,' I commanded Kaz. 'Now.' When I reached my hands out towards him, they trembled.

After a brief pause that felt like an eternity, Kaz gently placed the dragon egg back in my arms. Its weight was reassuring. Heavy, warm and smooth to the touch. It was the size of an overgrown pumpkin, with the texture of a river stone that had spent centuries being shaped by water. 'How long have you had it?' Kaz leaned against the wall, watching as I returned the egg to the hearth.

I let out a rough sigh. Kneeling before the fire, I stared into its crackling depths. 'Too long. As far as I know, it's the last egg in existence. I stole it from the nursery after I'd watched the queen have Migot, the dragon I used to ride, the one I was closest to, executed.' When she'd turned the courtyard red with dragon blood and my throat ragged from screaming.

Kaz's voice roughened. 'You were there? But you can't have been more than—' He cut off. When I glanced back him, I was surprised to see a flash of anger pulse through him. The storm howled outside, the elms moaning as the wind whipped through their boughs, rattling against the cottage. Kaz pushed off from the wall, running a hand roughly through his hair.

'I was nine. It's been ten years since she had the dragons executed.' Ten years since I'd watched Migot roar with pain and fear as the Angels of Death forced her down to the ground, in chains, my mother watching from a distance. Always from a distance.

I didn't share how I used to ride Migot every morning after sunrise, how she used to tuck me under her wing when I wanted to hide from the world and my mother's mountaining expectations. The little huff she made when I sneaked her a fistful of sugar cubes from the kitchens. With Migot I felt . . . No, I *was* unstoppable, soaring over the peaks of the Dragonspine Mountains and further still, to the point where Mazrovia met the Iron Sea in a clash of clifftops and grey-topped waves. She had been my best friend. '*Run*,' Pani Smok had told me fiercely, gripping my shoulders, her silver eyes hardened to iron. '*Run and save what you can, the last of dragonkind is in your hands now.*' A couple of Angels of Death had ripped her from me then, marching her away through the castle. I never saw her again.

Tears threatened and I blinked fiercely. Kaz's jaw clenched tightly as he watched me.

'Anyway –' I choked my grief back down into the dark pit where it lived – 'I managed to save this egg. There were more, but one was all I could carry and by the time I returned for another—' My voice cracked. By the time I'd returned for another, running flat out along the cold flagstones that led to the dragon nursery, it had been empty. No, not empty. It had been destroyed. I'd run as fast and as hard as my nine-year-old lungs could manage, fear pounding inside my skull with each slap of my feet against stone. The rest of the dragons were being herded for execution as I ran, pushing myself faster, harder, tears streaming as I forced myself to get there in time, even as I heard the dragons begin to make that awful sound, that high-pitched keening that signalled their pain and fear and grief. Even as my cheeks were hot with tears and my throat was hard and swollen, I hurtled back to the nursery to save another egg. But when I skidded in on the straw-covered stone, I saw nothing but broken shells and destroyed nests.

'My heart shattered that day,' I admitted quietly, looking up to Kaz's stare, burning into me. 'It broke so hard I swear to the gods I heard it. Like glass smashing in a silent room.' I was nine when I hardened my heart against my mother. When I first promised myself that I would have my revenge. When I learned how sweet the word *vengeance* tasted. But I lived in that castle with her, in silence, for another nine years before she cursed me.

'You were only a child; you couldn't have done anything else,'

Kaz said softly. His hand jerked, as if he wanted to reach out to me, but thought better of it. Then he sighed, disappointment turning him grave. 'Are you telling me that you've guarded that egg for the last ten years?'

'I have,' I whispered, staring back into the fire. Flames licked over the eggshell, turning it a dazzling ruby. 'I know it will never hatch, but I couldn't leave it in the castle. I couldn't—' I swallowed. Sorrow sat heavy in my throat, turning my words painful. 'I couldn't give up . . . hope.' Dragon eggs took a year to hatch, sometimes two. Ten years was too long, even for a dragon. And coupled with the trauma that the hatchling would have sensed unfolding around it? Well, I wouldn't be surprised if it had simply chosen never to hatch. I couldn't imagine the pain of being the last of my kind.

Kaz sat beside me. The firelight fell on his tawny hair, gilding it. 'You did the right thing, Elka.'

I sat back on my heels, watching the fire with him.

'Never lose your hope,' he said.

Turning my head to the side, I realised our faces were closer than I'd noticed. Close enough to count every one of his long black eyelashes. When his eyes searched mine, my heart gave a lone, sore thump. Reminding me that it still existed, battered and bruised, but whole. 'You're something special, Elka, do you know that?' he whispered into the space between us, so small that I could taste his words. That I could move a hairsbreadth and taste *him*. Kaz's gaze darkened as if he sensed my thoughts.

'Now it's your turn,' I said.

His brow creased in confusion.

'Since you are not a huntsman, I want to know exactly what you were doing in the forest the day I found you. How did you get attacked? And how did you know who I really am?' Had he been there earlier that day? Had he seen me traipse back to the cottage with a human heart in my hands?

Kaz's smile was slow. 'They say that Princess Elka is beautiful. With skin as luminescent as snow, lips as red as blood and hair as black as ebony.' He reached out a hand, as if he wanted to twine my hair round his fingers, before he thought better of it and clenched it shut. I swallowed, suddenly imagining his hands buried in my hair, craving his touch. I'd already felt his lips under my hand the night that the bauk had crawled onto my roof, so full and soft that I'd wondered more than once what it would be like to kiss him. Kaz's smile tipped up at one side as if he knew exactly how treacherous my thoughts had turned. 'They didn't lie. You are . . . exquisite.'

I scowled at him. 'I'm worth more than my looks.'

'Oh, I am aware of that. I've seen you fight. I've seen the way you care for the domowik when you think nobody's watching. I've seen the way you've guarded that dragon egg since I first entered your cottage.' He paused, his face still unbearably, intoxicatingly close to mine. 'You saved my life.'

His eye contact was so intense I almost forgot to breathe.

'There's also the matter of this.' He swept a notice out of his pocket, unfolding it to reveal a picture drawn on my seventeenth birthday. I looked like a trapped bird, my face stark in black and white. Underneath it the font spelled out: Missing Princess.

CHAPTER EIGHT

'It seems I'm not the only one in hiding.'

I screwed the page up and threw it into the fire. The notices had first made their appearance three solstices ago, a careful curating of the truth. An announcement from the queen that I had been taken by enemies to the One True Path. That only their prayers and obedience to the Shining Path would see me restored to the castle. In case that failed, there was a handsome sum promised for my safe return. 'Let's not get distracted now. We were talking about you.'

'And what would you like to know about me, princess?' His teasing tone was back, his shield sliding effortlessly into place.

'Stop being so charming,' I snapped, frustrated that it looked unlikely I'd get any real truth out of him now. After how open I'd been with him about Migot, sharing my traumatic memories of the day the Purge began, it galled me.

His grin only widened, irritating me further. 'So you admit that you find me charming?'

'Not any more.' I stood up, breaking the tense little bubble we'd been caught in together. The grin fell from his face, almost making me regret my sharpness. Almost, but not quite. 'If you wanted to know more about me then you could have just asked. I don't appreciate these games you're playing.'

He tilted his head to one side. 'Would you have told me the truth?'

Not for all the trees in the forest. Not unless . . . 'If you had been honest with me, if you didn't hide yourself behind those grins and remarks then, yes, I would have been.'

He looked up at me. 'I'm not hiding from you. It's just that—'

'Just that what?'

'That being with you, here, sometimes makes me forget everything else out there.' He gestured at the nearest window. 'You make me happy,' he said simply. 'If it makes you uncomfortable, I'll stop.'

Oh. 'No, that's fine.' I frowned. 'Hold on. If you were carrying that notice when you got attacked then—' My thoughts worked faster than my mouth, coming together in a jumble that I couldn't organise quickly enough to see the full picture forming before me. 'Then that means that you – you sought me out?' *He'd been looking for me.* The realisation hit like a thunderbolt. I staggered back under the weight of it. That was why alarm bells had been ringing over how he'd allowed himself to get attacked by a bauk when he was such a proficient fighter, how his stories about why he'd ventured this deep into Stary Bór didn't make sense. *I* was the missing link.

Kaz stood, too. 'Yes.'

'*Why?*' I demanded.

A chink of sincerity shone through his mask. I appreciated that he was trying, and decided to hear him out rather than toss him out into the storm. 'Because Mazrovia is a Queendom that's being driven out of control. And it's all down to one person.'

'Queen Serce.'

'Your mother,' Kaz confirmed. As long as you're alive, you are a threat to her.' He gestured to the missing notice, burning in the fireplace. 'I know there's more to that story than you're telling me, a reason why you're hiding in the forest with a dragon egg. You are every bit as much a heretic as I am – you cannot tell me you haven't entertained the notion of taking the queendom for yourself.'

I almost laughed. 'The queen was slaughtering dragons when I was nine years old, using their bones to decorate her churches. She has highly trained guards protecting her and her castle at all times. And besides those guards and her own power, she has a vast army at her disposal, which include the Angels of Death.' I gave an involuntary shudder. 'My mother didn't bring Mazrovia to its knees before her because she deserved it or because she was a great leader. No, the people saw her power, her strength, and they kneeled before it.' Kill or be killed. It was the way the world worked.

'You deserve that throne more than she does,' Kaz growled.

'I don't want it,' I said hotly. 'The only thing I'm searching for is revenge.' It slipped out before I could rein it back in, but Kaz didn't seem perturbed. He looked at me with that knowing gaze and that bottom lip I wanted to sink my teeth into, and I felt seen in a way I hadn't before.

'And then what?' Kaz asked. 'You'll step back and watch as the queendom is torn apart by greedy nobility, fighting for control, for land, for power? Could you really stand back while Mazrovia is ripped to pieces and stripped of its wealth by scavengers?'

'I didn't realise heretics were so matriotic,' I commented, ignoring my deep twinge of discomfort at the picture he'd painted.

Kaz looked at me curiously. 'You just admitted that you want the queen gone,' he pointed out. 'According to you, that's near impossible. So, if you can manage that, why shouldn't you then be queen?'

'Because it's more than figuring out how to defeat her.' I sighed. I felt like I was repeating myself to death. This must be what awaited me in Nawia; running around in circles trying to explain the same thing over and over to someone who refused to accept it. 'She has an entire religion of devout followers of the True Path who have renounced magic in her name. Do you think they would be happy to see me welcoming the return of magic to Mazrovia?' There was no point hiding my beliefs now, not when Kaz had admitted he shared them, not when he'd already seen my dragon egg. 'They'd call me the heretic queen.' Although that did have a poetic ring to it. 'And a thousand more reasons besides.

Seizing the throne is a political manoeuvre that would involve taking on the Angels of Death and overthrowing the One True Path. It would need a revolution. And revolutions need people.'

Kaz leaned closer to me as if he was going to impart a great secret, the culmination of his argument. I braced myself. 'There is an army in the forest.'

I inhaled so sharply I choked on thin air. 'You cannot be serious.' I gaped at Kaz when I'd recovered. '*That's* your plan? You're even more clueless than I suspected.'

He folded his arms, unyielding. 'It's a good plan.'

'It's a terrible plan. You want me to seek out the help of the forest demon himself? *That's* why you came hunting through the forest for me?' I couldn't help laughing out loud. 'You're delusional.'

'He has an army of fearsome creatures that follow his every command,' Kaz pointed out. 'And they say that the forest demon is one of the only things that the queen fears.'

'For good reason! He would devour us both alive, Kaz. No, you don't have a plan at all – you have a fantasy, a fairy tale, one that would get us both killed.'

'I would never do anything that would put your life at risk.'

'What you are asking is dangerous enough.' I rubbed my temple, pushing away any vestigial guilt at betraying my mother's greatest secret. 'Queen Serce is a witch.'

Kaz reeled back. 'Then the Purge—'

'She is not banning magic; she is stealing it.'

'This changes everything,' Kaz said. 'If you—'

Our conversation was rolling round in circles and I was tiring of it.

'You're welcome to stay here while you finish recovering,' I interrupted. It was only fair since I had poisoned him, prolonging his healing. 'But we will not be seeking out the forest demon and I will *not* be taking the queendom.' I stomped over to the table, leaving the bowls there for me to clean when I was in a better mood.

Kaz followed. 'But you do want vengeance, don't you?' His voice was low, his gaze smouldering. His words gave me pause. He'd pinpointed my desires and was whispering seductively to them, telling me everything I wanted to hear. 'You want to punish her for banishing you, for stealing the past few years of your life, for ripping away your future as the next queen. What could be more fitting than taking her throne in the name of revenge?'

'She did more than banish me.'

'What?' A muscle pulsed in Kaz's jaw. 'What did she do to you?'

Silently cursing myself for revealing more than I'd intended, I shook my head. 'That doesn't matter now.'

His hands braced on the table. 'What did she do to you?' he repeated roughly.

'She cursed me,' I whispered. Kaz was the second person I had confessed this to – Katia was the first – and it felt strange saying it aloud. I wanted nobody's sympathy, nobody's pity.

She cursed you?' Kaz stared across the table at me. 'What—'

he cleared his throat. 'What did she curse you with?'

'That,' I emphasised, holding my head high, 'Does not concern you.'

He looked very much like he disagreed. Before he could voice it, I picked up our bowls and returned them to the kitchen for an excuse to break our conversation. It was like there was a cord attached between us, taut and pulling. I couldn't stop looking at Kaz, and each time I stifled the urge to glance at him, I felt his eyes resting on me. The domowik rustled under the stove. When I blew the kitchen candles out, its eyes gleamed in the puddle of darkness that formed its body. Rain pattered down on the slanted cottage roof; the forest was drawing closer tonight. With a shiver, I turned to say goodnight to Kaz – and walked straight into his chest. It was hard and immovable.

An embarrassing yelp escaped me. 'What are you doing, sneaking up on me like that?' And how had I not heard him move? This cottage creaked more than a weary oak, yet his footsteps were silent.

'We haven't finished our conversation.'

'Yes, we have.' I stepped aside but he moved with me, blocking my way. Sighing, I folded my arms. 'Why does this bother you so much?'

'I find the thought of the queen hurting you . . . intolerable,' Kaz ground out.

'Oh.' Well, that was unexpected. And strangely touching. I wasn't used to people caring about me; I took care of myself.

'I can't go home until my curse is broken,' I confessed.

His eyes burned into me as if he knew. Knew that his life, the heart beating in his chest, could be the final piece I needed. The last key to unlocking the curse and throwing the castle doors wide open to me again. Presenting me with my vengeance and freedom in one swift stab.

'What can I do to help?' he asked instead. Since I'd blown out the candles in the kitchen, there was only one burning on the table, mirroring the dance of the fire, twin stars in the dusky cottage. In another life, it might have been romantic.

'Nothing. I'm close to ending my curse and I don't need your help or your worry.'

He leaned an arm on the wall, looking down at me with a peculiar expression. 'And if I can't help it?'

I sucked in a breath. 'Go to bed, Kaz. I'm tired.' I ducked under his arm. 'If you must fuss over something, the domowik wouldn't say no to another bowl of bigos.'

Behind my back, I heard him murmur under his breath, 'As you wish.'

I'd just closed my eyes when I felt a presence at the foot of my settee. 'Yes?' I asked without opening my eyes.

'I feel guilty sleeping in your bed now that I'm nearly healed. I'm doing much better since you've stopped poisoning me.' I opened my eyes to find myself fixed with a questioning look. 'Or, at least, lowered the dose?' he guessed.

I smiled to myself. 'Now that would be telling.'

He perched on the arm of the settee. 'Take your bed back, Elka.'

I stretched out languorously. 'Why, are you giving *me* orders now, *huntsman*?'

His surprise was more gratifying than I'd expected. It was chased by a look of pure delight. 'Oh, I would be more than happy to tell you what to do, princess.'

'I'm sure you would,' I told him. 'What a shame I'd never listen to you.' I closed my eyes again. Then reopened them. He was still there. 'Good rest will help you finish your healing and then you can be off on your way again and I'll have my bed back to myself.'

Kaz gave a stiff nod. 'I'm sorry to have troubled you for so long.' He made to get up, but I reached across and clasped his hand. It engulfed mine and I couldn't help liking that.

'Wait.' I swallowed nervously. His hand was warm, hard with callouses. 'I'm sorry, I didn't mean it like that.'

He relaxed, his spine easing as he softened. 'We could always share.'

A visual image of sharing the bed with Kaz flashed through my mind, warming my cheeks. 'That's fine,' I half squeaked, picturing his height, his breadth curled around me. 'I'll give you your privacy.'

A delicious smile swept across Kaz's mouth. 'A privilege I'd be happy to lose if I could spend one night with you.'

Gods. 'Goodnight, then!'

Kaz chuckled to himself. 'Goodnight, princess.'

I listened to his tread all the way upstairs, followed by the creak of him settling himself into my bed. When his breathing grew steady and deep, I tiptoed over to my trunk and retrieved my handful of maps and charts. Sitting next to the fire, as the storm died outside, I stabbed the point of my pencil at the queen's turret. There were only two ways to access it: magic or invitation from the queen. Since I had no blood magic beyond the simple workings anyone could do, that was out of the question, and I doubted I'd get an invitation from my mother into her innermost sanctuary anytime soon.

I circled the window. Maybe I could enter from outside? It was tall, but vines and ivy grew like a plague all over the castle; I'd climbed down them more than once when sneaking out of my own chamber. My rooms weren't as high up as the queen's, but hers were also too high for the gardeners to reach, leaving them unpruned. If I entered the courtyard without detection, the overgrown greenery would hide me like a green cloak, allowing me to climb up to the turret window. The best chance I had at taking on the queen, the *only* chance I had, was by surprise.

Nobody had underestimated me more than my own mother; she wouldn't see this one coming.

CHAPTER NINE

'Let me.' Kaz took my knife and ran it across the tip of one of his fingers.

As his blood swelled, I intoned, 'To the gods above and below, accept this tithe and let my will be done.' Taking his hand in mine, I squeezed seven droplets of blood onto my magicwork. It sealed with a hiss. Not enough to prevent anyone or anything from entering the cottage if they set out with that intention, just enough zing of magic to discourage any passers-by from deciding to peer through a window or knock on the door.

'You didn't need to do that,' I told Kaz, rolling up my bundle of sage and lavender and other, more nefarious herbs and berries.

'You paid the tithe for healing me. Protecting me.' He shrugged. 'I'm just balancing the scale.' Putting his finger in his mouth, he sucked it clean. My focus dropped to his lips. His tongue. Slowly lowering his hand, Kaz raised an eyebrow at me. 'See something you like there, princess?'

Flushing, I snapped back, 'Just the sight of you bleeding.' Things between us were still awkward and jagged, the broken edge of a shattered mirror, since we'd pulled truths out of each other like thorns last week.

His smirk grew more knowing. 'Don't worry,' he said, his voice deep and gravelly, 'I swore an oath not to lay a finger on you . . . I didn't say anything about my mouth.'

'*Gods.*' Shoving the bundle of herbs into my cloak pocket, I strode off before he could see my flush deepen. If we'd been in the castle, he would never have spoken to me like that. Even if he was just provoking me for his own entertainment, it gave me a small, warm glow. One that I couldn't help kindling even as everything inside me urged me to stamp it out. 'Come on,' I called back. 'It'll take us until nightfall to reach Sanok if you insist on dragging that massive ego along with us.'

His dark little chuckle followed me.

The forest smelled of green things, of life and death and moss and rot. My boots sunk into the waterlogged earth as I ploughed through the trees, leaping over a wandering tree root that slithered too close, ducking under low-hanging vines. What could be glimpsed of the sky through the verdant canopy was pale grey, feathered with thin clouds. Nightjars sang from branch to branch, lulling me into a sense of safety. It was never wise to venture to Sanok, the twin threats of being discovered as the princess and leaving my dragon egg unattended gnawed at me, but my meagre pantry had stretched as far as it could. I needed supplies and Kaz had recovered enough to escort me. We set out knowing that this would most likely be our last hours spent together.

'You know they say the forest demon will steal your soul, taking it from you bit by bit until you're a shrivelled husk, your skin turning to bark, your spine to branches, condemning you to live in his forest court and do his bidding for the rest of time.'

'Careful,' Kaz's tone was wry. 'This forest belongs to him; he might be listening.'

I scanned the unending treeline for one of his owls. 'Right. Well, what makes you think that he would ever consider helping me seize the queendom? Where does an idea like that even come from?' It was so audacious I'd never seen it coming.

Kaz swept a fern aside. It gave a menacing rustle, encouraging us both to pick up the pace. 'I happen to think that you each have something the other needs.'

Holding my cloak tighter round myself, I pushed past a thorned bush. 'What could I possibly have that the forest demon would need?'

'A legitimate claim to the throne. You're a beautiful princess; if the queendom knew the truth, they would rally for you. Fight for you.' His voice dipped seductively. 'Worship you.'

The thought sent a shiver straight through me. 'I don't need or want anyone's worship. That would make me no better than the queen and her preaching of the True Path.' It didn't escape my notice that he'd called me beautiful. I knew I was, my mother had crafted a potion the dawn she arose and knew life was quickening within her. Ruby-red crushed berries, a sliver of ebony wood and a handful of glittering white snow, sealed with blood fresh from her own veins. My mother made me beautiful. She crafted me like one of her intricate spells, calling on tutors to make me intelligent, to hone my body into a weapon as deadly as any blade. But even she could not make me a witch. All my power was in my face. *Snow White*. My mother's pet name for me had stuck like a tragic ghost, haunting me. Beauty made people lose their heads around you, that was all Kaz saw when he looked at me. Just the same as everyone else. At least my mother's strange silence, followed by an even stranger anger, was a refreshing change. I wanted someone to see past my face, to want me for *me*.

Jumping over a couple of snaking roots, I tuned back in to what Kaz was saying.

'You would inspire their loyalty. In a way that the forest demon could never. It's not like he could ever sit on a throne.'

'He doesn't need to; he has his forest court.'

Clambering over a fallen oak branch, Kaz raised his eyebrows at me. 'A court filled with wiła, forest spirits and other creatures that he has to terrify into loyalty? It must be a very lonely existence.'

I sunk into a patch of mud, ankle-deep. 'And why do you even believe that he would want me on the throne?' I asked grumpily, disliking how damp and boggy the forest was; the incessant rain had turned it into the consistency of a stew. Like a wet mouth. I pulled my foot from the mud only to leave my boot behind.

Yanking it out with a sigh, I used a stick to clean the worst of the mud off before putting my foot back in with a squelch and a grimace. 'What if he's a fan of Queen Serce?'

Kaz elegantly sidestepped the patch that had hungrily sucked my boot down. 'I don't see how he can be when the queen has spent the past decade purging the queendom of magic. The last pockets of magic are here, in Stary Bór, and in the Dragonspine Mountains.'

'And in the tundra,' I added automatically, thinking of the Witchlands in the far north, wild and ungovernable, near unreachable unless you wanted to spend half a moon cycle riding the sleighs that dared trundle up there.

'And in the tundra,' Kaz echoed. He gave me a serious look. 'But if she is truly stealing all this for herself then you must know that a greed like hers is never satisfied. It grows. She will never stop until her Purge has wrung every last drop of magic from the farthest reaches of Mazrovia. The forest demon may be the worst kind of monster, but he still needs magic to survive. Queen Serce threatens that.'

'So you think he'll just loan me his army to take down the queen and stop her leaching Mazrovia of magic?' I whirled round to face Kaz, startling him. 'You're forgetting something. She murdered the dragons. She's been stealing magic for the last decade, probably longer if my suspicions are correct. She's more powerful than an entire army.'

Kaz stared at me. 'So how exactly were you planning on getting close enough to her for your revenge? By yourself. Because that's your plan, isn't it?'

I turned and carried on ploughing through the forest, beating back the overzealous undergrowth with my stick.

'Elka?' Kaz sounded angry now. No, not angry, more . . . disturbed. 'Elka, talk to me.' He huffed out an irritated sigh. 'Gods, you've got more fortifications than the castle itself. Each time I feel like I'm getting closer to *you*, your walls snap down.'

'What makes you feel like you deserve access to me? That's a privilege, not a right,' I bit back. I'd been cursed to become a murderer by my own mother; I had wells of anger that ran straight down through the core of me, an unending tide that I would ride until it exhausted me.

'You're deflecting,' Kaz said. 'What are you scared I'll find out? Is it that you don't plan on confronting the queen and walking away to tell the tale?'

I brought my boot down on a passing tree root. It cracked like a bone, making me flinch.

'Or is it that you just don't want to share your plan with me? Do you still not trust me, Elka?'

I stopped. 'No, I don't. I don't know you, Kaz, not really. You're still a stranger to me, one that came looking for me with an ulterior motive. Yes, we've grown . . . close in the past week and a half.' His expression softened at that, a small tenderness I chose not to pay attention to. 'But I have enemies, I'd be a fool to give away my trust that easily. And that plan that you've come to me with, that you're so proud of?' A little sarcasm dipped into my tone and it was an effort to reel it back. 'It's nothing more than a gamble, an awfully risky one at that.'

Kaz shrugged. 'What's life without a little fun?'

A very un-princess-like snort escaped me. Kaz's mouth curled up at the corners as he definitely heard it. 'I wouldn't call risking my life fun.' Kaz had found me. That meant that others could. And if the queen was curating a narrative over my disappearance that called for my rescue, one that came with a rich reward, I needed to be more careful than ever.

'What would you call fun?' Kaz sounded curious. 'You've been living alone in the forest for, what, almost two years? You must have passed the time somehow.'

A flash back to that first winter here, the birds frozen to branches, ice creeping up tree trunks and between the joining in my cottage. The cold that sunk into my bones and refused to leave for months. 'Wouldn't you like to know,' I said lightly, skating over the subject.

'Actually, I would.'

The path widened and Kaz took advantage, lengthening his stride until he walked beside me. 'You spent most of your life in the castle, in the Amber City. Whatever did a princess find to occupy herself with in Stary Bór?'

I learned how to kill. How to peel back a person's ribs and seize the beating heart from within its bone cage. How to bake that heart into a pie that would make me forget where it had come from. How to leave out a flask of poison-spiked cherry wódka for a passer-by to pick up and drain, making my incisions neater as they couldn't fight back. Numbers Three and Four had both fallen for this trick. 'Living in the forest is hard work,' I told Kaz honestly. 'Finding enough food, learning where to go to trade for other things I need, like milk and cheese and flour, teaching myself how to forage and preserve so that I wouldn't go hungry, that took most of my time.'

'And the rest of your time?' he pressed.

I shook my head. 'You're relentless.'

'Thank you.'

'It wasn't a compliment.'

'Well, I decided to take it as one. After all, a huntsman needs to be relentless to stalk his prey.'

'Why do I get the feeling that I'm your latest prey?' I muttered dryly.

Kaz halted. The smile melted from my lips as he tensed, hand hovering above the hilt of his dagger, his gaze unfocused as he tilted his head. Listening.

I immediately froze. We'd been too relaxed, strolling through the forest as if it were a meadow filled with wildflowers, not harbouring some of the most monstrous creatures of Mazrovia. What had we been thinking? I knew the queen had spies everywhere and Kaz and I had been casually discussing our plans like a couple of godscursed fools. Still, I didn't hear anything, save from a distant raven and the whispering wind. 'What is it?'

I asked quietly, wondering what his trained hunter's senses could detect that I couldn't. I seriously hoped it wasn't another bauk.

He lifted a hand and I silenced. After a moment, his posture relaxed. 'A rusałka. Just passing by.'

A shiver rippled down my spine. Rusałki were undead water spirits, as malicious as they were beautiful. According to the books I'd read; I'd never seen one in the flesh before. 'They must hunt along the stream nearby.'

'There's no need to be afraid – I would have protected you.' Kaz winked at me.

Rolling my eyes, I supressed the urge to shove him into the mud and carried on treading our forest path. 'You saw me gut that bauk, what makes you think I need protecting? Besides, rusałki prefer hunting men.' I stifled a smile. 'They're fond of drowning you.'

When I glanced back, Kaz's reaction did not disappoint. He shuddered. 'In that case, I would have hidden behind you.' The corner of his mouth tipped up. 'I do enjoy watching your knifeplay.'

'You're a little bit violent, aren't you?' I commented.

His smile turned devious. 'Oh, I'm not watching the blade. You just happen to be very good with your hands. Sometimes you spin my thoughts wildly out of control.'

I whirled round, coming to a sudden stop that startled him, his eyes flicking behind me to check I hadn't spotted anything nasty. When I slunk closer to him, approaching him until my chin nearly met his chest, his gaze was on me and me alone. 'Do you really think you have what it takes to win me?' I murmured under my breath, peering up at him from between my eyelashes. 'Are you truly deserving of a future queen?' To my intense satisfaction, he inhaled sharply, his eyes swelling black. 'I thought so.' Smirking, I turned on my heel and continued along our path. After a beat, Kaz followed.

'Does it feel good?' he asked when he'd recovered.

'Tormenting you? Always.' My smirk grew as I sauntered along.

Kaz soon caught up with me. 'Calling yourself a queen.'

'I said *future* queen.' That robbed me of my smirk. I wasn't cut out to be a queen; I just wanted to break the curse and wreak my vengeance. The queen's heart. Then I could sail off across the Iron Sea into the sunset if I chose; I would be free to go wherever took my fancy. A collection of half-formed memories, long-forgotten and muddled together, shot into my head, like someone had fired an arrow of sentimentality at me. Of my mother, of soft hands, bedtime stories, curses and cobblestones running with dragon blood. It left a bitterness in my mouth that tasted like sorrow. 'I'm not interested in ruling a queendom. I just want her dead.'

Kaz leaped over a half-rotten trunk slowly losing itself to the thick carpet of moss running over it. 'Look.' He tapped the bark of a short, stout tree.

I squinted at it. A rudimentary symbol had been carved into it, three curving lines that were supposed to represent fire. 'Is that—'

'The symbol of the rebellion? Yes.' Kaz tapped it again. 'You have supporters everywhere; they're just in hiding, biding their time before they rally. You could be the match that strikes the fire they've been waiting over a decade for.'

I gnawed on my lip. I had no idea the rebellion had made it this deep into the forest, this close to me. The dracologists that lived in the castle had vanished that first night following the Purge; I used to fear that the queen had targeted them the same way she had the dragons, but now I wondered if any had made it out alive. If anyone I loved from my old life was also eking out a life in the forest.

Concern marred Kaz's brow in a way that I instantly disliked; it was too close a relation to pity. 'It's good to be cautious. More people in positions of power should fear the responsibility resting in their hands.'

'I'm not cautious; I'm unworthy.' Whoever the members of this rebellion are, they were older and smarter than me, had spent years if not decades plotting and planning their next move. Who was I to march in and try to take charge? I hadn't been living in the forest for two years yet – some of them must have been here for ten.

Kaz joined my side. 'You're worth far more than you realise.'

I twisted my lips to avoid replying; we were treading a dangerous path, one that wound up at the doorstep of my worst secret. I'd murdered and cannibalised six people since my eighteenth birthday, the day my mother had cursed me. After it became clear I wasn't going to respond, Kaz gestured ahead and we walked in silence. The forest was darkly atmospheric with glossy, green leaves and succulent berries, trails of fat mushrooms, wild garlic and nettles sprouting up every which way I looked. Ink-black beetles scurried past a thorned root that had stilled, sinister in the way it was waiting for its next prey to mistakenly lay a foot or paw on it.

'Out of curiosity,' Kaz shattered the silence, making me groan – what in the gods was going to come out of his mouth next? 'How are you planning on breaking your curse?'

'Nice try.' I gave him a smile that curved like the blade of a dagger. 'I'm not talking about my curse.' Or the terrible, twisted things I had done to thwart it. I only needed one more heart. Perhaps I'd find it today, if I could carve enough time away from Kaz to procure it. He might have been a heretic and a hunter, but I didn't think he was a murderer. That title was mine alone. Princess, murderess.

'Well, when you're ready to start thinking about things seriously, I can get you an audience with the forest demon.' Kaz shuddered. 'We've . . . met before. Once or twice. He owes me a favour.'

'Wait, I'm sorry – you *know* him?' I whirled round and stared at Kaz.

'Yes.'

Gesturing impatiently at him, I prompted, 'Are you going to elaborate? When did you meet him? What was he like?'

Kaz looked thoughtful. 'Strangely human,' he said at last. 'Which only made me fear him more.'

Before I could indulge my curiosity, Kaz spoke again. 'When we go our separate ways, just . . . think about it. For me.'

'Fine.' Loath as I was to admit it, he was right. Mazrovia deserved better than a witch queen who stole its magic, followed by a princess with a thirst for vengeance and nothing more. It needed a real queen. But I was just a cursed girl who devoured human hearts. I couldn't rule a queendom. Could I?

Spotting something, I swung out an arm, hitting Kaz in the chest and forcing him to halt.

A trained hunter, he fell back into a defensive crouch, alert at once.

I pointed a shaking finger at the line bisecting the forest ahead. On one side, lush undergrowth, speckled with mushroom caps. On the other, the plants were dusty and grey. A tree root had stopped mid-wander, its bark peeling as the magic which had sustained it had been bled dry. The queen had been here. 'She must have leached the magic here recently. It wasn't like this a few weeks ago.' My voice trembled as I stared at the evidence.

Kaz eyed the shrivelled plants. 'She'll cause another famine if she's not careful.'

We walked through the thinned foliage in silence. With each step, my heart sank further down my chest; the domowiki that lived in Sanok had probably already faded, leaving homes unprotected, which was a near death sentence living this close to the forest with its prowling bauks and rusałki.

Soon we caught our first glimpse of Sanok. On the sign that pointed towards the hamlet was hammered another notice declaring me missing. This one offered a handsome reward for my safe return. With a larger rendering of my face on it.

Kaz tore it down and folded it neatly, sliding it into his pocket. 'Another one to add to my collection.' He grinned.

Muttering several unrepeatable words under my breath that made his grin widen, I yanked up my hood. That notice hadn't been here the last time I'd visited Sanok. It rattled me with too many questions I knew I'd never find the answers for. Why would my mother go to all the bother of cursing me only to declare me missing almost two years later? I couldn't make sense of it.

A lone bell rang, slow and dull, its brassy song shrill though the treeline. A couple of ravens took flight, as disturbed as I was. That was new, too. Queen Serce and the True Path had well and truly sunk their claws into Sanok, edging ever nearer to the boundary of Stary Bór. To me.

CHAPTER TEN

Gloomy days suited the forest, wreathing it in spectral mist. They did not suit Sanok. The hamlet was a muddy, foggy wasteland, with just a smattering of stalls along a cobbled path, illuminated by the globes of oil streetlamps. A handful of people scurried along, weighed down with shopping baskets, dressed in drab greys: the further from the cities you travelled, the more colour leaked from outfits, and these people living on the edge of Stary Bór itself had long since learned how to dress to avoid attracting attention from anything hungry peering out from the bordering treeline.

'Well, this is a cheery place,' Kaz commented as we walked into Sanok. Although he blended in with his dark grey cloak, his height alone drew a few wary looks. With my chestnut-brown furred hood draped low over my face, I invited suspicion as well. But better suspicion than detection, since I'd just passed another of the queen's notices, hammered into the side of the first stall we passed. 'Are you sure this is a good idea?' Kaz asked quietly. 'What if someone recognises you?'

'Then I'll run like a demon.' I doubted anyone would chance racing into the forest after me.

'I should have come alone. This is too risky.' Kaz shook his head at an older man with a straggly white beard who held up a turnip from his wares as we wandered by.

I couldn't admit that I'd been worried he wouldn't return if I'd let him go alone, that I'd wanted to cling onto just a few more hours with him. Something about this huntsman had me twisted up with confusing thoughts and feelings. 'It's your fault we're having to make a supply run,' I said instead, sharper than I'd intended; I was only frustrated with myself, but my mouth was a runaway carriage. 'If you hadn't turned up, my food would have lasted longer, and I wouldn't have fed a domowik the last of my goat's milk.'

'No, you would have killed it instead.'

That silenced me.

'I'm sorry,' Kaz groaned. 'I wasn't thinking.'

'No, you're right. I would have killed it.' And added another body – however incorporeal – to my growing tally. Whenever I spotted the domowik's baleful eyes peering trustfully at me, my guilt thickened. I'd come so close to ending that little spark of magic.

'You weren't to know,' he said, gentler. 'Although there is one good thing to come out of all of this.'

'What's that?'

He grinned, patting his pocket. 'I come bearing gold. Whatever you need, it's on me. It's the least I could do after you've been such a gracious host.' He sidled a glance at me. 'Poison aside.'

He was right, that did cheer me. There were only so many gold coins I could get by pawning the fistful of jewellery I'd escaped the castle with, and I was running low. I thought I would have unbound myself from my curse by now, but most of my time in Stary Bór had been dedicated to not dying. Avoiding starvation, freezing or being mortally wounded by a wandering tree root took more time and effort than I could have predicted. 'Well, why didn't you say so earlier? I would have written a longer shopping list!'

'This isn't the Amber City; I think you need to manage your expectations.' Kaz laughed under his breath, a deep chortle that I never got tired of hearing. Luckily, he paused to consider a stall stocked with books, instead of my face, which was betraying that flicker of affection I couldn't seem to stamp out.

'Go on, then.' He set down a book on the history of dracology and we moved on.

I shot him a baffled look. 'What?'

His sigh was short, exasperated. 'Your list,' he said impatiently. 'What would be on it?'

I shrugged, running a hand over a chunky woollen shawl as we walked on. 'I've got used to living with less. There's no point wearing satin slippers or delicate jewels in the forest. I have a roof over my head and when the trees aren't scaring me half to death, I manage to forage enough food. I've gotten pretty good at cooking now, too.' I made a mean stew, and I was close to getting the hang of pinching my dumplings together hard enough so that my pierogi didn't fall apart in the pan any more. 'I guess we need some extra milk though, since the domowik seems to like guzzling so much of it.' I could probably do with baking more biscuits, and my vial of ground belladonna berries was looking a little low as well.

'That's an incredibly boring answer.'

I laughed. 'What did you expect? That I'd ask for a pretty ribbon for my hair?' I teased. 'I haven't even brushed my hair since I left the castle.'

His gaze flicked over me then darted away. 'Well, you look good to me,' he said, suddenly becoming very interested in a stall of pickled onions, though not fast enough to disguise the sadness that had filled his voice. It was uncomfortably close to pity.

I waggled my fingers. 'Who needs a hairbrush when you've got these?' Katia would have been horrified. She would happily spend hours braiding my hair in evermore beautiful styles while I read aloud. The longer and more intricate the better, so I would manage a decent chunk of a book without being interrupted; after all, nobody could question that being beautiful was one of a princess's duties. Even Pan Jedrick and Pani Smok never summoned me away from such primping.

'Are you following the True Path?' A middle-aged woman in a simple navy dress, overmended and too thin for the early spring storms, thrust a notice in front of my face. She sounded similar to the queen and me, all polished vowels and crisp consonants, signposting that she'd come from the Amber City. Although of course my mother's accent was like everything else in her life – carefully curated. Unbeknownst to her loyal citizens and followers, she hadn't grown up in the secluded summer palace down the river from the Amber City but in the wild Witchlands of the tundra, learning how to manage her magic. A fact she'd let slip one evening during a heatwave, after one too many glasses of iced cherry wine. I, however, had grown up in the capital, so I made sure to soften my speech and elongate my words like I'd come from the east, towards Mistport, when I responded.

'Oh, I, er—' I was distracted by the shiny pin flashing on her collar: A golden path shining through a clouded white space. The same symbol flew on flags above the castle, a sign that she'd been dispatched as an ambassador to help spread the faith.

Kaz smoothly intercepted the notice. 'Thank you.'

'May the One True Path lead you to glory,' the ambassador recited by rote, though her smile seemed genuine, burying her beady eyes in a sea of crinkles.

'And peace in the name of the Path,' we echoed back to her, a heretic huntsman and a murdering princess, lying through their teeth together. A few streets later, I exhaled. 'It's getting worse,' I told Kaz grimly. 'They didn't have a church the last time I visited and did you notice that—'

'She wasn't from here? Yes, I did.' He shook his head. 'That Amber City accent gave it away the moment she opened her mouth.' This was how Queen Serce had spread her control: through the burgeoning religion she'd latched onto, sending out ambassadors throughout Mazrovia to instil fear and obedience in each city, town and village. Now her reach had extended to the hamlets, and these poor people would be forced to register their households and renounce their magic, if they had any. Once registered, any use of magic or magical items, artefacts and harbouring magical creatures, all carried a steep punishment. Last I checked, it was fifty public lashings. Unless you fancied handing over any magical creatures you found, then you would be rewarded in gold. Hatred turned me cold. The queen's priests had lectured me on the importance of attending their church, but I'd refused to set foot in the building that had Migot's bones dangling above its doors. One good thing that came from the queen ignoring me – my unattendance went unremarked.

'Looks like we're not the only ones trying to keep a low profile.' Nudging Kaz, I jerked my head at a couple of cloaked figures bartering at a stall on the edge of the market.

'Those black cloaks,' he muttered as I craned my neck for a better view. 'They might be rebels. They could be here on Rebellion business.'

As I forged forwards, he grabbed my cloak, yanking me back to his side. Ignoring my glare, he adjusted my hood, checking that it covered my hair, my eyes. He gently tucked an escaped strand of hair back inside the hood, his fingers lingering on my neck, his touch warm and light and irresistible.

I sucked in a soft breath.

His hands fell away. 'You must not be seen.'

'I won't be, but I have to see what they're doing here.' Catching the caution in his face, I sighed. 'I won't draw any attention to myself.'

'No, you won't,' he said stubbornly. 'Because you're staying here. I'll go and see if I can hear what they're doing in Sanok. If they even are rebels, that is.'

Swinging my basket impatiently, I watched Kaz make his way over to the cloaked figures. If they were truly rebels, they were risking almost as much as me by being here. There had to be some great reason for their presence.

A few minutes passed before the reason made itself apparent.

Two Angels of Death rounded the new church. Their raven-feather wings and bladed helmets were a nightmare in the faded hamlet. A fresh horror pounded in my ears when I noticed what they were carrying: a fortified cage. My basket fell from my hand: shadowy tendrils were looped round the cage bars. They'd captured the last loyal domowiki, their weakened state suggesting they had not left when the queen had purged Sanok of magic but attempted to stay and protect their families' homes, even as they lost their form.

Across the market, Kaz very slowly and deliberately shook his head at me.

I took no heed.

Darting between shoppers, losing sight of the rebels, I stole closer to the Angels of Death. My pulse skittered with fear, but seeing those poor domowiki had angered me enough to want to rip out the Angels' spines.

In my haste, I bumped into someone. Their black hood fell down and a pair of brown eyes widened as the person beneath registered my identity. 'Will you free them?' I whispered, pleading to Perun that they were indeed a rebel, and I hadn't revealed myself to someone who would betray me.

'The cage is magic,' they whispered back. A rebel, then. My legs almost gave out in relief. 'We'd need more time than we can spare to free them. Our information was too late in coming and we didn't bring enough people.'

Bending down, I pulled a small knife free from my boot. 'Here.' I slid it into the rebel's pocket. 'This can cut through magic.'

'There are too many people here – it's still too risky.' They sounded panicked now. The crowd was pushing around us, swallowing us in one greedy gulp, hiding any trace of the other rebel. Or Kaz.

When I scanned the area, my heart pounded harder: a carriage sat waiting on the outskirts of the marketplace, embossed with the Angels' distinctive black-and-silver livery. 'I'll distract them,' I promised. 'I'll buy enough time for you to save them.'

The rebel gave me an appraising stare.

I tried and failed to summon an air of confidence. Time was slipping through my fingers and all I could picture was my domowik's wide, trusting eyes. 'Please. Please don't give up on them. They'll be killed if you don't save them.'

'Fine. But don't let me down,' the rebel warned.

Hurrying around the stalls, taking care to keep my hood low, my accent hidden, I quickly filled a basket with flour, butter, cheese and bottles of goat's milk, tossing coins at the sellers as I paced by, searching for a distraction.

I was glancing at a tray of poppyseed cake when the heavy tread of boots approached. Alarm flooded me, lightning-fast and searing. Whipping round, one hand braced at the knife hilt on my hip, everything within me was prepared to come face to face with one of the Angels of Death. Instead, I was greeted with a coffin. Four men carried a glass coffin on their shoulders, taking slow and measured steps as they passed through the marketplace.

'The eternal resting place is just up there.' The market seller gestured to a field next to the treeline.

When I squinted, I saw rows of coffins resting above ground. The clouds reluctantly drifted apart for a moment, allowing the sun to steal a look. All the coffins suddenly shone. Each one had been crafted from glass.

The market seller caught my reaction. 'Can't be too careful, living this close to the forest and all,' he said gruffly, his scraggly grey eyebrows drawing together.

The coffin bearers drew abreast with us. We fell silent. Inside the glass coffin was a young woman, who couldn't have been more than a few solstices my senior. Even in death, she was dressed in grey. And a large, roughly hewn stake had been hammered straight through her heart. My palms sweated.

'I thought you believed that following the One True Path would keep you safe,' I couldn't resist pointing out when the eerie procession had moved past us.

The market seller grunted. 'You'd have to be a godsforsaken fool not to follow the Path.' He cast a furtive glance to each side before lowering his voice. 'But it doesn't matter how brightly they paint that new church of theirs, it won't do a bit of good against the strzygi.'

I shuddered at the thought of that woman rising in the night, with an uncontrollable hunger for human blood. I'd never seen a strzyga, an undead person, but Katia's superstitious mother claimed she'd once seen one that had folded itself into a bat and flown away. Katia often found cloves of garlic deposited in her pockets, long after her mother had relocated them both to the Amber City.

'If you're worried about that sort of thing, then these will protect you.' After a quick glance to make sure nobody was watching, the market seller pulled out a small iron box. 'Be sure to keep it well hidden, mind.' Opening the box, he revealed a tangle of protective amulets, each leather cord strung with a chunk of amber.

It was a struggle not to react. Since our castle was the beating heart of the Amber City, my mother had gifted me a piece of amber every birthday, each one carved into the likeness of an animal that prowled our queendom. I'd left behind a small menagerie when I fled the castle, including the amber deer that I'd just received upon turning eighteen. It was a relic from another life. One that, according to Kaz, was mine for the seizing. I frowned at the box of amber from a once-life, a life that could be mine again if I only dared to dream bigger and bloodier. If I tapped into the darkness within.

'Will you be wanting one, then?' The market seller's patience had worn as threadbare as his tunic. 'It's real amber, straight from the amberworkers in the Amber City. Yours for only two quarters of gold.'

'Not today, thank you.' I made to move on. Time was running out for the domowiki and I'd already wasted too much.

But the seller followed me from behind his stall.

'Pity, that. Pretty girls like you can't be too careful.'

My smile pinched my cheeks.

'Have I seen you around these parts before?' the seller continued. 'There's something awful familiar about your face.'

There it was: my distraction. Oh, Kaz was going to be *livid* with me.

'I don't know what you're talking about,' I told him, letting my Amber City accent bleed through my words, my hood slide down a little.

The seller jolted back. *Five, four, three, two—* 'Hey, I've found the princess,' he hollered.

Slamming my hands down onto the wooden counter, sending

slices of poppyseed cake skittering like beetles, I vaulted over the stall and took off through the marketplace. My basket swung wildly, sending a couple of eggs smashing onto the cobblestones. I should have abandoned it, but a girl had to eat.

The market seller yelled something about a reward in gold for finding the missing princess.

I fled through the market, knocking over displays, hoping against hope that this would be a sufficient distraction for the rebels to liberate the caged domowiki. And that the Angels of Death wouldn't switch and come for me instead.

Another pair of bootsteps fell alongside me. Kaz. 'What in Nawia are you playing at?' he growled. 'You're going to get yourself caught!'

'You're too predictable – I knew you'd be livid.' I half laughed, flushed with my own success as we fled the hamlet, a gathering crowd hollering at our heels. Apparently, the amount of gold Queen Serce had promised for my return was tempting enough to brave Stary Bór. I should have paid better attention to the posters wearing my face – how much had she decided I was worth?

'Run faster,' Kaz snapped.

CHAPTER ELEVEN

Just as we neared the treeline, an Angel of Death reared up in front of us. My hood had fallen back as I'd fled, and I caught the instant he recognised me, his mouth falling open in shock that the princess had truly materialised in a tiny hamlet this side of Stary Bór.

It might have been comical if my situation wasn't so dire. If I hadn't also recognised him.

'You,' I clenched my hands into fists. 'You got me *banished*.'

Kaz snapped to attention.

A handful of villagefolk were approaching behind him. 'They're herding us,' Kaz said grimly.

I leaped into action, drawing my knife and advancing. But the Angel of Death drew his bayonet faster, swinging it towards my head as if he meant to knock me unconscious. My mother might have cursed me, but it seemed she wanted my return in one piece. To a castle, a city, I could not enter. Nothing made sense.

Ducking just in time, the bayonet whistled over my head. Before I could spring back up, Kaz appeared behind the Angel, grabbing his helmeted head in both hands and snapping his neck. He threw the Angel's body to the ground, then smoothed his cloak down as if he had merely rustled it on a pleasant afternoon walk, while I stared incredulously at him.

The horde of villagefolk were nearing us now. And they were not thrilled by this latest development. At least this was proving to be a momentous distraction for the rebels to both free the domowiki and get safely away.

Kaz grabbed my hand. A tiny zing of lightning zapped my palm and, for a heartbeat, we both glanced down at our entwined hands, before Kaz broke into a run, towing me along as I struggled to meet his long stride.

'Wait! This way is better.' I dug my heels into the waterlogged earth, pivoting and dragging Kaz towards the field of coffins.

My feet sunk into the mud with each beat, my head pounding with the effort of battling the sink and slide as I ran, holding onto the basket so tightly my fingers were numb. My focus sharpened on the rows of coffins in front of us. Each one filled with a body. Some still looked like bodies, others were far removed from the person they'd once been. Surrounded by a field of skeletons and rotting corpses, Kaz slowed. 'Elka—'

'They've slowed down, don't stop now.' I drove myself to battle these conditions, to run faster. My suspicions were right; the villagers didn't like to enter this field. Nobody wanted to witness their loved ones rot. We wove between glass coffins, not looking at their occupants, or the wood staked through each of their hearts. The first villagers resumed their chase with a valiant roar.

The wall of forest loomed before us.

We slipped between the first trunks like lost spirits. Tall pines surrounded us, turning the world green and shadowed as we lost sight of the thunderous grey sky. The villagers' shouts became muffled, the forest swallowing their sound.

We slowed, the trees silently staring at us with mournful knots in their trunks like whale eyes. The path grew twisted and mossy. 'Thank Perun you appeared when you did.' I clamped a hand to the stitch in my side. My roots were tight and painful; running with hard bark inside your veins was not a pursuit I'd recommend.

'What were you thinking, Elka?' Kaz wheeled on me with an expression I couldn't decipher. 'You could have got caught – you *did* get caught.'

'I didn't stay caught,' I pointed out brightly, trying to forget how that Angel of Death had reared up before us and the field of dead we'd trespassed through. I only hoped that we'd caused enough chaos to save the domowiki. To help the rebel cause. I wondered what else they were doing in the forest, if perhaps they would take me in after I killed the queen. Though maybe once I had taken the queen's heart, I would be removing their chief cause. They could help restore the magic instead then.

Taking my basket, Kaz swiftly transferred the milk bottles and paper-wrapped groceries into the knapsack he carried as we strode onwards. The eggs were beyond saving. The basket, too. Kaz tossed it aside. A thorned tree root slithered over, wrapping itself round the basket and squeezing until it collapsed with a sickening crunch.

'It was worth it to save the domowiki,' I told him.

He grunted in response. 'Nothing was worth compromising your safety.'

'Of course it was. They were innocent magical creatures; they needed help. What kind of person would I be if I turned a blind eye to them? I couldn't bear that on my conscience.' Not when it was already so burdened. Number Five's scream rang through my head. *'You've got a black hole where your soul should be.'* His had been the worst kill, the bloodiest. There had been no spiked wódka for him, not when he had snatched me from behind the trees when I was mushroom-picking, grabbing at my leggings. He'd fought hard; I'd fought harder. Funnily enough, it was not his kill that haunted me – it was his words. They'd skittered to the back of my skull, lurking there ever since. Each time they came out to play, I believed them a little more. 'When you lie in bed at night, it's the chances like these, the opportunities you had to help someone that will fester into regret. These are the moments that make you the person you want to be in this world and that is *always* worth taking a chance on, even if it comes at personal risk.' I would spend a lifetime atoning for those six lives I'd taken.

Kaz went quiet. I sidled a look at him, checking he was still listening. He looked lost. No, unguarded. 'I never thought of it that way,' he said eventually.

'I'm sorry I dragged you into it; for a moment I thought you'd left,' I admitted.

He crashed to a halt, the heat in his stare pinning me in place. 'I would never leave you without saying goodbye.'

'When are you leaving?' I whispered. We had agreed he would accompany me to Sanok, nothing more. He looked at me like a storm, fierce and beautiful and territorial all at once, and I wanted to hold onto him, to keep him by my side a little longer. But he had a life to return to and I had a curse to break. A soft crunching through the undergrowth alerted us. 'The villagers. They're coming through the forest after us.' After *me*.

Kaz tore his attention away from me, gesturing eastwards. With a nod, I ploughed on. Mist swirled around my mud-caked boots, obscuring jagged rocks and protruding roots, slowing our path, and still shouts echoed through the trees, and blades snicked as our pursuers cut down the undergrowth in their way.

At least the remaining Angel of Death didn't seem to be among them. I hoped the rebels had escaped his clutches.

'There are too many . . . we'll never outrun them all,' I panted, my rooted arm screaming, stiff and sore. It rubbed against my bone. 'Even if we did, one of them might be a tracker and we could lead them straight back to my cottage.' And I had seriously had enough of things prowling around my cottage when I was trying to sleep.

'Good point.' Kaz's eyebrows drew together, his expression as shadowed as the forest. 'Come with me.' Shifting his pack higher on his shoulders, he took off.

I followed him through knee-high weeds, past brambles and thorned berry bushes to a small, tightly winding river. As grey as the sky we could no longer see, and colder than my feet on a winter's night.

Kaz walked directly into it. I plunged straight in after him. It was colder than I'd anticipated. Following its narrow bends, the mud was slick beneath my boots, almost sending me into the deeper water racing through the centre more than once. Icy water swirled around my calves, my boots squelched with each step, and my toes were already numb. Gritting my teeth together, I forced myself to keep going, just one step at a time. Just another step, just one more—

A baying hound howled. Long and low, the sound cut through me like a knife, sending me crashing into Kaz in my hurry to escape. 'It will be all right,' he told me fiercely, grabbing my arm when I slid in the mud. 'I've got you.'

'They've brought dogs now.' Panic turned my vision red, fire behind my eyelids. Thank the gods I hadn't brought my dragon egg with me; it was safer left at the cottage. Safer without me there to endanger it. Everyone was safer without me. 'You should leave,' I told Kaz urgently. 'They won't follow you; you'll be better off going it alone.'

'What did I tell you about leaving?' he growled. He reached

out towards me and, for a moment, my heart stuttered, wondering what he was going to do, but he reached past and snapped off a handful of reeds from the riverbank. 'Take this, and put it in your mouth,' he instructed, holding one out to me. 'Breathe through the reed and go beneath the surface. We'll wait them out.'

I snatched one and crammed it into my mouth. Before ducking underwater, Kaz stretched across to the riverbank again, wedging his knapsack under a large fern. It was the last thing I saw before freezing grey water closed over my head, turning my bones to ice. Before Kaz sank down through the water next to me, turning until he set eyes on me. His tawny hair waved around him but I couldn't make out his face; the water was too murky, the forest canopy too thick and dark. I couldn't hear the hounds any more either, which frightened me; what if one suddenly appeared? I wouldn't have time to flee. My nostrils and ears filled with water, shutting down my senses one by one. Glancing behind, just in case, my breath coming faster and shorter, little huffs through the reed, I felt Kaz's fingers wrap round my wrist. When I turned my attention back to him, he slowly pulled me towards him and folded me into his arms. There, I felt a pulse of warmth through the teeth-chattering, almost frozen water – his heartbeat, pressed against mine.

As we hid underwater with a horde hunting me down, I counted our heartbeats until the villagers grew bored of wandering up and down the riverbank and through the forest, and returned to Sanok and its brick homes with iron doors that bolted shut.

When I crawled out of the river, I was a sodden, shivering mess.

'You're shaking,' Kaz said in that deep voice that curled my toes.

'It's spring, shouldn't it be warmer than this?' My teeth chattered, hard enough to split in two. I wrung my hair out, but I was frozen to my marrow and knowing the long hard trudge that awaited us before we'd be back in front of my fire made me want to cry. We'd rushed into the river in such a hurry, we'd gone in boots and cloaks and all, leaving nothing to dry ourselves with, nothing to bundle up in to relieve this bone-aching cold.

Kaz took a boot off, tipping it upside down. A small lake poured out from it. His laugh was indulgent, warm. I wanted to wrap it round myself like a blanket, and ask him why in Nawia he wasn't as cold as me. 'What's the matter, princess, missing your toasty castle?'

I flicked my hair at him, giving him a faceful of freezing water. He spluttered. 'Fine, I concede,' he said grumpily, taking off his cloak and slinging it over the crook of his arm. An idea wisped across his face. 'Follow me.' He set off into the forest, moving stealthily through the willowy pines and ancient oaks, careful not to step on any wandering branches or alert any beasts to our presence.

'This is the wrong way back to my cottage,' I hissed at his

back, trying not to notice the wet shirt clinging to his muscles, the way he moved, so elegant and sinuous, surprising for his height and breadth. He moved like a dancer or swordfighter, and it was impossible not to watch, not to feel . . . *something*. 'You're going to get us lost and I do *not* want to be lost in the forest when night falls.'

Kaz tossed an impish smirk back at me. 'Just trust me.'

'*Trust you?*' I lost my words, disorientated by his easy smile and wet shirt and the memory of his arms round me. Nobody had ever protected me like that before. I'd been guarded out of duty, but I'd never been held like I was something precious, like my thoughts and feelings were just as important and valid as my status, my face.

We walked through the gathering fog, shivering hard enough to make our muscles ache. Well, mine at least – Kaz didn't seem affected, though maybe he was better at hiding his feelings, or maybe he'd just grown up in an ice cave so didn't realise that we'd been in water in inhumane temperatures, I thought grumpily. I suddenly realised that Kaz had halted and was waiting for my reaction.

A soft bubbling met my ears. It hadn't been fog wending through the trunks: it was steam. Sunk into the forest floor, surrounded by jewel-green ferns and smooth rock, was a large hot spring. '*Oh.*' I gazed at the steaming pool reverently.

A self-satisfied look washed over Kaz's face. 'I thought it might meet with your approval.'

'Are you always this smug? You could go a day without massaging your own ego, you know.'

'Why?' He cocked his head to one side. 'Would you prefer to . . . massage it for me?' He gave me the kind of wicked smile that sent heat rushing to my cheeks. Then he stripped off his shirt and dove in. And, yes, I had seen him shirtless before, when the bauk had lanced through his side, leaving behind the horrific wound that I'd dressed, but I'd been focused on the spread of poison through his veins and torn flesh, not— My throat turned dry. His chest was defined, his stomach sculpted, and that deep 'V' beneath had me transfixed.

When I managed to drag my eyes back to his, he was far too amused. 'Are you going to join me?' he asked, raising an eyebrow. 'Or would you prefer to just stand there and stare?'

I pressed a hand to my stomach. My armoured corset was hard beneath my oversized shirt, and while it couldn't have been a surprise that I was wearing protection, with my shirt wetly plastered against it, my curse spilled down half of one arm and sprouted along my collarbone. I didn't want to remove my shirt and see Kaz's pity. He thought I was fierce and beautiful, the idea of him looking differently at me filled me with sadness and frustration. I shivered under the rising heat of the hot spring. It was just so very *cold*.

Before I could overthink it, I peeled off my wet shirt, giving Kaz his first look at the armoured corset I wore beneath. Of my curse, displayed at last. He stilled in the water, eyes locked on me, his jawline tensing. My chest hitched as I watched him drink me in, standing there before him, shivering. The leaf on my collarbone curled. His gaze fell to the only hardened vein of mine on view, the bark-brown branching down along my arm. It was stiff in the cold, each time I moved my arm, I felt its painful creak. Lowering my eyes, I kicked off my boots and yanked my leather leggings down, less embarrassed to reveal my simple black underwear than I had been my curse, and stepped into the steaming hot spring. Warm water rushed up my legs, swallowing me in heat. I breathed in deep lungfuls of steam. *Warm, at last.* My teeth finally stopped clattering, my bones stopped shaking, my hardened root-veins stopped creaking. I felt more like myself again.

Walking deeper, I approached Kaz. His brow was still furrowed, a storm brewing in his mood. A muscle ticked in his jaw as he clenched it. 'Who did this to you?' he demanded.

I raised my eyebrows at him.

Kaz swore. 'Your curse,' he said darkly. 'The queen cannot be allowed to get away with this, I won't stand for it.'

My eyebrows inched higher. 'I don't need a rescuer,' I told him. 'I am my own protector. The only person that's going to save me will be *me*.'

'That doesn't mean that I can't care,' Kaz ground out. 'Or that you should feel like you have to hide these things.'

'You're one to talk,' I retorted. 'Your secrets are your armour. You keep them wrapped around yourself so tightly that half of you is closed off.' Hidden behind that smirk and fiery temper.

Kaz hesitated. 'Is there something particular you wanted to know?'

'Yes.' There were so many things I itched to know. Like how he became a huntsman, where he was living now and when he was going to say that promised farewell and return to it. If he'd wanted to spend this time with me because I was the princess and his golden key to securing a position in the castle if I gained the throne, or if sometimes, when he looked at me like I was his air and he couldn't breathe without me, if that could really be the truth. In the end, it was the smallest itch that needed scratching the most urgently.

'How did the bauk manage to attack you unawares?'

Kaz let out a rough sigh. 'The week before my attack, I'd spotted you in the forest when I was hunting deer. You were picking mushrooms and your hair was—' He seemed lost in the mist.

'My hair was what?' I asked suspiciously.

'Beautiful,' he said simply. 'I recognised you at once.'

My pulse skittered.

'I spent the following days mulling things over, planning and plotting and wondering what you might be like. I figured that if you were roughing it out here, you might be made of tougher stuff than most people gave you credit for. That maybe, just maybe, I could help you along the path to something greater.'

I watched him silently, waiting for him to continue. Listening for any hint that he had witnessed something he shouldn't have.

'It was the night I had decided to walk straight up to your door and speak to you when the bauk took me by surprise. I should have seen signs that one was prowling nearby.' He shook his head ruefully. 'But I was too caught up in my own thoughts. In the idea of you. And by the time I realised my mistake, it was too late.'

I began to doubt he'd seen me with a stolen heart; I had taken it hours earlier that evening and it had been far from my usual paths. 'Why didn't you tell me that turning up near my cottage was no accident? I would have heard you out.' I spread my arms wide in the water, sinking a little deeper into the heat.

'I wish I had.' Kaz's voice pitched low. 'But being around you felt different than I'd expected.'

I glanced up, caught unawares by the change in his tone. 'How so?'

'I didn't expect to forget my duty to Mazrovia, to this forest. I didn't expect that I would lie awake, thinking of you. That the very notion of the queen cursing you would be so intolerable I couldn't imagine you going to war with her, didn't want to imagine it.' Kaz's gaze was intense, consuming. His wet hair was almost black, his cheekbones dewy from the hot water, his broad chest and shoulders wet, with steam billowing around him like a cloak of shadows. It was taking an immense amount of effort on my behalf not to jump into his arms. His strong, well-defined arms. Gods, what was *wrong* with me? When he spoke again, his voice turned husky. 'You take up a surprising amount of room in my head, Elka.'

My lips parted in surprise.

Kaz gave a rough sigh. 'Gods, don't look at me like that.'

I didn't know what was happening here, only that I was so very tired of fighting whatever *this* was. 'Or what?' I whispered.

His eyes dropped to my mouth. 'Or I might not be able to resist you much longer,' he groaned.

'Nobody said you had to resist me.' I swallowed my nerves, waiting. If he didn't kiss me soon, I might have to swallow my pride and take the first leap. I watched as Kaz took in what I'd said, as his pupils swelled, his throat bobbing up and down. Slowly, he came closer. 'I'm not a good person, Elka,' he breathed.

'I don't care.' And I didn't. The snap of my victims' ribcages echoed through my nightmares.

I saw that he didn't believe me. Guilt entered his eyes and, for a moment, I wondered what haunted him. How he'd snapped the Angel's neck with such cold precision – that had not been his first time. But even if Kaz had done something wicked, he could never be as awful as I had been. As I was. As I *am*. I decided I was right; I didn't care. I just craved his mouth on mine. I leaned closer. Wishing, hoping that he hadn't changed his mind, that he would give in to that desire that ran through us, that cord of attraction that kept tightening and tightening, drawing us ever closer. Whether we were fighting or fleeing or facing a fresh horror, every time I met his eyes, the air crackled.

And then the steam parted.

On the other side of the hot springs, a woman lay face down in the water, her hair billowing like seaweed.

CHAPTER TWELVE

She was rigid and unmoving.

'*Gods,*' I breathed, striking out across the water towards her.

'Elka, no!' Kaz shouted after me. 'She's a—'

I dipped underwater to swim the last distance, re-emerging beside the drowned woman. Placing a hand on her cold, stiff back, I rolled her over to check if she could be revived. I heard Kaz swimming towards me, hard and strong, but he was too late. We both were.

The woman's eyes snapped open. She smiled, revealing three lines of dagger-sharp yellow teeth. I screamed, throwing myself back just as Kaz reached me. 'Rusałka,' he finished. 'She's a rusałka.' One of his strong arms wrapped round me as he tucked me behind him. He stood defensively before me. 'Stay back, Elka.'

The rusałka preened at Kaz. Her skin held a greenish tint to it, her eyes were liquid pools of darkness and, as she unfolded her limbs and stood, I realised she was much taller than me. Taller even than Kaz, and slender, with ropes of muscles corded around her neck, shoulders and arms. Imbued with the strength to drown several people at once.

'Isn't she beautiful?' Kaz said dreamily.

She was beautiful. She was also a living nightmare. The rusałka stared at Kaz like she wanted to swallow him whole.

'Kaz, come with me.' I tugged at his arm, but the huntsman was an immoveable force of nature. '*Now*, Kaz,' I urged, panic setting in as the rusałka began to approach us. Teeth bared, she moved through the water like a snake, those black eyes never moving from ours, filled with hunger. A string of saliva dripped from her open mouth. 'I thought rusałki drowned their prey,' I said nervously, still trying to get Kaz to snap back to his senses, to realise that a rusałka was stalking towards us, closer and closer, to *move*.

'Drowning us makes it easier to feast on us.' Kaz spoke like he had a mouth filled with honey, slow and dreamlike.

To my intense horror, the rusałka then *spoke*. 'He's right,' she rasped, with a voice like nails down slate. 'There's nothing better than biting into a body filled with water. It bursts in your mouth like ripe fruit.' Her terrible, drooling smile curdled my blood.

If I didn't get Kaz to move now, I would be forced to fight her and I did not fancy my odds against those vicious teeth.

'Kaz!' I yelled at him. Nothing. I slapped him as hard as I could, right on one of his beautiful cheekbones, leaving a bright red mark behind. He blinked, once then twice, confusion muddying his features. 'Come on!' I screamed in his face as the rusałka reached out her elongated fingers and curled them round Kaz's arm. Her fingernails were long and jagged and stained with old blood. Drawing the knife at my hip, I plunged it through her wrist, driving it down with enough force that my blade didn't stop until it grated against bone.

The rusałka screamed.

Viscous algae-tinted blood ran down her arm. It stank like rotting weeds. As she cradled it against her chest, I turned and rammed myself against Kaz, using my body weight to physically shift him. I managed to push him onto the bank before I realised the mistake I'd made.

I hadn't been watching the rusałka.

Whipping round, knife in hand, I was already lunging forwards to defend myself – but she wasn't there. Steam drifted up from the water, cloud-thick, obscuring my view. I couldn't see my own hands through the haze.

My weapons master, Pan Jedrick's voice cut through my thoughts. *'The worst kind of enemy is the one you didn't see coming.'*

'What happened?' Kaz asked groggily, climbing out of the hot spring and extending a hand to pull me up.

I took it, scrambling out in a hurry. A rusałka could only venture so far from a water source, and as much as I'd welcomed the sight of the hot springs, now that I knew what was lurking there, I never wanted to see them again.

When my feet touched the forest floor, Kaz, who had bent to

retrieve our discarded clothes and boots, stiffened. 'What is it?' I automatically whipped round.

A row of rusałki were stalking through the steam towards us. Five of them, moving in tandem, their beauty melting from their faces like wax, revealing the sharp teeth and hunger and claws beneath. 'Hungry,' they hissed in one terrible voice. 'So very *hungry.*'

I swore loudly, digging my nails into Kaz's arm to keep him alert, afraid that he'd fall for their bewitchments again. '*Run.*'

'That's three times you've saved me now,' Kaz panted as we fled through the forest, leaping over thirsty tree roots and ducking under jagged branches. Something wild howled in the distance, an owl hooted softly, and behind the thick layer of cloud, the sun bled across the sky. The gloaming hour was upon us. All too soon, it would be chased by night, and we had no lantern. At least we'd long shaken off the villagers.

'*Four* times,' I corrected. 'The antidote, the bauk – twice – and the rusałka. However are you going to pay me back?' I said before I could help myself. Gods, it seemed like the flirting was catching. Kaz caught my grimace and gave a weak laugh. The day had been long and we were running against time itself now. Before darkness swallowed the forest and we were left stumbling along, lost in the blackness. We paused to pull on our still-wet clothes and boots; the rusałki would not be the sole hunters lurking around at this hour. My thighs ached and my root was taut through my chest and arm, groaning like the wind through the trees as I forced myself to keep running.

'The rusałki have grown hungrier since their hunting grounds have shrunk,' Kaz said.

'That doesn't surprise me,' I panted. Yet another reason why Queen Serce had worsened Mazrovia. As appalling as the rusałki were, they were spirits, not entirely unlike the domowiki; they both needed the ancient magic of Mazrovia to live. With the queen taking more and more of the magic, she was forcing all these magical creatures into smaller territories. Making them a bloodbath. I didn't understand why she needed all this power for herself, why the blood running through her own veins wasn't enough for her tithe. How she had even learned how to steal magic from the queendom itself. I didn't voice my questions aloud: Kaz would undoubtedly leave in the morning and my problems would be just that. Mine.

Finally, we passed a familiar curved oak, and there was my crooked little cottage, bracketed by its pair of wych elms. Smoke leaked from the chimney like mist, the sole sign of life behind the shuttered windows and bolted doors.

After unlocking the door, I almost cried at the warmth that immediately enveloped me – I had expected the fire to be reduced to embers, but it was burning hot and bright. My dragon egg was safe. A knot loosened within me. A wisp of shadow flicked by in the corner of my eye. The domowik. 'Did you do this?'

I asked, my voice trembling with exhaustion. It quivered in the doorway, its doe eyes deep and expressive. 'Thank you,' I said. It flitted over to the kitchen and back, as if it wanted to show me something.

There was a steaming bathtub in the kitchen. I shivered at the sight. Soaking in the hot springs was a distant memory now, undone by fleeing through the cold forest in wet clothes. I thanked the domowik again, almost falling to my knees with gratitude and relief and exhaustion, and, for a heartbeat, its silhouette firmed, its shadowy mass solidifying before it collapsed back down into its wispy form, disappearing under the stove. Had the other domowiki found safety yet? I prayed to the old gods that they had.

'You should go first.' Kaz gestured to the steaming water, flecked pale purple with fresh lavender petals. 'Unless you want to share?'

'What?' I half squeaked.

He shrugged, as if the idea of us taking a bath together was little more than sharing a cauldron of stew. 'You bathed with me in the hot springs.'

'That was entirely different,' I spluttered. 'This isn't big enough for two and I need to get out of these wet clothes and—' he looked delighted at the prospect. It sent a bolt of heat straight through me. But . . . the thought of his eyes on me, *all* of me, of removing my armoured corset and showing him how deep those cursed roots ran, made me shudder with more than the cold. 'No,'

I finished firmly. 'And since I've saved your life four times over, I think it's only fair that I go first.' I made a circular motion with my finger. 'You can turn round and wait your turn by the fire.'

'As you wish.'

He turned his back, stripping his shirt off as he strode towards the fire. The flames hissed when he wrung his shirt out. I couldn't help sneaking a look at him, even though I'd asked him not to peek. He braced himself against the mantle, his shoulders broad as great wings, his back sculpted with strength.

Shaking myself, I stepped into the bathtub, double-checking Kaz wasn't looking as I peeled off my clothes, leaving them in a sodden heap. All but my corset and underwear. Just in case he stole a look.

'That Angel of Death in Sanok,' Kaz began. 'You said that it was his fault you got banished. What happened?'

Since Kaz had been honest with me in the forest, I decided to return that trust. 'The queen stopped speaking to me the night she began her Purge. I was nine years old.' I eased myself into the hot water. When I glanced at Kaz, his back was rigid. 'She barely spoke to me for eight years and I never knew why. I still don't. I can count the number of times she actually addressed me on one hand. Like when she caught me sneaking out of the castle one night when I was fifteen.'

I'd been young and naïve, a princess who believed she was entitled to the castle she'd lived in. 'Plotting little acts of defiance with Katia kept me sane all those lonely years.' My smile was evident in my voice. 'Katia was my light, my pocket of joy. She always knew the right thing to say, how to bring a little adventure into life. Until we picnicked together the morning of my eighteenth birthday. Katia had chosen the spot: a meadow bursting with wildflowers, half a day's ride from the Amber City. But when we arrived, I walked ahead alone, leaving Katia to arrange the picnic she'd been trying to surprise me with.' My throat clenched.

'What happened in the meadow?' Kaz asked softly.

'I saw my mother. She was paying the tithe for magic with more blood than I'd ever seen before, bottles and bottles of it.' So much that she must have been letting her veins open, a little at a time, for more solstices than I could imagine. 'And when she'd paid it, when she started her magicwork, she—'

'You do not have to tell me if it is too painful.'

'No, I need to get this out.' Sinking deeper, the hot bath water eased my anger, washing away the pain. 'She pushed her hands into the earth and the entire meadow shuddered.'

'She was stealing the magic woven into the earth, the elements, the footsteps of the gods that had once walked there, and the magical creatures that still did,' Kaz said, as if he too was watching my memories.

'Yes,' I whispered. 'I'd believed her propaganda until then, that she was having the land purged of magic in the name of the True Path, but I knew then that that had all been another lie. And I had fallen for it, too.'

I could still see the queen's head flung back, her eyes unseeing as pure, raw magic flooded into her, her veins bulging as she struggled to take it all. My beloved wildflowers wilting, the colour leaching from them, and the tiny sprite that had run past my foot, fleeing as the magic left.

'I ran, not knowing what to do or what to tell Katia, only that I must. That people needed to know that the queen wasn't banning the magic as she'd claimed but taking it for her own secret purposes. But I didn't make it back to Katia. An Angel of Death, the same one we saw in Sanok today, seized me and dragged me before the queen.'

'Was that when she cursed you?' Kaz asked darkly.

'She had me brought back to the castle first. For the first time in years, she looked at me properly.' She'd had to, I'd been screaming at her. Confronting her with the truth I had stumbled upon. 'She knew I wouldn't keep her secret, that I wanted to tell everyone she was a witch, and she couldn't let that happen. Her secrets and powers were more important to her than I was. Than I am.' I breathed through the hurt. 'So she cursed me. It took root immediately, like I was drowning in air. I told her I'd fight it, but she didn't believe me.'

But that was a lie. I hadn't fought it to begin with. I'd fallen to my knees on the marble, pleading with her to undo it, begging her to let me stay. The image of her unmoved face was impossible to forget; I still didn't understand how she could have turned so vehemently against me. Why she thought it necessary that the price for discovering her greatest secret should be my own *life*. How she'd watched me choke on air, my heart spasming, and not felt something, *anything*. It was a betrayal I would never, ever recover from. When I finally realised that she didn't care about me, that she had no love left for me, I'd dragged myself up, holding onto the wall as my vision flickered and my legs shook, and spoke for myself. Decided that I would not break and cower and beg any longer. *'I'll fight this,'* I'd called after her, *'I won't let you be the death of me.'*

'Darling Snow White, my pure-hearted girl, you do not have what it takes to fight this. You're not a monster.'

'I wish to the gods I had been there that day,' Kaz said, breaking into my memories.

Pulled from the past, I looked at him. He was still standing before the fire, tension scored down the stiffness of his spine. All his muscles taut as if he were ready to take on an enemy.

I was torn; there were too many things I suddenly wished to tell him. That there was nothing he, nor anyone, could have done. That being there and defending me would only have got him killed. That I didn't need anybody to rescue me, though the sight of him, so outraged on my behalf, made something deep within me soften. That he was the only person who had seen the markings of the curse on my body, my soul.

That I yearned for him.

Before I could decide which path to tread, my curse reared its nasty little head once more. Gripped me in its talons as if it were punishing me for daring to speak of its moment of creation.

Crying out, I clung onto the side of the bath, the pain, sharper than I'd known before, slicing through me like I'd swallowed a dagger. *No.* These attacks were coming closer and closer together. I needed that seventh heart sooner than I'd thought.

'Elka?' I heard Kaz say as if through a dense fog. Then, his shout. 'Elka!'

'It hurts,' I gasped, tugging at my armoured corset as the world brightened then dimmed. I couldn't breathe. My corset was rigid, unyielding, crafted from the strongest leather, reinforced with iron and my own fear. And my curse was blooming beneath it, the darkest rose, entangled with thorns. Pressing, pressing, pressing against me. My ribs would give before the corset would. Snapping, one by one, the way I'd forced open the ribs of those six bearers of the six hearts I'd devoured. 'It's too tight, I can't—'

Strong fingers replaced mine, untying the tight straps that bound my corset round me like a second skin, protecting my heart from any that would steal it. Ironically, no armour would protect it from my own mother and her sly magic. Suddenly, my armour was gone, leaving me standing defenceless against Kaz, my pain receding as quickly as it had arisen.

He slowly reached out, tracing the newly hardened root that ran down between my breasts, his pupils swollen black. With anger or wanting, I couldn't tell. His touch was warm against my new soreness. I sucked in a trembling breath.

'What do you need to break this curse?' He met my eyes at

last, his hand dropping away as his finger reached my stomach. I half wished he'd continued its path, tracing heat down the core of me, making me feel good after the visceral reminder that my life was measured in roots and veins. And I was running out of time. The very next root could grow straight through my heart, stilling its beat.

Still, I couldn't tell him. Couldn't admit that I was one of the monsters lurking in the forest. I shook my head. 'That's not for you to worry about.'

A flash of frustration lit Kaz up like lightning. And I knew for certain that he didn't know about the man I'd killed mere hours before meeting him. I waited for Kaz to protest, to try to dig down to the root of the terrible things I had done. But he didn't. 'Lie back,' he said instead. 'The heat will ease your pain.'

I did as he ordered. My pulse skittered as I lay before him, in my underwear alone. But he made no comment, kept his eyes on mine. His throat bobbed up and down as he silently swallowed. Then he kneeled behind me and gathered my long, wet hair in his big hands. Reaching for the soap, he began to gently work it into my hair, his fingers massaging my scalp. Closing my eyes, I relaxed into his touch and the scent of lavender. Warm water ran down my neck as he scooped handfuls of water over my hair, rinsing the soap from it. 'You have beautiful hair,' he murmured, so quietly I wasn't sure if I'd heard it or imagined him speak.

I was verging on sleep, exhausted from the day and onslaught of the curse, when I felt him running a brush through my hair.

'Wait, I don't have a hairbrush.' Covering my chest with an arm, I turned to face him, confused. 'Where did you get that from?'

'I was buying one when you started tearing the market apart.' He looked almost shyly at me, as if seeking my approval. With his wet hair flopping over his forehead, he looked younger for a moment, vulnerable.

I touched his wrist, moved more than I could voice. 'Thank you. That was . . . very thoughtful of you.' And kind, and sweet, and considerate. If I wasn't careful, I was going to end up catching feelings for this huntsman I'd found in the forest.

He gave a nod. 'I didn't want you going without,' he said gruffly.

As Kaz bathed by candlelight, I sat before the fire, staring into its crackle and burn. Usually by this time of the night, my thoughts ran to darkness and despair, but Kaz had shone a lantern on them, sending them skittering away. The domowik deposited a mug of herbata, sweetened with berry jam, next to my foot. Sipping it slowly, easing the new tightness in my chest, I tried not to look at Kaz, even as I was hyperaware of him in my bathtub, how his hands had felt, sunken in my hair, his arms wrapped round me in the river earlier.

By the time he'd gone upstairs, a threadbare towel wrapped round his hips, I knew I wanted more tonight.

CHAPTER THIRTEEN

My hair cascaded down my back in damp waves. I rubbed a little honey into the ends to soften them with sweetness, which reminded me of Katia, laughing and dabbing her lips with honey before she'd run after the glassblower who had ringlets down to her waist. I honeyed my lips, too. My armoured corset, leather leggings and woollen cloak were drying in front of the fire, next to Kaz's clothes.

With my heart in my throat, I rummaged in my linen trunk. Digging past the maps and castle plans until my fingers hit silk. With a hushed breath, I pulled out the only dress I'd brought with me from the castle. Cream, with a fitted bodice and gauzy skirt, encrusted with hundreds of white crystals imported from the Edgestrand Islands. It had taken a pair of seamstresses twenty hours to stitch them all on by hand. I'd thought about pawning it for gold a dozen times, but something had held me back and now I was glad of that. As I lifted it over my head, just for a heartbeat I felt like a princess again. Like the forest had been a nightmare and I'd wake any moment now to see the familiar stone walls and canopied bed where I slept in the castle. I couldn't look in a mirror, but I heard my mother's voice the day she'd presented me with the finished dress. A day she had broken her silence. *A dress as beautiful as a winter's day, perfectly suited to my Snow White.* Sometimes hating her wasn't easy. Before the world crashed down between us, I veered wildly between loathing her and living for the odd kind word or gift during those unending months of silence. Maybe that was why I'd grabbed the dress when I'd escaped the castle.

The silk poured over my body like a second skin, softer than the velvet of the night sky. Hundreds of tiny crystals caught the candlelight as I approached the wooden stairs. At the foot, I paused. I could hear Kaz's movements in my bedroom above, measured by the creak and whine of the wooden floor. A low murmur of his voice seeped through the floorboards, making me smile. He was talking to himself. I was armourless. No iron-boned defensive corset, nor barbed tongue, just myself, all soft and vulnerable and open. With a sharp inhale, I went upstairs and pushed the door open.

'Elka.' Kaz started, knocking a pillow over as he spun to face me. A strange expression flitted across his face. Then he took in what I was wearing. 'What—' his throat tightened, one hand closing in thin air.

'Do you like it?' I asked shyly. My curse was bared, I was putting myself on full view, roots and leaf and cautious optimism all. Only this time, it was on my own terms, not because the curse was raging through me, rendering me helpless. White silk petals edged the top of my bodice, only a few shades lighter than my skin. It felt like I was wearing nothing at all. My hope was a soft trembling thing, begging for validation, for affection, to be wanted in the same way that I wanted him. *'I will never leave without saying goodbye,'* he'd promised me. If he left in the morning, these were our last moments together. Watching his chest hitch as he watched me, seemingly lost for words, I slowly slipped the delicate, petalled straps down my shoulders. Making it clear that, tonight, I was armour-less. 'How about now?'

'I thought you were cooking,' he said hoarsely.

I stalked towards him. 'I wanted to surprise you.' I ran my hands down the front of his shirt, feeling his heart thrumming hard and fast. 'Why, are you disappointed?' I laughed. 'Trust me, I'm better at this than cooking,' I whispered.

Guilt shadowed his face. So slight that I might have missed it if my chin hadn't already been tipped up towards his, waiting for him to kiss me, to feel that press of his soft lips and stubble against my mouth. But I did see it and I couldn't unsee it now. I stepped back, my confidence dripping off me like rainwater. 'What's wrong? Are you leaving tonight?'

'No, not until morning.' He shook his head, reaching for me. 'Come here.'

Suspicion bit deeper. There was something in his tone, in his face, that I distrusted. 'What were you doing when I walked in?'

I asked. The distance between us was a physical barrier, one I couldn't cross.

He looked confused. 'Nothing, I—'

'You were talking to someone,' I realised, putting the pieces together. 'Weren't you?'

He gave a forced laugh. 'I talk to myself sometimes. A bad habit for a huntsman, but—'

'You're lying,' I said flatly, folding my arms.

'Elka—' He looked at me helplessly. 'Please don't do this.'

'Fine.' I walked towards the door, making to leave. When I felt his posture relax, I lunged back, towards the pillow. Him knocking into it had seemed accidental, but Kaz was cleverer, more co-ordinated than that. He darted towards me, but I was faster, tossing the pillow aside before he'd even reached me. Underneath lay a small mirror.

Time fractured like shattered glass.

It was the same mirror I'd seen a hundred times over; a small glass oval, bordered with black stone mined from the depths of the Dragonspine Mountains: blast, a stone that had the uncanny knack of absorbing blood. In her private turret, my mother had walls filled with mirrors, each one holding a thimble of blood that connected it to an individual person. No matter where they were, each time that person looked through a mirror, if my mother was on the other side, pressing a bloody thumb or finger to the stone frame, the connection would spark alive, and she would be able to see them through their corresponding mirror. It was why

I kept mine covered, lest she spied inside the cottage itself. It was dangerous to keep, I should have rid myself of it, but I couldn't bring myself to sever that last connection between us. Only her most trusted guardsmen carried a small mirror to keep her up to date while on the move.

Kaz was no huntsman; he was working for *her*. He was a queen's guardsman.

'I can explain,' Kaz said in a hurry, reaching for me.

Purple-black smoke swirled across the glass. I jerked back, realising I was looking straight into the mirror. Before the queen's face appeared, I snatched it up and smashed it into the wall. Again and again, until the jagged glass cut into me, and blood trickled down my fingers, and it was reduced to glittering dust.

His knife lay nearby. I seized it before he could use it against me.

'Elka—' Kaz looked physically pained. Fine lines burrowed between his eyebrows, making him look as tired as I'd been before I'd discovered his betrayal. Now, I was riding a current of pure rage. 'Your hands, let me—'

I turned and slammed him against the wall.

He made no attempt to defend himself, though I'd stopped poisoning him days ago and we both knew he was stronger than me. He just looked miserable. 'I'm so sorry, but please let me explain – it's not what you think.'

Slowly, I brought the knife to his throat. He may have made

the mistake of allowing me the upper hand, but it was mine now and, by the power of Perun, I was going to keep it.

His gaze was hot against my face. It lowered to my mouth. A pang of wanting rippled through me. It was washed out by anger. 'Get out.'

He swallowed, the apple of his throat brushing against my hand clenched round my knife hilt. 'Elka, please.' He said my name like a caress.

I pressed the blade harder. 'You are going to leave and never come back unless you want me to slit your throat.' I should have taken his heart then and there, but my anger was not a simple one. It was bundled up tightly with humiliation and crushing sadness. Grief for the person I'd believed him to be, wanted him to be, and grief for myself. This marked a return to my loneliness. I'd known he was leaving in the morning, but a tiny shred of hope had been whispering in my ear that maybe, just maybe, he wouldn't go.

'I promised never to leave you,' he ground out against the knife. 'Not without a goodbye and not like this.'

My glare was as vicious as my blade.

'I'm not a guardsman; I only let the queen believe that I was working for her while I gathered information. I told you that I was a heretic, that I hated what the queen has been doing. That's why I pledged my services to her: I became a spy, not a guardsman. As soon as I discovered that you held the key to a better future, I came to seek you out instead. I wanted to tell you sooner, but I needed you to know me first or you never would have let me in. I give you my word that I am on your side.'

'Your word?' I laughed coldly. 'Your word means less than nothing right now.'

'Then I will have to prove it to you.'

'I want you gone.'

'Elka.' His whisper was anguished. 'We've spent too long together for you to not believe me now.'

'Do *not* make yourself out to be the victim here,' I snarled. 'I thought you were my friend. You had plenty of time to tell me the truth, but you didn't. Not until I caught you speaking to *her*.' The betrayal was as cutting as growing another root through my chest. 'Worse, you flirted with me. You made me feel—' No, that wasn't important now. I choked it down, my eyes burning. 'All this time, all the sweet things you said, how nice you were . . .' it was all an act. A manipulation. You just needed me to like you so that I'd do exactly what you wanted.' It was how I'd been treated in the castle; spoiled and pampered as long as I smiled prettily, obediently treading the path the queen laid out for me. Ignoring her terrible deeds for the small victories of my own private rebellions. The moment I'd come of age and discovered her secret, challenged her, she'd cursed me.

'It started that way, yes.' Kaz hung his head. He drew a sharp breath before meeting my eyes once more. 'I thought it would be easy to lead you in the direction I – *Mazrovia* – needed. I didn't expect—'

'What? That I was a real person? That I would save your life four times over?' I was shouting now. Registering my slip of control, I reined it back in. '*What?*'

'I didn't expect *you*,' he said simply. 'I thought this time with you would be a mindless task, setting myself aside to meet a princess's whims. Boring, but necessary.'

Anger seethed within me. Kaz hurried on. 'I didn't know how much I'd grow to enjoy talking to you, being there for you. I didn't expect that I would come to . . . care for you.'

'Pretty words,' I commented. 'Those kinds of words coming from a face like yours must have carried you far. I bet you got away with murder.' I leaned closer, ignoring the way his eyes flared with hope. 'But I'm not going to fall for your act again. Your days of manipulation are over. Whatever *friendship* we had is over.'

'I think we both know that whatever we had was more than friendship,' Kaz said quietly.

'It was nothing more than a lie.' I pressed the dagger harder against his throat, unsure for a moment if I would actually slide it deeper, slit him ear to ear. Kaz looked unsure, too. Even if he wanted to defend himself, he was incapable. My blade would be faster and he wouldn't dare risk his own neck. But I couldn't afford to be reckless now; I needed to be smart. The queen was so far ahead of me that we weren't even playing the same game. 'Why were you speaking to her? Did you tell her where my cottage is?'

'Of course not. I told her I'm staying in an old hunting cabin.

She sent me on a mission, I was trying to buy time before I confided in you—'

'Tell me what she asked you to do.'

Silence.

Somewhere below, the domowik softly whimpered to itself.

'Tell me!'

Kaz closed his eyes, slumping down against the wall. A trickle of blood ran down my wrist; I couldn't tell if it was from his neck or my fingers. 'She asked me to bring her your heart in a box.'

CHAPTER FOURTEEN

I stood in the forest as the sky opened and poured down on me. My rain-darkened silk dress was pasted to me, my raven hair blacker than ever. Anger beat a drum through my veins, as violently as the water thudding down through the canopy. The trees were alive with the sound. I stood in the rain and watched as the man I'd nearly given myself to stalked through the undergrowth, in pursuit of his prey.

He was silent, focused, deadly.

Ahead of us, a stag picked its way through the brambled undergrowth, its velvet antlers a majestic crown, held high as it wandered through the trees. Sensing something, it halted, pricking its ears. I watched it, detached. Knowing its fate did not bring me joy.

It didn't stand a chance against Kaz, edging silently closer, his wet shirt clinging to his back, his muscles coiled as he pounced. My nails cut half-moons into my palms as I looked on, Kaz's dagger slitting the stag's neck before the creature could react. In its final moments, it twisted its head back to stare at me with liquid eyes. Like it knew who was really responsible. Doing my best to honour its unwanted sacrifice, I forced myself to watch.

Kaz's swift execution of the stag, the way he expertly peeled back its skin and bones to steal its heart, sent chills through me. Was this what I looked like when I prowled through the forest, hands red with my victims' blood? Blood washed across the forest floor, muddying together with the earth and rainwater. For a moment, I wished my own blood had burned that day my mother had slit my palm open when I was seven, wished that witchblood surged through my veins, that I had been born powerful enough to wield my will upon the world. Then I would never have been forced to bear this curse, and Kaz would never have walked into my life. I should have killed him the first night I found him in the forest, but it was too late now. Besides, better the queen believe the stag heart was mine and I was no longer, leaving me free to devour my seventh and final heart, break my curse, and return to the castle without her knowing I was even alive. That's what I told myself. My decision had nothing to do with Kaz standing before me, with those sharp cheekbones and tousled hair, his shirt wet with rain and blood, his hands dripping scarlet as he grimly placed the stag's heart into a small wooden box. If the queen wasn't expecting his return, I could have killed him. *Would* have killed him. I never should have removed my armour for him. Physical or emotional. Never bared my scars, my wants and needs and fears. I'd begun to consider that he was a friend, perhaps more . . . but now I knew that he was nothing but a mistake.

Kaz approached me more warily than he had the stag. As if I were a small, skittish woodland creature that would shiver and quake before him. I held my head up like a queen. Panic hummed through me, but I refused to let him see my fear. 'I will return to the queen with this heart now. I'll tell her that you no longer live, that it is your heart which lays in this box. That I killed you and took it myself.'

'What did the queen promise you for my heart?'

He hesitated. Rain dripped down his face, washing the blood away. 'A bag of gold,' he said at last. 'But I will not be keeping that sum.'

I said nothing. How could I believe him now?

His green eyes burned into mine. 'After that, I will return to you. I swear on Perun and all the gods that I will come back, that I am true to you. I will find a way to prove that I'm on your side, that I would fight any battle for you.'

'Don't come back,' I told him.

Those expressive holly-green eyes filled with anguish. 'I am sorrier than you'll ever know,' he said quietly.

'I don't believe you.' Looking at him was painful and delicious all at once. He made me ache with fury, but still I ached for him.

His jaw tense, he nodded. 'I know. But you will.'

He took one last, long look at me then turned and walked away. Leaving me standing in the rain, alone again at last.

CHAPTER FIFTEEN

After watching Kaz walk out of my life, I ran back to my cottage. My cream satin slippers slid in the mud, my curse unveiled, unarmoured for all to see.

I slammed the cottage door shut behind me and bolted it. Muttering, 'To the gods above and below, accept this tithe and let my will be done.' I threw down sage and salt and lavender from the basket at the foot of the door before running a jagged nail across the tip of my index finger, unsealing one of the fresh cuts the shattered mirror had given me. Squeezing out a single drop of blood, I watched it fall to the floor, meeting the wood and salt and herbs with a hiss. A pulse of dark violet shadow ran out from it. If Kaz wished to return, he could; it was weak magicwork, able only to gently discourage anyone from entering, not bar them. But this would protect the cottage from my mother's spies until I was long gone.

Shadows rustled in the corner of my eye. I pivoted, blade at the ready. I wouldn't be taken unawares ever again.

It was the domowik. It hovered behind a table leg, peering out with wide, anxious eyes. 'You could have warned me,' I told it bitterly. It sadly curled up into itself.

With a scream of frustration, I ripped my dress off. Crystals skittered along the floorboards. I didn't stop until I'd torn the silk into rags. Then I curled my hair up into a tight bun, spearing it with the littlest knife in my collection, before picking up my armoured corset and tying it tightly on. I pulled on my leather leggings and boots, then flung open the trunk. With a lump in my throat, I pulled out the beaten knapsack I'd fled into Stary Bór with.

'It's time to leave,' I told the domowik.

I began to pack. If Kaz found a horse along the way, he'd be at the castle by tonight or tomorrow morning. The very instant he reunited with the queen I was in danger. I'd heard tales that there were powerful witches up in the wilderness of the tundra, ones that were brutal and vicious, who did not follow the laws in Mazrovia that the tithe to the gods must be paid in their own blood. Witches who stole blood from other people to feed their own power. Enough stolen blood to fly through frozen skies.

Fear settled into my chest like a rock. My mother had spent her childhood in the Witchlands – she would know better than anyone that the tithe did not need to come from your own veins. *The bottles of blood I'd seen in the meadow.* I cast my memory back, to the dress she'd worn that day and its short, fluttering sleeves revealing unmarked arms. I began to doubt she'd used her own blood that day – so whose blood had been in those bottles?

Horror spurred me on.

If Kaz's story was a lie, if he returned with her, I needed to be as far away as I could. Until I had devoured that seventh heart, I couldn't confront her.

I shoved a small handful of clothes and the last of the jewels I hadn't yet pawned into the knapsack. Then I found my hairbrush. That wave of emotion I'd been suppressing swelled, threatening to drown me. Leaving it behind, I turned and strode into the kitchen. There was no time for tears now. Cramming black rye bread and cheese into my satchel, I debated how much I'd need to keep me going over the next few days while I hunted my seventh heart. It was time. I wasn't going to let Kaz or the queen control what happened to me, to my life. I'd let myself be distracted for too long by that huntsman, no *guardsman*, and his infuriatingly perfect jawline and perfect chest and perfect arms and I was *done*. I would seize my own destiny and do what I'd been planning for all this time. Break the curse. Seek revenge.

The domowik watched sadly from beneath the settee. Folding my arms, I refused to be moved by the house spirit's feelings on the matter. 'Are you coming with me?' I asked. 'I've packed enough cheese for you as well –' I raised my knapsack – 'but I understand if you'd rather wait for Kaz to return and go with him instead.'

Poor domowik; it was from a broken home now. After a moment's hesitation, the domowik slithered out from under the settee and slumped next to my boot. It didn't seem happy about it.

Standing in the middle of my cottage, I took one long, last look around.

At the dark wooden floorboards and walls, the simple furniture, the stove where I'd taught myself how to cook, the hearth where I'd hidden my dragon egg. The bunches of dried herbs and lavender I'd grown myself, strung up like tiny broomsticks. Maybe I'd be back after I confronted the queen. The cracked shutters caught my eye and I shuddered, remembering the bauk. Maybe not.

Rolling up the castle maps and military plans detailing the size and location of the queen's troops and Angels of Death from two years ago, I wedged them down the side of my knapsack. I'd be needing them. Thank the gods I hadn't shared my exact plans with Kaz – I might have walked into my bedroom in a beautiful dress to seduce him, but I'd always kept enough self-preservation not to confide in him everything that I knew. Including the queen's greatest weakness, the real reason she'd loathed the dragons and hated me riding them: When I was seven, I'd learned that my mother was a witch and that I was not. Because my blood did not burn. *But hers would.* Witchblood went up like kindling. All I needed to do was break the curse, sneak into the castle and set the world alight, and her heart would be mine.

Finally, it was time for the last, most precious thing. The one that really meant that I was leaving. Because if not, I was risking this dragon egg for nothing. Closing my eyes, I rubbed my temples wearily. Maybe it was time to stop pretending to myself that guarding Migot's last egg was my duty. It wasn't. It was my punishment. Each time I looked at the dragon egg that would never hatch, I heard the sound Migot had made when my mother had had her executed. When I held the egg, I held the weight of my guilt that I hadn't been able to save her. Hadn't been smart enough, strong enough, magical enough . . . just not *enough*. Still, the thought of leaving it behind for the queen who had cursed me and the man who had betrayed me was unthinkable.

I kneeled in front of the fire. 'It's time to go,' I said softly, wrapping my hand in a thick cloth and reaching into the fire. Picking up the egg, I exhaled as its glowing heat burned through the cloth.

I pulled it out quickly but something jagged caught my wrist, cutting me. Crying out, I lost my grip. The egg fell from my hand. Ignoring the heat, I snatched it up, but my grip was unstable and instead of catching it, I accidentally sent it spinning away from me.

My dragon egg crashed onto the floor.

In shock, I stared at it, unable to move. It slowly spun once, then twice, but it was whole – it wasn't damaged. Surely it would be fine? Dragons were sturdy—

A whisper-thin crack zig-zagged through the shell. It widened and split it two. 'No, no, no, *no*.' I crumpled to the floor. 'What do I do?' I cried at the domowik, who had frozen in place, its wide eyes caught between me and the dragon egg. 'You have to do something!' I yelled at it. 'You have magic; you can fix this.' The domowik trembled, looking at me like it was a kitten I'd kicked.

'I don't know what to do,' I whispered. All the emotion I'd been suppressing broke free, running down my cheeks in salted floods as I gave up and sobbed.

The domowik sidled closer, resting a shadowy tendril on my knee. I couldn't feel it, but I understood the gesture and cried harder. 'I'm sorry I shouted at you.' My chest pinched as the tears came and came, as relentless as the moon dragging the tides across the seas. In response, the domowik lifted its tendril and pointed at the cracked egg.

The cracks had deepened, and several large fragments of shell had fallen off. It was the last relic of dragonkind in Mazrovia and I had ruined it. Crying harder, I almost missed the tiny snout that poked out of the eggshell.

It wasn't broken at all.

It was hatching.

PART TWO
The Forest

*The forest was a dark maw at night,
waiting to snap shut on its prey.*

CHAPTER SIXTEEN

Caring for Żar was as exhausting as I imagined looking after a newborn was. The hatchling consumed all my time, requiring feeding every couple of hours, even through the night. In the past few days alone, Żar had doubled in size. When he'd first hatched, he'd been the size of my hand, a tiny scrawny thing with a little snout and thin, ragged wings that kept unbalancing him as he tried to walk on his two back legs. His front pair of legs were like short arms, tipped with claws, that he'd hugged my thumb with when I'd first picked him up. 'I can't believe you're real,' I'd whispered to him, gazing at his sleek dark red scales, the small swirl of his tail flicking as he blinked back at me with trusting yellow eyes. Most dragons had orange, red or purple eyes; his were as special as him. Dusted across his snout was a black inkblot pattern, so like his mother's, Migot's, it was a punch to the gut. Then he'd let out a tiny puff of steam and I knew I loved him already, fierce and forever. *Mój mały Żar.* My little ember. Named for the glowing ember-red of his scales along with the embers of hope he'd ignited within me.

I'd spent the last few days feeding Żar goat's milk mixed with honey and a thimble of my own blood, my knapsack lying forgotten on the floor, as the domowik and I sat watching the miracle that had unfolded in our cottage. Transfixed as the first dragon in a decade walked over my settee, curled up in the fur-lined cauldron I'd set over the fire to sleep, tucking his tiny snout under a translucent red wing. I was besotted. And terrified. It was impossible to leave the cottage now, unthinkable to set off into the forest with such precious, vulnerable cargo, but if Kaz returned with the queen, that would be condemning him to a worse fate. My fear had been replaced with a fierce desire to protect the dragonkind that my mother had been determined to kill.

I awoke in the middle of the night on the settee, blankets twisted around me as I blinked, disorientated. An indignant huff came from the fireplace, where two pairs of eyes were watching me, glittering eerily. The domowik and Żar. 'Is it feeding time again?' I mumbled, stumbling to my feet. Żar was already the size of a kitten, but still tiny and thin enough for me to scoop up in one hand and take back to the settee with me. The domowik rushed over as well. I stroked Żar's glowing scales, the hatchling closing his eyes and butting his head against my hand. I could protect and care for him now, but when Żar matured and grew bigger and hungrier, I couldn't teach him how to live like a dragon. I couldn't imagine what it was like being the last of your kind. And I couldn't hide him from the world forever.

Żar huffed and bit my hand, his teeth tiny daggers. Wincing,

I let him feed on my blood as I stroked him, from head to the tip of his tail, until he'd satisfied himself and curled up to sleep some more. Now I was wide awake. Returning Żar to his warm, fur-lined cauldron, I cracked open a shutter. It was an unrecognisable hour of night, the trees colossal, silent sentries that stood in the blackness, watching me.

With a shiver, I bolted the shutter and turned to the domowik, who was standing next to me, raising a curious tendril in question. 'We need to leave,' I told it. 'Żar hatching distracted me, but we both know we can't stay here.' I still needed to break the curse, because, more than ever, I needed to put an end to the queen. It wasn't just about revenge any more – it was for Żar. He would never be safe in a queendom that hated him, and I couldn't leave him to the whims of the next ruler of Mazrovia. The realisation held me in a chokehold: the only way I could make sure that my hatchling, and all creatures like him, could be safe in Mazrovia would be if I took the throne myself.

A noise sounded outside. The domowik and I froze. It came again, louder, and this time, through my sleep-deprived fog, I placed it.

Someone was knocking on the door.

I unsheathed my largest knife. Żar poked his head up from the cauldron, watching with wide, unblinking yellow eyes. He swished his tail, sensing my rising dread. 'I'm not going to let anything hurt you,' I told him fiercely. Stalking towards the door, blade first, I prepared for the worst.

Until the domowik rushed towards the door like an overexcited puppy, and I realised who was standing on the other side of it.

'Elka? Are you there?' Kaz's urgent voice came through the thick wooden door.

Hearing his voice again weakened my knees. Sweat slid down the back of my neck as my dread grew and grew and grew. Days and nights had melded together since Żar had hatched and I'd lost track more than I'd realised – I thought I'd had more time.

Kaz's voice sounded again, 'I came back, like I promised.'

His promises meant nothing. I was willing to wager my last quarter of gold that Queen Serce was also stood outside. Just the thought of her dark golden hair and sharp features, eyebrows crooked with disapproval over hardened grey eyes, sent fear crawling through my veins. I hadn't seen her since she'd cursed me, and my armour and blades and meagre magicwork weren't enough to face her.

Gripping my knife harder, I tried to think. Fire. I needed *fire*. I couldn't kill her before I'd ended my curse as I'd remain cursed for ever. But witches burned faster than a wildfire raging through the forest; I could threaten her with fire before fleeing. Then it would be down to the old gods if I managed to outrun her. Shoving my knife back into its hilt, I grabbed a chair and brought it down on the settee to snap a leg off. Ripping the end of my shirt off with my teeth, I wrapped it round one end of the leg and raced to the kitchen, where I shoved it into my cooking fat.

With shaking hands, I snatched up a lit candle in my other

hand. Walking silently back to the door, I caught the tail end of Kaz's speech.

'Elka, please. Just let me know that you're alright.' His voice cracked. I slumped back against the wall. His voice still cut to the core of me. Flooded me with mental images: his arms wrapped round me, holding me tight against his beating heart as the river and villagers and hounds roared above us; brushing my hair as I lay back, bared before him; his eyes darkening when he'd looked at me, wanting me, both when I'd worn my prettiest dress, and after I'd slain the bauk, blood-soaked and exhausted.

Still, I said nothing.

The domowik reached out a hopeful tendril towards the door. 'Stop that,' I snapped under my breath. After all I'd done for the house spirit, it was hard to stomach it taking sides.

'Elka?' Kaz sounded uncertain now.

A tiny pinprick of hope sparked within. Surely if the queen was standing outside, I would have known by now? Would she not have already blasted the door off its hinges and strolled inside as if she owned the place? She was not known for her patience. But she was manipulative. Gripping my makeshift torch harder, I stayed put.

'Elka, *please*. How can I prove my loyalty if you won't let me in?'

He was a wolf outside my door. Whispering sweet nothings so that I'd let down my guard, lay down my blades. But it was too late; I'd already seen his teeth. Still . . . why was he waiting for me to open the door? I knew he could cross the weak magicwork protecting my door; cast only to divert casual passers-by; it wasn't strong enough to dissuade anyone with real intent from entering. For the most powerful queen Mazrovia had ever known? It was child's play.

'If you opened the door, you would see why you should trust me.'

The domowik turned its beseeching stare on me. 'Yes, we all know you love Kaz best,' I whispered angrily at it, 'But—' Another thought occurred to me. 'You love Żar just as much as I do,' I started afresh. The domowik's baleful eyes swivelled to the cauldron by the fire, then back to me. 'That's right. If Queen Serce is outside, she will kill Żar.' The domowik shivered, its wispy outline undulating. *'Is she outside?'* I asked in a trembling whisper.

The domowik rose up, sudden and strong, before collapsing down onto the floor, seeping out into a puddle with a pair of eyes, like it had melted. Its eyes slid along the puddle and squeezed under the door. The whites of its eyes bulged grotesquely, forcing me to look away. *Please, please let her not be there*, I silently begged the gods. *Please.* All too soon, the domowik was back, and dancing with excitement in front of me.

I opened the door.

Kaz looked as tired as I felt, shadows marking his lack of sleep, his hair mussed, stubble overgrown, and a fresh cut lancing down one cheekbone. But when he set eyes on me, he lit up from within. 'Oh, you're a sight for sore eyes,' he murmured, giving me a smile that radiated relief and gratitude and . . . happiness. His gaze ran down me, as if checking I was unharmed since he'd left me. 'I came as fast as I could.'

He made to step forwards before taking in the torch I hadn't yet lit and pausing, uncertain. His smile flickered with concern. I was unable to smile back even as his smile ruined me. Made me want to fling the door open wide and welcome him back into my life, into my arms, but he had proved nothing and so I stood there, knowing I couldn't lessen my guard, couldn't lower the candle I held, relinquish the torch I'd made. Not until I knew for certain that the queen was not prowling through the surrounding trees, just outside the hopeful domowik's reach.

'Elka—'

'You better have something really good,' I said flatly.

His smile sharpened. 'How's this?' Kaz stepped aside. Giving me a full view of the little wooden porch, the unending forest beyond, and the other person who stood there.

'Katia?' I breathed.

Her eyes shone with unshed tears. 'Elka.'

CHAPTER SEVENTEEN

I stared at Katia's auburn hair with the fringe that still refused to behave and the freckles that she hated and I adored, unable to believe that it was really her and she was really here. She stepped forward and we fell into each other's arms. 'Is it really you?' I sobbed into her hair.

'It's me, it's me,' she cried. 'It's really me.' Pulling back, she framed my face with her hands and smiled. 'Oh, Elka, when you left, I was so scared we'd never see each other again, but Kazimierz, he found me, working as a lady's maid in the Amber City, and brought me here.'

'He did?' I asked, half dazed.

Katia leaned forward and whispered in my ear, like we were fourteen again, 'I think he kind of likes you.' I heard the smile through her words.

Over her shoulder, I sought out Kaz. He had come back to me. His answering gaze burned straight through me, slow and steady, the distance between us crackling with awareness. I'd thought I'd severed that cord between us when I sent him away, but it had only stretched painfully tight over the distance, hurting and hurting until he'd returned, when it had snapped straight back into place like he'd never left. Stronger than ever.

'I told you I'd never betray you, Elka,' he said darkly.

My name in his mouth sounded like a sin. There were things that needed to be addressed, questions that were to come, trust that needed to be regained, but now that he had returned, had brought Katia back to me, I believed he was on my side. That flame of desire I'd been stifling suddenly set alight with an intensity that startled me, scaring me a little. It was harder than it should have been to look away.

'So, this is where you've been living?' Katia appraised the cottage. For a moment, I saw it through her eyes: a ramshackle wooden cottage, worn and weathered from standing in the deepest pocket of Stary Bór, with rickety furniture and a shabby little kitchen, each shelf crammed with jars and baskets. Herbs drying from every window, cracked shutters and a moth-eaten settee. Once it might have bothered me, but not any more. I'd *survived*. 'It's not much, but I've done alright here.' I shrugged, resting a hand against the doorframe. They looked haggard, the pair of them. They'd journeyed for days, my oldest friend and the man who'd left me heartsore, but still I was nervous to welcome them inside. Żar needed me more than anyone, and anyone I let see him had to be in my closest circle of trust. Did Kaz deserve to be there?

Katia gave me a confused look. 'Are you going to invite us in?'

'She still doesn't trust me,' Kaz said quietly. 'Do you?'

I twisted my lips. 'No,' I admitted honestly.

Katia rested her head on my shoulder. 'Let us in, Elunia,' she pleaded. 'At least let us talk inside. Kaz came for me, brought me to you. Why would he do that if he meant you any harm?'

I softened. My old pet name falling from Katia's lips sounded like my childhood – dandelion clocks and daisy chains, berries so ripe they fell off the bushes, and long, late nights whispering and giggling as we hung out of the castle windows and watched dragons soar through the sunset, their scales glowing like treasure. 'You're right,' I conceded, watching relief bleed across Kaz's face. 'But, before you both come in, I need to tell you something.'

'That's a dragon.' Katia was thunderstruck after I'd allowed them inside. 'An actual *dragon*.'

Kaz's gaze snapped onto me. It was filled with unspoken feeling, reminding me again of how things were very much unresolved between us. 'It hatched?'

'It hatched,' I softly echoed.

'What, how—' Katia's eyes were wide moons, her voice pitched high in surprise. 'That's not possible . . . I don't understand.'

I laughed. 'I know, it was a lot for me to take in as well. I've had Migot's egg for so long that I never thought it would hatch. I still don't understand how it *did* hatch.' We all looked at the hatchling who was peering curiously at us from the cauldron. 'But I'm glad it did,' I added gently, giving Żar my finger. 'His name is Żar.' Żar latched onto my finger and bit down, suckling at my blood.

Katia looked horrified.

'*Elka.*' Kaz's tone was sharp.

'It's fine,' I dismissed them. 'He just needs me while he's this little.' I gave them an exhausted smile, one that didn't reach my heart. 'He doesn't have anyone else – he's all alone.' But he'd never be truly alone while he had me.

'Pani Smok would have adored him,' Katia said gently, sensing my mood change. We exchanged a small smile.

Ignoring the dirty pots and dishes in my kitchen, I made the three of us cups of herbata, black tea, with extra spoons of berry jam stirred in. 'Tell me everything.'

'Oh, Elunia, things have been terrible. The queen runs the castle like a general marching into battle and, once you'd gone, well, I just couldn't stay there any longer.' Katia glared at her tea and I reached out a hand for hers. Guilt unfurled in my chest like fog; I'd left her there, all alone. 'So I gave it until the following solstice and then I found work as a lady's maid for a couple of sisters in the Glass Quarter of the Amber City.'

'That sounds nice,' I ventured. I'd never had a sibling, but Katia and I used to pretend we were sisters. Katia delighted in playing princess, but I just wanted a sister. A real one, one that wasn't paid to spend time with me. I loved Katia, but my mother had paid for Katia's companionship so that five-year-old me would stop tailing her like a second shadow. We'd become best friends, but I'd always wondered if she'd felt obligated.

Katia huffed a laugh. 'They were spoilt brats. But it was a nice house and safe . . .' she trailed off, pursing her lips at the cottage.

'It's alright, Katia,' I told her. 'I'm alright.' She nodded but her eyes were glistening, so I reached across the settee and pulled her into my arms. She seemed more fragile than the last time I had seen her, when she'd dispatched me to the forest with a knapsack, but warning me on the dangers of Stary Bór was worlds apart from venturing through those dangers yourself. 'We can talk more tomorrow, but you've had a long journey and I think you could do with some rest. Everything will look better after you've slept, I promise.' I squeezed her, feeling her hesitate for a moment before surrendering to my embrace. 'The bedroom's upstairs. Help yourself to anything you need.' I pulled back to smile at her. 'But you're here and we're together and safe and that's all that matters.' I'd worry about what this meant for my plans tomorrow.

'You're right. *Dobranoc.*' Wishing me good night, Katia set her cup down, kissed my cheek, and went upstairs to ready for bed.

Leaving Kaz and I alone together. The silence between us was as thick as fog, filled with all the things we weren't saying to each other. He watched me over the steam rising from his tea, his gaze burning with an intensity that threatened to steal the breath from my lungs. Taking my tea, I went and sat at the table with him. The single candle between us flickered, its soft glow gilding Kaz's tawny hair, shadows playing with the sculpted lines of his face.

The domowik rustled happily around Kaz's feet and I could have sworn its silhouette had firmed once more.

He slid a bag of gold over the table. 'I gave the deer heart to Queen Serce,' he told me. 'I didn't think it was wise to mention it in front of Katia. Does she know everything?'

I frowned at that. 'She does.' She did not; she didn't know I'd killed to unravel my curse, but then, neither did Kaz. If he suspected it, he'd never let on. But something else was niggling now. 'Did you not want Katia to know?'

'It's not that I don't trust her,' Kaz said carefully. 'I just don't know her. And the queen has eyes and ears all over her queendom. Elka, she could have followed us here.'

I went cold at the thought, glancing over my shoulder to Żar, softly snoring in his cauldron. Safe, but for how long? Returning my attention to Kaz, I whispered, 'Did the queen believe that was my heart in the box you gave her?'

'She seemed to. But who's to say that she hasn't discovered the truth since? Or that this is all part of some big game to her. I don't think she's aware that I joined her queen's guard just to dig for information on what she was doing in the forest, but she's diabolical, Elka. In my short time in her service, I learned that at least. When I returned to the castle, I claimed my family needed my services more than her and resigned. She didn't question me, but I do not trust that she believed me.'

Half lost in thought, wondering how much time I could eke out in this cottage or if it was wiser to leave as soon as possible, I murmured, 'Thank you.'

Kaz's brow creased. 'What for?'

'For putting your life at risk to try to protect mine.'

Kaz let out one of his dark little chuckles. 'Oh, princess, haven't you got it by now? There isn't anything I wouldn't do to protect your life.'

A glow rippled through me, beginning to thaw my suspicion. Something was stirring in the pit of my stomach, the back of my mind: the trust I'd had in him, that I'd thought lost forever, was rekindling. 'Why? You're taking on a battle that doesn't belong to you.'

'It does now. And this has always mattered. You . . . matter.'

'I was scared you weren't going to come back. Or worse,' I admitted, 'that you'd come back with *her*.'

Kaz's gaze was locked on me, his voice rough and ragged. 'I will always come back for you, Elka. The past few days without you, knowing that you believed that I'd betrayed you, that I'd been stupid enough to wait before I confided in you, that I could have lost you forever, were some of the hardest I've ever lived through.'

I watched him through the candle flame. Raw emotion flickered over his face, his chest hitching as he missed a breath, waiting for my response.

'I believe you now,' I told him. I wasn't sure when it had

happened, but it was true; he'd returned, not with the queen but with Katia. That had given me all I'd needed to know. Katia's instincts were sharp; she wouldn't have trusted him without good reason. 'You were right – you were stupid.' I gave him a reluctant smile.

He glanced down at the table, where his hands were knitted together. 'It was a mistake.'

'One that you won't make again,' I warned.

His gaze snapped back to mine. 'I raced through Stary Bór like the trees were going up in flames to get back to you. You were all I could think about. Rushing back to this cottage, to you, and—' he stopped, his throat bobbing up and down.

'And what?' I whispered.

He shook his head fiercely. 'Every time I close my eyes, all I can see is you standing there in that silk dress, offering yourself to me.' He placed his hands on the table and stood, transfixed on me in a way that had me standing too, mirroring him, that cord between us pulling tighter. Kaz slowly rounded the table, his intent clear. My breathing quickened. 'How I've never wanted something as badly as I've wanted to kiss you.' His voice was low, intoxicating. Like the sweet burn of cherry wódka. 'How I ruined it all the second you realised who I'd been talking to and how I'd have done anything to turn back the hands of time and told you the truth earlier.'

He reached me then, looking at me with a fiery intensity that blazed through my body. 'Kiss me?' I echoed.

He curled a finger under my chin, tipping it up towards him. His gaze was dark, hungry. Primal. 'You have no idea how much I regretted losing my moment with you,' he said huskily.

'Life is full of moments,' I whispered, scarcely able to breathe. 'If you wait long enough, another one will turn up soon.'

Kaz reached for me. His hands swallowed my waist, gripping me like he was about to lift me onto the table. My heartbeat was a wild animal, my stomach taut with yearning. His stubble was longer than I'd seen it before, his hair curling at the ends, smelling of forest and smoke and sweat as he looked down at me. I let out a little sigh, impatient with longing. His hands tightened round my waist in response.

'Elka?' Katia called from upstairs. 'Elka, are you coming up?'

Kaz closed his eyes.

'I'll be right there,' I called back to her.

'Go,' Kaz told me, 'I'm sure you have lots to catch up on.'

'But—' *Our kiss.*

'I will wait for the right moment.' Kaz released me, though he didn't step back. 'Because when I kiss you, Elka – and I *will* kiss you – I want to take my time.' Lifting a hand, he wound a lock of my hair round his finger, giving it a gentle tug. His voice lowered, his eyes searching mine. 'I want to learn every part of you before I devour you.'

'I'm tired of waiting,' I told him breathlessly, wrapping my hand round his wrist. 'Kiss me now.' I thought I'd lost him forever and now that he was back, I never wanted to let him go. I wanted him to grab hold of my waist again and keep holding on until we'd had a hundred kisses and even then never letting go.

Kaz groaned, tugging my lock of hair harder. 'Don't test me, princess. I am not a patient man.' The corner of his mouth tugged up. I traced it hungrily. 'But I happen to think that you're worth waiting for.' He released my hair with a wicked smile, filled with promise. 'Soon.' He removed my hand, holding it for a moment before bending his head and pressing a single kiss to the delicate skin on my wrist.

His lips were every bit as soft as I'd imagined. He glanced up from between his eyelashes, so unfairly long and thick and dark, and his gaze was swollen with such longing that I shivered.

He let my wrist fall from his hand, his mouth.

On unsteady legs, I went and picked up Żar. The hatchling glanced groggily up at me before curling back into his tail and falling asleep in my arms. Hesitating on the bottom step, I looked back at Kaz. He was touching his mouth as he watched me. It was a struggle to compose my thoughts when I ached to run back into his arms. 'I need to leave tomorrow morning; I can't lose my advantage now. I don't know if you intend to leave or—'

'I'm coming with you,' Kaz said.

I hid the thrill his words gave me. 'Good. Because there is much we have to discuss.'

Like what he'd learned from his period of spying in the castle, why in Nawia a huntsman from the forest had had the stupidity to go and infiltrate the queen's guard, and how he'd managed to get away with it. And the little fact that I'd had a change of heart: I didn't want to run any more, I wanted to fight. To *rule*. And, for that, I needed Kaz and his plan to craft an alliance with the forest demon.

'At first light,' Kaz agreed. 'I'll keep watch on the door.' As I ascended the ladder, the hatchling in my arms, I heard him whisper, 'Good night, princess.'

CHAPTER EIGHTEEN

'You've been gone a while.' Katia eyed me curiously. She was sitting on my bed, brushing her red-gold hair. As I sat beside her, she pivoted and began running the brush through my hair, as if we'd never left the castle.

I wrapped the sleeping hatchling up in a fur rug beside the bed. 'Just settling Żar down for the night.' Katia looked well. After my years of hard living in the forest, if either of us looked like a princess now, it was her. Her hair gleamed, as soft and bright as a burst berry, and her brown eyes were rimmed with some dusky sunrise colour that drew out their warmth.

'Tell me everything,' Katia said. 'I want to know what I've missed.'

In a wave of exhaustion and relief, I told her about the past few years about my forest life, meeting Kaz, my plan to find the forest demon and his army, and how I wanted to steal the throne. I did not tell her about the six people I'd killed. How they stalked through my nightmares each night, how I called them One and Two, Three and Four, Five and Six because I'd never wanted to learn their names, couldn't bear the idea of thinking of them with names and homes and families or I would start screaming and never be able to stop. How Five had still told me his. Stefan.

'Hmm,' Katia said.

'What?' I asked, self-conscious in a way I wasn't used to feeling with her.

'You've changed since the last time I saw you,' Katia said quietly. The brushing paused.

'It's been almost two years now since I left the castle.' I shrugged. 'I've been alone all that time.' Murdering my way through a list of victims had changed me. I was darker than I used to be, more cut-throat, vicious. Fiercer with the way I lived and loved, too.

'I don't know how you've managed living out here.' Katia gave a delicate shudder. 'Making the journey from the castle to Stary Bór was terrifying enough. We almost got savaged by a tree root.'

'I've done what was necessary to survive,' I said grimly. *The sound of a ribcage snapping, the look in Number Five's – the woodsman's – eyes when I turned his own axe on him and he realised his fate. The smell after I'd gutted the bauk. The rusałka's saliva-slicked teeth.*

'What about the curse?' Katia whispered. 'It's been years. Have you started trying to break it yet?'

The question I'd been dreading hadn't taken long to rear up. I'd never told Katia the cost of breaking my curse. If she'd been the one cursed, I doubted she'd have taken one life, let alone seven. She'd have lived out the rest of her days, coming to terms with her fate. Not that anyone would have had any reason to curse her in the first place – she was sunshine and blue skies and the dream you never wanted to wake up from. I was the nightmare you never expected. 'I'm close enough,' I told her, making it clear I held no desire to discuss it. She brushed my hair in silence for a short while, but I knew it wouldn't be long before she—

'Kaz is handsome, isn't he?' Katia commented.

I smiled to myself. Katia hated the silence worse than she hated mushrooms or frogs, a peculiar fear that had spawned after she'd fallen into a pond when we were seven and emerged with frogs stuck in her hair. I'd pulled them off, one by one, and she'd been afraid of them ever since. 'I hadn't noticed,' I lied. The back of my neck warmed; every time I was around Kaz I burned. Like I might die if he didn't touch me. I didn't know if kissing him would quench my fire or if it would make the flames roar more fiercely.

Katia giggled. 'Well, some things haven't changed – you're still a terrible liar.' Sitting beside me, she put the brush down. Its polished wood and soft bristles was a world away from the basic hairbrush Kaz had found in Sanok. I was glad that I hadn't tossed it in the fire after he'd left; every time I looked at it, I felt his heartbeat pressed against mine as we hid underwater and my fear dissolved in his arms.

Downstairs, he was rustling about, speaking to the domowik,

and probably feeding it far too much. No wonder the domowik preferred him – I would, too. The warmth spread from my neck to my cheeks. 'Fine, he's . . . handsome,' I croaked, my throat dry.

Katia peered at me more intently. 'You have feelings for him.'

I groaned, burying my face in a pillow. 'Not on purpose.'

She giggled again before sobering. 'Is that why you're following this plan of his?'

I emerged from the pillow to Katia's puckered forehead; Katia didn't wear her heart on her sleeve, she displayed it on her face. Taking my silence as permission to continue, she twisted my thready blanket as she spoke. 'It's just that seeking out the forest demon, going hunting for a battle, doesn't seem like your idea. Before you left, you wanted to travel the world, explore what was beyond the reaches of Mazrovia, all the way to the Iron Sea and further, to Glenwich and Alvor and all those lands overseas, off the edges of the map.'

'I still want all of that. But I want more now, too.' I let out a rough sigh. It had taken Katia a while to bring up the plans I'd confided in her, and now I knew why. She disapproved. 'I'm not the same person you knew in the castle. Life there was hard, my mother made sure of that. You know better than anyone what it was like for me growing up there.' A pulse of sadness flashed through Katia's eyes. Undeterred, I ploughed on, needing to share who I was now. 'I'm cursed, Katia. I've carved out a living for myself in this cottage, this forest, but it's been harder than I could tell you. I'm ready to leave, to fight to protect what's mine and to try to make things better for everyone. Otherwise, what kind of person would I be?' My breath hitched. 'It would be selfish to fight only for myself when I'm not the only one the queen's made suffer—'

Katia's hand found mine. 'It's alright, you don't have to talk about it if you're not ready.'

I managed a nod.

'But you don't have to go along with Kaz's plan if you don't want to either. You do have other options.'

She smiled at me, the kind that felt like sunshine, reminding me that our friendship would weather these changes and emerge stronger than ever. It gave me the confidence to stand, to tell her, 'I have no other option, Katia. I'm not just going along with Kaz because he's handsome and I've been lonely; I want to work with him because I believe it's the right thing to do. As I confided in you years ago, my mother is a witch. She purged the queendom of magic, murdered the dragons and banished me with an unspeakably cruel curse.' I drew my head high. 'I refuse to allow her to continue along this dark path; the people of Mazrovia deserve better. Their villages are being sapped of life, and they live in fear for their families.' I took a deep breath. 'And I deserve better, too. So I will ask Kaz to take me to the Forest Court and I will address the forest demon himself. This –' I gestured around me, as if my arm was encompassing all of Mazrovia and its many, many problems – 'has gone on long enough. It's time Mazrovia had a new queen.'

Katia looked stunned. 'Do you really think that the forest demon will loan you his army?'

'Yes,' I said, with more certainty than I felt because Katia's doubt was frustrating me, making me question my own choices and feel guilty for my scheming. But she didn't know what the past few years had been like for me and sharing them would only upset her; she didn't see the world in the same way I did. She'd never loved the dragons like I did. And she didn't know Kaz. 'We share an enemy. I need an army and he needs a new ruler for the queendom. I think we can come to some kind of agreement.'

Katia hadn't blinked since I'd begun my little speech, my attempt to convince her. Her wide eyes were tinged with fear, her voice higher pitched. 'They say the forest demon is descended from the devil himself. That he's charming and seductive before becoming the worst kind of monster you can imagine.'

'I've heard the stories,' I said grimly. They varied wildly but all agreed on the central theme; that the Forest Court was a pit of sin and debauchery.

'Are you sure you're brave enough to seek him out? I know you've survived Stary Bór so far, but –' Katia spread her hands – 'the Forest Court is very different. They say when you walk into it, you've stepped into a living nightmare.'

'Yes,' I lied, trying my hardest not to look my fear in its face. 'He might be a demon, but he's never met *me*.' I deliberately omitted that he had met Kaz; Katia was unsure enough about Kaz without adding fuel to those flames. 'I'm not asking you to come with me though,' I added. 'You should stay safe, far away from any battles.'

Katia's smile wavered. 'When Kaz turned up, I grabbed a few of your things from the castle – with the help of one of the cooks.' She held out a small linen sack. 'I thought you might have missed some things from your normal life. You left in such a hurry. I wasn't sure what we'd forgotten that you might need. I only spotted your hairbrush after you'd gone.'

'That's alright.' I smiled to myself. 'I have a new one now anyway.'

'Oh, you're in trouble,' Katia said softly. 'Don't let him break your heart.'

That wasn't a conversation I was ready to have. 'Ah, it's too well protected for that.' I patted my armoured corset under my shirt.

'Well, you might want to take that off, because I brought you this.' Katia pulled out a lovely dress. Blue as the sky after it had been washed clean by a storm, with white satin laces that crisscrossed the back, and a skippy hem that would flounce around my calves. 'It's beautiful.' I stroked the fabric, knowing it would be thick and well-made before I'd even touched it. But it didn't feel like me any more.

'Try it on,' Katia urged.

Hating the awkwardness that had settled in between us, the sweet ease of our friendship turned brittle as glass, I put the dress on straightaway.

Katia sucked in a breath when I bared the telltale marks of my curse. Flushing, I turned my back to her. 'Tie me up?' I asked quietly, hoping she wouldn't mention the roots.

Katia silently tied the laces. 'Do you have a mirror?' She glanced around my bedroom.

'It's under there.' I pointed at the old mirror I'd covered the instant I'd stumbled on this cottage. 'No, don't!' Katia froze, her hands still on the covering. 'My mother will be able to see us, remember?'

'Of course.' Katia left it covered. 'Oh.' She softened, gazing at me. 'There's the princess that I remember.'

My smile turned brittle. I hadn't been a princess for a long time, and I held no desire to return to being a princess. I was ready to be queen. Although when Kaz called me princess, which he did purely to rile me, in that deep, spine-tingling voice of his, I didn't seem to mind it at all. My thoughts whirled so fast, it took me a moment to realise that my discomfort wasn't just in my own head. Something strange was happening.

CHAPTER NINETEEN

I breathed deeply, trying to ease the strangeness that had sunk into my bones.

Katia frowned. 'What's the matter?'

'Something's wrong.'

Something was very wrong; I was struggling to breathe. But the dress wasn't too tight, and it wasn't my curse. It was something *else*. Like something insidious had wormed its way inside my lungs and was slowly closing them. My head banged and my stomach rolled violently. 'I—'

'Are you choking? Did you eat something rotten or—?' Katia wrung her hands, flapping around me.

My knees hit the floor. My lungs were squeezing tighter and tighter, my body turning weak and unfeeling, my fingers numb. 'Help,' I whispered through my closing throat.

'I don't know what to do!' Katia screamed.

Just as my vision was flickering out, as I was plummeting towards a wall of blackness, my terror blinding, I heard Kaz's boots thundering upstairs. 'What happened?' he demanded, crossing my bedroom in two strides and dropping to my side.

I tried to grab his sleeve but my hands refused to obey me. I was trapped inside my own body. 'I—' My throat shuttered. I gagged for air, choking on an unseen malevolent force. Terror set in.

'Is it the curse?' I heard Katia cry.

I didn't hear Kaz's response. A dull rushing sound rose up; I was drowning in my own lungs. This was it; this was how I died. On the floor of a cottage in the woods before I'd even ended my curse.

The glitter of a blade shone through the descending darkness. Kaz was holding a sword. He sliced my dress clean off.

Sweet, sweet air hit my lungs.

Before I could register what was happening, Kaz had torn the shirt off his back and wrapped it around me then scooped me up into his arms. He carried me downstairs like I was an injured bird and placed me gently on the sofa. I missed the warmth of his arms round me, his chest pressed against me, the moment he let go. Until he sat next to me. Closely. And pulled a moth-eaten woollen blanket over us both. The domowik rushed over, startling Katia. Between Żar and the domowik, this was more magic than she'd witnessed in an age.

'What happened?' My teeth chattered. I felt like I'd been pulled from the riverbed, half-drowned and spluttering for breath. My lungs ached viciously.

'Where did you get that dress from?' Kaz asked.

I looked to Katia, who clapped a hand to her chest. 'I brought it from the castle,' she whispered, her eyes flitting between mine and Kaz's. 'Before I left with Kaz, I went back there for some of your things. I'm friends with one of the cooks—' Her voice caught. 'Elka, I'm so sorry. I had no idea or I would have never brought it here—'

A cursed dress. 'The queen,' I said flatly. 'She knew you were lying to her, Kaz. That you would return to me. She must have known that Katia had entered the castle as well, and realised that you were both coming to me.'

Kaz swore, leaping up and throwing the remains of the dress onto the fire. It hissed, turning the flames incandescent violet, until the fabric charred and blackened, releasing a coppery tang; the tithe that had bound a curse to fabric, the blood price of magic.

Kaz leaned against the mantle, his back bared. I tried not to stare at it. His shirt was still draped round me; it was warm and smelled like pine and smoke and salt. Like him. 'You're not safe here.' He turned, the firelight casting shadows over his cheekbones, highlighting a bone structure the gods themselves would have envied. 'Pack your bags tonight; we're leaving at dawn.'

'She's not in any fit state to travel,' Katia argued, gesturing at me. 'Look at her, she's in shock! She needs hot food and a warm bed, not to go gallivanting through Stary Bór. Do you know what kinds of things prowl through this forest?'

'Yes, I do.' Kaz gave her a disapproving stare. 'And so does

Elka, since she's been living here for almost two years. Alone. You care so much about her well-being? Where were you then?'

Katia looked like she'd been struck.

'Stop arguing,' I sighed. 'We'll leave first thing.' Catching sight of the concern flooding Katia's face, I added, 'Don't worry, it'll take more than a cursed dress for the queen to stop me.'

She nodded, knowing well that when my mind was made up, there was nothing she nor anyone could do to change things. 'I'll brew a fresh pot of herbata.' She swept away into the little alcove of the kitchen and began bustling around.

'Your companion is very opinionated,' Kaz remarked.

'She's more than my companion,' I told him. 'She's my oldest friend. The one person who was always there for me at the end of the day, no matter what kind of day I'd had.'

'Then I'm glad she's here for you.' He ran his eyes over my face, as if evaluating me. 'Are you sure you're alright?'

I was rattled. Frustrated that the queen had seen straight through Kaz and manipulated Katia into being the carrier for her little dose of deathly magic. Wasn't cursing me once enough? 'You were right,' I told him. 'Mazrovia needs a new queen. And I am going to be that queen. Take me to the forest demon. I'm going to burn it all down.'

CHAPTER TWENTY

'Are you ready?' Kaz asked.

No, I was not ready to take on the forest demon and seize the queendom after what was sure to be a long and bloody battle. My mother would not ease her grip on ruling so easily but, if I didn't challenge her, I would lose the last dragon to walk Mazrovia. 'I'm ready.' I turned my back on the cottage I had found when I'd fled into the forest, scared and alone, not knowing how I would fight the cursed magic bleeding through my veins like tree sap. The domowik touched my leg, reminding me that the spirit of this home I'd forged for myself wasn't something I was leaving behind. I would be carrying it with me.

Hoisting my knapsack higher on my back and adjusting the woollen sling I wore strapped to my front, keeping Żar warm and safe, I took the stick Kaz held out and set off, taking the lead. I heard Kaz then Katia follow. Our little travelling party of three. Plus one domowik and a hatchling I would have given my life to defend.

Making our way through Stary Bór was slow progress.

The further we ventured, the more we spotted signs of magical activity, not lost, after all, but in hiding. Little sprites, hardly bigger than a daisy, that peered from beneath toadstools with sharp, beady eyes. 'Oh, how adorable,' Katia had cooed at one until it grinned at her, its jaw unhinging and splitting its face in half, revealing more teeth than a rusałka and a black gullet. She'd fallen silent after that, even when I realised we were walking towards a tree with something large and spindly clinging to it, that looked tree-like but was, in fact, something other.

'Wiła. Tree spirit,' Kaz said when I startled. 'The Forest Court is filled with them,' he added in an undertone, the wiła lifting its face to watch us pass. Its eyes were two hollows carved from bark and, as it moved, it creaked like an ancient oak. Like my roots, creaking with each swing of my arms as I marched deeper and deeper into the forest.

We didn't pass the time with conversation. Too much was at stake to risk being overheard. Tales of the Forest Court claimed that when you walked through the forest, tree branches would steal strands of your hair, thorns would rob you of pinpricks of blood and the moss would soak up every drop of sweat that fell from your brow. The forest learned your scent, letting the forest demon track you through his territory. He already knew we were coming. But that didn't mean he had to know our strategy or that the other spies hiding somewhere in the trees, the ones belonging to the queen, could learn our plans.

The day grew late before we stopped for a well-earned break, finishing our first bottles of well water – we'd avoided any fresh water sources, still troubled from our run-in with the rusałki.

'Elka.' Katia pointed a shaking finger up at the nearest branch. A white owl perched there, one eye glowing white, the other black. Watching. There were no mirrors in the forest, but there might as well have been corridors of them; my mother's spies were everywhere. I cursed, drawing my hood low and checking that Żar wasn't poking his snout or tail out of the sling, but it was too late, the owl took flight on silvered wings. 'Gods,' I swore. 'It's probably already on its way back to the castle.'

'It won't need to go that far,' Kaz said. 'I'm willing to bet the queen has Angels of Death stationed at every church around the forest.' He surveyed the trees hemming us in, his expression wary, guarded. 'We need to move faster.'

'How far is it?' Katia asked. 'The evening's already drawing closer.'

Kaz glanced at the gold compass he'd been using to pinpoint our path, occasionally altering our direction if we veered too far off. 'It's further than I remember it being,' he admitted with an apologetic wince.

'Great.' Katia sighed. 'We're going to have to spend the night in the forest, aren't we?' Kaz opened his mouth to speak, but Katia continued, 'At least it's not the Forest Court.' She stepped into a patch of boggy mud with a look of horror. I grabbed her wrist and hauled her out before she lost a boot. 'Thanks,' she muttered. A couple of beetles and a small frog perched on her shin, unwanted passengers from her detour.

'Oh, let me get that for you,' I went to remove the frog before she yelped in fright, but she shrugged and brushed it off herself. 'It's fine,' she huffed. Frowning to myself, I almost didn't see Kaz come to a stop and caught the back of his heel with my boot.

Kaz gestured up at the trees. 'If we're spending the night in the forest, we should sleep above ground. It'll be safer.'

I nodded in agreement; I'd seen the things that wandered through Stary Bór, and the later the hour, the hungrier the forest. 'Bauks can climb though,' I pointed out.

'But the roots can't,' Kaz countered, 'and those are the most common threat.' He didn't add that there was nothing we could do right now to hide from a bauk. At least to my knowledge, we were far enough away from the waterways slicing through the forest to avoid any rusałki that might happen upon us while our defences were down.

Katia scrunched up her pert nose. 'What if we move in our sleep and fall out of the tree?'

'I've got rope,' Kaz said. Sizing up the nearest tree, he ran and leaped, catching hold of a branch and pulling himself up. He wasn't wearing a cloak and the back of his shirt rode up, exposing the taut muscles beneath. With a grunt of effort, he swung his legs over and climbed higher.

I caught Katia staring with the same expression I suspected I was wearing. She gave a sheepish grin. 'Well, no one ever said you had bad taste.'

I snorted, making us both laugh. It was freeing, reassuring that a spot of awkwardness didn't mean our friendship was lost. A rope uncurled from above and I gestured for Katia to climb first.

Żar prowled over the thick branch Katia and I were sitting on, exploring the unfamiliar terrain. His dark crimson scales glittered under a lost ray of moonlight that had worked its way through the leaves above. 'Does it ever scare you?' Katia asked as Żar chased a line of ants.

'What?' I smiled as Żar huffed steam at the ants, almost sending himself toppling off the branch. Reaching forward, I scooped him up, shaking the cup of milk and blood I'd mixed for him.

Katia grimaced as I fed Żar the mixture, his trusting yellow eyes staring back at me. 'Knowing that, one day, he'll grow up to be dangerous. Maybe it's a good thing that there aren't any dragons left in the skies of Mazrovia. It's safer.'

I gave her an incredulous stare. 'I didn't know you felt that way about dragons.' I knew some people did, but not Katia, who had watched me ride Migot a hundred times and been my partner in crime, stealing pots of sugar cubes for the other dragons. Wiped the tears that refused to stop falling after we'd watched my mother have Migot executed. 'Where is this coming from? Tell me you're not following the True Path now.' I gave a dry laugh. Until I spotted the guilty twist of Katia's mouth. 'Katia, you know it's not a real religion.' I looked at her more seriously now, my tone turning lower, urgent. 'It's a means of controlling the citizens of Mazrovia, of keeping track of their movements, influencing their thoughts. It's my mother consolidating her power.'

Katia shrugged. Deep purple shadows mottled her eyes, marking her with exhaustion. 'It's been a long two years, Elka. A lot's changed. You're not the only one who's had to endure hardship to survive.'

It took me a few minutes to gather myself enough to respond calmly. 'I'm sorry you've been through a hard time, Katia,' I told her. 'Genuinely, I am.' I clasped her hand, as familiar to me as my own. 'But Żar isn't to blame; he's just a hatchling, and I owe it to his mother to keep him safe. Dragons aren't dangerous unless they're threatened.'

'People could use them as weapons,' Katia argued back.

Black spots danced in my vision. 'Just like magic, or money.' Some Mazrovians had always believed that dragons were inherently dangerous, but dragons were loyal and protective. Of course you had the occasional accident, but hunting dogs killed more Mazrovians each year. I'd never counted Katia as someone who didn't believe we should live this closely with dragonkind.

Katia sighed. 'You're right, I'm sorry. I know what dragons meant to you. I don't know why I'm so jumpy tonight.'

'You're out of your comfort zone,' I offered, trying to make the peace, even as her words still thumped in the back of my skull.

'Oh no, not at all. Whatever gave you that impression?' She gave me a small smile in return.

I snorted. 'This is just like the trees we used to climb in the summer palace gardens when our governess wasn't looking.'

Katia grinned then. 'If we'd had rope back then, maybe you wouldn't have fallen out of one and broken your wrist.'

We laughed quietly together, careful not to rouse curiosity from anything passing by beneath. We talked about our childhood in the castle, about old friends and teachers past, until Katia's responses began to slow and she faded into sleep. But sleep would not come for me. I was haunted by the things Katia had said and the things yet to come. Each time I closed my eyes, I saw the forest demon imprinted on the back of my eyelids. I didn't know what he looked like, few people did, but the pictures in the books I'd read on Mazrovian lore painted him as fearsome, more beast than man, darkly powerful with abilities to uproot the entire forest if he so wished. I didn't know which fate I feared most; that the forest demon would bend to my will and grant me an army to confront my mother with. Or that he'd kill me where I stood for such an audacious request.

Sleep was a spirit that eluded me. Eventually, I gave up and climbed over to the neighbouring branch with Żar strapped to me, asleep in his sling. Kaz looked up as I walked towards him, holding onto the branch above me for balance, evading the vines that traipsed down from higher branches. 'What's wrong?' he asked, sitting forward, his green eyes gleaming under a single ray of moonlight.

'Nothing.' I sat opposite him, steadying myself on the branch. 'I just couldn't sleep.' He must have heard mine and Katia's conversation, but I didn't want to dwell on it any longer.

Kaz leaned back against the mossed trunk, resting a forearm on his knee. In his other hand, he held his gold compass, idly flicking the lid open and shut, its soft snick mingling with the rustle of leaves, the scuttle and trill of creatures in the trees. 'Me neither. I keep worrying about what will happen tomorrow, when we finally reach the court.'

I raised my eyebrows at him. 'I don't think I've ever heard you worry about something before.'

Kaz shrugged. 'There's a lot at stake here.' His voice dropped. 'I don't want to lose your trust again.'

'Then don't,' I whispered. Fear prickled down my spine, but I chose to ignore it. Kaz hadn't betrayed me to the queen; he'd just made a stupid mistake in not trusting me sooner, but I knew now that there would never have been a good time for him to have told me. That he'd been scared of losing me. Stupid, but forgivable. If he betrayed me again, it would be a crushing blow, bruising my heart. Moonlight toyed with his hair, landing on his white shirt, that bottom lip I wanted to sink my teeth into. 'Who are you when you're not the huntsman, the heretic?' I asked in a bid to distract myself. 'Tell me about Kaz.'

He gave me one of his crooked smiles that made my stomach flip. 'What do you want to know?'

'Everything. You said you were a huntsman, so how did you manage to infiltrate the queen's guard? How can you afford to carry a compass made of gold?' I nodded towards the compass in his right hand.

'This was my father's.' He flicked it open once more, showing me an engraving that curled over the golden patina: *Moje kochanie*. 'My love. He gifted it to my mother after my birth, shortly before he walked out of her life. She didn't want the reminder of his desertion, so she gave it to me. It's the only thing of his I have.' He pocketed it with a casual shrug that masked the pain radiating from him. Not wanting to prod old scars, I waited patiently. Kaz tipped his head back, looking up through the canopy. 'As for the queen, when the Purge spread like a cancer, reaching the forest and stealing everything I loved about it, this beautiful, deadly, magical forest, I couldn't ignore the state of Mazrovia any more. I felt compelled to act.'

I was familiar with the feeling.

'I went to the Amber City. Applied to be a queen's guard and spent a few months in the castle, learning everything I could—'

'What did you find out?' I interrupted.

Kaz gave a slow smile. 'That you –' he held out a hand towards me – 'were the answer to everything.'

A heady rush swept over me. I knew he'd meant it only in terms of saving his beloved forest, of overthrowing the throne, but a secret wish dug its talons into my chest, making me imagine, just for a moment, that he'd said it about me and him.

Kaz continued, unaware. 'I began positioning myself closer and closer to the queen until I finally was able to plant the seed in her head. That I knew my way around the forest, that I was a huntsman. That I was loyal to her, discreet.' He hesitated, guilt marking his face as he continued to watch my response. 'That I had a cruel streak.' When I said nothing, he finished, 'The seed took root. Not long before we met, Queen Serce summoned me to her throne room in the dead of night, gave me a mirror and dispatched me to Stary Bór, to return with your heart in a box.'

'But you didn't take my heart,' I said.

'I would sooner rip out my own.'

The forest hushed as we stared at each other, all my fears, worries and concerns fading away until there was just Kaz and me, sitting in a tree in the darkest part of the night. He bit his lip. It fascinated me, his teeth sinking into that plush lip. When I dragged my gaze back up to meet his eyes, they'd sharpened. He'd noticed me notice him. 'I still haven't managed to kiss you yet,' he said huskily.

My breath caught. 'You don't need an excuse to kiss me.'

Had his face always been this close to mine? The gold flecks in his eyes were like molten stars. He was looking at me in a way that whispered of want and need and a lick of danger. Like if I let him, he would claim me, body and soul. And, oh, how I wanted to let him. 'You sure about that, princess?' he murmured.

'Queen,' I whispered back. Watching as his lips drew into a sultry smile, as his pupils darkened, turning his gaze black. Hungry.

'Even if you didn't have a throne waiting for you, you would be a queen.' His tone was fierce on my behalf, the lines of his body taut with that same unbearable tension that was crackling through mine.

I sucked in a breath. 'You're not going to flirt with me? Tease me, find devious little ways to amuse yourself?'

'No.'

'Then I guess I'll say goodnight.' Brushing off my leather leggings, I made to stand up. Disappointment cut me to the quick.

Faster than a hunting tree root, Kaz caught one of my wrists, tugging me back round to face him. His hold steadied me on the branch. 'I'm not going to tease you because I want you to know that this isn't a game for me. This is more real than anything I've ever felt before and I won't have you doubting why I kissed you.'

He pulled me onto his lap, covered my mouth with his and *oh*.

He kissed me like it was a primal need. Like he would die if he didn't. I sighed into his mouth as his hands slid up my neck, knotted in my hair. The soft scrape of his stubble against my face made my ache deepen. I held onto his upper arms, my legs resting either side of his as we clung together in the branches. It was hard to resist pressing against him; I needed more, would have begged for more, but Żar was in his sling, bundled against my chest. And Katia was asleep the next branch over. Until Kaz deepened the kiss with a groan, tasting me.

'Gods,' I moaned, any cares I had evaporating as Kaz trailed kisses down my collarbone, his breath coming harder and faster against my skin, grabbing my waist in his hands to keep us balanced on the branch. When my shirt rode up, his thumbs stroked my stomach, stoking that desire burning inside me. I hadn't realised I'd sunk my hands into his tawny hair until I was dragging him back onto my mouth again, kissing him roughly.

I'd thought our first kiss would be slow and soft and sweet. It wasn't. It was a collision. A raging wildfire. His lips and tongue meeting mine. Now I knew what he felt like, what he tasted like, I was in trouble.

CHAPTER TWENTY-ONE

The next morning I was woken by Żar trying to claw his way free from the sling. I opened my eyes to dawn gilding the sky and the taste of Kaz on my lips. *Kiss* felt too small a word for the way we'd collided last night; his touch had seared me, marked me in some irrevocable way. It had been an effort to tear myself away. My shirt smelled like him now, woody and smoky. My stomach twisted with *want*. 'Alright, alright,' I muttered as Żar's snout worked its way free, popping out the top of the sling, making a little rasping sound that sounded like a whisper of a roar. 'Breakfast time it is.' After I'd freed Żar from the sling, Katia blinked awake.

'Is he . . . bigger than yesterday?'

I cocked my head at Żar, who mirrored the gesture, peering back at me. He'd grown again. Now he was as big as a cat. Instead of slitting my finger with my knife, I dragged it across my palm instead, squeezing blood into the bottle with the last of the goat's milk we'd brought with us, until it turned dark pink. 'You're lucky you're adorable,' I told Żar, feeding him the bloody milk.

Katia grimaced. Before she could pass comment, Kaz came to join us. Our branch creaked with the sudden addition of his weight. Holding onto a higher branch to stabilise us all, Kaz looked at me. My face was stubble-sore, my hair tangled from his fingers. 'We're out of milk.' I managed to drag my thoughts away from his mouth long enough to tell him.

'I don't know if we'll find anybody selling their wares this deep in Stary Bór,' he said. 'It might be time to wean him.' He jerked his head at the canopy, each breath of wind revealing a glaring orange sky. Sunrise. 'Let's get moving.'

'What exactly happened between you and Kaz last night?' Katia whispered. 'You've been blushing all morning and he's been staring at you so hard I'm surprised he hasn't walked into a tree yet.'

That gave me a tweak of satisfaction. 'We kissed,' I admitted, low enough that Kaz wouldn't hear me, but, trundling along beside my boots, the domowik tilted a tendril in my direction. Little eavesdropper.

'And?' Katia asked impatiently.

'And what?'

'And I need details!'

A furious blush ignited my cheeks. I glanced at Kaz, prowling through the forest like a panther, wielding his walking stick against the thistled and thorned undergrowth, clearing a path. 'It was unreal,' I whispered. Katia tucked her auburn plait behind one ear, listening intently. 'I can't stop thinking about it. About him.'

'That good, huh?' Katia frowned into the distance.

Concern tickled me. 'What?' I asked, self-consciously.

'Oh, nothing.' She smiled at me. 'Just . . . be careful, won't you? You know you're special.' Her smile warmed as she nudged my shoulder with hers, before sobering once more. 'But you have enemies everywhere, Elka. It comes with the territory. You're a princess, beautiful and rich, everyone wants a piece of you.'

I cast my eyes down before she saw them prickling. She didn't mean to wound me; she just worried, and it would have hurt her if she'd realised I'd taken it to heart. 'I know,' I said quietly. 'But Kaz makes me forget all of that.'

She smiled again, but it was tighter, seeping with worry. We continued walking through the emerald forest, greener than ever after the spring storms, bursting with ferns and fronds and moss, smelling of verdancy and rot, life and death bound together.

'I think I see someone over there.' Katia suddenly pointed to the left, past a silver birch with peeling bark.

Though I squinted, I couldn't make out what she'd spotted. 'Where?'

'It looks like a market woman, she's carrying baskets!'

Before I could warn her on the dangers of people not being who they seemed – the rusałka incident still fresh in my mind – Katia had darted away.

'Kaz,' I called out. Still a little way ahead, he'd paused, turning back as he'd heard Katia leave. 'Can you go after her?' I would have done it myself if it wasn't for the hatchling strapped to my chest. Żar's safety came first.

With a nod, he sprang after Katia, leaving me alone in the forest.

Żar growled under his breath, sensing my anxiety. 'It's alright,' I whispered, reaching into the sling to give his scales a reassuring stroke. Their smooth warmness calmed me, as I waited and waited for Kaz and Katia's return. Soon, I began to pace. 'What's taking so long?' I asked the domowik, who tilted its head at me. Scanning the surrounding treeline, I spotted the edge of something carved into a nearby trunk, half obscured by moss. I walked over and pushed the moss back. Three wavy lines; fire reduced to its most basic representation. The symbol for the rebellion. 'They were here.' Though the carving was old enough to be covered by fresh growth, its existence gave me courage, reminding me that I had allies, even if the forest demon did not care to be counted as one. I wondered if I could sneak away before we reached the Forest Court; somehow I needed to take a seventh heart without Katia or Kaz knowing.

Twigs crunched. I whirled round, hand whipping to my hilt, but it was Kaz, followed by Katia, who looked victorious. 'It *was* a market woman and, look, she even had milk.' She presented me with a large glass bottle. 'For Żar.' She dropped her voice to a hush as Kaz walked on, continuing to clear the path ahead. 'I shouldn't have said those things last night. I was tired and wasn't thinking clearly. I know you'd never do anything to put anyone in danger.'

Guilt snapped its jaws round me. The faces of my six victims rolled through my head, one after the other. If the forest demon joined our side, if he lent me his army, then I would need to be un-cursed. That meant a seventh victim.

Katia seemed unaware that my head was elsewhere. 'And she was selling these combs too, aren't they lovely? She told me that her husband carves them and she paints them.' Katia held out a wooden comb, patterned with cheerful flowers. 'It reminded me of the daisy chains we used to make together.' She slid it into my hair. 'Pretty,' she smiled.

Thanking her with a matching smile, I looped my arm in hers as we strolled on.

The comb began to pinch.

I ignored it, not wanting to be ungrateful. And then it began to cut. I yelped, trying to remove it with one hand, then both, but, to my horror, it was *moving*. 'It's cursed!' I yelled. Katia tried to tug it free as Kaz ran back towards me. Blood ran down from my scalp like tears. It was dagger-sharp as it crawled over my head, until I saw it reach my temple from the corner of my vision. Panic hit, hot and overwhelming. 'Get it off,' I screamed.

Kaz yanked at it, his mouth set in a grim line, the fear in his eyes turning my legs to water. 'Oh gods,' I whimpered as it sliced into my temple. A fresh trickle of warm blood coursed down the side of my face. Kaz's fear turned to horror as he realised first that the cursed comb was moving again: it was making its passage towards my eye. 'No no no *no*,' I screamed, clamping my hands over my face. The comb hit my little finger, digging its wooden claw under it, trying to burrow its way down. '*Kaz*,' I cried.

'Hold still,' he instructed in an icy, calm tone.

Cold metal met my fingers: his hunting knife. Fear dribbled out of my mouth in an incoherent moan. With a click of metal against wood, I felt Kaz leverage the cursed comb off my face. A sliver of remaining magic hissed as it hit the forest floor and vanished beneath a stone like a wounded reptile.

I fell into Kaz's arms. They clamped round me, holding me tighter than ever, until my panic ebbed. He pulled away to look down at me. Using both thumbs, he wiped away the blood under my eyes. 'I won't let anything happen to you,' he promised, his voice gravel. 'The market woman.' he turned to Katia. 'What exactly did she say to you?'

Taken aback, Katia stuttered, 'I-I don't remember. I just asked her if she had milk and then she showed me her combs—'

'That wasn't a market woman,' I whispered. 'The queen likes her disguises—'

Kaz drew his sword. 'I'm going to hunt her down.' Wild and furious, he stalked away like an avenging god.

'Stay here,' I yelled back at Katia, already breaking into a run after him. 'Kaz, *wait*.' He didn't wait for me; he was too far gone to even hear me. But if the market woman had been the queen in disguise, he couldn't face her alone. And if it had just been a messenger of hers, well, then I would claim my seventh heart as payback.

CHAPTER TWENTY-TWO

When I caught up with Kaz, he was standing still, every muscle coiled to strike, his senses trained on something I couldn't hear. 'You shouldn't have followed me,' he ground out from his tensed jaw, pacing on.

'Nonsense.' I pursued him. 'This is my battle, not yours. Besides, there are things that you don't know.' Like I might die soon if I didn't take another heart, devouring it like meat to feed the dark curse that twined through me, living and breathing magic that threatened to end me if it didn't get a taste of human flesh.

That caught his attention. 'What don't I know?' He snapped round, his fury spilling out from him like smoke. '*Elka*, what don't I know?' A nearby tree rattled its branches, echoing his anger, his pent-up frustration.

But he wasn't the only stubborn one. I glared at him, my lips sealed.

'Fine, don't tell me. I'll figure it out eventually,' Kaz said, shaking his head and muttering, 'I swear you'll be the death of me,' as he turned to survey the tangle of surrounding trees.

I rolled my eyes behind his back.

A raindrop fell on my face. Warm and thick. Then another, then another. But you didn't become a heart-devourer without becoming very closely acquainted with the smell of blood. 'Kaz,' I whispered, wiping the new blood off my face.

His nostrils flared at the sight of my bloody face. Wielding his sword faster than a whip, he gestured for me to get behind him.

But I'd already seen what was above.

Her face contorted into a horrifying rictus, the market woman was silently screaming down at us, her dead body hanging from the tree.

'Is that the woman Katia bought the cursed comb from?' Bile seeped up my throat as I scrubbed my face with one of my sleeves, trying to wipe her blood off me. Żar shifted in his sling, scenting blood, but he could sense my fear, too, and stilled, staying hidden, thank the gods.

'It is. And her throat's been cut.' Kaz craned his neck to examine the body, careful not to step under its drip, drip, dripping wound.

Her throat gaped like a second screaming mouth.

'She was just a messenger, then,' Kaz said grimly.

A thick tree root slithered past my boot and lunged for the dangling body. The tip of its thorned root punched straight through the body's open throat and began to make a sickening gurgling sound. Drinking.

Kaz went to pull me away as more roots appeared, wrapping themselves round the poor market woman. 'Kaz.' I grabbed his wrist, the onset of my panic catching his attention faster than my touch, faster than the tree roots swarming the body. Usually, I would have fled from the sight but the storm inside my own head was louder than the snap of the body's spine giving way. Whatever apparent remorse the queen had suffered after cursing me that had led her to plaster Mazrovia with missing posters was long gone. And the only reason I could see was standing in front of me. I had an ally now. And this threatened her.

'The queen's still trying to kill me.'

Kaz met my eyes, following my thoughts as if they were his own. Anger and fear flashed through him. 'Then she knows that her last attempt, the cursed dress, failed.'

'She's watching us,' I whispered, horrified. Stumbling back, I scanned the nearby trees, looking for owls, for a mirror dangling from a branch, for any explanation of *how* she was spying on me, *how* she'd managed to get such an intimate and close look into my life.

Kaz seized my hands. 'I won't let her hurt you, Elka,' he said fiercely. 'She'll die before I let her lay a single hand on you.'

I shook my head, tears slipping down my cheeks and mingling with dried blood. 'Kaz, she knows we're going to the forest demon, she must do, that's why she's trying to kill me after those posters offering gold for my return. She—' I gulped for air. Terror and sadness gripped me by the throat, suffocating me with the awful, awful truth as the pieces fell into place, one by one.

'She's *here.*' I took a step back, then another, breaking into a run.

'Oh, there you are.' Katia shot me a worried look when I emerged back through the trees. Then she got a proper look at my face. 'Is . . . is that fresh blood?'

Before she could come to her own realisations, I drew my knife and charged at her, ready to carve her heart from her chest and eat it raw, gods be damned that it would trigger my curse into killing me. I would take her down first.

She whispered out of existence. I crashed into the moss and earth. She reappeared behind me just as Kaz came hurtling into the clearing, sword in hand.

'Ah, the gallant knight to the rescue,' Katia laughed. It was thin and cruel. Far from the infectious peal of a laugh that the Katia I knew had. The domowik hid behind a tree.

'Katia?' Uncertainty rippled across Kaz's face. When he glanced to me, I gave him a terse nod. His uncertainty hardened into hatred.

'There it is.' The thing wearing Katia's face smiled then. 'What's the matter, Kazimierz? Did you fail to recognise your queen?' She wheeled on me. 'And you.' Her smile exuded triumph. 'How long did it take you to realise you'd been spending the past few days with your own mother?'

I was carrying Żar in his sling. I'd been keeping him at my side day and night, protecting him – when would I learn that being with me was what endangered him most? My heart thrummed faster than a bird's, my fear for him reaching dizzying heights. Thankfully Żar must have sensed it, felt my heart racing against him, as he continued to stay still and silent. *I should have known.* The queen always did love her disguises. And Katia, my Katia, was beautiful and bright and *brave*. A fact the queen seemed to have dismissed. Or perhaps she never knew, the same way she'd never known that Katia was deathly scared of frogs. I'd been too willing to believe that Katia had been returned to my life that I'd overlooked the glaring truth, and now we were all at risk.

'Ah, ah, ah.' Not-Katia held up a finger. Kaz, who'd been stealing ever closer to her, stilled. She gave him a smile, dripping with honey. 'If you kill me while Elka's curse still lives in her veins, she will die.'

My breaths came shallower, my pulse thready. We were locked in an impossible situation, the battle already lost.

Kaz's jaw hardened. He glanced at me, his every reaction tied to mine, like he couldn't not look at me even as every one of my instincts screamed at me not to take my eyes off the queen. 'It's true,' I whispered to him. 'If she dies now, I die.' A muscle in his jaw ticked. I wanted to run my fingers over it, smooth it away, tell him it would all be alright, but I couldn't. I didn't know that it would be.

'And we all know you couldn't bear that to happen, could you?' the queen continued, more confident now.

Kaz said nothing. Neither did I. There was nothing to do, no way to beat her. I had no fire. All I could do was plead to Perun and all the gods that she wouldn't remember Żar.

'You both thought you were so clever.' Her lip curled in distaste. 'As if I wouldn't know the difference between a deer heart and the heart of the daughter I birthed from my own body.'

'Why waste your time?' I folded my arms, thinking desperately hard. We wouldn't be able to take her on and live, not here, not now. If she so wished, she could slaughter us both before we so much as blinked. The fact that she hadn't meant she had an ulterior motive. This, then, was another game to her. But two could play my mother's game. 'Surely the ruler of Mazrovia has better things to do with her time than to spend days wandering through the forest.'

'You will not goad me into revealing my secrets. My darling Snow White, I had you raised more intelligently than that.'

My heartbeat was as thin and ragged as a moth wing. What could I do? *Think, Elka.*

'And him.' Not-Katia tipped her head at Kaz. 'He believes he's always the most sharp-witted in the room. It amused me to keep him as a guard for a while, sending him off on spurious errands, letting him think he was the greatest of spies to walk Mazrovia. I knew he would never take your heart, but, I have to admit, he surprised me.' She fixed me with that shrewd look of hers I feared most from my childhood. 'I thought he'd return to his own life. I didn't suspect he would seek you out. Then when he had the audacity to come back, filled with lies, I took one look and I saw straight through him. Down to his lovesick heart and the traitorous blood that beat through it. Curious. So very curious.'

'Why would you care who I spend time with?' I asked without thinking. And when my mother's satisfied smile carved across Not-Katia's face, I cursed the name of every god I knew for falling into her trap.

Kaz shot me a desperate look. His eyes blazed brighter than ever, his wrath burning golden, as furious as the sun and, for a moment, he looked different to the Kaz I knew. Sharper, stronger, vibrating with power.

'That's the funny thing about falling in love,' my mother said softly, making me distrust whatever was about to spill from her lips. 'In some ways it softens you, makes you weak. After all, you're walking through this world with your heart beating outside of your own chest. In other ways, it makes you desperate. You see, there's nothing more tragic than an unrequited love. But what if the person you love doesn't know who you really are?'

I shifted my gaze onto Kaz, confused. Then he closed his eyes, and I knew. This was never *my* trap. My skin turned clammy; what had Kaz kept from me now? What painful secret had he guarded closer than a jewel, keeping it locked away in the dark until my mother had found the key and prised it open?

'What if you're worried that they wouldn't return your love if they knew the truth? Wouldn't that be an unbearable twist of fate? So you tell a little lie, craft a charming tale, so that this person you've set your sights on will ease their guard on their own heart and give you a chance. When they eventually find out that they've fallen in love with nothing but a pretty story, it will be too late. They'll have already lost their heart.'

'Stop talking. Now.' Kaz clenched his hands into fists, his control slipping as the queen goaded him, his eyes blazing golden once again as whatever he didn't want me to know threatened to reveal itself.

Thunder cracked above us, sudden and alarming.

'What's the matter, darling?' the queen cooed at Kaz, turning my stomach. This was a carriage crash I couldn't look away from. 'Is your love too fresh and new to withstand the truth?' She turned to me and I braced, my roots like iron bolts through my chest. 'And you. I raised you better than to be this naïve.'

'You didn't raise me.' My pulse was deafening in my ears. 'You had me raised by nannies and tutors.'

The queen surveyed me through the eyes of my closest friend. My stomach rolled, hoping the real Katia was alive and well and far from the queen's reach. 'I would almost be disappointed if I had any expectations of you.'

'I would rather be cursed than living back in that castle with you,' I spat.

My words couldn't hurt her, not when she didn't care what I thought or didn't think of her. I was powerless against her. When she next spoke, I knew it would be the killing blow. 'That huntsman you've been having a little . . . *dalliance* with? He is—'

Kaz roared, lunging for the queen with his sword. I could have told him not to bother; no blade would end her. Only fire. But then, he already knew he couldn't kill her, not unless he wanted my death on his hands. He was bluffing, desperate to distract her from whatever she knew about him that I did not. With a delighted, vicious laugh, the queen vanished in place, leaving the earth smoking where she'd stood. Kaz staggered through the violet smoke as his target disappeared. And reappeared right in front of me, close enough to kiss my forehead. Slowly, she reached out for a loose strand of my hair, curling it round her finger as I forced my feet not to move, my knife at the ready if she even hinted at an intention to take Żar. It wouldn't kill her, but by the gods I would make sure it hurt. Her eyes softened within Katia's face, her voice sweetening. 'You've grown even more beautiful than you were a few years ago. Be careful, Snow White; he's not who he claims to be. You've been sneaking around with the forest demon himself.'

Then she vanished again for good.

Leaving Kaz and I staring at each other.

'Elka—' he uttered, a world of desperation clinging to my name, a silent plea in his eyes.

My knife-bearing hand clamped tightly round Żar's sling, I ran before I could hear the rest.

CHAPTER TWENTY-THREE

I didn't get far before Kaz caught up with me.

'Leave me alone!' I screamed at him. 'You're a trickster god, a demon, the scourge of the forest. Wicked and cruel and *never* to be trusted.'

The pain in his eyes nearly cleaved me in two. 'You know me,' he said quietly.

'Actually, I don't know you at all,' I said bitterly, shaking my head as I backed away. 'Do not follow me. I want nothing to do with you. Not now, not ever.'

His face flashed with alarm. 'Elka, it isn't safe in the forest; the queen won't stop trying to kill you. You can't strike out on your own like this!' he called after me as I ran again.

His cursing followed me through the trees. I didn't know where the domowik was hiding, but I could feel Żar cowering in his sling. Dragons were deeply empathic animals; I was heartsore that the hatchling was feeling each one of my tempestuous emotions. A brown owl watched me pass, its head swivelling as I fled deeper into the forest. A second owl took flight several trees later. Her spies were everywhere. Once I was sure that no more remained, that I'd run long enough, I slowed.

I was standing next to an old yew, tall enough to scrape the clouds. Leaning back against it, I caught my breath, tugging my unspooled thoughts back into one neat knot. Sunset was imminent; there was a low-hanging moon already in the sky, curved like a hunter's scythe.

Kaz entered between two trees, his gaze seeking me out at once. The *forest demon*. Part of me had always suspected that there was a deeper layer to Kaz to tease out. Magic attracts magic and there had never been so much magic in my life since the day I'd met Kaz. He was there when the domowik first appeared; he'd been staying with me before Żar hatched. There had always been that energy crackling under the surface of his skin, that darkness that played through his gaze. The way he'd never shied from the terrible things I'd done because *he'd done worse*. The way he loved the forest. Still, I'd never expected *this*.

'Elka—' he rasped, guilt shining like a beacon through his face.

'Are there any of my mother's owls around?' I asked steadily.

He hesitated, confusion tugging at his brow. 'I'm sorry?'

'You have magic,' I said impatiently. 'You're powerful enough to know every creature with a heartbeat that walks through your territory. Are there any of her spies here?'

'No.'

I nodded to myself.

'Elka, I'm sorry.' Kaz inhaled sharply. 'But this changes nothing. We still need each other.'

'I know,' I said quietly.

'You have no army, no magic that belongs to you. Your followers are a half-formed domowik and a hatchling that can't yet fly. Not to mention the small matter of that deadly curse you're still afflicted with.'

'I said, *I know*,' I repeated, glaring at him.

'I— Oh. You do?'

I pushed off from the tree. 'Yes, I do. That little show was for the queen's benefit. I guarantee she was watching from afar, eager to see the effect her *revelation* had on us. I needed her to believe that I hated you, that we were no longer allies.'

A vein pulsed in Kaz's throat. 'Does that mean that you don't hate me?' he asked gruffly, but not gruffly enough to cover the note of hope that sang through him.

I stalked towards him, burying any misgivings I had about the forest demon – about *him* – down deep. Now was the time to be strong. The battle to become queen began here. With him. 'Let me get one thing straight. I still want to be queen, and to do that, I need your army. I like my chances better now that I've realised who you really are, but that doesn't mean I have to trust you.'

Kaz closed his eyes for a beat. 'I understand.' His mouth pinched with sadness, with the same sense of loss that coursed through me. Yes, I needed him, but he was a trickster, a demon, and I would do well to remember that. His eyes flew open, the intensity shining there startling me. 'But, Elka? I *will* make you queen.'

I stopped just before him and tilted my face up, close enough to kiss, proving to him – to myself? – that I didn't fear him. I wanted the throne and, damn it all to Perun, I would make a bargain with the demon himself to get it. 'And then will you worship me like the rest of them?' I whispered, watching his eyes rest on my mouth. 'The princess who stole the glass throne from her mother. Or will I be beholden to you just the same way that my mother controlled me?'

His eyes swelled with fury. 'We would form an alliance.'

'An alliance.' I gave a sardonic laugh. 'I wonder who would lead that.'

'We would.' He closed the distance between us, his chest almost meeting my chin. 'Together.'

I wasn't sure if I wanted to kiss him or kill him. I knew I didn't trust him, but that didn't mean we couldn't be allies, provided I ignored the way he made me feel. This coming battle was too important to muddy the waters with anything else.

'You scared me, running away like that,' he admitted. 'I thought you'd never speak to me again.'

'It was tempting,' I glanced up in time to see his wince. 'But I knew the queen would have been spying. There was no chance she'd have missed watching the aftermath of her chaos.'

'Clever,' Kaz murmured, careful to keep his voice tender, as if afraid I'd bolt again when I realised who was speaking. It was the furthest thing from my mind. Maybe I had a death wish.

'Now I need to know one thing,' I demanded.

'Anything.'

'I've been living in the forest for almost two years. And, before that, I was in the castle itself. Why did you wait so long to come to me?'

'I had to be sure that you were ready.' Kaz's smile was touched with sadness, but there was something else there, too. This was a man – a demon – who spoke in half-truths and evasions. I needed to keep my wits sharper than a sword; each conversation was a duel, and I could not lose sight of that, even as the memory of our single kiss taunted me, as he stood close enough for me to hear his heartbeat, smell the forest on him.

'No, I don't believe you. You're hiding something from me again. There must have been another reason.'

With a sigh, he rubbed his face. 'You've heard the stories about me. They're all true. I'm a demon, Elka. You want to know the truth?'

I swallowed nervously. 'Yes.'

His voice lowered, until his words were a secret between me and the trees and the moss-slicked ground. 'After I left the queen's guard, I spent days keeping an eye on you in the forest. Checking in from afar. You were just a young princess; I didn't know if you could be queen. But you weren't what I expected. You were fiercer, stronger, tough enough for the coming war, for the battle for the queendom, but you—' he hesitated.

'What?' I whispered.

'You cared. I was thinking about knocking on that cottage door when the bauk attacked me. I'm the demon of the forest, the ruler of this territory and I was so distracted by the thought of *you* that I didn't see it coming until it had already ripped through my side.' He ran a finger down my cheek. 'Then you came,' he said simply. 'And you were brave and kind and—' He dropped his eyes. 'I came so close to telling you to run from me instead.'

My heart pounded. 'Why didn't you?'

'Because I'm a selfish demon.' He gave me a crooked smile. 'Because I wanted to talk to you and see if I could make you smile when you thought nobody was watching.' His smile faded. 'Because your destiny was racing towards you, and I couldn't let you meet it unprepared.'

His finger halted on my cheek. I pushed it away. There was still so much that I didn't understand, knowledge I needed to equip myself with before I allied myself with Kaz. 'The Purge began ten years ago. When I was just a child. You're a demon.' My throat squeezed around the word, hardly able to believe my own daring at standing here with him. 'Why didn't you make a move against the queen years ago?'

'I always knew Queen Serce was a witch.'

I nodded. 'Of course you did.'

'She may believe she has kept her true nature hidden from the world,' Kaz continued, 'but I have kept an eye on the rulers of Mazrovia for years; there is very little my spies do not know. Secrets are like water; no matter how hard you clench them in your fist, they will leak from your fingers. The Purge was troubling; as soon as it began touching the edges of the forest, scattering magical creatures and draining the land of everything which sustains it, I knew I needed to investigate myself. So I went to the castle.' A vein pulsed in Kaz's neck. 'You already know I spent a few months spying there. It took over a week before I managed to discover her plans: she intends to build a city in the forest. She doesn't have a trade deal with Stary Bór, there are no minerals in the forest like there are in the Dragonspine Mountains, no whales for oil that live around the Witchlands. Once Stary Bór is fully purged of all magic, she wants to raze the forest to the ground and rebuild it as hers.'

Her audacity stunned me for a moment. *What was she doing?* 'I don't know why she didn't kill me,' I admitted to Kaz. 'It doesn't make any sense. She disguised herself to come to my cottage, to give me a cursed dress, a cursed comb, and still she didn't kill me when I realised it was her. *Why?*'

'Honestly? I don't know.' Kaz frowned.

'There has to be a reason; I must be missing something. And if I'm missing something, if I'm two steps behind, then that's bad, Kaz. Really bad.'

'Let me take you to my court,' Kaz said.

I had no choice, I was a walking death sentence that needed an army. I needed Kaz, the forest demon. The one person that the queen feared – though she hadn't seemed afraid when confronting him, I'd noticed she hadn't dared lay a finger on him. She'd lashed out with words alone. Another mystery. But if I stayed with Kaz, I would be under his protection until I figured out the queen's plans. And what I needed to do next. 'I will consider allying with you on one condition.'

He cast a wary eye over me.

'Show me who you really are.'

He stiffened with apprehension.

'You've been deceiving me since the day I first met you,' I said. 'Yes, I know you had reasons for that,' I added before he could interrupt, 'but that doesn't excuse your lies. If you truly want an alliance, then we have to be on equal footing. Show me your true face, not the one you think I want to see.'

'I don't want to lose you.' His whisper was low and anguished and *real*. 'The things that I've done, Elka, I am beyond forgiveness. Unlovable. They call me a monster and they are right to do so.'

'No.' I shook my head fiercely. 'I don't care about any of that, and you know it. If you ever want me to consider trusting you again, then you have to show me all of yourself now. There can't be anything left that I don't know, that someone else could use to blindside me with.'

Kaz paled to the shade of goat's milk. 'Will you give me your word that you won't run?'

'I will.' And I wouldn't break my promise, not when I knew

how hard it had been to strip my armour off in front of him. To break those walls down and let another person in. I couldn't give in to my aching for him, couldn't trust him yet, but I still cared.

Mist wreathed around Kaz as he dropped his mask at last. I stepped back, my arms wrapped round Żar as a deep creaking reverberated through the ground. It intensified as Kaz unleashed his power, until I felt it in my bones, my teeth clashing together. Still, I refused to tear my eyes from Kaz, even as I could no longer see him through the mist, even as the surrounding trees all shuddered, bending towards him. Like they were bowing down to him. Thick patches of moss and mushrooms sprouted up from the earth, and the entire forest trembled for a moment before stilling.

When the mist receded, I stamped out any apprehension, determined that Kaz would look back at me and not see one hint of fear in my eyes. The way he'd looked at me after I'd slain the bauk.

He slowly raised his head, tawny hair falling back as he met my stare.

He was a star glimpsed through the canopy, sharp and jagged, and so luminous that I couldn't look away. I would have let him set me alight and thanked Perun for the sweet pain as I burned. His holly-green eyes turned burnished, bronze, as everything within him crackled with the wild magic of the forest. Sap-green ink rushed down his corded arms, painting them with ivy, brambles and thorns, marking him with the territory he ruled.

When he spoke, his voice was deeper, rougher. 'Do you still wish to form an alliance with me?'

'You can't scare me away that easily.' I lifted my chin higher, meeting his fiery stare.

He stepped closer and the trees turned their branches towards us, the forest reshaping itself around him and his power. 'Maybe I should. Maybe you should run, far away from me, my court and this impending battle,' he growled.

'Don't lash out because you're afraid not to wear your mask around me. I know you need this alliance every bit as much as I do, and seeing you, the real you, has not changed that.'

'I see your mask, too. The one that you think I don't see, the one that covers your fear because you are a queen marching into battle without an army,' Kaz fired back. 'I know you can't walk away from me now you've seen my true face. You need me too much for that.'

'Am I supposed to feel lucky that you came to me and offered me your army?' I demanded.

The dark green ivy wending up above his collar bristled, his fingertips crackling with raw magic as his temper frayed. His golden eyes blazed with the strength of the sun, stunning me. 'No. You're supposed to take it and prove that you're worthy of it. I don't want your gratitude; I want your fury. I want the darkest parts of you that you've hidden away from everyone else because you think they make you unlovable and I want to worship them.'

I could hardly breathe.

'I want to see you rule,' he said, reining back in his temper, his control, the magic that had seeped from him as he revealed more than he'd intended. 'Like the queen I know you are.'

CHAPTER TWENTY-FOUR

Before I could respond, the domowik reappeared, its shadow-form pooling together in front of a silver birch. Drawing my attention to a carving on the moonlight-white bark: three curving lines. *Fire.* 'The rebellion.' I went to examine the symbol, ignoring the heat that still radiated between Kaz and I. 'They were here, too.' When I glanced down, I spied several silver curls on the ground. *Bark.* Kneeling, I picked one up, feeling its freshness. 'They were here *today.*' A thrill of anticipation licked my spine. 'They have to be the same ones we spotted in Sanok – they must be living in the forest nearby.' I stood, holding the bark out to Kaz as if I needed evidence. 'Wait – you can tell me where they are. You know, don't you?'

Kaz's power rippled through him. 'This is my forest,' he said darkly. 'I know everything that happens in it, every footstep, every flight, every tree root.'

'I need to meet them.' I tossed the bark aside. 'If I'm to be queen, I'll need more allies than you alone.'

Kaz gave me an evaluating look. 'The rebellion has been

living in Stary Bór for longer than you; some of them have lived through both the Purge and the great famine. They won't be easy to recruit to your cause. If they'd wanted to, they would have approached you years ago.'

'I have to try.' I tightened my cloak round myself, adjusted the hilt. 'They accepted my help in Sanok; that must have bought me some goodwill with them.' *Please let those domowiki be somewhere safe now.* 'I know they can't be far. Take me to them now.'

Kaz's eyebrows rode up his forehead.

'Why are you looking at me like that?' I demanded.

'No reason at all.' He coughed into a fist but I spotted his lurking grin. 'Your inner queen is showing.'

'Good.' I snapped my cloak behind me, impatient to set the cogs of my plan whirring. To set aside the tension brewing between us that I refused to address since Kaz had broken my trust, yet again. 'I'm tired of hiding her.'

I followed Kaz's silent prowl through his forest, trying not to stare at his solid height, at the inked ivy peeking over his cloak collar. At the magic that wreathed around his hands, spitting sparks like he was carrying a thunderstorm. The domowik slithered along at his feet. Calmed by my own mood settling, Żar had sucked blood from my wrist until he fell asleep. I hoped there was somewhere safe for the hatchling at the Forest Court; he was growing by the hour and would become too heavy for the sling I wore. Soon his appetite would grow too big for me as well: I was already weaker than I'd like, reminding me of that first hard winter in the forest. The one that had almost killed me.

Night was falling like a velvet cape.

I continued to follow Kaz, who led the way without need of a lantern. Until he declared, 'We're here,' and that thunderstorm rolled up his arms and over his face, masking him with magic once more. 'Just in case the rebellion doesn't take as well to dark magic as you have,' he told me.

I rolled my eyes.

'There.' Kaz parted two curtains of fronds, revealing a large patch of cleared earth where several trees met. In the middle, a group of people huddled round a campfire. Candles burned in little lanterns that dangled from every branch, all the way up the trees. There were more people up there, too, on wooden platforms that looked like they'd been cobbled together.

'Can we help you?' An intimidating woman strode into view, blocking our observation of the camp. Her stare was piercing, her silver hair cropped short, showcasing her long umber neck. She was petite yet muscular, her hands gripping her hips as she waited for us to respond, in a manner that was all too familiar.

'Pani Smok?' I gasped.

Her hands slackened as she took in my black hair, my milky skin, my red lips. '*Elka?*'

*

'Pani Smok taught me how to ride on dragonback,' I told Kaz in an undertone as we followed the dracologist into the heart of the rebellion camp.

They were nestled close around a fire, hugging its warmth as they shared out bowls of bigos, along with hunks of black rye bread. Two women shuffled apart on a fallen log, making room for Kaz and me to sit between them. We were passed bowls of stew and a fistful of bread immediately. One of them nodded at me, her warm brown eyes all too familiar: she was the rebel I'd spoken to in Sanok. Now that her hood was back, her hair spilled over her shoulders, straight and bark-brown. 'Are the domowiki—'

'Safe.' She fished a knife from her pocket and handed it me; it was the one Pan Jedrick had gifted me, and I slid it into its empty hilt, glad to have it returned. 'Thanks to your help.' She turned back to her stew before I could ask her anything else. Disinterest seemed to be the common mood and I glanced to Kaz, automatically seeking out his reassurance.

'Give it a moment,' he said beneath his breath, digging into his stew.

Pani Smok did not sit with us, nor did she want to speak with me privately first. Worry churned my stomach, making the single bite of bread I'd taken sit there like a stone. I set my stew aside, it just occurring to me that Pani Smok had been a woman at the height of her career, spending her life with the animals she loved and revered. She hadn't been my friend. And, when the Purge occurred, when the dragons had been killed, she'd fled into the night without a second thought.

It was only when she stood and clapped her hands together, once, commandeering the attention of everyone in the circle, that I realised: Pani Smok was the leader of the rebellion. I shifted uneasily as more and more people came to listen to her, dropping from the trees on vines, gathering around us until they were around a hundred strong. More than I could have imagined; they must have been steadily recruiting over the years.

'It seems that we have an esteemed visitor,' Pani Smok announced, her piercing eyes slicing straight through me. 'Princess Elka is not as lost as the castle wants us to believe.'

Kaz nudged my knee with his. 'Get up there,' he said, scarcely loud enough for me to hear. 'Take the control back.'

With an internal groan, nerves crowding in, I stood. 'Dobry wieczór.' I wished everyone good evening as if I was beginning a royal speech. 'I've been wanting to meet you since I realised you existed.' The women who had handed me the stew looked offended and I winced. 'That is to say, I—' Gods, this was harder than I'd been expecting.

'Why are you here, princess?' Pani Smok said impatiently.

With a deep breath, I drew myself up straight. It was time to be honest and face things head on. 'I'm going to take the throne for myself and I need allies. Since you all loathe Queen Serce as much as I do, I was hoping you would join my cause. Help me, in whatever way you can.' I gave them a bold smile, owning my power, my position.

Silence. I hadn't been expecting applause, but I'd been expecting some reaction. A clue as to which way they stood.

'And why would we do that?' The offended-looking woman drawled. Kaz's fingertips crackled with blackness. Clasping his hands together, he gave me a steely nod.

'Because, right now, I'm your best chance at overthrowing the throne,' I replied calmly.

Pani Smok stared at me. 'But then you would take it for yourself?'

'Well, yes—' I said awkwardly.

A murmur of disapproval rumbled through the campsite.

'Then we are still beholden to the crown and castle,' Pani Smok said. 'And a young queen who knows nothing of ruling.'

My cheeks heated. 'Yes, I'm young,' I said evenly. 'I'll be the first to admit that I don't know what I'm doing.' Kaz sat up straight, tracking the slightest movement in the crowd, keeping watch for any threats. This gave me the courage to forge on; I had one ally already, a powerful one. 'And, yes, I'm sure there is a better, fairer way to rule but, right now, I don't have time to worry about that. My mother needs to be stopped and I am your *best chance.*'

Pani Smok gave me an evaluating look.

Before, I had considered showing her Żar, knowing that she would have delighted in meeting him, on learning that a hatchling had *survived*, that dragonkind was not yet extinct. Now, I feared that she would take him from me. Thankfully, he was fast asleep, his body moulded to mine, my cloak thick and luxuriant enough to wrap round us both.

Eventually, Pani Smok sighed, the lines around her eyes deepening. 'I'm sorry, Elka, I believe that your heart is in the right place, but you are wilfully naïve and I can't risk my people walking into a bloodbath on your account.'

Disappointment ripped through me.

'Nor can I take them into battle to fight for a cause we don't believe in. This rebellion won't rest until we have a republic who welcomes magic and representation of all beliefs.' She softened, as much as Pani Smok was capable of softening. 'You're a smart girl and I valued our time together when you were growing up, but that does not mean you have the right to rule over us, and I will not betray my own ideals simply because I'm fond of you.'

It was an effort to speak over the hard lump wedged in my throat. 'I understand,' I said quietly. I held a hand out for my knapsack. Kaz rose, passing me it at once, his concern apparent in the jut of his chin, the way he looked as if he wanted to protect me from disappointment, from disagreement. But these were good conversations, ones I needed to have. I wanted a better Mazrovia for everyone, not just myself. I slid out the maps and castle plans that I'd pencilled my thoughts over, marking out the secret passageways to the castle. 'Here.' I handed the roll to Pani Smok. 'For when you make your move.'

Her hand met mine on the paper. After battling her own curiosity, she gave me a firm nod. 'Good luck to you, Elka.'

'Thank you, all, for listening to me,' I said before exiting the camp, Kaz at my back. The domowik rematerialised, trundling along beside me, knee-high.

Kaz took my knapsack, slinging it over the same shoulder on which he carried his own larger bag of supplies. 'You didn't tell them the queen is a witch.'

'No.' I sighed, wondering if that was a mistake. 'Information is power and, right now, that's all I have. I'm saving it for the right moment.'

Kaz held a hand to the small of my back, guiding me through the pitch-dark forest, which rumbled and shook around us as he unveiled his massive power once more.

'Tell me about your court,' I asked. It was dawning on me that soon I would be seeing the Forest Court for myself, and the only time I had learned about it from my tutors was to instruct me to stay away, lest I wanted to step into Nawia itself. I didn't believe anybody from the castle had set foot inside. If the stories were to be trusted, I also didn't believe many people that *had* set foot inside had also then left to share their story. My fear was tempered only by my curiosity. 'If we are to be allies, I must know what to expect. Who your closest advisors are, who you might distrust.'

'The Forest Court is ruled by an inner circle, a council of four. I form the head of that four. Tosia is my second in command, though it should have been Bereza.' Kaz's sigh was audible through the darkness.

This was exactly what I needed. 'Tell me more,' I instructed. 'Tell me everything.'

'Bereza is the eldest of us all and a distant cousin of mine on my father's side. He's steadfast but can be stifling with his adherence to traditions. He is also part demon and more powerful than the other members of my council.'

'But not as powerful as you?'

Kaz paused. 'No.'

I nodded to myself, digesting the things he told me and the things he did not. The gaps in the conversation that needed to be prised open to reveal the secrets hiding within. 'You must have had reason to put Tosia in that position instead?'

'I did, but that does not dull Bereza's resentment of the fact.' Kaz continued to guide me through the night as he spoke. 'I told you once that I had had a younger brother?'

'I remember,' I said softly. He'd told me the story before I'd known he was more than human, but it was easy enough to infer the rest. 'Your mother and your brother were human, weren't they? That's why they died?' Now I was leaving things unsaid. Kaz was either immortal or close to it. I was not.

'They were. My power manifests in two different ways. I have power over the forest itself, a power that was bestowed upon me when I was given the court to rule over. One that is not inherently mine.'

This was news to me. I listened more keenly, ignoring the fear that came with treading through a darkness so thick I couldn't see my own feet.

'My own power is elemental,' Kaz said quietly. Almost a confession. He was still worried I would run from his darker, demon side. Perhaps I knew him better than he knew me, now. 'It manifests in storms, in fire, in earth and water and air. I am stronger with some than others, but I have some ability to heal as well. One that appears tied to my own emotions: the more strongly I feel about a person, the more I can help them. This was enough to keep my family well and strong for a while. When a horse trampled my brother, shattering the bones in his leg, it was not a death sentence. Neither was the terrible fever that haunted my mother every winter for years. But I couldn't save them from everything. Not from their own mortality.' He fell into a silence I had no intention of breaking. 'But I am grateful they lived long human lives. Enough for Filip to have his own son. To see his grandchildren. And when he died, I looked after them from afar.'

'Tosia is your . . . great-niece?' My head whirled, wondering precisely how old Kaz was.

'Niece is fine,' he said, a little tightly.

I smiled, knowing I had hit a sensitive spot.

'It's remarkable really. She has the same eyes as he did, in the darkest shade of blue that misses nothing. The same calm manner with a streak of underlying stubbornness, always so sure that she knows best.' His smile was nostalgic. 'The same keen mind. Sometimes she feels badly that she has no powers, that she herself is not magic the way the rest of us are, but her shrewd intelligence is a greater gift.'

'Then it makes sense why you chose her for your second,' I said. 'And the fourth member?'

'I took Mirosław under my wing when his parents begged me to let him live at the Forest Court.'

Interesting. 'Why?'

'He was having problems learning how to use his gifts. In time, he proved himself worthy of joining my council.' That triggered many more questions, but Kaz continued. 'Szafir is the fifth, unofficial member of my circle. You will meet her first.'

'Why unofficial?'

Kaz chuckled under his breath. 'She refuses to be part of any official council business. Claims that the meetings are so boring they would sap her spirit away. I ask her every solstice – I think she enjoys refusing me now. It's become something of a tradition. I still have a seat saved for her though, just in case.'

'She must be powerful for you to keep asking.' Especially if she felt comfortable turning the forest demon down. 'Why do you want her there?' It was curious to hear Kaz talk about the people he spent his days with, and who and what he valued. I thirsted to hear it all. To know him every bit as well as I knew myself.

'She's a friend,' Kaz said simply.

'Then I look forward to meeting her,' I told him, feeling his hand tighten on my lower back in response. Igniting that deep ache that slumbered inside me, even as I'd promised myself I would not act on it. Kaz was an itch I could no longer scratch and it troubled me that I didn't seem to care that he was the forest demon himself. It only made me ache for him more. Perhaps darkness was drawn to darkness. It mattered not; we were to be allies and allies alone.

'You told me once that you knew nothing of your father,' I said in an attempt to distract myself from more . . . wicked thoughts. 'If Bereza is your cousin, if you've inherited your father's court, how can that be true?' Or was it another lie?

'Bereza's mother and my father were estranged half siblings,' Kaz said. 'Centuries apart in age, they never knew each other. And, when I inherited the court, only wiła, the forest spirits, lived there, none old enough to have remembered my father. Everyone else had already departed with him, gone to wherever the old gods vanished to. The day I inherited the Forest Court, I was summoned there by magic,' Kaz continued. 'Another half-demon sibling of my father's awaited me to explain everything. He was the one who informed me of Bereza's existence, and I sent an owl with an invitation to my council that same day.'

I nodded to myself, digesting this all.

After we'd walked through half the night, Kaz's hand fell away from my back. I still couldn't see a thing, but I knew we'd arrived, the tang of magic hung thick and heavy in the night. It was different to the queen's magic, fresher and earthier with a hint of smoke. It smelled like Kaz.

'Welcome to the Forest Court, princess.'

CHAPTER TWENTY-FIVE

Kaz threw his arms up and a hundred pyres ignited, revealing his court.

The Forest Court was a web of ancient ruins, choked in a wild tangle of forest growth. A giant oak tree rose above it all. As we neared, my throat tightened with nerves. Żar stared up at me from his sling, wide-eyed and vulnerable. I fastened my cloak, concealing him once more, and prayed to Perun that I wasn't making a terrible mistake.

As I tried to match Kaz's long stride, we strolled along a fire-edged stone path, leading to an arched entry. Above, pairs of trees formed a gnarled tunnel. 'From the moment we walk in there, hide your fear,' he instructed me in an undertone. 'Choke it down deep or they will devour you alive. You must not be fooled by our veneer of respectability; this court answers to bloodshed and the laws of the forest above all else. And –' a warning lanced through his eyes that sent my heart rate racketing up – 'do not let them see that you're afraid of me.'

'I'm not afraid of you,' I reminded him.

'But you will be.'

I ignored the prickle his warning gave me; I was in too deep now. Emerging from the tree-tunnel, we were faced with great stone ruins embedded within the forest itself, leftovers from an ancient civilisation whose name was long lost to the winds of time. Great trees grew through the cracked stone. A creaking noise dragged my attention away. The branches draped over the ruins were moving. Another few steps and I stopped abruptly. They had eyes. And they were all looking at me. Wiła. They were creeping and crawling over the exterior, their limbs cracking like broken bones, and as we passed under the arch of two meeting oaks, I noticed a couple clinging to the underside, watching us. A nest of maggots squirmed where one of the wiła's knees would have been if they'd been human. I quickly looked away.

'No fear,' Kaz reminded me.

I held my chin higher. 'No fear,' I murmured back.

The challenge blazed in his golden eyes. 'Perhaps the interior of my court will be more to your liking, princess.'

'Interior?'

He lifted an eyebrow. 'You didn't think we all lived outside, did you?'

'No, of course not,' I scoffed. Kaz was amused, sensing the lie.

We reached the great arched door set into the centre of the ruins. A torch flamed either side of it, illuminating a series of carvings on the walls. I halted; I'd never seen anything like them before.

'They're older than the recorded history of Mazrovia.' Kaz

rested a hand on the smooth dark stone, next to the curled carvings that were either pictures or some form of early writing. Beautiful but unknowable.

I stared at them, humbled by how much I had yet to learn. Maybe Pani Smok and her rebellion were right to question who should rule over this land, but I couldn't lose my confidence now. First, I would secure the throne and ensure Żar's safety. Then I could ponder what was best.

Kaz swept his hands out. Stone screeched against stone as the immense door slowly opened. 'Show off,' I muttered, hiding how his power affected me, a girl born to a witch with no magic of her own. Though Kaz's abilities were vastly different to the witches': he had no need of a tithe – his magic did not carry a blood price. Being a demon, he was magic himself.

We entered the Forest Court together, the hatchling sleeping in his sling, the domowik at our heels.

A single torch revealed wide stone steps, running down into darkness. With another flick of Kaz's hand, more torches flamed to life, rippling down and down and down. Holding my chin high, I set off, Kaz at my side. As we descended, something else occurred to me. 'You told me that your name is Kaz. Kazimierz.'

'It is.'

'But do your court know that?' We'd only seen the wiła but I wasn't so naïve to believe that I was entering the Forest Court with the ruling demon himself without anyone watching. I hoped they weren't listening, too.

'Some.'

'So what should I call you front of them?' I pressed. How did one address a forest demon? My etiquette lessons at the castle had failed to prepare me for this. 'What does everybody else call you?'

His lips curved into a delighted, dark little smile. 'They call me master.'

At the bottom of the stairs, the space widened out to an atrium. Pillars carved with the same ancient language supported an earthen ceiling. Roots rippled through walls, jostling for space with decorative wall panels, carved from stone and cracked with age. On the far side, a waterfall gushed down from the ceiling, filling a rocky pool before wending out into miniature streams. Small lanterns bobbed along their current like wandering stars. 'This is not what I expected.' I couldn't help gaping at it all. I'd braced myself to walk into the nightmare that everyone said the Forest Court was, but this . . . this was a dream I never wanted to wake from.

Kaz's smile twisted my stomach.

It had been an age since we'd left my crooked cottage, but I hadn't expected Kaz to escort me directly to where I'd be sleeping. I knew we'd be staying here a short while, firming up our plans and debriefing the army, but I'd also expected to meet the key players of the court on my arrival. To put faces to the names – Bereza, Tosia, Mirosław and Szafir – not be ushered along the passageways that coiled round the court like earthworms. 'Is there a reason you don't want anybody to see me yet?' I demanded when we stopped, the domowik traipsing along behind us.

The smoke and sparks twining around Kaz's hands gave a warning flash.

'You are the leader of the Forest Court, aren't you?' I asked sharply. 'You weren't lying to me about the army, were you?' I knew of the existence of an army, buried deep in the forest from the plans I'd stolen from the castle, but the texts I'd read on the subject were short on the details.

'I am,' he confirmed. 'But it's an unruly court.' Glancing to either side, he stepped closer, lowering his voice. 'I cannot say more just yet, only that you should think on what I told you earlier. I have been away and my position is . . . coveted. If this is done the right way then we'll both get what we want, but we can't rush into it.'

I folded my arms. 'So this is why you picked me to be your queen, why you just happened to have an army standing by for me; it was all to serve your own greater purpose.'

Kaz gave a rough sigh, rubbing the back of his neck. 'Elka, this is why I sought you out in the first place; I knew we would make powerful allies. But it's one thing to be powerful, it's another thing entirely to *stay* powerful.'

'Fine,' I conceded.

'Elka.' Kaz's gaze softened on my face. 'Thank you for coming here. I was terrified you'd never trust me again.'

Żar grumbled, whipping his tail inside the sling.

Kaz chuckled. Then he caught sight of my expression. 'What is it?'

'I don't,' I whispered. 'I don't trust you.'

His shields slammed back down. Once, at the cottage, I had questioned how he had veered between teasing and flirting, to turning serious in the blink of an eye. *You make me happy*, he'd claimed. Judging by the thunderclouds crawling up his forearms, that happiness was a distant memory now. As was keeping his power a secret; since we'd entered his territory, he had reverted back to his demon self. I hoped that signalled the end of any secrets between us. 'I understand,' he said.

But he didn't. I trusted that he wanted an alliance, that he too raged against the Purge and wanted the queen dead. I did not trust my own feelings. My longing was an insatiable beast that I could not tame and, when I was around him, did not *want* to tame. I'd told Kaz I didn't trust him, but, really, I did not trust that he felt the same way as I did. The queen had called me naïve and she'd been right; I knew little about the ways of men. I'd been taught to guard my heart and here I was, being careless with it in the Forest Court, with the forest demon himself. And that was a weakness, in a place I couldn't afford to have weaknesses.

Kaz opened a door I hadn't noticed. 'Szafir will take care of anything you need; I'll send her your way in the morning. You'll be safe here.' He strode away without a backwards glance.

'What gives you the impression that I need protecting?'

I called after him, desperation staining my voice. *Come back. Show me you feel the same way I do. That you like me for me and not because you would prefer me on the throne.* 'Was it when I gutted the bauk? Or when I saved you from the rusałka?'

His tired laugh echoed back along the passageway. I knew, even without seeing him, that it had not softened his gaze, his mood. That I had hurt him.

With a sigh, I walked through the door.

It was a cosy chamber, carved from the earth. A white stone floor was polished to a pearl, and a large bed sat in the centre, with cream canopies, similar to the ones I'd slept under in the castle, though those had been embroidered silk and these were thick and warm. Toeing off my boots, I collapsed into the heap of woollen blankets and cushions, hugging Żar close to my heart.

CHAPTER TWENTY-SIX

A brusque knock on the door roused me from a deep sleep. I snapped to attention, tossing a blanket over Żar. 'Yes?' I called out. The domowik appeared from under my bed.

A half-wiła, half-human entered. She was petite, with patches of bark vanishing under the straps of her yellow dress, and a shock of cerulean hair tumbling around her shoulders. Wild owlish eyes, with sapphire-bright irises, blinked at me, and a mischievous smile lurked on her face. 'So you're the one that's drawn the master's eye.'

I spluttered for a response.

With pursed lips, she looked me up and down. 'Not bad.' Her smile grew more devious. 'But I can do better.'

'I'm sorry?' I managed to find my tongue.

'Cute dragon.' She glanced at Żar, who'd escaped the blanket and was regarding her curiously, his scales glittering blood-red, then whipped a tape measure out from one of the many pockets sewn into her dress. 'Now, let's put you in something that will really bring out the fire in his eyes.'

I stood warily, all too aware that the person I'd believed was Katia, my dearest, oldest friend, had been the queen in disguise. 'Who are you?'

'I'm Szafir.'

That was unexpected. From what Kaz had said about begging her to join his inner circle, I had not presumed she would be the one dressing me. 'Ah, I see the master told you about me.' She cocked her head to one side, her mischievous smile tipping up at one corner; on the other, a thin scar bisected her mouth. 'How delicious.'

'You're not curious about what he said?' I couldn't help asking.

'Curiosity is the first step to Nawia,' she retorted, evaluating me every bit as keenly as I was her.

'Well, he seems to think very highly of you.'

She scoffed. 'As he should. Now, the master sent me to help with anything you might need. And this –' she waved a hand at my leather leggings and loose shirt buttoned over my armoured corset, rumpled from days of hard travel – 'is a desperate need.'

'I don't look that bad,' I grumbled, giving my shirt a cautious sniff as Szafir rummaged in the alarmingly large bag she'd dragged in with her. Standing beneath a bleeding corpse and trekking through the darkest corridors of Stary Bór had not been kind to me. The sides of the domowik rippled.

'I don't know why you're laughing,' I whispered, 'You don't smell any better.' It stopped at once, making me snort. The domowik was not fully corporeal yet; I didn't even know if it *could* smell bad.

'Right, then.' Szafir straightened, fixing me with her owlish stare. Her delicate nose wrinkled. 'I think you'd better have a bath first.'

'There are baths here?' I was too excited to mind the insult.

I scooped up Żar and followed Szafir through the hallway and through the door beside mine. With the lack of windows, my sense of time was disorientated; I could have slept for two hours or twenty. *And where was Kaz?* I wished we could return to the easy friendship we'd shared when we'd been locked inside my cottage while a storm raged through the forest. Before all our secrets had come tumbling free.

The bathroom walls were crafted from the same kind of stone as the ancient ruins outside, but the ceiling was open to the forest above. Peering up, I glimpsed mossed trees interwoven with crumbling statues of gods I didn't recognise, obscuring anyone's view if they happened by. In the centre of the floor was a large sunken square filled with frothing water, big enough to swim from one end to the other. In my arms, Żar squeaked with excitement, stretching his talons towards the heat.

When Szafir left, I undressed, cautiously shedding my armoured corset, although I laid my largest knife next to the bath. Just in case. A splash sent water my way. 'Żar?' Alarm fired through me like a warning shot. But the hatchling was lazily floating in the water. He gave one huff of contentment before closing his eyes, fragrant pine-scented steam flowing over his scales. Smiling, I slid into the water and joined him, easing the stiffness from my muscles.

My fingers had pruned when I heard voices outside. Lowered voices. Not heeding Szafir's earlier warning about curiosity, I reached for a nearby robe and left Żar floating in the steam with his eyes closed as I crept to the door, snatching up my knife en route. I was at a disadvantage here and, by the power of Perun, I was determined to claw a little information for myself before I stood in front of the court and asked for their help.

I pressed my ear against the wood.

Two voices battled in a dangerous rhythm of discontent. One was brittle and sharp, in a way that made me distrustful before I caught the threatening tone. I tensed, reaching for the door though I didn't want to reveal myself.

The second voice belonged to Szafir. 'Leave me alone,' she snarled, loud enough that they were the first words I'd caught.

I ripped the door open.

Szafir wheeled round, her bright blue eyes locking with mine. She must have been guarding the door. Her eyes widened in warning.

'You must be the princess.' A sharp-toothed young man was standing too close to Szafir, to me, to the bathroom that sheltered Żar. I silently closed the door as he surveyed me through wide-set, mossy eyes. His slanted cheekbones were similar to Kaz's, but his nose was long and proud, and he was leaner and closer to my height. 'How . . . underwhelming.'

'Is there a problem here?' I asked, ignoring the slight.

Szafir slid her hands into her pockets, raising my suspicions that she had more than tape measures stashed in them. 'Bogdan was just leaving.'

'Is that so?' Bogdan leaned against the wall, lazily watching us both. 'I don't recall saying anything of the sort.'

'If Szafir asked you to leave, I suggest you leave,' I told him. My knife was burning in the pocket of my robe. I itched to bury it in Bogdan's chest, claiming my seventh and final heart from the man who had managed to rattle Szafir.

Bogdan showed no inclination of moving. 'You are not the ruler of this court, *princess*.' He called me 'princess' the way some men called women 'girls'. Who sneered at the things women smiled at, who turned their beauty, their intelligence against them. Belittled them.

I gave him my prettiest smile. Then I slowly drew my knife. Bogdan watched as I flipped it from hilt to blade, blade to hilt, taking in how experienced I was with the weapon. 'No. But I will be the ruler of this Queendom. Do you really wish to make an enemy of me?'

Bogdan scoffed. 'I doubt you'll ever sit on that glass throne,' he said. But wariness tightened his mouth and he sauntered out of sight.

I turned on Szafir, who looked as relieved as I felt. 'What was that about? Why was he threatening you?'

Szafir fidgeted with the pockets of her dress. 'Bogdan is the son of Bereza.'

I frowned, trying to follow the twisting currents of court

politics. 'Does that mean that he's part demon, too?'

'Yes, but only very slightly. His magic is negligible. Any power he holds is by the name of his bloodline alone, but that doesn't stop him from strutting around the court as if he were entitled to it. And he *loathes* me.' Szafir's smile reappeared, crueller than the one she'd flashed at me earlier. I liked her already. 'He can't abide that Kaz keeps asking me to become the fifth member of his council, that the last seat is reserved for the day I might change my mind.'

'Let me guess,' I said dryly, 'he thinks it ought to belong to him.'

Szafir pulled a face.

'So that's why he belittles you, bullies you.'

'Yes.'

'You threaten him.'

'I'd do a great deal more than that if I could get away with it,' Szafir growled.

She hadn't told me how Bogdan had threatened her and I didn't ask. But the thought of it happening again was unacceptable. 'Have you told Kaz? Surely he would offer you some kind of protection.' If not ridding the court of Bogdan altogether.

'Without a second thought.' Szafir began fidgeting again. 'But he's been away for solstices and, though Tosia has been ruling in his stead, she is only human in a wicked court, and Bereza has been gaining considerable influence.'

It took a minute to take in the implications. 'Then Kaz is right to be concerned.'

'I believe so,' Szafir confirmed. 'And since Bereza has the ears of the court, so does Bogdan to some extent. It's made his behaviour worse. Even now he's back, Kaz's hands will be tied.'

I began to worry. For Szafir, for Kaz. For me. The future of Mazrovia was tied up in this alliance and if it wasn't built on the steadiest rock, everything could come crumbling down.

The Forest Court rivalled the castle with its twisted loyalties and scheming rivals, but I had been born to the castle; that language had been my mother tongue. Here, I would have to learn fast.

'Don't worry,' Szafir said, missing nothing. 'I can handle Bogdan. He's all bluster and no storm. Be careful, though – you've drawn his attention now, made him look weak in front of me. He won't like that.'

I looked at my knife, shining in hand. 'I think I can handle him, too.'

Szafir's eyes took on a knowing gleam. 'Oh, we are going to be *good* friends.'

Back in my room, I fed Żar almost an entire vein's worth of blood, until the domowik floundered in panic and I realised how dizzy I'd grown. Szafir passed no comment but sent for a hearty lunch to be delivered since I'd overslept breakfast. It arrived on a silver tray: a hot pile of crispy pierogi with fluffy cheese-and-potato filling, reminding me of Kaz's laughter when mine had collapsed back in the cottage, a lifetime ago now. I wondered where he was, if the balance between us had shifted now that we were on his territory, where his power peaked.

On the gloaming hour, Szafir draped silk around me in luscious holly-green, the colour Kaz's eyes had been when I'd believed he was just a huntsman I'd found in the forest. I'd spent only one night and day apart from him and I was seeing him in everything. Ever since I knew how he kissed, I craved him.

'What's the Forest Court like?' I asked Szafir.

Szafir smiled around a mouthful of pins. 'It sounds like you've already heard the stories.'

'It's a little hard not to,' I said wryly. The one about the court being a pit of debauchery sprang to mine. As did an older tale, one I'd forgotten about till now, that I'd overheard, whispered between two members of the queen's guard in the castle. That in vengeance for some slight, Kaz had seduced both princes in Glenwich, a neighbouring kingdom, almost triggering a civil war.

'No need to worry,' Szafir said brightly. 'Only half of them are actually true.'

'It's which half that has me worried,' I muttered.

'Those princes had it coming.' Szafir sniffed. 'Glenwich had the biggest illegal magic markets, selling magical creatures into captivity before he . . . distracted them.'

I twisted my lips, reframing the stories I'd heard.

'We're done.' Szafir gave me a satisfied nod. 'You can look now.' She lifted a polished sheet of thin metal to show me – it seemed there were no mirrors in the Forest Court. Wise, since Kaz had parted with a thimble of his own blood to forge his connection with my mother's mirrors. Any mirror he or I looked into would be seen by the queen.

'It's a masterpiece, even if I do say so myself.'

The moment I caught sight of myself in the mottled reflection, I yelped. 'What have you put me in? I can't wear *this*.'

Szafir's satisfaction slid off her face. 'What's wrong with it?' she demanded, her hands coming to rest on her hips.

'I might as well be walking into the court wearing nothing at all!' I stared at the verdant green silk that dipped sinfully low, revealing the roots that wreathed my chest, ran down my arm. The straps were cobweb-thin, straining to hold the dress up before it plummeted down my back, low enough to trace my entire spine. It would be impossible to wear my armoured corset beneath this, or any undergarments at all. The silk hugged my slight curves, leaving nothing to the imagination.

Szafir lifted a shoulder. 'Well, that's your choice. You wouldn't be the only one, but the master had instructed me to make you a dress so I assumed—'

'I was being sarcastic. Obviously I'm not going to be naked.' I glared at her, trying desperately to ignore the fact that she'd mentioned others would be – I'd assumed the stories of how debauched this court was were . . . embellished. Now I fretted that they were not.

'Just wait until the master sees you,' Szafir whispered seductively, her blue gaze meeting my hazel eyes in the reflective metal. 'He'll lose his mind.'

'He doesn't think of me that way.' Even as I said it, his voice filled my head, deep, rich and silken. *I want the darkest parts of you.* The leaf on my collarbone trembled.

Szafir smirked like she knew exactly what was running through my head. 'Are you sure about that?'

I failed to answer her.

'I thought so,' she said smugly. 'Anyway, I thought you came here because you needed an army to walk into battle with? Because you wanted to be queen?'

'I do.'

She held the metal sheet up again. 'Tell me you don't feel like a queen in that dress.'

Steeling myself, I gazed at my reflection, studying it properly for the first time since I'd left the castle. My face was more angular than it had been two years ago; I was taller and thinner. My ebony hair was longer, too, and Szafir had brushed it until it gleamed, leaving it loose and wild. She'd exaggerated the redness of my lips, painting them darker, bloodier.

'When you walk into the court, every eye will be on you.' Szafir gave a particularly vicious smile. 'And the master will want to gouge every single one of them out simply for looking.' She dusted a golden powder over my eyelids and cheekbones until they shimmered in the candlelight.

A knock sounded on the door. 'The master is waiting for her,' a gruff voice announced.

I picked up Żar, his scales warm from the fire, and held him tightly for a moment. Knowing that this was coming hadn't made it any easier to prepare for. The domowik had vanished, probably to seek out Kaz. Or the kitchens.

Szafir cocked her head curiously.

'I've never left him before,' I admitted.

She held her arms out. 'I'll take good care of him, I promise.'

Still, I hesitated.

'It isn't magical creatures who fear the Court,' Szafir said. 'Stary Bór is a haven for those who don't have a place elsewhere. Żar being the last hatchling means something here.' Her gaze was steady, earnest.

'Aren't you coming as well?' I asked.

'Not for all the bark in the forest.' She shuddered. 'I prefer to spend my time alone. Now, hand him over.'

I let Żar go, taking a deep breath and turning for the door before I could regret my decision. Nerves fluttered in my stomach. I wore no armour, no weapons; Szafir and I had decided it would be better to demonstrate my trust in my new allies. Weapons didn't scream trust.

'Oh, and, princess?'

I glanced back at her. 'Yes?'

Szafir fidgeted with the pockets of her yellow dress. 'I want you to be queen,' she said in a rush.

'Oh.' Well. I hadn't expected that. 'That's very sweet of y—'

'I want to make your coronation gown,' Szafir interrupted,

giving me a shrewd look and folding her arms over Żar, her sharp elbows jutting out like dagger hilts. 'So, if someone eats you, I'm going to be annoyed.'

I hid any hint of a smile. 'I won't get eaten.'

Still eyeing me, Szafir sighed. 'It's my own fault; I made you look too delectable.'

'Er, thank you?'

'Don't thank me.' Szafir flapped a hand at me. 'But try not to die either,' she called after me as I gave up and made for the door.

It was time to prove myself to the Forest Court.

CHAPTER TWENTY-SEVEN

A guard escorted me down a dark tunnel. Tree roots whispered through the earth, the stone floor shuddering as they passed by, unseen, somewhere below. The guard was half wiła like Szafir, but the forest had left a greater imprint on him, with patches of moss alongside his bark and skin. A single mushroom sprouted behind his left ear. Globes of light lit our way towards a pair of carved marble doors, flanked by another two guards. More wiła.

As I strolled towards the doors, they were whisked open, revealing a cavernous ancient temple, all stonework and trees and waterfalls tumbling down ivy-clad walls. Lush with plants and mosses and ferns in a hundred shades of green, from the lightest grass-green fronds to emerald leaves glossed with a patina so dark it looked black.

And it was filled with people.

More half-wiła danced with beings I didn't recognise, the floor writhing as one, satin slipping from shoulders, hands dipping low and lower, lips roaming in dark corners, where shadows moved like syrup, and several people seemed to have given up on the idea of wearing anything at all. I scanned the crowd, looking for the crackling centre of power, the flaming heart of the court himself.

Kaz stood beside a tower of glasses, flowing with a sparkling liquid that looked like molten starlight. He was not alone. Three other beings stood with him, the four of them drawing constant glances from everyone else. That, then, was the council. A strain of haunting music sang out, sending goosebumps trailing down my bare arms.

I strode inside like I already wore a crown.

Kaz's head jerked up, sensing me. Standing there, I let him come to me. Kaz thrust his glass into the chest of one of the council, and stalked towards me like a stag through the forest. King of his court. The other three watched silently.

I inhaled sharply; this was my chance to secure our alliance, the army I needed to make myself a queen. But, gods, he looked good all in black, his formal suit hugging his broad shoulders, his white shirt hinting at the sculpted chest beneath.

Kaz trailed his gaze down me. 'That's *quite* a dress you're wearing.' His golden eyes blazed fiercely.

'I wanted to make a good impression.' I gave him a wry smile, trying to ignore our audience.

'Well, you've certainly drawn their attention,' he murmured, lingering on the hollow of my throat as if he wanted to feast on it. 'Now, come.' Taking my hand, he led me to the centre of the hall. The dark beating heart of the forest. The air was rich with petrichor. A group of musicians lifted bows to their stringed instruments, playing something deep and slow and heady, sending lovers into each other's arms. A fleeting glance over Kaz's broad shoulder revealed that the three key players of the court were still fixed on us.

'Your council are watching,' I told Kaz, placing my hand in his. 'Let's show them how secure our alliance is.' Never mind that the music and magic were entrancing. That Kaz was under my skin, in my blood, that every part of me sought him out like a flower tipping its head towards the sun. I craved him.

Kaz drew me closer, holding me tightly against himself, his hand tingling against my bare back. 'Agreed. Let's show them all who you belong to.'

'I'll dance with you, but the only person I belong to is myself,' I whispered up into his ear, my breath hot against his neck. 'This is an alliance and nothing more, remember?'

'We'll see about that,' he purred back.

Kaz led me through the pattern of unfamiliar steps, until I sank into the rhythm of them; a princess had to dance well and I'd been instructed in the art. I wouldn't have found the footwork as easy had I not also been secretly continuing my lessons in swordplay at the time. When Pan Jedrick was ordered to stop instructing me in favour of becoming the queen's political advisor, he risked everything to spend another eight years turning me into a weapon.

I was good, but Kaz was *good*. He danced as effortlessly as breathing, his steps as fast and slick as a river. Each time he whirled away, holding his hand out for me, I met him there, sinking back into his arms, moulding myself to him.

It did not escape the notice of the three, who hadn't looked away once. I stared back at them, challenging them. The heart of the Court. The inner council. I needed to win them over to my cause. I had to show no fear, no lick of desperation. I memorised their features: one bore traces of Kaz's features on his older face, surveying me with dull green eyes over his glass as he drank; this must be Bereza, father to Bogdan. The second had short blonde hair and seemed to be smiling faintly to herself. Tosia. And the third was the youngest, around my age, with one eye black, the other white, and a smirk, who could only be Mirosław.

'Everybody's watching,' I whispered to Kaz. I was out of my depth here in a way I'd never been in the castle, even when things had been bad, when my mother refused to speak to me for years, and I'd lain awake wondering if it was possible to die from loneliness, I'd still belonged.

'Good,' Kaz growled. 'Let's give them something to watch.'

A shiver trailed down my spine. 'I thought I was here to garner support from your court?'

'Forest politics is nothing more than one big show. If we show them that our . . . *union* is solid, then they have nothing to fear allying themselves with the throne and Mazrovia will be more united than it's been in decades. Stronger than ever.'

'I don't understand why you're going to such lengths for me.'

Gods, had that really just slipped out? 'I know it benefits you, too,' I added in a rush, 'but we still have an alliance without you needing to pretend that you were erm, *interested* in me as well.' My face burned. I was glad Kaz's arms enveloped me, concealing me from his penetrative gaze.

Until he dipped me into a backbend, his golden stare locked on my face as he bent over me, holding me up with a single arm. His other leg crooked under my knee, raising my leg as we came to a dramatic finish. My dress spilled over him, revealing a hidden slit running up to my upper thigh. I saw the moment he noticed, the tip of his tongue wetting his lips. Sending a pulse of desire shooting through me. When he spoke again, his voice was gruff. 'Is this why you pulled away after learning I was the forest demon, after seeing my true form?'

'It was part of it,' I admitted, a little breathlessly.

He snapped upright. In the same beat, he pulled me up and into his arms. 'Do you really not know how I feel? Can you not tell?'

His gaze flicked to my mouth and back. My chest hitched, the memory of our kiss haunting me, teasing me with the ghost of his lips on mine, his tongue plundering my mouth. Tearing his eyes away, Kaz tightened his arms round me as if I was a precious treasure he needed to hold close, and continued the dance, leading me over the polished stone floor. 'When I close my eyes, I see that day when you bared yourself and lay down in the bath in front of me. Hurt and vulnerable and strong and beautiful, all at once. I don't think you realise the effect you have on me.' His hand flexed on my back, like he was resisting gripping me harder. 'When I sank my hands into your hair, I foolishly let myself imagine for a moment, just a moment, that you might be mine one day. That you would come to me, not because you needed help but because you wanted me. And then later that night, when you sought me out in that dress.' His breathing grew ragged. 'Knowing that you did want me, then realising that I couldn't let myself have you, not yet, was hard. You're almost impossible to resist. But you needed to know the truth. Leaving you was even harder, the hardest thing I've ever done, and I have lived a long life.'

My pulse feathered. The way Kaz's voice altered when he spoke to me, the things he'd confided in me that he no longer needed to say to convince me, not now that I was in his hall, that I'd seen his true face and was still dancing with him, proved that there were feelings there. Feelings that I wasn't sure I wanted to understand. Feelings that were becoming impossible to ignore, even as they scared me. 'I did want you then,' I confessed.

Disappointment crested his face. 'Will you ever forgive me for keeping my identity from you?'

'Which time?' I asked lightly, regretting it the moment pain bled through his expression. He lifted me, his arms flexing as he whirled me around, the music fast and wild, dancers' skirts and suits and tunics spinning in a garden of colour.

Slowly, losing the beat of the music, Kaz lowered me. 'I have forgiven you,' I told him, his eyes searching mine. As soon as I'd said the words, I realised they were true. If the forest demon had shown up at my cottage that night, I never would have listened to a word that poured out of his mouth like a silken night, charm and darkness entwined. I would have met him in a clash of blades and fear. I understood that Kaz had needed to build my trust in him before shattering it, but I didn't have to like it or stop wishing that he'd done it a different way. 'But you are a demon, a trickster, and I would be a fool to trust you.' I needed to remember this, even as he made my blood sing, my stomach throb each time he entered my sight. My own body was too eager to betray me.

He inclined his head. 'I understand.'

'Though sometimes it's much more fun to make bad decisions,' I added with an impish smile. I was tired of denying myself: I had an alliance with Kaz; there was no reason to abstain from anything more. Not when doing so only punished myself as well. I was going to be queen . . . Surely I could keep my wits sharp when it came to him. His gaze snapped back onto me with an intensity that almost stilled my lungs. 'And, Kaz?' I ran my hands down his arms. Slowly. Sultrily. 'I never stopped wanting you.'

His golden eyes ignited. His hands tightened on my waist like he wanted to pick me up and carry me away from the hordes of his people watching us dance. 'Careful, princess,' he growled, 'You wouldn't want to make me lose control. Not here, not now.'

I caught his earlobe between my teeth. 'Try me.'

His growl deepened, thrilling me.

'*Gods,*' Kaz groaned when he noticed the thin silk of my dress refusing to hide my desire. The trees wrapped round the ruins shifted as his power slipped, the ancient stone rumbling a threat.

I grabbed the front of his shirt and pulled him down onto my mouth.

He tugged me up, onto my toes, seeking more, with that mouth I could get lost in. Lips I wanted to kiss for days. Running my fingers through his hair, I gave it a soft, insistent tug. Felt his groan vibrate through my mouth as he deepened the kiss, claiming my mouth with his tongue.

I hadn't planned on kissing him, but his little speech had cast a spell. He may be the forest demon, but I was a murderess. I'd lied every bit as much as he had; who was I to judge him? Him who wanted me, darkness and all.

I didn't see the blonde woman approach, I was so caught up in our unravelling, the ribbons of time slowing to a flutter as I gave up pretending that I didn't want Kaz. Until she spoke and we peeled apart, a small thunderstorm crawling along Kaz's shoulder. 'I think you've proven your point already.'

The stone beneath us shuddered. 'Back off, Tosia.'

'Careful,' Tosia said mildly. 'You wouldn't want to bring your own court down.'

'Fine,' Kaz ground out, tearing his eyes away from me long enough for the ancient temple ruins to steady. For my pulse to calm. His hands trailed down my arms, giving my hand a quick, reassuring squeeze before he let me go, Tosia watching like a sentry. I had a feeling that nothing escaped her notice.

'Are you ready to play your part?' Kaz asked.

Apprehension needled my spine. 'I'm ready.'

CHAPTER TWENTY-EIGHT

Tosia. Mirosław. Bereza.

The council that, together with Kazimierz, formed the inner workings of the Forest Court. Tosia, who had interrupted Kaz and me, was calm and still, a well-suited second in command with keen dark-blue eyes and cropped golden hair that gave her the air of a pixie, though I knew she was the only human to sit at the council. Her dress was a sleek, stylish smoke-grey, and she looked to be in the middle of her twenties. Mirosław's black and white eyes were so striking it took me a beat to register the rest of his face; he'd tied back his long hair, the same golden brown as his skin tone, and his mouth quirked to one side, giving him a permanent impish expression that I suspected he used to his advantage. He looked the closest in age to me, though that could well be an effect of his powers, whatever they might be. And Bereza, the eldest of the four of them, was a shadow of Kaz, his features paler, sharper, leaner. Though, unlike Kaz, both Bereza and Bogdan, his son, shared the same long, proud nose.

Kaz introduced Bereza as his cousin and third in command.

'It's a pleasure to meet you.' I smiled at Bereza, determined to give him a fair chance despite what I'd heard.

He surveyed me before turning to Kaz, dismissing me in a manner that sent a hot wash of anger over me, my smile sticking to my face. 'No,' Bereza said.

'Give her a chance. Listen to what she has to say,' Kaz said in a warning tone. 'To what *I* have to say.'

'Ignore him, Bereza's an old bore,' Mirosław interrupted, taking my hand and pressing his lips to it, grinning when he heard Kaz's sigh. 'And the pleasure is all ours. The missing posters do not do you justice. No wonder Kaz took his time returning to us.'

The hall gave a slight rumble.

'Stop goading Kazimierz,' Tosia said evenly.

Kaz and Bereza were locked in a silent match. 'One might question where his priorities lie.' Bereza slid a disapproving look in my direction.

'The court will see that allying with Princess Elka gives us our best chance at taking down Queen Serce,' Kaz replied.

'Much time has passed since you last deigned to address your court.' Bereza folded his thick arms. 'You might be surprised at how their allegiances have shifted.'

Mirosław's white eye flitted nervously between Kaz and Bereza, while Tosia maintained the same impassiveness she'd held from the start.

Kaz stared at Bereza. 'I would hope that *my* court's loyalty is not so fickle as that. I trust them to have good judgement.'

I watched a nerve tic in Bereza's jaw. That parting shot had rankled him. Kaz held out his hand to me. 'It's time.'

My anxiety returned threefold. 'Aren't we adjourning to another room, to have some sort of council meeting?'

'Things here work differently to the castle,' Kaz explained in an undertone. 'In the Forest Court, our decisions and rules and debates are all publicly heard. Anyone is free to pass disagreement, to voice their opinion.'

'Fantastic,' I groaned, eyeing the horde of part wiła, demons and other creatures I held no name for. 'I'm sure they're going to have plenty of opinions on this.'

Kaz's jaw was set. 'They usually do.'

Kaz strode up to the base of the great oak tree that speared through his entire court. There was an old stone dais set before it, engraved with the same ancient language that marked the rest of the ruins, and a throne, crafted from the remnants of another old oak. Kaz took his seat as I stood at his right-hand side. The court silenced.

'As you know, I have spent the past few months away from court,' Kaz began, idly trailing his hand up the smooth bark of his throne. The oak shivered as if his touch were connected. I supposed it all was; Kaz was more than the forest demon, he was part of the forest himself. Resting his forearms on his knees, Kaz leaned forward to address his people. 'It was not a decision I took lightly, but at the time I believed it was of the utmost importance to discover exactly what was occurring under Queen Serce's rule. We knew her Purge was worsening, felt that drain of magic as she turned her sights to Stary Bór, and it was imperative I found out what her next plans were.' He paused, turning grave. 'They were worse than we'd feared. The queen plans to raze Stary Bór to the ground, to make room for a brand-new city under the crown's control.'

The court voiced their disapproval, cursing the queen and calling for action.

'In light of that, I have allied the Forest Court with Princess Elka. With her alliance, the forest will rise up to overthrow Queen Serce, ending her theft of magic, and put a new queen on the throne.' He held a hand out towards me. 'One who will be a friend to the Forest Court and have our best interests at heart.'

This was it, the moment I'd been waiting for. I stood tall under the court's scrutiny, refusing to let my confidence waver. Yes, I needed them, but they needed me, too.

'Are there any objections?' Kaz finished.

I tensed. A chill undulated through the hall. One of displeasure, distrust. One that I'd felt towards Kaz too many times not to recognise when it was targeted at me. Perhaps Pani Smok had been right and I was wilfully naïve, assuming that I'd have no problems borrowing an army to march into battle because a man with perfect cheekbones had promised it to me.

'I have a better suggestion.' Bereza strode forward. The way the crowd parted for him turned my palms clammy; he commanded enough respect to unsettle me.

Kaz gestured to the court. 'Share your opinion.'

'It's high time that Stary Bór stopped pandering to the whims of the castle.' A whisper of agreement swirled through the court. Kaz's back stiffened. Bereza gave a thin smile that never reached his moss-coloured eyes. 'This is the Forest Court. We do not want nor need another queen dispatching orders from afar. What we need is leverage to ensure that we get what we want.'

It was an effort to keep my contempt hidden, knowing exactly what Bereza was intimating.

Bereza gestured at me. 'Queen Serce's daughter walked into our court of her own accord. I think we need to determine if she's here for the reason she states or if she's here at the behest of the queen.' He raised a glass to me. 'Who else could make such a perfect spy?'

The whisper of agreement morphed into a roar of contention.

I glared at Bereza. 'I am no spy.'

Bereza's stare skated over my head to land on Kaz.

'I can confirm that she is not a spy,' Kaz said firmly.

Bereza had dismissed me once more. I was beginning to understand why Bogdan acted the way he did. It was only surprising that Bogdan himself had not yet added his voice to the crowd. 'You can't prove that,' Bereza continued. 'The girl has seduced you, that much is plain to see after your little dance.'

Now I was angry. Bristling. And deeply afraid. Our dance had started as a show of togetherness, but it had ended elsewhere. We'd betrayed a weakness.

Kaz matched Bereza's stare. Lightning flashed up his sleeve; he was rattled, but not surprised. When I looked out over the court, the thick crowd amid the ruins and trees and waterfalls, I didn't see allies that would fight on my behalf. I saw a threat to Kaz.

Kaz broke his stare with his third in command to address me. 'You may be heir to the cities and castles, but here in the forest, I am king. And you will kneel before me. Show this court your loyalty to me.'

Kaz's golden eyes blazed with something I didn't recognise. 'Face the court you wish to ally with,' he instructed, his command swelling to fill the hall. *His* hall.

Fear slammed into me. It didn't matter if this was the right move; I had no choice. Kaz was challenging every fibre of that thin trust I'd handed back to him.

My throat trembling, I kneeled in front of Kaz's throne, my back to the forest demon. Kaz rested a hand on each of my shoulders. He gave me a secret, reassuring squeeze. 'I trust her implicitly,' he continued in that deep, commanding voice, 'And as you are all under my rule, have accepted my authority in exchange for your safety living in this court, I suggest you do the same.'

I heard the threat rumble through the ruins.

'Or would you question my intelligence?' Kaz's tone lowered dangerously.

The court quieted.

'It is not your intelligence we question—' Bereza began, his bushy eyebrows drawing close together.

Tosia, who had been leaning insouciantly against a column, pushed off. 'That's enough, Bereza,' she said with calm authority. 'You have made your position clear. Let someone else speak now.'

'I stand with Bereza,' a wiła suddenly said, crossing her bark-skinned arms, carved with thorns. 'Even if she's loyal –' the wiła looked directly at me – 'she's more valuable to us as a hostage than an ally.'

Bereza slowly smiled.

And with that, the tide turned against me.

'She doesn't need to be alive to be a hostage.' Bogdan came to stand beside Bereza. He gestured at the banquet table, a long oaken table heaving with platters of roasted meat and pitchers of dandelion wine. A trio of forest sprites with pointed teeth were scooping the marrow from a pile of bones with elongated fingernails. 'Seems a shame to waste her,' Bereza's son continued, meeting my eyes with a flare of malice.

It slowly dawned on me that the bones were human. Fear slid down my spine like a hot knife. 'You're welcome to try to seize me,' I bluffed, standing up, one hand falling to my thigh. It hit silk. I wore no armour, no knives. 'But I can assure you that Queen Serce does not care about me. My ransom would be less than worthless to you. In fact, you'd be doing her a favour.' I trailed my left-hand fingers down the long root nestled between my veins of my right arm. 'She had a witch curse me.' I omitted that the queen had been that witch; that information was too valuable to share if they were not going to fight for me. 'So ask yourself again why you should ally with me.'

Doubt flitted through the part-wiła standing closest to me. Bogdan looked unconvinced. 'If your own mother would rather have you killed you, then you seem more trouble than you're worth.' When I blinked, he was fingering a long, curved blade.

Kaz slammed his hands down on either side of his throne and stood, his considerable height on the carved stone dais formidable. A colony of bats took flight from one of the pointed arches, the trees shuddering in their wake.

'Anyone who dares lay a hand on the princess will lose that hand,' he thundered. The hall fell silent. I shivered despite myself. His voice dropped, low and dangerous, his tone promising violence. 'We will discuss this further tomorrow. This court is adjourned for the night.'

'Well, that was a disaster.' Kaz stormed away from the hall, leading me gods knew where. 'Bereza's always been a thorn in my side, but I thought showing up here with you would quell any bid for power he'd been making in my absence. I underestimated him. Him and his nuisance of a son.' His eyes cut to mine. 'Bogdan. He's grown sharper-tongued since I last had the pleasure of encountering him.'

I bit back any mention of Szafir's earlier encounter with Bogdan; that was not my tale to tell. She'd claimed that he was a bully, but I saw now that he was more than that; he was a mouthpiece for his father's opinions. All infections began at the root.

'Since I tried it your way, with the dress and the subservience and it didn't work, tomorrow I will be doing things my way,' I informed Kaz, striding after him as he paced up a circular staircase, winding round a thick, mossed trunk. I was grateful for the deep slit in my dress now that it allowed me to keep up with him, who was a walking thunderstorm.

Ink-black clouds scuttled over his arms. 'Fine.'

I didn't know if I should still be following him; he was incensed, his power raw and wild, and the further we went, the less I remembered where my own room was. But he hadn't told me not to come, and I needed to figure out what my next move would be. I needed this army. I could challenge my mother without it, but if I wanted the throne, the crown, the safety those things would bring to Żar and the domowik and every other magical creature who was clinging onto life by their fingernails, talons and claws, I needed that army.

With a snap of Kaz's wrist, the wooden door crowning the top of the stairs flew open.

I followed him through, not considering that he might want privacy; if I let him go his own way now, who knew where his thoughts would lead. Yes, I needed the army onside, but I needed Kaz more. And right now, he needed me.

The sky opened up before us. Spangled with stars, in a night cut from the richest velvet. It had been years since I'd seen the glitter of so many constellations. 'Where are we?' I whispered, awed, as if the stars were reverent beings.

'This is where I sleep.'

I'd been too enraptured with that sighting of the night sky to notice where I was standing. I noticed now.

We were in the uppermost branches of the ancient oak that speared through the court. A circular room had been built in smooth, honey-tinted stone, a long time ago if the carvings here were the same ones scattered over the rest of the ruins. A private crown in the sky for the master of the court himself.

'You can relax now.' Kaz strode over to a sideboard, poured something berry-dark into two flutes and handed me one. It smelled like cherry wine. 'My chamber is the safest place in the Court. It's bound to my powers; only those I permit can enter. No one can harm you while you're here.' He jerked his chin towards the column of fire in the centre, smoke trailing up into the dark like lost clouds. Lying across a fur at the foot of the fire, curled into his tail, was Żar. 'I ordered Szafir to bring your dragon here the moment I sensed you might be under threat.'

'Żar.' I rushed to scoop up the sleepy hatchling. Relief hit me like a hunting bauk; leaving him alone in this court had been harder than I could have predicted.

Kaz ran a hand over his thickening stubble. 'Elka,' he sighed. 'I brought you here on the promise of giving you an army, but things with Bereza are worse than I thought. The fact that his son felt confident enough to threaten you was our first warning;

he wouldn't have if Bereza hadn't garnered substantial support while I was away. If Bereza seizes the court—'

'We won't let him,' I said fiercely, lowering Żar back onto his fur and crossing the floor. 'This court is yours, *you* are the forest demon, you're bound to each other, are you not?' I didn't understand the intricate workings, but I recognised Kaz's power, laced through the court itself. It lived and breathed in tandem with Kaz; the two were inseparable. I lit up with a spark of realisation: this was why I had been able to poison him, why he hadn't defended himself suitably against the bauk after it had attacked; the Forest Court was both Kaz's greatest strength and weakness alike. A second realisation trailed off the back of the first: Kaz would never be able to stay in the castle, in the Amber City, with me. He couldn't sustain a life away from the court for that long. Whatever relationship we engaged in – if we ever did – was doomed.

Kaz gave a terse nod.

'What gives Bereza the right to challenge your rule?'

Kaz downed his glass and put it down. 'I chose Tosia over Bereza despite her being human, and Bereza has never gotten over that. But Bereza is right.' Kaz tilted his face to the stars. 'It should have been him. I was young and foolish when I was given this court to rule over and the almighty powers that came with that. I chose poorly; if anything slays me then Bereza's next in the bloodline to inherit the court and all the power that entails since our parents were half-siblings.' When he poured himself a second drink, his hand trembled. It touched me.

'I would argue that you chose wisely,' I countered. 'Tosia reminds you of your brother, of the mother you shared. The one who taught you how to be kind, caring, considerate.'

Kaz's voice turned hoarse. 'What makes you say that?'

'The way you held me against your heartbeat when we hid in the river together,' I told him. 'How you remembered I had no hairbrush and didn't want me going without.' I took in a shaking breath. 'How you washed my hair in the cottage.'

He looked at me for a long moment.

I sipped my wine. 'You mentioned your father vanished wherever the old gods went – why would a demon and half the Forest Court accompany them?'

Kaz's smile was slow, satisfied. 'My father was a god. *Demon* is a new word, one that the True Path have spread through Mazrovia like a cancer, seeding distrust in the old gods.'

I opened my mouth to speak, but nothing came out.

'The word you want to know, what I *am*, is a demigod.' Kaz's smile turned dark, playful. 'Now, since my way didn't work as I'd had hoped, come nightfall tomorrow, you are free to unleash yourself on my court however you like.'

'I won't be wearing one of your dresses,' I said automatically.

He clapped a hand to his chest. 'Are you trying to break my heart, princess?'

'I mean, they're just so impractical.' Standing in a way that revealed the thigh-high slit, I slowly dragged a finger up my leg, parting the dress.

Kaz tracked every inch it travelled, sucking in a breath. 'Szafir will be distraught.'

'And you?' I asked softly. 'How will you feel when I take charge in your own court rather than kneeling before you?'

Slamming his glass down, Kaz stalked over. He tipped my chin up, his gaze molten with desire. My lips parted. 'I would much rather kneel before you.' Before I registered his words, he'd pushed me back onto the wooden desk behind me. His hands rested on my thighs, his touch burning. That ache buried deep inside me flamed alive with vengeance. I was on fire. Still, he waited.

'Then kneel before your future queen,' I said, permitting him to quell that ache, to give me what I needed, what I wanted from him.

A devious grin crept across his mouth. 'There is no future. You are my queen, now and always, and I will gladly worship at your temple.' Slowly, keeping his smouldering gaze on mine, watching as my chest rose and fell, faster and faster, he sunk to his knees.

Taking a fistful of my satin dress in each hand, he ripped the skirt of my dress up to my waist, letting out a low moan when he realised I was wearing nothing underneath. 'Gods,' he swore, his eyes darkening with hunger. 'Are you trying to kill me?'

My smile curved like a dagger.

Until he ran his hands up my thighs, my breath trembling as my legs fell open, granting Kaz his first glimpse of me.

'Beautiful,' he murmured, gently parting me with his fingers. I sucked in a trembling breath, watching him look at me. His gaze flicked back to me as he lowered his mouth and feasted on me. His tongue was warm with cherry wine and I let my head fall back, giving myself over to him, body and soul.

CHAPTER TWENTY-NINE

Kaz's sheets smelled like him. Pine and rain and smoke. Thick smoke. As if I was sitting too close to a crackling bonfire. With a start, I snapped awake, leaping out of the bed. It was on fire.

Grabbing a jug of water sat on the bedside table, I tipped it over last night's dress, using the wet silk to staunch the flames. It was torn anyway. A little growl sounded. I looked over the remains of my dress to where Żar was sitting on Kaz's pillow, disgruntled. He hiccupped, showering the pillow with sparks.

Lunging to pick him up, I sat the ever-growing hatchling on the floor, thanking Perun that the floor was stone. Fireproof. 'This would be much easier if you had a dragon parent,' I grumbled as he sent another spray of sparks over my arm. Żar regarded me through wide, yolk-yellow eyes. Guilt rose up my throat like bile. I would never stop mourning that more dragonkin hadn't survived, that Żar hadn't grown up in a nursery of hatchlings.

Before I could wonder where Kaz was, he stalked into his room. With a fresh deer carcass strung across his shoulders, its eyes liquid night and unblinking. 'It's time you stopped feeding Żar from your own veins.' Kaz dropped the carcass in front of Żar. Żar poked it with a talon, his tail swishing back and forth, his scales catching the light. Sunlight. We were still above the canopy, where sunshine spread across the sky like butter. I idly wondered what happened when it rained. 'He's growing too big and fast for you to sustain and, one of these days, he'll drain you.'

'I know,' I admitted, dropping to the floor and trying to coax Żar to breathe his newfound fire onto the deer carcass; dragons preferred their meat roasted. I sneaked a glance up at Kaz, who was surveying his blackened bedsheets with amusement.

'Don't,' I sighed.

Kaz shot an affronted glance at me. 'I didn't say anything.'

'Yes, but I know exactly what was running through your mind,' I told him, ignoring the blush that skulked across my cheeks.

Kaz tracked it with interest. 'I have to confess, I like seeing you like that.' He closed the distance between us, his hands sinking into my hair. 'All flushed and pink and pretty, begging for my touch.'

'Nobody was *begging*,' I said in a higher pitch, making his wicked smile deepen.

'Oh, but I bet I could make you beg,' he murmured into my ear, his lips drifting down my neck.

Turning my head, I sought his mouth out with mine, feeling

his surprised smile press against my lips. 'Is that right?' I whispered, catching his bottom lip between my teeth and biting down until he groaned. 'Maybe I'll be the one to make you beg.'

'I don't doubt it,' he chuckled, his hands finding my waist.

I did. I knew I'd be the one to cave first; everything about this man, this demon, this demigod, called to me. I burned for him.

When Kaz lifted me up, I wrapped my legs round him, my nightdress slipping up my thighs. I frowned, drawing in a steady breath. The heat was growing too intense, sharper, almost as if—

What's wrong?' Kaz murmured against my mouth.

'Nothing.' I shook my head, running my hands up his corded arms as if I could forget the world if I only focused on Kaz enough, filling myself with him until those devious little monsters whispering the blackest of thoughts and fears left me alone.

The pain reared up again, immense and inevitable. I slammed a hand against my heart, my chest threatening to tear in two. Gasping for breath, my legs turned boneless.

'Elka?' Kaz grabbed my waist as I slid down, peering at me with a concern that grew until the great oak we stood in, shook. 'What is it?'

'Curse,' I ground out.

Żar cried, shrill and anguished. I hated that I couldn't comfort him, couldn't promise that I would be alright. Because, this time, I didn't know. The pain was carving deeper than ever, slicing directly towards my heart.

Kaz carried me to the bed. 'Tell me what you need to break the curse. Name it and I'll bring it for you.'

'No.'

When I gasped and shuddered from the pain, spreading through my chest like a wildfire, his face tightened. Branches thrashed around his room.

'*Tell me.*' His voice was a deep rumble, a command I didn't have the strength to resist. Or maybe I was just so very tired of keeping secrets.

The fire intensified, spreading out along my ribcage, burning away my inhibitions, my care. 'She made me a villain,' I bit out. 'She turned me into a murderer. She—' I fought through another wave of rolling, blistering pain, gripping Kaz's hand, tight enough to splinter his bones. He rubbed my back with his other hand, silently encouraging me to continue, to share the darkness tarring my soul, the black pit in the very core of me, where my worst secret lived. 'I need seven hearts. I need to—' It was too horrible to voice. If I said it aloud, that would make it real, make it impossible for me to wash away those blood-stained nights in my cottage kitchen, slicing up a fist of muscle to eat, knowing the face it had once worn.

'Nothing you say could make me see you any differently,' he said softly. 'Nothing could ever change the way I see you.'

'What—' I struggled to breathe, the pain searing my heart. My pulse fluttered weakly. 'What do you see?'

He stroked my cheek. 'I see a beautiful soul that's unfairly shouldering a cruel burden because of who her mother happened to be. I see a vindictive, scared queen who used your greatest strength against you, trying to turn it into a weakness.'

His face slipped in and out of focus. I clung to his words as if they were a life raft, like I might drown if I didn't hear what he said next. 'My greatest strength?'

'You are kind, Elka,' Kaz said simply. His arms wrapped round me, anchoring us together. Like I belonged in his arms. 'Kind and caring and loving and protective. You've spent the past decade fiercely guarding a dragon egg you believed would never hatch; you gave the last of your milk to the domowik without thinking once that you would go without.' His gaze was locked onto mine, those golden eyes a beacon of strength, of safety. 'You took me in when I was injured and poisoned and brought me back to full strength, even knowing I could be a wolf in sheep's clothing.'

Guilt ensnared me; even now Kaz did not know how close I came to killing him.

The pain receded, leaving a fifth root spearing up in front of my heart. 'The queen calls me Snow White. For my ebony hair and lips as red as blood, skin as white as snow. For how pure-hearted I once was. She did see my kindness, that's why she cursed me. She never believed I would break it; she thought I was too pure-hearted to ever take another's life.' I was too exhausted, too hurt to cry. Kaz interlaced his fingers with mine, my hand small within his. With his other hand, he lifted Żar onto my lap, the hatchling rending the foot of the bed with his talons, trying to roar in his frenzy to reach me. I held him against my chest, his snout tickling my neck as he curled round me, quieting now that I had survived. This time.

'You *are* pure-hearted,' Kaz said fiercely. 'The queen miscalculated. You are kind, but you are strong and fierce, too. Though what she did was terrible, she made you stronger, thirsty for vengeance, self-reliant. She turned you into a threat.'

Anger painted my vision red. 'I'm going to kill her.'

'First, you have to break the curse, or . . .' The pain in Kaz's voice engulfed him for a breath. 'Or you will die, Elka.'

I closed my eyes. It was all or nothing now – I'd come too far on this journey to let the curse kill me just as I was on the verge of getting what I'd come for. 'I need to devour a heart. A human heart, killed by my own hand. Seven hearts is the price of ending this curse; I need just one more.' Wincing, I peeked out from between my eyelashes at Kaz.

He was watching me steadily, his hand still clasped round mine. 'You may be dark, but I am the darkness itself. We can live in the shadows together.' And with that, he leaned across and kissed me. Slow and soft and deep, until I forgot the world.

I attended the morning court proceedings in my leather leggings and armoured corset and all of my knives. It was a smaller affair than the revelry of the previous night. Kaz lounged across his throne, seeking me out every few minutes as he listened to his peoples' woes and settled their affairs.

I leant against a stony wall, half watching Kaz, half looking at the ancient symbols engraved next to me. I wished I could read them, wondered how many stories were carved into the temple the Forest Court had once been that were now lost to time.

'Dzień dobry.' Tosia appeared at my side, handing me a silver cup as she wished me good morning.

My stomach churned. 'Oh, no thank you.'

'It's herbata. With extra berry jam.'

I took the tea gratefully. She was wearing a dark green suit with her hair slicked back. Tiny gold earrings climbed up the shells of her ears, and she was taller than me in her black, pointed boots.

'They –' Tosia jerked her head at Kaz, now conferring with Bereza – 'might be able to drink their body weight in wine at any given hour, but I'm much happier drinking tea.'

'And here I just thought you had a remarkably strong stomach.' I laughed.

Tosia's chuckle startled me; it was so like Kaz's. No wonder she reminded him of his brother. 'Only when it comes to the amount of cheese I can eat,' she confessed. 'Ah.' She straightened. 'Speaking of strong stomachs, I hope yours is equally robust.' She nodded to Kaz, who had just stood, holding a hand up at the two men who had sought his counsel.

I clenched my cup, my nervous system still flooded with emotion. 'What's happening?'

'They're old friends who have been competing to wed the same woman.'

I resisted rolling my eyes. 'Why doesn't she get to decide who she marries?'

Tosia looked wary of my reaction. 'She has decided. She's said she will marry the winner.' She shrugged. 'Such is the way of the Forest Court; here, power is everything.'

Kaz lowered his hand. Daggers were drawn.

'They're not . . . they're not fighting to the death?' I couldn't look away as the men sprang at each other, the court urging them on. Kaz glanced at me.

'The rule is to first blood,' Tosia said carefully. 'Though it often escalates.'

I had seen too much pain already today.

'Would you care to take a walk with me instead?' Tosia asked.

'Did one of your parents sit at the council before you came of age?' I asked, fascinated with Kaz's human relative.

'No, my mother didn't care to be aligned so closely with the Forest Court.' Tosia cut a thick slice of plum cake and set it on my plate. After accepting her offer, we'd strolled up a short stone staircase, taking us behind one of the waterfalls. Now we were sat at a table in a tearoom, carved out behind the curtain of water, muffling the bloodbath below. 'She wanted me to marry and give her a crop of rosy-cheeked grandchildren, but that never interested me. This did.' Tosia gestured at the Court, her keen eyes scanning the proceedings below. Satisfied, she forked a large bite of cake into her mouth, chewing neatly before continuing. 'I'd known Kazimierz since I was an infant. He'd always taken an interest in our family, but my mother had kept him at arm's length. It was my aunt who sat at his council before me. Who brought me to court when I ran away at the age of fifteen and begged her to teach me everything she knew.'

'It must have been hard being one of the only humans here.' I picked at my cake, my stomach still unsettled, my chest sore.

'The only one,' Tosia corrected. 'Until you.' She toasted me with her cup of tea. 'We must stick together.'

I smiled, tapping my cup against hers. Having both been thrust into powerful positions with no innate power of our own, we were more alike than I'd first realised, and I was happy to get to know first Szafir and now Tosia of my own accord. Kaz was no longer the sole ally I held at this court, I was certain of it.

'What's wrong, princess?' Bereza suddenly appeared behind Tosia, making me start. 'Unable to stomach how things are done at Court?'

Tosia sipped her tea, ignoring him. As confrontational as Bereza had been towards Kaz, he must have been worse when Tosia ruled in Kaz's absence.

'Not at all. Would you care to join us for some tea?' I might loathe him, but I had been raised with impeccable manners.

He pulled out a chair and sat heavily. Tosia did not pour him a cup of tea. After a tense silence, Bereza poured his own cup. My heart felt like a stone buried in my chest. Kaz's court was a powder keg, and my chances for seizing my queendom rested on top of it. But I wasn't done fighting yet. 'Why don't you tell me about yourself, Bereza?' I inquired. 'Did you grow up in Stary Bór?'

'The only thing you need know about me, princess, is that I refuse to ally myself with anyone who sits on the glass throne in the Amber City.'

'How fortunate that is not your decision,' I said.

Tosia sat tall and silent.

Bereza leaned forward, lowering his voice. 'I would not bet on that.'

'Careful,' Tosia warned him. 'You're beginning to sound mutinous.'

'Am I?' Bereza stood, draining his tea before slamming the cup down between us. 'Fancy that.' He left as abruptly as he had arrived.

Tosia pushed the remnants of her cake away. 'Suddenly I have no appetite.'

'Will he mutiny?' I stared through the rushing water, down to the Court below.

'I don't know,' Tosia whispered, raking back her short hair. It was the first time I'd seen her composure break, and it was more disquieting than I could have expected. 'But I'll die before I see Bereza take the forest throne.'

*

I drew my eyeliner thick, black, and sharp enough to kill my enemies.

Szafir had brought her bag and endless pockets up to Kaz's rooms, only to be told that I would not be requiring another dress from her. Thankfully, she recovered quickly, rallying to my cause.

'Bereza and his fanged son are the worst.' She sniffed, dabbing red paint onto my lips until they gleamed. I'd filled her in on my tea with Tosia and Bereza's declaration. 'The master's right to ally with the castle, to put you on the throne; if we go against Queen Serce ourselves, we'll lose, and we *cannot* let her win. I'm part wiła, like half the Forest Court. If the queen drains the rest of Stary Bór of its magic, I'll die.' She glanced at the domowik then, its form almost solid now. It had shown its true face for the first time this morning, after my curse had reared up and Kaz had determined it was safer for me to stay in his rooms after the debacle of the previous night. The domowik looked like a small woodland creature peering out of a short human body, with wide baleful eyes and large, pointed ears. 'There'll be nothing to sustain us magical creatures, to keep the domowiki in physical form, to keep the wiła alive.'

'What will happen to you if the Purge reaches the court?' I couldn't help asking.

Szafir hesitated, meeting my gaze. 'I'll ossify,' she said. 'All the wiła will. We're forest spirits. Magic beats like a living heart through the land of Mazrovia, veining through its forests, rivers and mountains. It sustains spirits like me and the domowik, lends life to the undead, like the rusałki, and gives the sprites their magic. Only the gods and demigods would be unaffected – their power is their own.'

'The witches, too,' I added quietly.

'Of course.' Szafir nodded. 'Their power is in their blood.'

I pressed my lips on a cloth to set the colour. 'What do you know of the witches up in the tundra?'

Szafir painted a second coat onto my lips. 'I've never been to the Witchlands, but I've heard the same stories that I'm guessing you have. That they're more bloodthirsty than the Forest Court.'

'I heard that half the witches don't pay the tithe for their powers from their own veins, that they hunt other witches down for their blood instead.'

Szafir tilted her head. 'Some people are fated to never be satiated. Always seeking more; more power, more influence, more riches.' Her hands fell from my face. 'Is this about your mother?'

I looked at my blotting cloth. It was stained red, like my cleaning cloths after I'd brought another heart back to my cottage. All this time with Kaz had distanced me from the men I'd killed. Sweetened my dreams until they ran red with heat, with wanting. My newest root gnawed against my ribcage, reminding me that I urgently needed my seventh heart. I was down to the final grains of sand in the hourglass of my life. 'What makes you say that?'

'The way you sounded when you spoke about witches—'

I squeezed the cloth in my hands. 'How did I sound?'

'Like a child who has been wronged.'

I flung the cloth away from me. 'You're right. Queen Serce is a witch.' Szafir watched me thoughtfully as I continued. 'I have only told you and Kaz. To my knowledge, the rest of his council does not yet know.'

'The council knows,' Szafir said matter-of-factly. 'And I did, too. Kaz told the four of us when he learned, some years ago now. The rest of the court have no idea.'

I nodded to myself, unsurprised. 'We've all been wronged, Szafir. The queen is stealing Mazrovia's magic for her own use. A use that I cannot imagine because I'm beginning to doubt that she paid the tithe for that theft herself. I think she used somebody else's blood.'

'Are you so surprised that a queen who would curse you, who would steal magic, would also kill?'

'Not any more.' I stood up. 'I will get this army and take the throne.' Twisting my hair back, I speared it with my sharpest, smallest knife. 'And then I'll make sure you're all safe.' I glanced at Żar, his talons snarled around a charred deer leg. Now that he was eating solid food, he'd be growing at an alarming pace – soon he'd be too large to curl up on my lap and drape round my shoulders, and even as nothing would make me prouder than to see him grow and take to the skies, I couldn't imagine how much I would miss him being little. By the time he grew, I had to ensure that Mazrovia was safe for him. It was a non-negotiable deadline. But I needed to be un-cursed to make it happen.

Szafir's smile was tinged with sadness. 'I'm completely behind you, but Bereza's never going to approve loaning you that army. Tosia and Mirosław would, but you've seen for yourself how Bereza thinks. He's obsessed with the idea of stealing the court from Kaz.'

'Surely Kaz can overrule him?' I frowned, disliking Bereza more and more. Szafir stood. 'Bereza has a lot of support in the court. He and Bogdan have been cultivating it the past few months while the master's been away. Making promises they couldn't hope to fulfil, feeding the bloodlust until Kaz's more rational way of ruling looks weak now that he's returned. If Kaz overrules him now, he'll risk the court swaying towards Bereza. His position is more precarious than he understands.'

I reached for Szafir's hand as her panic caught. 'Is Kaz in danger?' The pair of men who had been ordered to fight to first blood occurred to me; I knew that Bereza had mutiny on the mind, but I had not taken into consideration how he might go about achieving succession.

'If you love Kazimierz, you must do what he cannot,' Szafir whispered, clenching my hand.

Yes, Kaz was in danger. I stared at her, horrified. 'But Kaz is immortal, or near enough—'

'Only from death by natural causes. And Bereza is a lesser demon; he will not survive that long and he does not intend to wait.'

I swallowed, the full implication of her words hitting me. 'I never said I loved Kazimierz.'

Szafir relinquished my hand. 'You don't need to say the words for it to be true,' she pointed out. 'I've been watching you both since he brought you here; I see it in the way you look at each other. If you fell, he would catch you, if you bled, he would kill your enemies. One man stands in your way. Only one.'

I began pacing. Pausing only to check, 'Kaz is bound to this court, isn't he?'

'Yes.'

I nodded to myself. Everywhere I trod, I slammed against hard, impenetrable walls. Ending my curse, killing the queen. Being with Kaz. I was tired of never getting my own way.

'I once dated a half demon from the Mountain Court, over in the Dragonspines,' Szafir offered helpfully, watching me pace. 'We took turns visiting each other.'

'Did it work?'

'He fell in love with the descendant of a rusałka.' Szafir rolled her eyes. 'I went up there to surprise him and found them in bed together. She was eating his arm.'

I barked out a surprised laugh.

'I stopped dating men after that.' Szafir gave my nose an

affectionate tap. 'You look perfect. Now walk in there and don't leave until you've got what you want. Remember; shedding a little blood always makes them sit up and pay attention. This court respects violence.'

'Trust me, Bereza won't know what's hit him tonight,' I growled, sliding my favourite knife into my hip hilt, another into my ankle boot. 'How do I look?'

Szafir took in my outfit. I was back in my leggings and leather-and-iron corset, but, this time, I wore no shirt to disguise my armour or the knives I wore, strapped to my hip, thigh and ankle. My black hair spilled around my shoulders in loose waves and I'd darkened my eyes. All the better to glare at them with. Last time, it had thrown me that I was appearing in front of the entire court, not a small council of select members. I'd followed Kaz's lead, kneeling before him in front of everyone to prove my loyalty, and though he'd more than made up for that afterwards, this time, things would be different. A queen bowed to no one.

Szafir nodded in approval, her sapphire eyes glinting. 'You look like a queen.'

My smile felt like a weapon.

After pressing a kiss to Żar's snout, I slipped my hand into Kaz's waiting one and followed him down the spiralling stairs and into his court. Before we strode through the double doors, he hesitated. 'Are you sure you're prepared for this? My most reliable spy informed me that Bereza will be making his move tonight.'

'Tonight? You're sure?' I willed my pulse to slow, my heart to turn cold and unfeeling.

'If you're having second thoughts, if at any point you do not want to be here, just say the word and I will move the court itself to get you out of there,' Kaz vowed, his hand on my arm. Not as a mark of possession but as reassurance. His eyes glittered. 'But, rest assured, I won't be giving up my court so easily.'

'Good.' My thoughts turned to Szafir's bloodthirsty request. 'Do you trust Szafir?'

'With my life,' Kaz replied.

Silently counting my blades, I gave him a nod. 'Then I'm ready.'

'I have made my decision. Do I have your vote of confidence to move forward with my plans?'

The gathered court was a wall of silence. Broken only by the splintering of bone as a horde of sprites feasted.

'Well?' Kaz drummed a hand on the polished oak arm of his throne. Bogdan was standing near the front, the half wiła that had spoken yesterday at his side, their joint stares promising violence. 'If there are no further objections, Tosia, Bereza and Mirosław, you three will join me in the council room to map out our attack.'

Mirosław's one white eye swivelled between Kaz and Bereza,

his nervous smile stretching too wide until Tosia gave him a cool shake of her head.

'Here's an alternative plan.' Bereza spoke at last, stepping up onto the dais where Kaz lounged on his oaken throne. 'If the court no longer holds faith in Kazimierz, your forest demon, your *master*,' the emphasis he placed on the word turned it sour. 'Then perhaps it is time to elect a new ruler of this court.'

'This court is mine, Bereza.' Kaz continued to drum his hand on his throne. 'And I would thank you to remember that.' His voice was midnight, a dagger wrapped in silk.

'I am tired of being underestimated, Kaz,' Bereza snarled. 'Of sitting back and giving in to your ludicrous machinations of power. Your head has been turned by a pretty face –' When he threw a gesture my way, I fingered the dagger at my hip, tracing its cutting edge until I calmed. '– Leaving you nothing but a puppet belonging to the castle. Does anyone here want a puppet sitting on this throne?' Bereza's voice sang loud, rising to fill the cavernous court.

Half the court yelled their feelings of dissent. Stamped their feet. Slapped a hand against the swords I'd only just realised they'd brought here tonight. Fear crawled inside my mind. *Half the court.* They'd come ready for battle. While I'd been whiling away the night in Kaz's arms, Bereza had been readying his troops. I glanced at Tosia, who looked steadily back at me. She wore a silver suit this evening, but she had a sword at her hip, too. She had not come unprepared. Neither had Mirosław, who was shadowing Kaz, his sword already drawn.

Kaz rose from his throne. Throwing his arms wide, he curled his fingers into fists and *pulled*. A low groaning ground out from the flagstones underfoot as that ancient temple, the tree-twisted ruins we stood in, rippled like living water beneath our feet, sending the sword-bearing court to their knees. 'I am no puppet, I *am* the Forest Court,' Kaz roared, sending branches whipping through the air, forcing his people to duck, to scramble out of the way before they lost an eye. A lone scream echoed through the court, signalling that someone had been too late.

'Fine, you've proved your point,' Bereza said when the court had stilled, eyeing the green ink on Kaz's skin, now dripping thorns, the cluster of menacing thunderclouds rolling over his shoulders, the jagged bolts of lightning that flashed on his forearms, promising the power that he was reining back, that he would unleash on Bereza if needed. But, according to Szafir, doing so would only win Kaz this battle. Not the war. 'Sever ties with the princess and you will regain our trust. She doesn't belong here with us. The moment she steps foot back in that castle, when she starts thinking like the rest of them, about their land and their money and their resources, this alliance will be a distant memory.'

'You're wrong,' I uttered, drawing the eye of the court. It was time to remind them who I was and what I stood for.

For the first time that evening, Bereza looked at me.

My stare brimmed with challenge.

Until a familiar sensation tingled in my veins. The curse. It was about to strike again. Panic curdled my stomach: I'd never had two attacks from my curse in the same day, and since I was still sore from this morning, my new root carving a path up the front wall of my heart, a soreness I felt with each beat. I knew this one would be my last. Dread seeped through me, icy cold and awful. Reminding me that my time was too short, too precarious, drip, drip, dripping away, like water in a clenched fist; impossible to hold onto. There was no delaying the inevitable any longer: I needed a heart and I needed it *now*.

Bereza unsheathed his sword and pointed it at me. The tip came to rest against my throat.

The world slowed to a crawl, the ribbons of time fraying.

As one, the court froze, uncertainty and doubt tearing through them. Tosia's impassiveness drained away as she drew her sword in tandem with Mirosław, who almost vaulted up onto the dais, to stand beside Kaz. And Kaz. He was the air before a storm, his power crackling at his fingertips, hundreds of lightning bolts flaring over his skin, lighting him up.

Pain reverberated through me, ground against my bones.

'You say that Kaz underestimated you?' Bereza's sword cut into my throat as I spoke. 'That's ironic, considering that you never stopped to consider if you might be underestimating *me*.' Before Kaz could unleash that great power, before anyone could spark the flame that ignited this trembling tension, I clamped my hands on either side of Bereza's blade and shoved his sword back, ramming the thick handle straight into that long, proud nose of his.

The crack of Bereza's nose breaking brought me no satisfaction; pain was still rolling through me, building and building, and all I knew was that I did not want to die. But Bereza needed to, to keep Kaz safe and on his throne. I stared down at Bereza. His eyes were filled with an emotion that chilled me; there was no hatred there, no temper, no heat. Only cold calculation.

Bereza spat a bloody glob onto the stonework. 'Bitch.'

I laughed. Long and low. 'How original.'

I plunged my knife into his chest. Deep enough to cleave him apart. Shallow enough not to graze his heart. After all, I was an expert by now. The court watched on, in silence. Even Bogdan refused to utter a word, though his eyes were filled with hatred.

When I reached into Bereza's chest with both hands, wrenching his ribcage apart as he breathed his dying breath, the snap filled the entire hall. Like a tree falling in a silent forest. I tore his still-beating heart out, blood running down my elbows, and I stared back at Kaz, at the court, at Bogdan, as I took my first bloody bite.

The cutting claws of my curse slowly receded.

I hid my revulsion at the taste, forcing myself to bite again and again, swallowing it in hot slick lumps that slid down my throat.

They watched me eat Bereza's heart raw.

And then they laid down their swords.

CHAPTER THIRTY

Swallowing my last mouthful of blood, I swiped the back of my hand across my mouth. Left it pressed there for a moment to hide my gagging.

It tasted disgusting.

It tasted like freedom.

I reeled back from the body at my feet; Number Seven. I was stunned at my own daring, at the horror of what I'd done, in front of an entire court, who stood staring back at me, their swords abandoned at their feet. A silence thicker than any I'd known pounded in my ears. I didn't look back at Kaz, didn't check if he was horrified. I didn't care. I was *free*. It had taken years, but I no longer bore my mother's curse. My banishment had ended. My life was my own once more.

'Tosia, Mirosław, let's adjourn to the inner chamber. The rest of you –' Kaz swept a hand towards the banquet tables, the feast laid upon them near untouched – 'eat, drink and dance yourselves stupid. Come tomorrow, the Forest Court will be at war with the crown of Mazrovia. We fight with Princess Elka.'

He stalked towards the far end of the temple ruins, where the widest waterfall streamed down into a stone pool.

Tosia winked at me before following Kaz.

'Come on.' Mirosław held out an arm. 'You're coming with us.' His arm stayed behind my back as we walked together, never touching but never leaving, symbolising that I was shielded by the council of the court, now reduced to three.

When we'd caught up with Kaz, he flicked a hand, opening a tall door embedded in the pale stone. It groaned open, splitting the waterfall in half, cascading down each side of the door.

å

Swallowing the lingering blood on my tongue, I walked between the split waterfall and into a low-lit stone chamber.

Inside it was circular, as if it had been carved into the hollow of a tree, with a round stone table in the centre, at standing height. 'Are you alright?' Kaz asked, his, Tosia's and Mirosław's focus all pinned on me.

'I am now.' Seven hearts, at last. Tinged only with the disappointment that my roots hadn't melted away. They were still strung through me, stiff and hard, reminding me of their presence every time I moved, like deep-rooted scars. 'And I will never be eating another human heart again. It's time I channelled my energy into ruling instead. I'm ready to be the fair, merciful leader the queen never was.'

'Good. Because you're more terrifying than you look,' Mirosław told me, giving me a chagrined look.

I gave him a bloody grin, enjoying myself a little too much when he grimaced. Kaz grinned back at me, pride seeping through his expression. He didn't fear my darkness. He revelled in it.

Tosia braced her hands on the table. Her short blonde hair swung forwards, framing her face. 'I have a question,' she stated, giving me a considering look.

'What is it?' I swiped my bloody mouth with the back of my hand.

'We've spent years spying on Queen Serce, infiltrating her ranks –' she nodded to Kaz – 'and prying information out of her messengers. And not once have we discovered *how* she is purging Mazrovia of its magic. We know she is a witch,' Tosia admitted.

'I have always kept the council abreast of our enemies,' Kaz told me, confirming Szafir's information. 'Though none outside the council know this, I will not have our information leaking; it is better that the queen is unaware of how much we know.'

'I'd wager my last purse of gold that Bereza told Bogdan everything,' Mirosław said darkly, eliciting a curse from Kaz.

'That doesn't matter now.' Tosia steered us back on track. 'I want to know what she's using as her tithe.' Tosia's dark blue gaze pinned me in place. 'It has to be considerable; I doubt she's using her own blood, not for the amount of magic that she would have to be channelling to strip the land of its intrinsic magic.'

I caught my lip between my teeth. 'I don't know,' I admitted, 'She keeps her secrets too closely guarded. I saw her once, the day she cursed me—' My voice faltered. 'The day she cursed me,

I caught her draining a meadow of magic. She didn't pay the tithe from her veins; she used bottles of blood instead.'

'Then she must be draining Mazrovians of their blood, like the witches up in the tundra.' Tosia inferred what had taken me years to believe. I'd been clinging too hard to who I still wished the queen was to see how deep her crimes ran.

'She's covering her tracks well, though – we haven't seen anything since we've started watching her,' Mirosław said. 'Maybe she's offing prisoners in the dungeon?'

Kaz raked back his hair. 'I have no idea. We've never learned her tithe and we've been observing her for years.'

Tosia fell into silence, thick with thought.

'How will we disarm her if we don't know her tithe?' Mirosław frowned to himself.

'We don't need her tithe,' I stated. Three pairs of eyes fixed on me. 'You know that the queen is a witch. Well . . .' I drew a deep breath. 'Witch's blood burns,' I whispered. 'Faster than a forest fire.'

Kaz stiffened, a predator sensing a weakness.

Guilt burned the back of my throat as I betrayed all witches' deepest secret, kept closely guarded, passed down from witch to witch. The one which would cost my mother her life. The one I wasn't supposed to know, not being a witch myself.

Tosia stared into the distance, as if seeing her thoughts and ideas and plans play out.

'I also know how we can enter the castle and take her by

surprise, but I can't overthrow her reign, her council, her religion, by myself. She has a political advisor, Pan Jedrick, who will have been co-ordinating her masterminding, but we can turn him to our cause. He used to be my weapons master; I trust him.'

'The attack must be done in tandem.' Kaz pulled out a long scroll from a hidden shelf, spreading it out over the table. It was a large map, beautifully detailed, marking the magical currents that rippled through the forest like rivers, where the rusałki and wiła tended to lurk, and every village skirting Stary Bór, before spanning out to take in the Amber City and the Dragonspine Mountains as well. 'Otherwise, the first attack will clue them in to what's coming.'

'Counter point.' I tapped a finger on the castle at the heart of the Amber City. 'We take out the queen first. Cut off the head of the snake so that the queen's guards and the Mazrovian Army, including the Angels of Death, are unsure who they're fighting for. Some won't bother if the queen's already dead. It will be quicker.'

'How are you planning on reaching Queen Serce without an army to fight your way in?' Mirosław gave me a curious look.

'I am so glad you asked.'

Tosia raised her head, listening intently. She was a woman of few words; when she spoke she was measured, considered. Perhaps her mind was a hidden maelstrom.

'Queen Serce likes spying through her mirrors. I think she spends more time watching them than anyone realises, a fact

I found out three years ago, when she caught me on the verge of sneaking out of my bedroom at midnight.'

Kaz looked mildly amused. 'What happened?'

'The moment she saw me pulling a hood over my face, she guessed what I was up to and—' I remembered it like it was yesterday. The hand that had shot through the glass, seizing my wrist, making me shriek in fear. 'She reached out through the mirror and *pulled me through to her side.*' The seconds I'd spent travelling through the magicked glass had been slow, filled with a dense pressure that had made my ears pop and ring, until I'd been yanked out into my mother's turret to directly face the consequences of my sneaky actions. Her turret held more mirrors than I could count, of all sizes, from the smallest pocket-sized looking glass to two identical mirrors, each larger than a horse, mounted at the centre. One of them was bound with my blood, the other, I suspected, belonged to my father, though she never told me who he had been.

Mirosław's mismatched eyes flashed with interest.

Kaz smiled at me, his index finger tapping a slow beat on the map.

'Does that mean—' Tosia frowned to herself.

'We're going to need the largest mirror we can find,' I said, turning to Kaz. 'Have you got one?'

'There haven't been any mirrors at court for a long time,' he said. 'But aren't you forgetting something?'

I frowned, not following.

'You may have broken your curse,' Kaz said softly, 'but the moment you look into that mirror, asking Queen Serce to bring you through, she will know you are no longer banished from the castle.'

'She knew the second I shattered her curse,' I told him. 'She would have felt that cursed connection between us snapping, known that she no longer holds that power over me. She can't keep me away from my own home any longer.' A thrill ran down my neck: I had broken myself free. I could walk back into the castle this very moment if I so desired. It was time to seize the throne, to be *queen*. And then nobody could have power over me ever again.

'If she already knows then we must make haste,' Tosia said. 'She'll be expecting Elka to return, but hopefully not this way. We'll have to find a mirror large enough though.'

Kaz turned to Mirosław. 'Can you handle this? I don't want anyone to catch word that we're procuring a mirror; the queen's spies have been unusually active in the forest lately.'

'Of course. Will any mirror work?' Mirosław asked. 'Or am I looking for something in particular? Remind me how they work again.'

'Queen Serce has rows of mirrors lining her turret,' I explained. 'Each one was made with blast, which is a black stone mined in small quantities in the Dragonspine Mountains.' The magical qualities of blast were not well known; most Mazrovians believed it was nothing more than a pretty crystal. 'It can hold power.

With the queen's mirrors, it holds a thimble of blood belonging to each person she seeks a connection with. For instance, there's been a large mirror hanging in her turret that has held my blood since the day I was born. Whenever the queen wants to see me, she'll pay the tithe for her magic to open the connection, and then she can see me through whatever ordinary mirror I happen to be looking into at the time.'

'Then you'll be the one baiting her,' Mirosław said, cutting a wary look at Kaz, whose hands had stiffened on the table, crumpling the edges of the map.

'Exactly,' I continued, licking the blood off my lips before grinning at him, at Tosia, at Kaz, whose clouds had thickened, swelling with the promise of that coming storm he had yet to unleash. 'But, at the time, I was holding one of the kitchen cats and it *came through with me.*'

Their attention sharpened.

'Good,' Kaz growled. 'I refuse to let you go by yourself. You need backup.'

'Take me with you as well,' Mirosław asked Kaz, who grunted in agreement.

Tosia pored over the map again. 'It'll take our army a couple of days to reach the castle; what if things turn nasty after you kill Queen Serce?'

Kaz's storm clouds rolled over his biceps, funnelling magic through the chamber. The heavy stone table rocked in its wake like a sapling caught in a strong wind. 'I won't allow anyone to lay a hand on Elka,' he said in a gravelly tone.

'Noted,' Tosia said lightly.

'Then we have a plan,' Mirosław said.

Tosia gave a curt nod. 'I'll update the court.' She hesitated, her gaze sliding over me to Kaz. 'And give the order to remove Bereza's body.'

'Leave it,' Kaz snapped. 'He betrayed me. Let him rot as a warning to anyone else who would do the same.'

'If that is your will.' Tosia inclined her head and exited.

Kaz let out a rough sigh. 'Mirosław, go and check the perimeter and check in with your sources; the last thing we want are any surprises. Everything must go smoothly. And make a start on finding that mirror.'

'Aye aye, captain.' Mirosław saluted Kaz before winking at me and sauntering after Tosia.

'I wish he wouldn't do that,' Kaz grumbled. Rubbing a hand over the back of his neck, he shot me a rueful glance. 'Are you alright?'

'I broke the curse,' I whispered. 'Why do I still have roots?'

Kaz gathered me into his arms and held me like he'd never let go. 'Perhaps they'll fade, perhaps not. If they don't, there will be some magical cure we can seek out to help ease their pain.'

'I'm sorry I killed your cousin.'

Kaz's thumb rubbed my back in small circles. 'I don't want you to worry about that. I will grieve the person he once was, not who he became.' His sigh was saddened. 'I regret that it needed to come to this, but there was no other way, and I won't have you feeling any remorse over your actions. You were brave and fierce and you did what I could not, removed the obstacle in our path. And you have a bright, shining path ahead of you, Elka.'

'Careful,' I said wryly, my voice muffled against Kaz's chest, all warm and broad and pine-scented. 'You're starting to sound like an ambassador for the One True Path.'

Kaz laughed. 'Gods, I hope not.' He leaned back, surveying me intently. 'Come, let me show you something.'

CHAPTER THIRTY-ONE

'This is the true heart of the Forest Court,' Kaz said, after he'd taken me on a hike to the farthest reaches of his court. We stood behind another waterfall, in a lush woodland. Glossy green plants and azure rocky pools filled a large pocket of the ruins, entered only through a series of steep steps, hewn into rock. Water spirits swam through the network of pools, diving out of the waterfall before reappearing through the fresh spring that fed the pools. Sprites flitted through the air like carnivorous bees.

'Where did they all come from?'

'All magical creatures have been fleeing the Purge for the past ten years. To the highest peaks in the Dragonspine Mountains, up to the tundra with the witches, or here. To Stary Bór.'

'I don't understand.' Looking around, I spotted a large pair of slitted purple eyes hiding just below the surface of the water, a long tail slithering up a holly tree, its body rustling in the leaves. 'Why have they all been waiting here for so long? You already have an army.'

'Isn't it obvious?' Kaz said gently. 'We've been waiting for you.'

'Me?' Expectation pressed down on me, thick and heavy, impossible to escape, even if I'd wanted to.

'Until you were ready to be our queen.'

If Żar hadn't hatched, this would have been the moment I'd realised I was ready. That I needed to be queen. A familiar little figure darted into view, tugging at my heart. Our domowik. 'So this is where you've been hiding.' I kneeled down. 'And here I thought you'd been in the kitchens all this time.'

Kaz chuckled. 'Oh, he's been there as well.'

'Stay here,' I told the domowik. His head cocked to one side. 'Stay hidden. When it's safe, I'd love to have you at the castle with me, but only if you want to.' He looked at me a moment longer then darted away. Just before he vanished from sight, I caught a glimpse of another domowik running alongside him.

'This is what Mazrovia looked like before the famine started chipping away at us and Mazrovians turned on magic. Before the Purge began, signing a death warrant for these creatures that rely on magic to live.' Kaz brushed his thumb against my lower lip, hardened with blood. 'This is what you're fighting for.' With his other hand, he pressed something into mine. I pulled back to look at it: it was a small piece of black stone. 'The queen's not the only one who can stow magic in blast,' Kaz said. As I held it, the stone began to flame. 'Now you have fire at your fingertips.'

He'd given me a greater weapon than any blade.

'You will be a mightier queen than any I've seen,' he vowed.

'And how many queens would that be?' I teased, slinging my arms round his neck.

'Wretch,' Kaz growled, scooping me up into his arms. 'I'm going to make you pay for that.' He ran his teeth down my neck until I shivered and squealed, secretly delighted as he carried me out of the sanctuary and all the way back to his chambers, like he wanted to devour me alive.

'Are you sure?' Kaz rested on his elbows above me, staring down as if he couldn't believe his luck. I wanted to tell him that I was the lucky one, that being with him felt like a gift, but he was shirtless and so was I, and I couldn't wait any longer.

'Yes,' I panted. 'I'm tired of waiting.'

He pressed me down, his gaze searching mine. 'Tonight, you're *mine*.'

'What did I tell you?' Summoning my core strength, I flipped us both over. Kaz moaned beneath me, his hands tightening on my thighs. 'I belong to myself,' I told him, sitting up with a wicked little smile.

'Shouldn't we be preparing for battle?' I murmured later, lying beside Kaz, his fingers feathering up and down my spine.

'Yes.'

'Then I should get dressed.' I made to rise, but Kaz pulled me back down.

'Not yet. The battle can wait another minute.'

His warm touch melted a path down my skin, but it was

impossible to relax. A hundred questions were warring for attention and I'd spent too long ignoring them while we secured the Forest Court's army. I didn't know why the queen hadn't killed me when she'd had a chance, why she hadn't taken Żar, why, if she was afraid of Kaz, had she not killed *him* when he'd been right under her nose in the castle for months? None of her movements made sense and that terrified me more than the impending battle.

Propping myself up on one elbow, I studied Kaz. 'They say that you are the only thing my mother fears.'

'They do,' Kaz said softly.

I ran a hand over his chest. 'Do you know why?' Because I did not.

'Not until yesterday.' Kaz's hand stilled on my back. 'Queen Serce guards her fears close to her chest, careful not to let her weaknesses known. My spies are older than hers, have been watching her for a very long time, since her mother stashed her away in the Witchlands and pretended that she was being raised in the Summer Palace instead. I knew the queen was a witch, but it wasn't until yesterday that I finally realised why she fears me.'

My heart skittered wildly.

'I never knew that witches burned,' Kaz admitted. 'Elemental power courses through my veins; I have some influence over water, air, earth, some healing abilities, too, and—'

'Fire,' I breathed, looking at the firestone he'd gifted me, lying beside my knives. I should have realised earlier.

Kaz nodded. 'Fire.'

I wished my mother had told me stories of the Witchlands, but I only read about it in her secret journals. She'd never told me who my father was either, but that was more common; Mazrovia was a queendom, the lineage ran straight down through the female bloodline, incorporating those who were gender-fluid into their ranks; it was men and men alone that Wanda, the first queen, had distrusted. 'Do you know who my father was?' I suddenly thought to ask Kaz.

He hesitated. 'No.'

But there was something else there, some grain of knowledge. 'What do you know?' I asked instead.

'I believe your father was a witch.'

I believed this as well; according to her journals, my mother had returned from the Witchlands already expecting me. With that kind of heritage, I should have been a powerful witch myself. Had it skipped a generation or simply ended with me? An old disappointment tore through me.

'I also know that she has two fears,' Kaz continued, stroking my back again. 'Me. And you.'

A surprised laugh escaped me. 'My mother isn't afraid of me. That's ridiculous,' I continued. 'She has the kind of power I could never dream of. Unreachable.'

'And yet you are the only thing she cannot control. You have youth on your side. Beauty. All the gifts she bestowed on you, thinking that she would be able to manipulate you, to use your magic if you inherited her witchblood. To use you to her political advantage if you did not.' My thoughts fell silent. 'But she underestimated you. Your iron will, your fearlessness. How old were you when you first rode a dragon?'

'Three,' I whispered. Pani Smok had walked into the castle one day, plucked me from the royal nursery and taken me into the dragon nursery. There, she'd placed me on the back of a hatchling. It couldn't have been more than the size of a small horse, but to me it had felt massive. I still remembered stroking those scales as we'd left the floor behind, flying around the dragon nursery together. Those grass-green scales were my very first memory. When the queen had found out, she'd been furious. Now I reframed that emotion, the wildness in her face as she'd lost her temper at both me and Pani Smok. She'd been afraid. Of a stronger ruler rising from beneath her. Of the day that the throne would be mine.

'And were you scared?' Kaz asked.

'Of dragons? Never. The only people who fear them are the ones who don't understand them. I never had any magic of my own, but I felt powerful when I flew on dragonback. Like I'd been given a magical treasure to guard.' I used to sneak out and ride Migot without a saddle in the dead of night, when nobody could see me risking my neck. I raised my head to glance at Żar, lying across my feet like a contented kitchen cat. Speaking of power – 'Do you know which god fathered you?'

'I think you already know.' Lightning crackled down his arms, tingling against my back.

'*Perun*,' I breathed. God of thunder and chief of all the gods. 'Is that the god carved into your hunting knife?' I asked, remembering the tiny bolts whittled into the wood, the ones which I had assumed were daggers or branches – they'd been lightning all along.

Kaz's golden stare burned through me. 'Yes.'

He sat up. Taking his gold compass from the side, he handed it to me. 'All I know of my father is this compass.' I traced the engraved letters of love to his mother as Kaz spoke. They hummed beneath my fingertips. 'And that he tied my power to the Forest Court, effectively chaining me to this place for some purpose I've never learned.'

'This feels like magic.' I passed the compass back to him. 'But different, too.' It sang with something I'd never felt before, something old and strange, almost a memory of magic.

'It's godtouched.' Kaz slid it back into its drawer. 'Anything that once belonged to a god feels like that.' He cast me a curious look. 'You may not have powers of your own right, but you're sensitive to magic. You can sense power more than ordinary humans can.' He took in my surprise with a touch of amusement. 'You didn't know?'

'No.' I frowned, filing that away to think over later.

An owl swooped down, landed on Kaz's maple desk and neatly folded its wings back. It was tawny, its feathers rich shades of oak and chestnut, but its eyes were ghostly lanterns, one white, one black. 'What's the report?' Kaz asked.

I blinked, taken aback – I'd always known that both the queen and the forest demon alike used owls as spies, but I'd never imagined them speaking before.

With a flutter of feathers and a clack of its beak, the owl shuddered, the smell of magic leaking out as its wings hardened into arms and its talons stretched into feet. My jaw fell open as I stared at Mirosław, now sitting where the owl had been, fully naked and grinning back at me.

'I— What?'

'Mirosław is a shapeshifter and my best spy.' Kaz gestured for Mirosław to speak.

'Two Angels of Death have been spotted on the hunter's path, just a couple of hours west of here.'

Kaz reached for his trousers and pulled them on as he stood, raking his hair back and searching for his shirt. 'They've never come this deep into the forest before.' He swore loudly. 'They're searching—'

'For me,' I whispered, curling my fingers round the bedsheets. Żar huffed and prowled closer, protective at once.

'I won't let them have you. You're safe here,' Kaz said, still searching for his shirt.

It was on his desk. Mirosław held it out, his grin slanting into dangerous territory. I blushed furiously, glad beyond measure that Mirosław hadn't glimpsed the scratches on Kaz's sculpted back. A *shapeshifter*. I'd always known of their existence, rare as they were, but to my knowledge had never met one. 'Yes, I am safe here,' I said slowly. An idea was taking root.

Kaz looked troubled. 'I don't like the look you're giving me.'

'I have an idea.'

Kaz groaned.

'You need to draw them away from here. Lull the queen into a false sense of security. If we can convince her that nothing's happened between the two of us, that I never forgave you for hiding your true identity as the forest demon, that we never allied, she'll let her guard down.'

'I am not leaving you,' Kaz said flatly.

'She has a point,' Mirosław began before Kaz glared at him. 'Shutting up now,' he said, shuffling awkwardly.

'I don't want you to leave either,' I told Kaz, 'but this is a good plan and you know that. Right now we need any edge we can get and this? This gives us an edge.'

Kaz closed his eyes for a beat, rubbing his eyelids. 'Fine.'

Mirosław and I exchanged a victorious look.

Kaz pressed a kiss to my forehead, his hands framing my face, thumbs gently stroking my cheeks as he looked at me for a long, heated moment. 'I won't be gone long, but don't leave my rooms before I return. You and Żar will be safe here.' His throat bobbed up and down as he swallowed. 'Promise me that you won't leave?'

'I promise,' I vowed.

'Good. Because you are my everything.' He kissed me urgently.

My hands fisted in his shirt, wishing that I could keep him here, safe with me forever. 'Be careful.' I shot Mirosław a look, brimming with worry. 'Both of you. I want you back in one piece.'

Kaz rested his forehead against mine. 'Wild dragons couldn't keep me away.'

Żar gave a disgruntled rumble and blew a spurt of hot air onto Kaz. He chuckled. 'It looks like we're making someone jealous.'

I gave Żar's scales a reassuring stroke.

Kaz slid his boots on and clapped Mirosław on the back in a brotherly manner as they both made for the door. Apparently, I was the only one who minded Mirosław's lack of clothes. Kaz threw one last look back at me. 'Oh, and, princess? Don't bother getting dressed. I want to see you wearing my bedsheets when I come back to you.'

I threw a pillow at him. It hit the closing door with a soft thump, but I heard his laughter through the wood.

Seconds later, the door opened again. Szafir bustled through with a large tray, heaped with plates. 'Time for breakfast,' she sang, giving me a cheerful smile. 'I asked for extra servings; I figured you'd need to get your strength back since you're staying in the master's rooms now and I've heard he has *quite* the appetite.'

I covered my face with a pillow and groaned.

Szafir laughed and wandered up the couple of steps to the adjoining bathroom I'd discovered yesterday with glee.

Smiling to myself as she sang over the gush of the taps, I examined the plates. 'This one's for you.' I placed a raw cut of meat in front of Żar, before pouring myself a cup of lavender tea, deciding what to eat first. Pillowy slices of black rye bread with honey and creamy goat's cheese, delicate rose-petal cakes, or wild berries, plucked fresh from the forest.

My eyes settled on a luscious red apple.

Gleaming and glossy, it tempted me first. I picked it up and took a bite.

PART THREE
The Castle

I'd fallen in love, raised a dragon and ripped seven still-beating hearts from seven chests. I was here to claim my eighth.

CHAPTER THIRTY-TWO

Sweet juice burst over my tongue. It wasn't until it trickled down my throat that I tasted the magic it carried. Like the deadliest thorn, buried deep beneath a blood-red rose. 'Szafir!' I cried out.

She came running.

I threw the apple down, fighting the sudden urge to close my eyes, the sweet little voice that whispered how wonderful sleep would be. 'I've been poisoned,' I said, eyelids drooping.

Szafir's expression tightened. 'What can I do?'

'Bring Kaz back.' Fighting the growing compulsion to sleep – *sweet, sweet sleep* – my limbs growing heavier and heavier, I thrust Żar into her arms. 'But take Żar to the sanctuary first – whoever did this will be coming for me and they *cannot* see Żar. Please keep him safe.' My voice splintered, fear showing through the cracks. Between the loyalty of Kaz and Szafir, I'd managed to keep Żar undetected in the Forest Court, and I intended to keep it that way.

Żar let out a low, mournful whine, thrashing his tail to break free of Szafir's hold, to return to my side, but Szafir held tight. 'I swear it on the old gods,' the half-wiła said fiercely. 'And I will find

Kaz, but you must fight this, princess. Fight it!' she called back over her shoulder, already running Żar out of Kaz's chambers.

Relieved that the hatchling was safe, I fell back onto the pillows. Letting my eyes close at last.

I wasn't dead yet.

I came to after an immeasurable lump of time to the real horror that greeted me: I couldn't open my eyes. Couldn't move. I was locked in an all-hearing, all-feeling state of paralysis.

And I wasn't alone.

Footsteps approached. Desperately trying to move my arm, my hand, my finger, *anything,* I lay there, rendered powerless as an unseen stranger peered down at me. *Who was it?* Had my mother struck first before the Forest Court army mobilised?

'Princess Elka,' a voice spoke in my ear. Brimming with malice. 'The most beautiful princess to grace Mazrovia. You look mighty pretty in a glass coffin.'

My lungs squeezed tight with panic. I was lying on a cold, smooth surface, and my dress was damp against me, the air stale and thick with rot – I'd been moved somewhere else. Somewhere that I hadn't been before, judging by the smell. And if Kaz couldn't find me . . . There would be no saving me. Grief and anger rushed through my veins, my pulse skittering out of control. *Whose voice was that?*

'Of course, my father hasn't been granted the privilege of a coffin,' the voice continued bitterly, enabling me to place it:

Bogdan. I should have seen this coming, should never have underestimated the power of grief. 'I'm taking him to be laid to rest with the respect he deserves. I've heard that sleeping curses are the worst way to die. Flooding your veins with poison until they reach your heart. Gods, I hope that's true.'

His footsteps retreated.

Leaving me alone to die.

Only, as time ticked by, the poison felt as if it was receding. I twitched one finger, then another, wondering how I'd managed to survive. Then realisation rushed over me: it was my curse. The roots had grown over my heart, locking it in a cage of flexible bark, less brittle than bone, strong enough to resist whatever fresh curse that apple had been riddled with. My mother had accidentally saved my life.

A rumble of distant thunder grew and grew.

'Elka?' Szafir's urgent tone was the sweetest sound I'd ever heard. 'Elka, can you hear me? We're here. We found you. You're safe now.'

Kaz's voice, his woody, smoky scent rolled over me. 'Oh, Elka,' his voice cracked. 'I should never have left.'

'I'm fine,' I managed to mumble.

Żar squealed, pushing his snout into my hand. Letting out a shaky laugh, I flexed my fingers, stroking Żar.

'Mirosław, go to the kitchens. Find out where that apple came from. See if anyone knows how in Nawia Bogdan managed to get hold of it,' Kaz ordered.

I opened my eyes.

Kaz was staring down at me, his golden eyes glimmering. He blinked hard, tucking my hair behind my ear. 'Welcome back, princess.'

'I was here the whole time,' I whispered, looking around. We were in some kind of earthen, underground chamber. Water dribbled down the walls, thick with moss, and fungi sprouted in the corners.

'I know.' Kaz gathered me in his arms. With an indignant squeak, Żar clambered onto my stomach. 'Like I'd leave you behind,' Kaz murmured under his breath as he lifted us both out of the glass coffin.

He looked wrung out, his inked vines faded, his stormclouds missing. His tawny hair was awry, shirt torn and bloodied, but he'd never looked better to me. 'How did you find me?' I asked.

'I sent my army to search every inch of this court. I will always find you, Elka.'

My eyes filled.

'I love you,' he said simply.

Warmth rushed over me. 'I love you, too.'

CHAPTER THIRTY-THREE

The mirror was taller than me. Wider than a tree. It was stood a stone's throw from the distinctive ruins and gnarled tree entrance of the Forest Court and covered with sacking. When I looked into it, I alone would peer into the glass, with no hint that the core council of the court was standing at my side. Minus one member. Yesterday, Mirosław had returned without information. 'It seems Bogdan has been operating on his own, out of revenge,' he'd told us all as Kaz swore. 'He was last seen fleeing the court with his father's body.'

We fell into formation.

I stood before the mirror. Just out of frame was Kaz, his power a menacing growl as we readied our attack. Tosia and Mirosław were to his side, accompanied by two fighters, Borsuk and Wróbel, lean and lithe, identical part-wiła twins, dressed in night-black, like a pair of living shadows. 'Assassins,' Szafir had hissed before taking Żar into her arms – they would form the tail of our group infiltrating the castle through the mirror. I was heartsore at the notion of taking Żar with us, but it wasn't safe to leave him behind. Anxiety knotted in my throat; this *had* to work. Too much counted on it to fail.

On the other side of the mirror stood the Forest Court army.

Wearing bark armour, they moved like the forest itself, armed with swords and daggers, along with a unit of sharpshooters, clad in dark-green armour, better disguised to steal up high into tree branches and shoot unsuspecting enemies below. Behind them stood hordes of wiła with crossbows fixed to their arms, each arrow tipped with poison from the deadliest mushrooms that sprouted in Stary Bór. The wiła wore no armour; Szafir had assured me that their own bark-skin was sufficient protection. Clouds of sprites whizzed around like wasps, sacks of poison-dipped acorns strapped to their backs, and deeper into the forest were other beings. Beings that slithered and clambered between the trees, like every nightmare I'd heard about the court come to life.

'Forest Court,' Kaz's order rolled out like thunder. 'The moment we step through the mirror, we will have entered the castle. We will remove Queen Serce from her throne at once. The second you see the last of us –' he gestured at Szafir, holding an inquisitive Żar in her arms – 'vanish into the mirror, you march. I am counting on all of you.' He surveyed his court, standing to attention. 'It's time to fight for what we believe in, to defend our forest, our home, and to secure a better future for ourselves,' he roared.

The army roared back, slamming their swords on their shields in a battle cry that could have raised the gods. Until Kaz threw up an arm and they silenced once more. He signalled to me.

With a steady hand, I reached out and dragged the covering off the mirror. My own pale face stared back at me, my raven-dark hair pulled severely back into a bun and speared with a knife. I wore a loose, soft jumper over my armour in pretty pastel blue, borrowed from Szafir. A disguise. My roots had not yet vanished and my chest was tight and uncomfortable. At least I could move easily in my leggings and boots, and I'd suffered no lasting consequences of biting into a poisoned apple.

I hadn't seen the queen's real face for almost two years. Maybe I'd been optimistic and she wouldn't appear at all. In front of me, the forest army, hundreds strong, stood silent, watching. The forest was eerie, the trees themselves still. Not a trace of wind nor birdsong nor creeping roots sounded.

Silver glass darkened, clouded with violet smoke. *Magic.* I couldn't breathe for a moment as the connection formed and then she was standing there, and I was facing the queen herself. She was unchanged. The same dark golden hair, neatly twisted up into a functional yet stylish seat for the simple glass crown she'd designed for her coronation. Her sharp bone structure and her clear light blue eyes gave her the intensity of a hunting eagle, her focus pinned on me.

'Hello, Elka, darling.'

Anxiety and guilt and sadness unfurled within me like a great pair of wings.

'This is quite the surprise after our encounter in the forest,' she said.

That *encounter*, when she'd worn my best friend's face, was hard to reconcile with seeing the queen, the glass crown glimmering on her head, surrounded by her mirrors. In her inner sanctum.

I pasted a smile on my face. There was no feigning how small it was, how tentative. 'I was hoping that we could talk.'

Her eyebrows were still arched as highly as I remembered, forever pointed, disapproving. 'We are talking.'

'Face to face,' I clarified.

She waved an impassive hand at the glass in front of her.

Beside me, out of sight, I felt Kaz shift, the weight of his eyes on me. Gods, I seriously hoped that I was right, that I could bring him and the others through the mirror with me. The forest demon, *son of Perun himself*, was substantially larger than a kitchen cat. And then to pull through another five beings and a hatchling? Maybe I was a naïve, optimistic fool. Or maybe, just maybe, this would all work and that crown would be sitting on my head by dusk. 'Bring me through the mirror, mother. I need to talk to you and I refuse to do so through glass and magic and this, this . . . distance between us.' Sighing, I softened my tone. 'Please.'

A hint of disappointment crested her face. 'Very well, then.' Before I could ponder why, she thrust her hand towards me. It came through the glass, the queen's hand extending through the mirror, into the forest, bridging the gap between us. It was soft and smooth, the hand that had stroked my brow when a fever had ravaged me in childhood, smoothed away my nightmares, turned the pages of my favourite storybooks until they wore thin. The hand that had signed the execution order for Migot.

I took it.

With a tug of magic, the queen began pulling me through the mirror.

Quick as a flash, I seized Kaz's hand, knowing that he was already clasping the hand of Tosia at his side, who held onto Mirosław, then the two assassins, before Szafir was pulled through at the tail end, Żar across her shoulders. I wanted the hatchling there last, hoped that I would have already lit the flame that would burn down Queen Serce's reign by the time he emerged through the glass. It was a daring plan, audacious. But it might just work.

The glass turned to the consistency of algae, sucking me into its marbled depths, time slowing to a syrupy pull as I forced myself forwards. Onwards and through. With a muted, bubbling sound, I shot out through the other side, stumbling towards the queen, who backed away at once.

The second my feet hit the castle floor, I knew it was a trap. But Kaz was already coming through after me, Tosia after him, until our entire chain stood there, unlinking and looking around.

At the dungeon we were standing in.

The trappings of the queen's turret, the thick creamy carpet, the silk wallpaper and mirrors had never been real. The queen had glamoured the mirror I'd spoken to her through, showing me exactly what I'd wanted to see until it was too late. Damp stone and thick iron bars penned us in. We were inside one of the cells.

I raced for the cell door before it swung shut, Tosia and Kaz at either side. With a roar of defiance, Kaz dragged one of the queen's guards inside with us, his dagger against the man's throat, as Tosia and I pushed back against the closing door. It widened a crack, then another. 'Let me go first,' Tosia whispered, jerking her head at her sword hilt, the same sharp silver as the suit she wore. 'I'll take out the guards and get you out.'

Before I could warn Tosia that the queen was watching, her smile curled with amusement. Tosia squeezed her tall, lithe frame out through the small gap, leaving me to slow the heavy iron door by myself. 'Hurry up, Tosia,' I groaned as she turned to face me through the bars.

'Sorry, Elka. Kaz.' Tosia slammed the door shut. A guard slid the bolts home, imprisoning the six of us, along with one captured guard and Żar in the largest cell, at the end of the dungeons.

I gaped at her.

Kaz threw the guard he'd seized back to the part-wiła twins, Borsuk and Wróbel, who unfolded blades from their sleeves, pressing them against the guard's throat at either side.

'Tosia?' Kaz's voice was pitched low, danger carved into each of his muscles. 'What is the meaning of this?'

Tosia gave Kaz a levelled look. 'Do not pretend that you have been acting in the best interest of the forest,' she said. 'You were so desperate to seek an alliance with the future queen, a precocious princess scarcely older than a child, impulsive and naïve and bloodthirsty—'

Her words hit me like arrows. Each one notching deeply into my heart, my lungs, my soul.

'Yes.' Tosia's measured gaze shifted to mine. 'You may not care to admit it, but I watched you plunge your knife deep inside Bereza's chest. I witnessed your lack of remorse.'

Shaking my head, I staggered back a step. 'You're wrong.'

'It was all too easy to whisper into Bogdan's ear, to hand him that apple, passed through a mirror from the queen herself,' she continued.

My eyes slid to the queen, watching me steadily through the bars. I ought to have known that apple was another one of her creations.

I was sinking into despair; we'd walked straight into a dungeon where the person who'd sought our death held the keys.

'Stop talking.' Kaz's power rushed up his arms. 'Start explaining yourself. I have known you your entire life, Tosia. I made sure you were provided for, kept well and healthy. I gave you a seat at my council, opened my court, my home to you, and *this* is how you repay me?'

Storms hissed at Kaz's fingertips. I waited for his power to build, but it fizzled out.

Tosia gave a nonchalant shrug. 'You claim that you have the

court's best interests at heart, but you never once attempted to forge an alliance with the *current queen*. The true power of Mazrovia. You ought to be proud; all your training made me loyal to the court, even above you. *I am the one who holds the Forest Court's safety at heart.*'

Kaz looked devastated. 'Filip would have been disappointed in you.'

'Filip is a man I never met.' Tosia's composure began to fracture. She pushed her choppy hair back, its neat ends falling out of place. 'You have allowed your own sentimentality to interfere with far too much for far too long. I am my own person, not a memory of the brother you once had. Bereza was right, he should have been your second in command.'

'How could you be so unfeeling?' I whispered. I hadn't known Tosia the way Kaz had, but I hadn't expected our tentative friendship to incinerate.

Tosia whirled on me. 'Do you truly wish to compare our actions, Elka? At least *I* have never taken a life.'

Guilt snarled at me. Queen Serce's attention sharpened.

'You've been the puppet master all along,' I realised, staring at Tosia. 'It was your views that Bereza was parroting. You knew that manipulating him would get him killed and you did it anyway.'

'Coward.' Kaz slammed his hands onto the bars.

'Are you quite finished?' Queen Serce asked, smoothing down her steel gown.

Kaz flung his arms wide, his muscles bunching as he attempted to tear the dungeon apart. The walls rumbled like thunder, but did not yield.

He roared in frustration, slamming his hands back onto the bars.

'It looks like I've caught myself a forest demon.' Queen Serce braved approaching the bars since it was apparent that we were caught fast. Disappointment was crushing, like she'd stepped on my lung. The queen tapped the stone that had refused to answer Kaz's call. 'Blast. Stone imported from the Dragonspines. It's remarkably resistant to magic.'

She was lying; blast had the ability to be soaked in blood, in magic. I eyed it, noting the crimson veins threaded throughout each block. *Blood.* Did it belong to my mother or had she used someone else's to pay for this tithe?

Her pupils glittered as she stared through the bars, knowing her power imprisoned us. 'You will never break free from its grasp.'

Kaz's glare was unflinching, silently surveying her.

'We'll kill your guard if you don't release us,' Mirosław threatened.

Queen Serce pivoted on one heel. 'Any guard of mine foolish enough to get captured is deserving of death,' she called back over her shoulder.

'Home sweet home,' I said bitterly, slumping against the bars.

My mother paused, her spine stiffening. 'Do not dare lash out at me when you know you did not come in peace.'

I wrapped my hands round the door, curling my fingers around the bars as if I could pull them off. 'Please, Mother, let's talk. Just the two of us,' I pleaded, a last effort to try to wriggle free.

'No. You lost that privilege the second you tried to betray me.' Turning, she pointed an elegant finger at me. 'You disappoint me, Elka.' Her finger shook.

After all that had happened between us, after the curses and the secrets, her words still cut to the core.

Queen Serce exited the dungeon with Tosia and her contingent of guards. Leaving me alone with the worst mistake of my life and the others I'd condemned along with myself. My one solace was that Szafir had managed to shrink herself down into the shadows at the back of the cell, hiding herself and Żar in the darkness clustered there, the pair of assassins shielding them with their own bodies.

Before the door finished closing, I heard a gasp and a spurt of blood hit the wall. The guard we'd seized dropped to the floor, dead. Moments later came the sound of a series of successive iron doors slamming shut, sealing us away in the stone pit beneath the castle.

CHAPTER THIRTY-FOUR

I leaned against the bars, stewing in guilt. Kaz paced furiously, his jaw clenched tight enough to crack his teeth. 'I should have seen this coming,' he seethed.

'How could you?' Mirosław slid down the stone wall slick with algae and rested his forearms on his knees, any hint of his mischief I'd come to adore stamped out. 'I spent more time with Tosia than anyone. She was my mentor, and I had no idea. She played Bereza, Bogdan, she played us all.' He eyed Kaz uncertainly. 'It doesn't make sense that the queen is leaving us down here. Why she hasn't killed either you or the princess when she's had more than enough chances?'

Kaz growled under his breath.

'She could be listening,' I whispered. 'Waiting for us to talk to give her information.'

Mirosław gave a curt nod, falling silent.

Żar had fled to me the instant Szafir had loosened her iron grip on him. He was in my arms now, deeply unsettled, firing the odd spurt of hot steam from his flared nostrils. Szafir was silent. The assassin twins stalked the shadows, eyes glowing under the oil lamps as they stared at the remaining guards; a pair on the door, who stared straight back. I didn't recognise them, but I'd avoided the dungeons when I'd lived in the castle. It was a dank pit of despair that stank of death.

'I'm sorry,' Szafir suddenly said, drawing mine and Kaz's attention. 'I told you to kill Bereza.' She winced. 'I should have known it was Tosia. Instead, I told the woman you love to kill your cousin.'

I began shaking my head, but Kaz beat me to it. 'That's enough,' he said. 'Bereza deserved what he got and Tosia will deserve everything that's coming to her. Even if it means ending my family line.'

I wanted to wrap my arms round him, numbing his hurt. But his anger was too fresh, too consuming. The hurt would follow.

Szafir fell silent again.

I needed to *think*. It was near impossible with the throaty grumble of stone as Kaz tested the limits of his power, cut off at the knees by the queen's own magic – oil lamps a bleary flicker, dirty water dripping down the walls and the echoing voices of other prisoners. 'He's waking up,' one whimpered, their chains clinking as they rocked back and forth. 'He's waking up.'

And one voice that stilled my whirlwind of thoughts, ripping me back to my childhood of daisy chains and climbing trees and storybooks with pages worn thin with adventure. 'Elka?'

I ran to the bars, squinting through the dimness. 'Katia?' I breathed. 'Is that you?' I'd watched the queen leave; surely it couldn't be her, tricking me again.

'Oh, I missed you so much,' Katia cried out from the neighbouring cell. 'But what are you doing here? Why aren't you safe in the forest?'

'It's a long story,' I said cautiously, catching Kaz's slow shake of his head. Nerves crept down my spine. 'What happened to you?' Another, awful thought reared its head. 'How long have you been here, Katia?' Her auburn hair hung in dirty strands, her fringe grown out, freckles faded.

'I-I lost count. Sometimes I think it can't have been that long, that the days just run longer here, but other times it feels like years have passed.' Quiet anger threaded through Katia's voice. 'But when I get out, the queen is going to pay for this. I don't care if she's your mother, I have had *enough*.'

She certainly sounded like the Katia I knew.

'There were *frogs* in here, Elka,' she added, horrified.

I smiled to the darkness. 'It's really her,' I told Kaz. 'That's my Katia.' I slid down the bars, reaching out as her arms came through the generous gaps. With the slick iron between us, we held each other tightly like we'd never let go.

'Is that a dragon?' Katia half laughed, half cried.

'Migot's egg hatched,' I told her, Żar's gaze flitting between us, moon-bright. 'But why are you here?'

'I don't know.' Katia's gaze shifted as Szafir handed me a

bottle of water that we'd brought with us before sitting beside me, watching Katia curiously. 'One day I was working as a lady's maid to two sisters in the Amber City, the next I was seized by the queen's guards and thrown down here.'

'The queen disguised herself as you in the forest,' I told Katia, passing her the water. 'I bet that was when she had you brought down here; she couldn't risk anything messing with her plan.' I sighed raggedly. 'I'm so sorry you got dragged into this.'

Katia gave the water back, holding onto my hand as she did. 'None of this is your fault, Elunia,' she said firmly. 'I'm just happy to see you with other friends, allies.' Her eyes swung to Kaz, pacing in a storm of his own creation, to Mirosław speaking in a hushed tone with the assassins, and finally to Szafir, where it lingered.

'This is Szafir,' I told her, noting a spark of interest glimmering there. 'When we get out of here, and we will get out of here,' I whispered as quietly as I could, 'I want the pair of you to take Żar and hide somewhere.'

'I will *not* leave you again,' Katia said. 'Whatever danger may come, we will face it side by side.'

'I'd defend you, princess,' Szafir offered.

Katia's laugh was tired. 'I'm not a princess, only Elka's companion.'

'There's no *only* about that,' I said sharply. 'You're my closest friend. You mean the world to me.'

Szafir cocked her head. 'You look like a princess to me,' she said simply.

I lowered my head to hide my smile as Katia blushed.

'They will want to remove the body,' Kaz muttered to Mirosław and me some hours later, when his storm of anger had dulled. 'The instant they open that door, be ready.' His golden eyes burned. 'And say nothing to each other about anything else we discussed before we stepped into that mirror.'

'It doesn't matter if we do,' I pointed out. 'Tosia will have told the queen everything. She already knows our army is marching on the castle.'

Kaz closed his eyes.

Mirosław clapped him on the back. 'We'll be free before then,' he said. I nodded, wanting to believe it, too. Hopefully they would remove the guard's body soon. It was starting to smell.

My belief guttered when two guards entered the dungeon with a small axe. Katia vomited into the corner of her cell as they quickly and efficiently dismembered their fallen comrade's body, pulling the pieces out through the bars rather than opening the door. 'Didn't think we'd fall for that one, did you?' one of the guards winked, hauling a thigh over his shoulder as I stared back at him, refusing to be goaded. I itched to draw my knife and throw it through the bars, burying it in his chest, but I needed to save my blades and bide my time. Kaz, silent at my side, seemed to be of the same mind.

*

A day later, we were still locked up. Bread and water was brought twice a day. Time began to distort, each hour dragging its heels until I couldn't tell how long we'd been incarcerated in the dark and dank. The bucket in the corner began to overflow. The smell burned our noses. And our spirits plummeted. Wind sighed through gaps in the stone, and the forest army marched towards an ambush.

I curled into Kaz, his arms folding round me, holding me close. Żar slept on my lap; the hatchling had been growing increasingly restless since we'd been locked down here with no room to spread his growing wings and tail. Without any meat, he was hungry. And it was getting harder to hide him from the guards, though they seemed more interested in a game of chance and a bottle of wódka than us. 'Maybe I should give her what she wants,' I wondered aloud. 'Play her game. It might set the rest of you free.'

Kaz's arms tightened round me. 'It wouldn't,' he said. 'And I would burn the world down to blazing embers before I allow her to lay a single hand on you.'

'I should never have left the forest,' I whispered into his neck, trying to lose myself in his scent of pine and smoke and salt. 'Even if I'd managed to take the throne, you couldn't have left anyway. The forest is in your blood, the court tied to your power. I should have never tried to take you away from it.' Not when he had his own battles to fight there, too.

Kaz tipped my face towards his. 'Look at me, Elka. It matters,' he said fiercely. 'We *will* get out of here and you will take that throne; all is not lost yet.'

'I'm still right though – you need to live in the forest, don't you?' I was half afraid to voice it, wanting to dwell in fantasy a little longer. But we were in the dungeon and my fantasy had already tarnished.

Regret, pain and longing filtered through Kaz's expression. 'Yes,' he said after a long pause. 'I could never live in the castle with you. But that doesn't mean that we won't see each other. We will find a way. Love always finds a way and I love you more than you could imagine. For me, Elka, you are it. My everything. My reason for waking up each morning. I resent every second I spend apart from you, even in sleep, because nothing, *nothing* feels as good as being with you. A hundred lives together would be too short but know this; if anything did separate us, I would pull open the gates to Nawia myself to come and find you, so, no, I am not worried that I cannot live in the castle. I will find a way to fight for us.'

'I love you more than that,' I managed to croak, my throat swollen with emotion as Kaz pressed a kiss to my forehead, to my eyelids, to my nose then, finally, to my mouth, where he paused, murmuring, 'Not possible.' Then he gently kissed me, distracting me from the dungeon and the pain hollowing out my chest.

✳

I awoke with a start. The wind whistled a mournful song through the dungeon, its chilled fingers creeping under my cloak, and my stomach was an empty void. When I blinked, Żar's yolk-yellow eyes stared back at me. I smiled at him, rubbing the sleep from my eyes. Something felt off, but I couldn't place it. Until my eyesight adjusted to the dim light filtering through the dirty lamps: Żar was on the other side of the bars.

I leaped to my feet with a gasp of terror. The others stirred. 'Żar.' I held my hand out through the bars. 'Come here, come back to me.' I couldn't add 'where it's safe' – it wasn't. Neither was it safe out there though and, least of all, in the castle itself, where the rest of dragonkind had been slaughtered. Did the hatchling know? Had he sensed that this was where his egg had been laid, felt the violence as hundreds of dragons were lured into the courtyard in chains? Dragons were empathic and as intelligent as the great horned whales that swam through the depths of the Iron Sea.

Katia sucked in a breath, awake in the cell beside me.

'I know you're hungry,' I told Żar, 'and I'm sorry I dragged you into this.' He looked at me with wide eyes, huffing softly. My heart ached for him. 'But please don't give up on me yet. Do you want blood? I can feed you.' I fumbled to roll my sleeve up.

Kaz's hand seized my wrist. 'Stop.'

'Kaz, I have to, Żar needs—'

'He needs meat. If you offer him your arm now, he'll get confused. It's too dangerous.' Kaz softened. 'I understand how much you care for him, but to keep him safe you have to keep yourself alive and well first. What good would it do Żar if you sacrificed yourself for him?'

Fear slid through me like a knife. 'Żar.' My tone sharpened, making the hatchling glance back in alarm. I held my arms out to him. 'Come back. *Please.*' My voice cracked. He trotted back towards the bars, a hairbreadth from my fingertips, until I could almost reach out and pull him back through. Guilt snarled at me: I hadn't realised he was small enough to squeeze through the bars.

One of the guards shifted. 'Quiet down there,' he snapped.

Żar ran.

'No,' I whispered. '*No.*' My hatchling clambered up the far wall, his talons skittering over stone, making one of the guards stand, searching for the source of the noise.

Żar reached the barred window, high above, and squeezed himself through. I watched in horror as the last flick of his tail vanished from sight. He was gone. The last of dragonkind was wandering around by himself in the Amber City, the home and heart of the One True Path, who'd dedicated themselves to eradicating all traces of magic and magical creatures. And I was powerless to save him.

Crumpling to the floor, I gave up.

The dungeon was a dark throat, but I didn't care if it swallowed me whole. Kaz held me, smoothing my hair back as I drowned. My heart hurt. Katia squeezed my hand through the bars as I sobbed until my throat turned ragged, my voice hoarse.

And, all the while, the Forest Court army marched closer and closer to their deaths.

CHAPTER THIRTY-FIVE

'Just eat a bit.' Szafir waved a heel of bread under my nose. 'You have to keep your strength up.'

Mirosław snorted. 'I doubt a chunk of mouldering bread's going to do much good.'

Szafir glared at him. 'Not helping.'

'Have some water.' Katia slid the almost-empty bottle through the bars to Szafir.

I was lying with my head in Kaz's lap, eyes sore and pinched. I had no more tears left. The bars groaned as Kaz flexed his powers, experimenting with how far he could move the metal under the queen's magic-inhibiting stone until Mirosław spoke again. 'Save your energy,' he said grimly. 'We'll need it for when we eventually crack our way out of this place. Then they'll get what's coming to them.'

'Fine.' Kaz let his hand fall to the floor.

I gave in to Szafir and Katia's fussing and drank a couple of mouthfuls of water.

A guard's footsteps echoed along the worn stone path that

cut through the centre of the dungeons. Something whistled through the air, followed by a soft *snick*. The guard dropped to the floor. Blood pooled around him.

Kaz pushed me behind his back. He and Mirosław and the two assassins silently sprang into action, forming a line of defence at the front of the cell. Through the gap, I stared at the dagger protruding from the guard's throat; he hadn't stood a chance. But we were the ones behind bars. I heard Katia's quiet gasp, felt Szafir's shiver of fear as we waited to meet our fate.

The second guard drew his sword. 'Who's there?' he said sharply. 'Show yourself.'

A second dagger flew through the air, sinking into his neck, hilt deep. Gurgling in panic, the guard scrabbled at his throat, dropping to his knees before his eyes rolled back into his head and he collapsed.

Pani Smok sauntered into view.

I exchanged a stunned look with Katia before I remembered; Katia had no idea that Pani Smok had fled to the forest and become the leader of the rebellion.

'Fancy meeting you here,' Pani Smok said, flicking her fingers at the darkness behind her. Three members of the rebellion, distinctive in their night-dark outfits, wearing no armour but clothes that stretched and gave, crept into the dungeons behind her.

I stepped clear of Kaz, who hadn't altered his protective stance. 'What are you doing here? I thought you didn't agree with the idea of another royal on the throne?' Out of the corner of my eye, I watched two of the rebels ferret through the guard's pockets for his keys.

'Oh, I don't,' Pani Smok said. 'Make no mistake, princess, this is not my endorsement.'

'Then why are you here?' Kaz stared her down, Mirosław standing firm at his side.

'There are interesting rumours filtering through the forest; strange sights if you know where to look. Who to listen to. That a huge army has been moving through the forest.' One of the rebels unlocked our door with a dull *thunk*. Pani Smok threw it open, her iron gaze pinning me down before I could walk free. 'That inside the ancient walls of the Forest Court, something was spotted. Something very important to me.'

My heart spasmed. I knew the words that would trip off her tongue before she spoke them.

'Rumour has it that you have a hatchling.'

I refused to let any emotion show. 'Then you see why the queen, responsible for executing the rest of dragonkind, has to go.'

'I do. For this, for the last hope of dragons, my rebels will join your cause.' Pani Smok's mouth twitched with excitement before she sobered. 'Elka, I am the top dracologist in Mazrovia. You must allow me to help. Rearing a hatchling is a serious job.' She craned her neck to peer into the shadows in the dungeon. 'Where is it? Do you know what its parentage was?'

'His name is Żar,' I said, sharing a bittersweet smile with her. 'I rescued his egg from Migot's nest the night the Purge began. He's been with me since he hatched in the forest, but he slipped out between the bars and escaped yesterday.'

Pani Smok gave a curt nod. 'Then let's not waste any time.' She signalled to two rebels, who passed the keys to her before running silently back to the main dungeon door, where the third was keeping watch. Pani Smok smiled at Katia as she unlocked her cell, though it was flecked with worry, the creases around her eyes burrowing deeper as she took in Katia's dirty, tangled hair and the hollows of her usually plump cheeks. 'It's good to see you again, girl,' she told her.

I walked out of my cell, followed by Kaz and the others. Mirosław looked particularly relieved.

Katia flew out and gave me a ferocious hug, the force of which made me stumble back. 'I thought I'd never see you again,' she mumbled into my neck, in an eerie echo of when my mother had worn her face. I decided against mentioning that little anecdote just now. We were *free*. Now I just needed to find Żar. Terror slunk through my veins, poisoning my thoughts: what if I was too late? The hatchling had fled the dungeon yesterday; judging by the murky light peering in through the single window, that was an entire night and morning ago. My pulse drummed as I raced towards the dungeon entrance; the castle was the most dangerous place in Mazrovia for a little dragon.

The dungeons were sealed below the castle with a series of

thick, iron doors that dated back to the Dark Dragon Ages; they were dragonproof. Now, they were all open, a rebel stationed to each door.

'How did you find your way in here?' Mirosław asked the rebel who'd sprung us free.

'The princess gave Pani Smok a set of plans for the castle with some very useful annotations penned on it.'

Ah yes, the secret tunnels. That explained how the rebellion had stolen into the castle. I was thankful they'd decided to come and liberate us first before going to the throne themselves.

'We still need her though.' The rebel nodded to me, her short black hair swinging around her chin. 'Nobody else knows how to get past the queen.'

'Correct.' Pani Smok took long strides, staying abreast of me. Almost as if she was guarding my side. 'You said you had a plan?'

'Yes, I do.' The army was on its way, the forest demon at my side, and I had my secret weapon in my pocket: a firestone. I eyed Pani Smok. 'It's time you knew, Queen Serce is a witch. This Purge, this religion she endorsed and encouraged, it's all a lie. She's stealing the magic of Mazrovia for her own gain.'

Pani Smok's mouth thinned. 'Then the situation is more dire than we'd thought. Tell me your plan,' she demanded.

Kaz shook his arms out. Now that we were free of the queen's restrictive magic, his powers were cracking open an eye after slumbering inside his skin. Black clouds thickened along his forearms, rolled off his shoulders like the storm he was desperate to unleash. 'Update us first,' he commanded Pani Smok, who narrowed her eyes before deciding he wasn't worth arguing with. I didn't blame her; he was fury incarnate. Now that I knew he was the son of Perun, I didn't know how I hadn't guessed before; with each long stride, lamps flared and flagstones quaked. His hair was in disarray, his jaw thickly stubbled, eyes on fire. I'd worried for him in the aftermath of Tosia's betrayal; I ought to have been there for him, but I'd fallen apart when Żar had escaped and instead he'd wrapped his arms round me and held my broken pieces together. I vowed that once I'd found Żar and won the throne, I would be putting Kaz first. It was about time somebody did; it was surprising his shoulders didn't cave in with the weight of all that rested on them.

'We followed in the wake of your army,' Pani Smok informed us. 'They're biding their time, hiding in the trees just outside of the city.'

Relief flooded my thoughts.

'Thank the gods,' Kaz breathed before turning to Mirosław and the assassin twins. 'When we exit the castle—'

'We'll take the secret tunnel,' I interrupted. 'The entrance is just beyond the last door –' I gestured to the next iron door in the stone passage, set on a steep slant. 'It lets out just behind the stables.'

Kaz nodded. 'Then Elka and I will find a way to reach the queen. Mirosław, I want you to locate my army. Lead the main attack on the castle. 'Borsuk and Wróbel,' he addressed the assassins, 'you're to stay inside the castle. Take out as many of the queen's guards from the shadows as you can.'

We reached the final door. Here, the stone was laid with carpet runners made by artisans in Mistpoint, the lamps were set into gilded sconces that lined the walls, thick with tapestries that wove stories of Mazrovia – from the first queen, Wanda, through the bloodline to my mother. Running over to the nearest one, I lifted the bottom, revealing a small wooden door. 'Here,' I whispered.

Kaz and Pani Smok ushered Katia and Szafir forwards. 'When we get out the other side, I want you both somewhere safe.' I glanced between them. 'Away from the battle.'

'I can fight.' Szafir looked stubborn, fingering a long, curved dagger I hadn't noticed her carrying.

'As can I,' Katia interrupted.

'Oh, I know you can.' I smiled. 'But you're the ones I trust most and I –' my throat roughened. 'I need people looking for Żar. He's out there all alone and—'

Katia pressed a hand to my arm. 'We'll find your hatchling, Elunia. He can't have gone far. He's probably just in the stables, hungry for the horses' food.'

'Or the horses.' Szafir shrugged.

That, I didn't want to consider. But Żar was a growing hatchling with no one to guide his path, and I was a princess who'd ripped a man's heart from his chest and eaten it raw. 'Go,' I urged them.

The rebels that had been staged along each of the iron doors leading down into the dungeons crowded closer. 'What's the biggest threat inside the castle?' Pani Smok asked.

I thought hard and fast. 'Besides the queen? The sharpshooters. Archers will be stationed along the ramparts to the north, east and west. Defences are down on the south, where the mountain cuts away to the river; it's nearly impossible to penetrate the castle from that direction.'

'Not for the forest army.' Mirosław's black and white eyes unfocused as he schemed. 'I'll send a troop of wiła around the back, they'll be able to climb straight up the castle walls.'

'Good.' Pani Smok nodded. 'Then we'll take on the sharpshooters.' She pulled out the scroll of maps I'd given her and pointed them at me. 'Strike first and hard. Do not give the queen a second to regroup. Remember, magic is more powerful than any weapon, but *not as fast*.' Before I could thank her or wish her luck, she ran on through the castle, the rebels following like a pack of wraiths.

'After you.' Mirosław held the tapestry up for me. I ducked to enter.

'Hold it right there,' a voice snapped, cold as steel.

I froze in place, Kaz and Mirosław either side of me, just the three of us left in the passage as I heard the unmistakeable sound of a sword being drawn.

CHAPTER THIRTY-SIX

Power ripped through Kaz, that cord between us tightening as I sensed the guard training his sword on him.

'I can raise the alarm faster than you can kill me,' the guard said, the steel in his voice straining, covering his fear. But that voice – it was familiar.

Frowning, I pivoted to face him. His impish dimples weren't showing, but those sky-blue eyes, that sweet, handsome face that had crept into my castle bedroom, showered me with memories. 'Piotr,' I said, feeling Kaz's eyes snap onto me. Piotr's face was thinner than the last time I'd seen it, cut with tiredness.

'Princess Elka.' He swallowed hard, his initial surprise chased by regret. His sword wavered. 'I don't want to hurt you.'

'Oh, Piotr.' I sighed, ignoring Kaz's hiss of alarm as I walked straight towards the tip of his sword. 'That's not the kind of thing you should be saying to me.'

'My apologies, princess.' He shuffled uncomfortably, taking in the twin threat of Kaz and Mirosław.

Another step closer. 'You should be begging me to spare you.'

Those eyes that had once stared down at me, bewildered and swollen with lust, widened as he registered my words, just as I arrived at his side, close enough to thrust my blade into him if I so wished. I didn't. There would be enough senseless loss of life in this battle and, if I wanted to take the throne, I needed people left in the castle. Alive. 'Run,' I whispered into his ear. He fled, fast enough for his boots to mark the stone.

'He'll raise the alarm now,' Kaz fumed. 'You could have at least knocked him unconscious.'

'Jealous, Kaz?' Mirosław chuckled to himself.

Kaz's storm clouds darkened. 'No.'

I shot a grin back at him before ducking under the tapestry.

The three of us hurtled down the secret passage. Narrow and winding, it swept through the thick castle wall before letting out under a storm drain behind the stables. 'How did you discover this?' Mirosław whispered as I pushed the drain open and climbed out.

'I'm not sure I want to know if it involves sneaking around with the guards,' Kaz grumbled, shoving Mirosław ahead before clambering out and easing the drain closed.

'I thought you weren't jealous,' I whispered, crossing the short distance to the stables and pausing, my back to the rear wall. Nerves clustered, each one alert as I scanned the vast courtyard shadowed by high defensive walls. Katia and Szafir were nowhere to be seen. Neither was there any hint of the rebels, the forest army or the two assassins we'd unleashed on the castle. Kaz and Mirosław joined me, peering out from behind the stables. 'Angels of Death,' I murmured, taking in both the old iron gate that led outside the walls and the towering hammered-iron doors that marked the entrance to the castle itself. Both were heavily guarded with Angels of Death, their raven feathered wings and bladed helmets an omen. There was no way Żar could have breached either defensive line. Perhaps my mother had him, maybe she'd already—

'Stop.' Kaz's hand found the back of my neck, his touch sure and soft and warm. 'You're forgetting that Żar is a dragon,' he said as if he could read my mind. 'Dragons are intelligent; he won't have endangered himself.'

'He's only a hatchling.' The words dried in my throat. We were standing in the courtyard where the rest of the dragons had met their death. Where the cobblestones had run red with their blood and the sound of the dragons had rent the air with despair.

'Raised by the cleverest, fiercest person I know.' Kaz's hand trailed to my cheek, cupping my face. 'Now stop worrying and start owning your destiny.' He nodded to the castle behind us, its amber spires gleaming, turrets towering up to the cloud-strewn sky, ivy strangling the honeyed stone. It looked like a picture from an old storybook. 'Your birth right.'

I let my simmering anger burn hotter, brighter. Until it turned into a wildfire. Glancing behind us, I eyed the ramparts. Nocked arrows glinted in the sun. 'Kaz, can you create a distraction?'

When he nodded, I continued, 'When the rebellion hits the ramparts, Kaz, you unleash it and, Mirosław, you clear a path to the gates.'

'What are you going to do?' Kaz's brow pinched with concern, but his gaze burned steadily into mine.

I slowly smiled. 'I'm going to open the gates and let the forest army inside.'

A gut-curdling scream echoed through the courtyard. I whirled round fast enough to catch the moment that a sharpshooter hit the cobblestones, his skull exploding like ripe fruit.

The Angels of Death snapped to attention. Rather than entering the castle to disable the threat, they stood tight. A flash of light sparked from one of them and I squinted at it. 'Mirror charm,' I said. 'Queen Serce is giving them orders to stay put. Then she knows we've escaped. We need to be careful; she could materialise around any corner.'

'Distraction it is, then.' Kaz rolled his neck and grinned. 'I hope you're watching very closely.' His grin turned a lick darker. 'It might inspire you later.'

I stared at him. 'Are you deliberately being stupid? There's a battle—'

Kaz kissed me. Long and slow, making me lose the trail of my thoughts. Then he pulled away, rubbing his thumb over my bottom lip. 'I couldn't resist making you smile one more time, princess,' he murmured. 'Your smiles sweeten my dreams.'

I scowled at him. 'If this is a goodbye—'

'Never.' Kaz's voice turned hoarse. 'There are no goodbyes between us. I would tear the world apart before I allowed anything to happen to you. You are my heart and soul.'

'I never knew that love could feel like this, but these days my heart lives outside my chest, with you.' I rested my forehead against his for a beat.

Until he gathered my hands in his and pressed a kiss to my palm. 'Stay safe,' he told me. With that, he unfurled his powers.

Mirosław pulled me back from Kaz. 'Shield your eyes.'

It started with a creak. Deep below the mountain on which the castle stood, a sentry perched atop the highest point of the Amber City, its long, circling path surrounded by woodland that trailed into countryside on the east, eventually meeting Stary Bór and forging together. Behind was the River Wanda, and to the north and west was the Amber City itself, with its rosy dawn gates and empty dragon hangers.

The creak grew to a roar.

When I peeked between my fingers, the tips of the trees visible behind the walls began to tremble.

Kaz blazed with golden light, his green ink running over him like scrolling vines as he channelled the might of the Forest Court.

My jaw fell open as the ground shuddered and quaked, loose stones falling as the entire woodland began to creep closer to the castle. Moving as one, in eerie judders, their roots pounding the earth. With a colossal crash, the first tree smashed against the wall. The Angels of Death turned their attention to the trees marching on the castle. 'How did you do that?' I marvelled, glancing at Kaz, at the power surging through him. Blood trickled from his nose. '*Kaz.*'

'Come on, we need to open the gates,' Mirosław urged. 'It's time.'

'But Kaz—'

'Has only so much power this far from the court. Do not let it be in vain.'

I ran across the courtyard, hugging the wall farthest from the Angels of Death and the trees slamming against stone, carving my distance from the castle at my back, where the sound of fighting drifted down. Now and then, another sharpshooter fell to a screaming end. Rebels, too. Forcing myself to run faster – to cross that immense distance that once was capable of holding an entire wing of dragons – my feet pounded into the cobblestones. Three Angels of Death remained guarding the gate. I drew my knife without slowing, ducking under the first Angel's sword to slash his throat. As Mirosław took on the other two, I ran to release the mechanism for the gate. It was old, but kept in good condition, the gears running smoothly as I cranked them, panting for breath. It usually took two guards to open the gates, but, with Mirosław otherwise occupied, I had no choice. My roots and muscles strained; if it wasn't for my armoured corset keeping everything bound together, they might have snapped like fallen branches.

The gate began to lift. One hand higher than the cobblestones, then two, and then, claws curled under it, making it easier to crank open as creatures began pushing the gate up from the other side.

Once it was at head height, the Forest Court army streamed inside.

Huge flagstones suddenly shifted aside as the Mazrovian Army climbed up from hidden passages below the courtyard, swarming the Forest Court.

The armies collided in a scream of swords and shields.

Kaz's trees smashed through the wall, marching through the courtyard on thick, gnarled roots before trembling in place and collapsing, burying Mazrovian soldiers beneath their vast trunks. *Kaz.* I didn't want to think what that immense power had cost him. Running back towards the stables, dodging the battle unfolding around me, my senses were in overdrive. Blood had already been spilled across the cobblestones, reminding me of the slain dragons as I scanned every wall, every stone for a hint that Żar had passed that way. I had to find my hatchling. My courage wobbled at the thought of him hiding, lost and scared. I also needed to find the queen; the longer she had to prepare for whatever she was about to unleash, the worse it would be for all of us. She could finish my attempt to overthrow the throne before it had even begun.

I reached the stables, skidding on the cobblestones as I rounded the corner too fast. Kaz wasn't there.

In the courtyard, a wiła released a soul-shrinking scream as an Angel of Death hacked at her with an axe. My blood froze. More and more of the Mazrovian Army were pouring into the confined space, vastly outnumbering the Forest Court. Arrows rained down from the ramparts, the remaining sharpshooters that the rebellion hadn't managed to pick off were targeting the Forest Court from above, herding them towards the Angels of Death.

We were losing.

This, then, was why the queen had not intervened. The battle was of little consequence to her, so why bother? Frustration needled me.

A zing of metal sounded behind me. Ducking and rolling away, I came face to face with a pair of shiny black boots. An Angel of Death snarled down at me. 'Careful,' I warned her. 'You don't want to maim the heir to the throne.'

She hesitated, uncertainty warring in her gaze.

I leaped to my feet, unsheathing my knife. The Angel of Death stared at its embossed hilt, at the mountains and moons. 'This?' I twirled it. 'It was a gift from Pan Jedrick. And so was *this*.' I charged forwards, but she outmanoeuvred me with ease.

I landed with a force that robbed my lungs of air, my knife clattering beside me. Before I could snatch it up and roll to my feet, I spotted a crumbled patch of stone in the base of the nearest castle wall. There were hundreds of tunnels weaving in and around the castle and the mountain below, though most of them were like this, unusable and impossible to traverse. Dangerous to even attempt as the passage might cave in at any point, burying you alive under a wall of stone too dense for anyone to hear you cry out. But the entrance to this tunnel was surrounded with blackened stone. *Scorch marks.* Small ones. Finally, I'd picked up Żar's trail.

A sword clanged on the stone next to my face. 'Gods,' I muttered, staggering back to my feet, ignoring the wave of dizziness that roared in my ears.

The battled raged around us. Out of the corner of my eye I saw Tosia and Mirosław prowling around each other, swords raised, giving me a fresh surge of worry. A thin, ragged scream rent the air as a long creature with a tail met the end of another Angel of Death's sword. The red livery of the Mazrovian Army swarmed everywhere. There were far fewer soldiers in bark-brown. I'd brought an entire army from the forest to fight for me and they were dying in droves.

The Angel of Death came racing forwards.

Parrying her quick volley of blows, I found myself quite evenly matched. Frustration bubbled in my veins. I needed to get to Żar and secure him before taking on the queen and ending this battle before any more blood was spilled. Dodging her blade, I grabbed her sword arm and span to elbow her in the face. Hard. She dropped at once, her helmet thudding against the cobblestones.

Seizing her sword, I took off for the crumbled tunnel. With the blade, I prised the scorched stones apart, until I could enter.

It was dark and cramped inside. I heaved myself along, my roots rubbing as the tunnel swallowed me. Deeper and deeper I went, until it was ink-black and I wasn't sure I could get back out again, let alone if Żar was here somewhere. Sweat slid down my corset, slickened my hands as I felt the weight of the earth pressing down on me, burying me alive.

Was it my imagination or was the air growing too thin? I paused, considering if I should start inching back out – I couldn't abandon the Forest Court, the rebellion, *Kaz*, for a hope, no matter how desperately I wanted it to be real.

A small light flared ahead.

Pushing myself harder, I crawled towards that tiny spark, pleading with the gods that it had been what I thought it was. It went out, leaving me in the pitch black. Still, I charged blindly ahead.

When it sparked again, I was close enough to see the glitter of sunset scales, the bright yellow eyes that widened as they spotted me. 'Żar!' I cried out, relief crashing down on me.

Żar let out a small roar, leaping towards me and burying his snout in my hair.

CHAPTER THIRTY-SEVEN

'Thank Perun you're safe.' I sighed, running my hands over Żar, checking that he wasn't injured. He preened under my touch, puffing happily. A small flame spurted from his throat; the fire that I'd spotted. 'I was scared to death I'd lost you.' I blinked dust and tears from my eyes. 'Let's get you somewhere safe now.'

I creeped backwards, bit by bit, waiting for him to follow. He did not. 'Come on, Żar,' I called. 'I know you're hungry. Szafir has food for you.' If I could even find Szafir. I hoped she'd made it out with Katia, but I had no idea where the pair of them had vanished to. At least Żar had apparently run out of the dungeons and straight into a tunnel; Kaz had been right, I'd underestimated him. My heart gave a painful thump. Not knowing where Kaz was, if he was safe, gnawed at me.

Żar grumbled and turned away, swishing his tail. With a sharper huff, he summoned a weak stream of fire, illuminating what he had fixated on: the tunnel was blocked in front of him.

I tapped the rock in front of my nose. 'Come this way.'

I was ignored. Żar scraped at the rubble with a talon. 'You're not going to let this go are you?' I muttered, pulling myself towards the blockage at the other end of the tunnel. 'Fine, let's pull this out of the way and then you'll see.' Tossing a couple of smaller stones away, I dug my fingers around the largest stone and heaved.

It shot out towards me. I grabbed Żar, flinging an arm over my face as the blockage fell in front of us, raining pebbles and dislodged earth.

When it stopped, Żar wiggled loose and, with an excited little roar, took off through the cleared passage and abruptly vanished from sight.

'I guess the tunnel runs deeper than I thought, then.' With a weary sigh, I crawled on my forearms after Żar. The tunnel narrowed, hugging my hips and shoulders. I would *not* lose him again.

The battle rumbled in the distance as I wended deeper and deeper into the pit of the earth, further away from confronting the queen and facing either her death or mine. I couldn't keep delaying the inevitable. Was this some devious distraction that the hatchling had spawned to keep me away from the battle he heard raging above? Maybe we were crawling deep below the castle because Żar wanted to protect me.

A louder rumble reverberated through the tunnel, forcing me to duck as clods of earth fell. I exhaled a shaky breath, hoping it had been Kaz, that his powers were still firing after he'd summoned half the forest to march on the castle. I needed to get to the queen as soon as possible, before the Mazrovian Army wiped out the Forest Court.

Chasing Żar round a tight elbow turn, I opened my mouth to call him back for the hundredth time when I realised his scales were shimmering. 'What the—' I stared at the glowing end of the tunnel.

Żar squeaked, the roar he'd been working on deserting him entirely as he bolted towards the distant flames.

Fire.

The tunnel shook, forcing me to move quicker. Several pulsing heartbeats later, it abruptly ended, spitting me out into a cave. Stalactites and stalagmites formed a pointed maze, sparkling as I wound through them, searching for the light source – there had to be a faster exit than going back through that tunnel again.

I raced into the next cave.

Where my world shattered apart.

It was like I was under the sleeping curse again, living a waking dream, a cruel taunt. Reeling from what my eyes were telling me, what my brain refused to believe, I couldn't move, speak, *breathe.*

Żar was at my side; he'd been waiting for me at the cave entrance. As if from a great distance, I felt a concerned talon prod my boot. It wasn't until I blinked that I felt the tears running down my cheeks, the hard lump of solid emotion wedged in my throat, the way the stalactites clinging to the roof of the cavernous cave glimmered in and out of focus as I stood there, dizzied by what lay in front of me.

Dragons.

Fully matured, grown dragons. Dragons I recognised from my childhood in the castle in greens, reds, purples and blacks, more than I could count. It hadn't been the battle I'd heard rumbling through the tunnel, it had been *dragons*.

'This isn't possible.' I'd witnessed Migot's execution. Heard the dragons that were slain after her, the courtyard awash with blood as I'd run to the nursery, where I'd saved Żar's egg. In the days that followed I'd been too distraught to speak. But I'd listened. Learned that the slaughter of the dragons, these highly intelligent and empathic creatures, had been too difficult to stomach watching, that most of the queen's supporters had left the scene, one by one. Leaving Queen Serce alone with the Angels of Death, her tongueless soldiers who could tell no tales.

She must have only killed a handful for show before hiding the rest away from the world. Had they been trapped here for ten years? Unable to stretch their wings, to fly? It was unthinkably cruel. My blood bubbled with rage. *Why?*

Żar was clinging to my ankle, the hatchling clearly nervous at being presented with a cave filled with grown dragons. I rested a hand on his head. He wasn't the last of his kind. The nearest dragon, a veridian green one, shifted in her rock nest, giving me a glimpse of smooth scales resting beneath her. *Eggs.* I inhaled sharply. The green dragon swung her head in my direction. A dark orange eye fixed on me. Like a wave gathering momentum, the rest of the dragons stilled, suddenly registering my whirlwind of emotions. A cave full of glowing eyes stared at me.

Żar darted behind my legs. My heart ached for him; I'd raised him, fed him from my own veins. I was what he knew, I'd been his home since he hatched, but this . . . this was what was best for him.

'It's alright,' I murmured, meeting the dragons' stares without flinching, showing them I was unafraid. Dragons weren't a threat unless they themselves were threatened. Or hungry. But these had been trapped underground for years; they must have been fed.

An amethyst dragon took an experimental step in my direction. Her scales were scarred. But the scars weren't shaped like dragon bites; they were too precise, too small. They were knife scars. I staggered back under the weight of the truth: all magic carried a blood price. The more powerful the magic, the greater the cost, and Queen Serce, powerful enough to drain an entire queendom of magic, needed the highest cost of all: bottles and bottles of blood: *She was using dragon blood as her tithe.*

A menacing snarl erupted from the amethyst dragon. I'd broken eye contact, fallen into my anger again. Deep wells of endless anger that the dragons were now sensing, shuffling unhappily around me. A stocky, coal-black dragon jerked his head, drawing his leathery wings in tighter. Pani Smok had instilled in me the warning signs that dragons gave before they attacked, but she'd never taught me how to defend myself against one: you couldn't.

Żar quaked behind my leg. Was I fast enough to pick him up and run back into the stalactite cave? Or would I be scorched the instant I turned my back? As I warred over what to do, the dragons prowled closer and closer.

I looked around, wildly hoping that something would occur to me.

From the darkest recesses of the cave, a set of eyes suddenly gleamed. Rising up, the dragon that had been slumbering there awoke. Noticed me. Began walking towards me on its back legs and wing joints, the rocky floor trembling beneath its weight. When it passed through a shaft of light, its dark golden scales were set aflame.

' Ogień,' I whispered aloud. The biggest, most foul-tempered dragon in Mazrovia. Even Pani Smok had never dared to venture close to him, let alone ride him; none of the resident dracologists had. Nobody had known why he'd chosen to reside at the castle – before Queen Serce had endorsed and spread the True Path, dragons had roamed wherever they liked. The ones that stayed did so out of their own preference. Like Migot, who had loved bonding with humans, and fistfuls of sugar lumps. But a dragon like Ogień? He could have ruled the skies if he wished.

The other dragons lowered their heads, hiding their throats as Ogień stomped past them. He was a king among dragons, his size would have been daunting in the training fields or dragon hangers but, here, in this cave? It was terrifying.

Ogień glared at me. And showed no signs of slowing.

I froze.

Ogień thundered towards me, the cave quaking under his great, taloned claws. He wasn't going to stop. He was going to snap me up in his jaws without pause, devouring me in a single bite. Or maybe he'd roast me first.

He stopped.

Fear threatened to stop my heart as he peered down at me, fire rolling in the back of his throat, each tooth as long as a sword and close enough to touch.

Żar peeked out from behind my shaking legs. I pushed him back out of sight.

Ogień rolled his huge neck back and roared. My eardrums threatened to burst, bones shuddering as the cave shook. Stalactites fell like icicles, smashing on the ground. His eyes were incandescent, as fiercely blinding as the sun. I blinked, trying not to break eye contact, not to show weakness, even as I reeked of fear. Those bright yellow eyes. Rare among dragons, who tended to have orange, red or purple eyes.

Żar craned his head round my knee, peering up at Ogień. With those same yellow eyes.

Ogień stared down at him.

Reeling, I dropped to my knees. I hadn't known that Ogień was Migot's nestmate, but the truth was undeniable. 'Żar, you have a family.' My voice broke on the last word as I hugged the hatchling close to me. 'You're not the last of your kind any more;

you'll never be alone again.' Picking Żar up, I slowly stood before holding him out to Ogień. 'I believe he belongs to you,' I said, calm and steady.

Ogień sniffed Żar before huffing, blowing a gust of hot air that sent me staggering back. I stood still as rock as Ogień reached a talon out. It was bigger than me, but I knew I wasn't the one he was interested in any longer. He'd never been hungry for me; he'd smelled his long-lost kin, returned at last.

Slowly and carefully, Ogień curled his talons round Żar. My heart accelerated as they grazed my sleeve, at how small and insignificant I was in the face of this creature. Żar squeaked happily as Ogień lifted him the way dragons carried their young when they flew, caged in their talons. I stepped back with a quiet sob. It was time to let Żar go.

Ogień bowed his head in return. Swinging his heavy body around, he slowly lowered himself to the ground before staring back at me. Waiting. The other dragons stilled, as stunned as I that the king of the dragons, the dragon that would never let a soul near enough to touch him, was inviting me to ride him.

CHAPTER THIRTY-EIGHT

My sweat-slick hands slipped against Ogień's dark golden scales, chest pounding with excitement and shock at my own daring. *Dragons existed.* Happiness sang through me, brighter than I'd ever known, shining down into that pit where my anger and despair lived. Giving me more reason than ever to seek out the queen and end this.

I climbed onto Ogień's back and sat there, waiting to see what would happen next. I hadn't flown on dragonback for over ten years, but this was a cave; there would be no flying here. So why had Ogień wanted me to mount him?

Once I was settled, he rose. Wind swirled past my face as he stood tall, reminding me of the times I'd climbed into the highest branches of a tree, tilting my face to the clouds, letting the wind and rain rush over me. Of riding Migot.

Ogień set off at a swift pace to the far side of the cave. There, the shadows receded, revealing a massive iron door. A small window was set into the stone above; the light source I'd wondered about. 'So that's how you were hidden down here,'

I realised as Ogień lowered himself.

Sliding down from his back, I went to examine it. The iron door held no lock. In place of a keyhole, there was a fist of black stone. Blast. Probably bespelled to be unlocked with the queen's blood. Ogień huffed impatiently. 'I know, I know,' I said absentmindedly. 'I wonder if—' I bit my thumb. Hard enough to bleed. And then I pressed it to the stone. I might not have witchblood, but I was still the queen's heir.

Something jolted, and with a screech of grinding gears, it clanged open. Sunlight beamed through, shining down on the dragons for the first time in years, setting their scales gleaming like jewels.

The dragons hesitated, looking between Ogień, and the door to their freedom. Fresh air vined through the cave, scented with the River Wanda, which curled below like a green snake. We were halfway down the mountain; the only way in or out was to fly. Only the queen could have entered this cave in the past years; I'd seen her fly once when I was a child, an eerie, slow rising as she manipulated the air with her magic. Dragons had paid the price for that magic – it had been their blood in those bottles I'd seen the day she'd cursed me, their blood lending her power. But why then did she need to steal more magic from her own queendom? I needed answers. I needed to return to the castle.

'I understand if you can never trust humans again but, please, know this. I want only what's best for you. So go, go back to the Heartlands, be wild and free,' I told them all, raising my voice to reach every last dragon, letting my emotions sing through my words to make them understand. 'Go!' I yelled, stepping aside, even as my heart throbbed, sore and heavy, at the thought of Żar leaving, too. But he was where he was meant to be. After all, he had never been mine.

The green one was the first to walk towards the door, holding her eggs gently in her talons, her spine rolling in the uneven gait of dragons. She spread her wings and leaped into the air. After that, dragons jostled for space, flying free one after another, away from the mountain and over the riverbanks, soaring high and higher, filling the skies with dragons again, at last. The way Mazrovia was always meant to be. The way I was going to keep it.

I soaked in the sound of those leathery bat wings beating the air, watching as the dragons luxuriated in their first flight in years. Then, slowly but surely, they began to peel away from the castle, striking out towards the Dragon Heartlands, the cradle of dragonkind in Mazrovia.

The cave seemed smaller now that the dragons had left. Except for Ogień. Żar was lying stretched out in his father's talons, his eyes half-lidded with contentment, lazily surveying me. 'It's time to say goodbye now, little one.' Reaching out a hand, I gave him one last stroke behind his ears, ignoring that I'd threaded my arm through Ogień's talons to reach him. 'Stay safe and don't forget to visit when you've found your wings.' I sniffed back a sob, smiling at him. 'I will *never* stop loving you.'

Bracing myself for Ogień to turn and fly away, follow the others away from the castle and their trauma to the emerald Heartlands, my heart stalled when, once more, the colossal dragon lowered himself for me.

Riding on dragonback tasted like freedom. Like kissing Kaz for the first time. Like seeing the castle and knowing I wanted it for myself. Like surging into the sky was where I was meant to be, who I was meant to be: a girl on borrowed wings who lived and loved fiercely, whose rage could have torn the sky in two. Once, I would have struggled under the burden of that anger, its heat, its intensity too much for me to carry. Now, I embraced it.

I expected Ogień to drop me off somewhere near the castle before following the rest of the dragons. He did not. Gliding on vast, outstretched wings, he flew straight to the battle raging on around the castle. Giving me a dragon's-eye view of the chaos: the rebels fighting the sharpshooters across the ramparts; the Mazrovian Army facing off against the Forest Court, who were holding up a line of defence even though they were horribly outnumbered. Angels of Death flitted through the courtyard, hunting down the larger forest creatures, those of pointed talon and tooth, picking them off one by one.

I screamed a war cry like an avenging god.

The rebels on the ramparts looked up. Pani Smok's jaw fell open as I glided overhead on dragonback. It was sweetly victorious. '*Run!*' she yelled to the rebels, who dived for cover.

The sharpshooters were slower as they hadn't registered the sound of dragon wings beating the air.

Ogień rained fire down on them.

Their bows and arrows were incinerated, the sharpshooters turned to ash. I raised my fist in the air, pumping it in triumph.

I no longer needed to kill to battle my curse – I was still in the first precious days of freedom – yet here I was, killing again. I waited for guilt to engulf me. It never came.

Ogień glided lower, over the courtyard. Just outside the open gate, I spotted a familiar pair. 'There.' I pressed Ogień's scales next to his right-wing joint, urging him to angle down, where Katia and Szafir, having ignored my instructions, were fighting back to back, surrounded by Angels of Death. Despite her bravery, Katia was not a strong fighter. Szafir was, but she was tiring in the vicious onslaught. Ogień swooped down. I clung to him, sliding down his scales as he dropped his right wing, turning.

'*Move!*' I screamed at Katia and Szafir.

Katia's head jerked up, the sword she was using falling slack as she stared back at me. At Ogień. Szafir hit her like a runaway carriage, barrelling them both out the way without hesitation.

The Angels of Death began to run.

Ogień unleashed an unending river of fire, flames charging across the flagstones and onto the fleeing Angels of Death, who blazed alight at once. With their feathered raven wings, they hadn't stood a chance.

Ogień circled back over the courtyard, firing down on the

Mazrovian Army as I held on, my eyes and nose streaming. It had been an age since I'd ridden a dragon and I was unpractised, especially without a saddle.

I spotted Mirosław, his cloak torn, one sleeve cut open and bloodied, refusing to allow his injuries to slow him as he danced around his opponent, wielding his sword with a skill that Pan Jedrick would have envied. I wondered where Tosia had gone. Had he killed her? Sadness needled me; I'd liked her. Kaz had loved her.

Nearby a small gang of sprites were attacking a Mazrovian soldier's ankles until they felled him, cheering out in a high-pitched squeal I couldn't decipher before climbing onto his chest and rushing towards his throat.

But there was one familiar figure I couldn't see.

'Where's Kaz?' I yelled down at Mirosław, searching through the battle, my heart twisting with fear.

Mirosław's eyes flashed toward the castle. 'He's with the queen.'

My fear sharpened into a blade. 'And Tosia?'

Mirosław lowered his sword, his gaze. 'Dead.'

Something whizzed past Ogień's wing.

Ogień roared out, banking sharply left. Squeezing my legs tighter to keep my seat, I scanned the ramparts, looking for the source of the attack. Arrows wouldn't penetrate dragon hide, but that hadn't looked like an arrow.

A second attack came, this one glancing off Ogień's talon. Żar cried out.

'Żar!' I screamed, scrabbling over Ogień's back to check he was unharmed. If anything had hurt him— Ogień let loose a guttural snarl. He brushed a wing back, pushing me back into place. I glared up at the castle, squinting against the sun to see . . . *there.*

Pressing my hands down on Ogień, I urged him up to the ramparts. It had been ten years since dragons had been spotted in the skies of Mazrovia and many, many more years since the Dark Dragon Ages, when dragons had hunted people as prey. No weapons that targeted dragons had been crafted in a long time. Only relics were left. Which was exactly what the antique weapon sitting on the ramparts was: a relic that fired iron bolts, designed to pierce dragon wings and drag them from the sky. A cluster of soldiers frantically worked to reload it as Ogień hurtled down.

Iron bolts volleyed towards us.

'Watch out!' I yelled at Ogień as he folded his wings back and *dived.*

The soldiers scattered. But dragonfire was faster. The stench of burning flesh filled my nostrils as Ogień cooked them alive. Spreading his wings at the last moment, my head whipped back as Ogień soared away. In our wake, ash fell like snow over the courtyard.

Ogień flew over the castle, circling higher and higher until we reached the tallest turret, the sharpest spire piercing the sky, visible from any street in the Amber City. The pinnacle of Queen Serce's rule.

'Thank you,' I patted Ogień's flank. 'Please come if I call for you?' I asked. I hoped I wouldn't need him, but I wanted to give myself my best chance, so I filled my words with emotion, staring into his yellow eyes. 'Please stay here.'

I leaped off his back, onto the turret. Grabbing onto the ivy, I glanced back at Żar, still nestled between Ogień's talons. Relief thrummed through my veins; he was fine. Before I lost my courage, I climbed down to the single window and kicked in the glass, throwing myself through its frame.

I landed on thick carpet. The very same that the queen had conjured a likeness of to trap us in that horrid pit. A hundred mirrors of varying sizes threw my reflection around the rounded room. I was covered in dirt, an angry, wounded, wild thing.

Magic flew through the room. The queen was bleeding, her dark golden hair as unkempt as mine as she unleashed spell after spell at Kaz, the air ripe with the scent of magic and blood. Kaz looked little better; he was fading fast. Still, he evaded her magic, sending his own power surging back at her with fast lightning strikes. One landed, making the queen hiss in pain and fury and not a little fear as she leaped away from an errant spark.

I scrambled out of the way. Kaz reached down and yanked me up. 'Light the firestone, Elka. Burn it all down.'

I turned to face the queen, who was watching us both warily. Her fingers dripped blood, ready to pay the cost for whatever fresh curse she sent my way. But I had survived all she had given me, taken it all and kept living. I'd fallen in love, raised a dragon and ripped seven still-beating hearts from seven chests.

I was here to claim my eighth.

CHAPTER THIRTY-NINE

'This ends now.' I pulled my firestone out from my pocket. It flamed at once.

'Wait!' the queen cried, her chest heaving, breathing ragged. She was as exhausted as Kaz, her hairstyle fraying, her silk plum dress torn.

Kaz had elemental power; he could have burned the queen where she stood if he so wished. But this was not his fight. He'd been distracting the queen from the battle, waiting for me to arrive and seek my revenge.

'Do it, do it now,' Kaz growled.

My hand stilled against my will. Most often, I found myself calling Queen Serce 'the queen' as if I could distance myself from who she really was – my mother. It was a peculiar feeling hating someone you were born to love. It turned your emotions murky. Things were never black and white, but this grey was a thick fog that obscured everything. 'You trapped the dragons underground for ten years, made me believe that they were all dead, that you'd killed them all.' I slid my eyes to Kaz, who looked unsurprised; he must have seen them fly free. 'You were using them as your tithe.' I needed answers more than I needed death.

'Yes,' my mother replied.

Well, if she was answering questions then I had plenty more. 'Why?'

No response. She shifted on her feet, boredom coasting over her face.

'And if you had the dragons as your tithe, you didn't *need* more power, you could never have managed to channel all the magic the dragon blood would have given you as well as the magic you plundered from your own queendom. So what benefit could you have possibly reaped from stealing magic, from spreading hatred against magical creatures? Or was it all about power?'

The boredom drained out of her face, leaving it stark. We were too high up to hear the battle, but she knew everything that happened in the castle; she must have known they were losing. Unless she was that confident that she would not lose here, in her turret, the final battle and the only one that truly mattered.

'My darling daughter,' she began, her words pinching my heart. 'My beautiful Snow White, you are as naïve as you are lovely. Did it never occur to you why I needed this much power?'

'No. Not when taking it was wrong. You leached it away from creatures that need it to survive. Magic is the life breath of the forest, the mountains and the tundra and you, you—'

'I did what I had to do to protect them.'

'Another mind game, mother? This time I won't fall for your

manipulations.' I held the flame higher, triggering her fear, and something else, too – a sadness, a grief I couldn't begin to guess at.

'You will die without me,' she said quietly.

'Why aren't you fighting me?' I yelled. 'You have all this power and I've never seen you use it.' *I'd never seen her use it.* Not her stolen magic, and not the amount she'd taken. Nothing beyond the magic she already held as a witch. I stared at her, fighting for breath.

She gave me a slow smile as if she knew how far she had pushed me, how infuriated I was. 'You will die without me,' she repeated.

My laugh sounded hysterical, even to my own ears. I caught Kaz's flinch from the corner of my eye. Pitch-black clouds rolled along his arms. He looked like he would carve the world in two for me. But this was my battle and I loved him more for letting me fight it alone.

'I would already be dead if you had your way.'

A flicker of some emotion – remorse? – crossed her face. Just as quickly, it was swept away. 'They were only warnings. I knew it would take more than that to kill you.'

'I nearly lost an eye!' I snapped, 'which you witnessed yourself, when you were pretending to be my best friend.'

Her lips curled with amusement. 'I was rather proud of that disguise,' she admitted. 'Nevertheless, believe me; if I'd wanted you dead, your body would still be in that glass coffin. Each curse was set to expire before your death. They were warnings only.

Warnings to deter you from the forest demon and the dangerous path you were treading.'

I shook my head. 'I don't believe you.'

She stepped forward, reaching a hand towards me, to the roots that still wormed through my chest, thick and hard and painful.

Kaz raised a hand, wreathed with lightning, moving to block her. 'Touch her and I'll burn you alive,' he snarled.

She hesitated, her fingers curling into a fist as if she had to force herself not to touch me. I stared at that hand, that had smoothed my headaches away, run magic over my broken wrist until the bones knitted together again. *You made me better*, I'd whispered in awe. *That's impossible*, she'd told me. *You are perfect just as you are.* The hand that had cursed me.

'That apple could never have killed you,' she said now, meeting my burning gaze. 'It was my curse that protected your heart from its poison, would have protected you from any weapon. *I protected you.*'

I shook my head bitterly. 'You are unbelievable.'

Her temper frayed. 'So you believe that you would make a better queen? That you could take a vast, wild queendom like Mazrovia and reign over it?'

Holding my head high, I met her gaze head on. 'I would do better than you.'

'Ah, I miss the arrogance that came with youth.' The queen smiled to herself in a way that I disliked.

'Why a church though?' I blurted out. The flame was warm

in my hand, a reminder that we could not stand here talking for much longer: the battle was raging on and I had promised both the Forest Court and the rebellion that I would cut off the head of the snake. Win the war, seize the crown. I hadn't wagered on my curiosity burning brighter, an unquenchable fire. 'Why endorse the True Path, why send out ambassadors to spread it through Mazrovia? I know you don't believe in their message.'

'No,' my mother admitted. 'You're right, I've been using the Path for my own means.'

'Why?'

She met my gaze, honest and true and unflinching. 'Because the old gods are not who you think they are. War is coming. Do not be on the wrong side of it.'

I stilled; I hadn't expected that.

'What war?' Kaz asked, interrupting the back and forth my mother and I were firing at each other, unspoken truths and secrets leaking out like curses.

She fell silent, her gaze flicking to the nearest mirror.

If she was done answering questions then it was time. I raised my firestone again; it had burned low but I didn't need it. My mother's reign had been a lonely one. Once I'd been lonely, too. Now my greatest strength was in my friends, my allies, the magical creatures I cared for.

My mother gave me a sad smile. 'So it's come to this, has it?'

I swallowed hard, blinked harder, forcing my pulse, my hand, to steady. My tears not to fall. Shoved my emotions into a box and locked them tightly away. 'I'm afraid so.'

She uncurled her bloody fingers. Pani Smok's advice echoed through me: *Her magic is more powerful than any weapon, but not as fast.*

'Ogień!' I screamed.

The largest of all the dragons, king of his wing, crashed through the wall of the turret, carving my mother's inner sanctum open to the skies. Żar was no longer in his talons, but there was no time to wonder where he was. With a low growl that raised every hair on my arms, Ogień opened his jaws. The back of his throat glowed orange as fire rose—

'Roots!' my mother cried out.

'Hold your fire.' I rested a steadying hand against Ogień's leg.

'*Elka.*' Kaz's voice filled with warning.

It ran against every instinct I had, my gut screaming at me to let Ogień breathe fire until the turret was a charred memory and the throne was mine, but my mother's eyes were silvered with unshed tears. For me or for herself, I did not know. But I did need to hear her last words otherwise it would haunt me for the rest of time, wondering what they would have been.

'I gave you roots as your curse. To remind you where you came from, who you belong to. You've forgotten that now, too swept up in your forest demon and your own righteousness to listen to the truth, to understand why I did the things I did.'

'You ignored me for *years*,' I half cried. 'I was a child, I *only* wanted your love, your attention. I would have happily listened to whatever you wanted to fill my head with because I only wanted to be good enough for you, deserving to be your daughter.'

She closed her eyes, reeling back. 'You are right.'

My eyes stung.

'I have failed you. I failed you both.'

I felt Kaz stiffen at my side before I registered her words. 'What?'

She ran her index fingernail, sharpened to a point, against her thumb until a fresh bead of blood swelled. I watched, dumbfounded, as she strode across to where my mirror stood, one of two largest in her turret, the central focal point, and walked on to the second one. She pressed her bloody thumb to it.

Violet mist swirled through the glass, parting to reveal a young woman looking into her mirror, unaware she had an audience. She looked the same age as me. 'I cast a spell the morning I awoke and knew that life was quickening within me,' my mother said, licking the blood from her thumb. 'I felt you even then, two souls curled up together like fishes. A spell of ruby-red berries, ebony and snow for beauty. A spell of dragon scales, bone and river water for power. When you were born, you were a rare beauty. When your sister was born, the castle shuddered with knowledge of her power.'

Twins. I staggered back, unable to tear my eyes from the mirror. From my sister. With her fine silver hair and clear lake-blue gaze, she looked nothing like me. She looked everything like my mother, from their sharp features to their arched eyebrows.

Even if I couldn't believe every word my mother was spilling, their likeness was undeniable. 'Which one of us was born first?' I ripped my attention away from the mirror, a new fear taking root.

My mother smiled. 'It was never my intention to fight you, Snow White. This was not the way things were meant to happen, but you have left me no choice now—'

My chest tightened. *'Who was born first?'*

Before I could begin to make sense of it all, my mother's stance changed. 'I cannot stay here a moment longer. Not now that you have failed to heed my many warnings. I did not expect my own daughter to betray me.'

'Now, fire, now!' I yelled to Ogień.

His throat glowed orange again, the molten fire rising.

My mother leaped through the mirror.

'No!' I screamed. Ogień turned his head, blasting his fire out of the broken window instead and I raced towards the mirror, ready to follow my mother through, to set fire to the world, to save my sister from our mother, to burn it all down, I didn't know and I didn't care.

The glass turned black.

I slammed into it.

'We're too late; she turned her magic on the linked mirrors. The connection is shattered now,' Kaz said grimly.

'Where was it?' I wheeled on him. 'Did you see where that mirror led? Was it in Mazrovia?'

He gave a slow shake of his head, his lightning fading. 'I don't know. It wasn't anywhere I recognised.'

I turned back to the mirror. 'I have a sister. My mother didn't even tell me her name.' *Or if she was the true heir to Mazrovia.* 'I will find her,' I vowed, glaring at the mirror. 'I will find them both.'

'Elka,' Kaz's voice was gravelly. 'Queen Serce has abandoned her queendom. You need to make your move now.' He crossed the turret, taking my hands in his. 'It's time to seize the throne.'

CHAPTER FORTY

Kaz's chest pressed against my back as we flew on Ogień. Żar was in his talons once more; he'd been grumpily waiting on the turret roof, less than pleased about being left behind.

Sister, I had a *sister*. A twin, no less. Had my mother gone to retrieve her because this twin was the rightful heir to Mazrovia? Was that the real reason she had fled? And were her suggestions about the gods significant or just a misdirection? I didn't know what I could believe, not when she'd declared that she'd cursed me for my own protection. My path forward was murkier than ever, but I had started along it now and I couldn't stop. Not if I wanted to protect the dragons and save the last vestiges of magic clinging to Mazrovia.

I leaned back against Kaz as the wind tore by, burning our cheeks. 'You can do this,' he said into my ear.

'You never needed me to kill Queen Serce,' I shouted, clinging onto Ogień's scales as we soared over the castle.

'No,' he agreed. 'But assassinating her would have only put a stop to half the Purge. To end it properly, I needed a queen who would stop this distrust, this hatred of magic. A queen who would take Mazrovia in hand and give them hope again. I needed you.'

Below, the last dregs of the battle forged on. 'I don't know if they'll accept me on the throne. I didn't kill the queen—'

'She escaped. She didn't stay and fight,' Kaz said firmly, his arms, his thighs tightening around me, holding me together on dragonback. 'And our army, the dragon you found and freed, have conquered hers.'

'Then why do I still feel like an imposter?'

'Because this corset—' Kaz's fingers drummed against my armoured stomach. 'Isn't the only armour you're wearing, princess. Your heart is locked up tight because you're afraid to let people in, because you fear that they won't love you if they see who you really are underneath it all. You think that you're unlovable.'

I gave a terse nod as we swooped lower, the wind whistling past. There wasn't a monster buried deep within me, I was the monster. But the curse was ended. The battle won. I never needed to kill again, never needed to taste another heart slipping down my throat again. Maybe I didn't need to be a monster any more, maybe I could just be . . . me.

'The queen can rot in Nawia for making you believe this.' Kaz's voice came again when Ogień's wings had levelled out. It was ragged, worn thin with fatigue and anger. 'She was wrong. *You* are wrong.'

'What are you saying?' My thighs burned as Ogień swept round the central turret of the castle, where my mother's new flag fluttered, the silver path at its centre shining out like a beacon.

Kaz's breath against my neck made me shiver. We were filthy and exhausted from the battle, the dungeons, yet still I wanted him. 'I love you, Elka. I have loved you since the moment I saw you stumble through my forest, scared and alone, carrying a deeper courage than anyone standing in my court. And I will love you until the last breath I take. You are imprinted on my heart, and I will never not love you.'

I drew a trembling breath, but he hadn't finished.

'I've been around for a long time,' Kaz admitted, his stubble grazing my earlobe, his husky voice curling my toes. 'I've seen hundreds of love stories. Enough to know that the way I feel about you doesn't happen often. Meeting you redefined my life. You are my guiding star, the brightest day to my darkest nights.'

'I've murdered innocent people, Kaz.' Guilt stained my mouth; if he kissed me now, I wondered if he'd taste it. 'My soul carries that darkness with me every day and my dreams are nightmares.'

'Oh, princess, you don't know the things that I've done.' Kaz swept my hair behind my ear, his fingertips dancing down my neck as if he wanted to peel my clothes off, right here on dragonback. I glanced down, but we were still circling the flag. Ogień must have sensed the emotion playing out between us. 'I don't need you to be good, I just need you to be mine.'

'I want to take everything you have to give and give you even more. But first, I need to do this.'

Kaz's arms fell from me as I stood up. My arms spread wide for balance as the wind snatched at me, I walked along the dragon's back. Ogień's growl of approval rumbled through my legs. He hadn't been giving us a moment, he'd been waiting for me to claim my victory.

As Ogień circled the turret one last time, I reached out and snagged the flag. I wondered if Ogień had been there the day the new flag had been flown, if he had smelled the dragon blood running between the cracks of the cobblestones, remembered the flag flying high as he'd been herded into the cave that would imprison him for years.

Wrapping the material round my fists, I braced as Ogień shot away. Kaz's hands clamped round my ankles, holding me fast to the dragon as I stood on his back, the flag ripping from its pole and flying raggedly behind me like my own set of wings.

We landed in the courtyard.

'*Surrender,*' I ordered, holding what was left of the flag high as I walked down Ogień's back onto solid ground. 'Queen Serce has abandoned her position and the battle is won.'

I scanned the courtyard imperiously, 'Surrender now and serve your new queen or forfeit your life.' I threw the flag onto the cobblestones and nodded to Ogień. A stream of flames incinerated it. Blackened stone marked where Ogień had roasted Angels of Death alive. Ash coated everything like grey snow, the fallen trees that Kaz had uprooted to march into the courtyard had thrown everything into chaos, with Mazrovian soldiers, Forest Court soldiers and rebels fighting in isolated pockets. I set eyes on Katia and Szafir, Mirosław now at their side, with no small relief.

A queen's guard with sky-blue eyes dropped his sword. It clanged to the stone, slicing through the silence. Piotr. 'I serve Queen Elka,' he declared. Kaz, who stood at my back, silently defending my blind spots, let out a sigh. Other soldiers quickly followed suit, swords dropping like pennies down a wishing well.

Only the Angels of Death exchanged significant looks. If you were willing to sacrifice your tongue to fight for the previous queen then your loyalty ran deeper.

'This could be a problem,' Kaz muttered, storms wreathing his shoulders. His forest powers were overstretched; he flexed his fingers, awaiting that rumble of stone and wood obeying his call, but nothing came.

Before I could comment, a metal screech sounded behind.

The great doors to the castle were opening.

Emboldened by the distraction, a couple of Angels of Death sneaked forward, swords at the ready, aiming straight for what they'd correctly identified as mine and Ogień's greatest weakness: the hatchling curled up inside his talons.

I charged forwards, unsheathing a blade in each hand, roaring out as I met the first, the woman who I'd knocked out earlier. 'You,' I snarled. 'I should have killed you when I had the chance.' Keeping

Żar at my back, I met each blow of her sword, moving faster than wildfire. I gave her everything and when she paused, sweat and panic coating her face, I parted with my favourite knife, the one Pan Jedrick had gifted me, throwing it like a spear. It sunk into her throat, that soft spot between her bladed helmet and her shiny black armour. Choking on blood, she dropped.

Ogień roared, thrashing his tail, as furious as me. The remaining Angels of Death hesitated but they had no chance to surrender. Ogień breathed fire onto them all. I dropped to the stone, arms over my head as flames rushed over me, onto the Angels.

The last soldiers surrendered swiftly. As did the queen's guards who had managed to survive the rebels and assassins stealing through the castle. They exited now, laying down their arms. Behind them walked Pan Jedrick.

He crossed the courtyard, bent to pick up the knife he'd given me and offered me the hilt. I took it. Pan Jedrick looked just as I remembered him, short and stocky and elegant, his grey eyes resting on me with fondness and not a little pride. 'I was wondering when you'd come home,' he told me.

'Piotr.' I turned to the old queen's guards, the soldiers, what was left of the Angels of Death. 'Since you were first to lay down your sword, I want you to lead the queen's guard for now.' I needed the castle protected as a matter of urgency; this was when I was at my weakest, my grasp on the throne tenuous. Piotr nodded, picking up his sword and sheathing it. 'Soldiers—' I waved at the chaos of the courtyard. 'Your first order of business is to clear this mess and rebuild the fortifications.' I glanced at the wall that Kaz's tree army had marched through, feeling his ego swell a little as he considered it, too. 'Angels of Death.' I looked through the survivors. There were only a handful; the notorious raven-feathered killers had been the first target of the Forest Court and Ogień alike. 'You are all dismissed from your services pledged to the castle and crown. I no longer have need of you.'

Before they could react, I strode through the courtyard and out of the gate, Kaz, Katia, Szafir and Mirosław at my back, following without a second thought. After a moment, the ground began to shake. I smiled; Ogień was following me, too.

On the mountaintop and surrounding gaping holes where Kaz had commanded the woodland to tear their roots from their ground and march on the castle, people had gathered. Ordinary Mazrovians had come to see what was happening. They staggered back as Ogień bent to fit through the gate, staring up at the great dragon with fear and no little awe.

I reached the church. Capped with an amber dome and bearing a large, thick iron door, once it had been a temple to the old gods before the queen had reclaimed it for the True Path.

Above the door hung Migot's bones, vast and yellowed with age. Even now, seeing them stung. 'Cut them down,' I ordered.

A couple of soldiers scrambled to obey and soon the chained bones were brought to me. Ogień roared at the sight of them. Tenderly scooping the remains of his nestmate up in his free talon, he huffed in my direction and launched himself into the sky. Cries of alarm and wonder mingled together as the Mazrovians watched the colossal dragon soar over the castle. Kaz's hand found mine, our fingers interlinking.

'I never knew the dragons had survived,' Pan Jedrick murmured.

I turned to the crowd spilling down the mountain, more gathering with each breath. 'People of Mazrovia,' I called out, 'Queen Serce has abandoned her throne. I am your queen now. You are free to follow the True Path if it brings you joy, but it is no longer mandatory and will not be endorsed by the castle. What will be enforced is the freedom of all magic and magical creatures anywhere in this queendom. I will not rest until Mazrovia is a safe haven for magic once more.' Throwing up an arm to gesture at Ogień, his sunset wings gliding into the distance, I continued, 'Harming the dragons is prohibited and will carry a weighty sentence.' I'd never made a speech before, never been trained in how I might one day reign. Doubt knotted my thoughts into a tangle; maybe I was going to all this effort only for my sister to steal the throne back. *She was the powerful one.* I felt the first stirrings of envy; I'd always been desperate for magic of my own. I pushed all my fears and doubts away. I'd come this far – nothing was getting in my way of the crown, the throne, the queendom now. It was *mine*.

Kaz cleared his throat.

'Thank you,' I finished.

Silence rang. A couple of uncertain claps rang out, then a volley of applause. When Kaz looked at me, exhausted and wrecked, all I saw was his pride. I didn't know if they clapped because they felt they should, but I hoped they clapped not for me but for the return of magic. For a new era in Mazrovia.

'It seems congratulations are in order.' Pani Smok fell into step with me as I headed back to the castle. Her silver hair was crusted with blood, her rebels collecting around her, readying to leave.

'I take it you'll be travelling to the Dragon Heartlands now?' I asked.

'Of course.' The dracologist's gaze misted. 'And I give you my endless gratitude that you found and freed the dragons. This is a good day for all of us. But don't think I'll be taking my eye off the castle.'

I raised an eyebrow at her. 'Planning another revolution?'

'No . . .' Pani Smok trailed off before shooting me a smile with a hint of warning. 'Just watching for the time being. You can think of me as your conscience.' With that, she inclined her head, nodded to Kaz, and strode off.

For the first time in over ten years, I walked through the front doors of the castle, the demon, the demigod I was in love with at my side.

Home, at last.

CHAPTER FORTY-ONE

'Make it gold,' I stared at my reflection in my old castle bedroom.

After I'd walked into the castle for the first time in years, I had forced myself up endless stairs to my mother's turret, where I'd plunged my favourite knife into the mirror that bore my blood. The knife that could cut through magic. One by one, I destroyed her magic mirrors until relief coloured my thoughts with joy that I was back, that I'd faced my mother and survived.

Now, for the first time in my life, I looked into a mirror without worrying I was being watched.

Szafir removed the measuring tape from my waist. I had declined offers from the resident seamstresses at the castle in favour of Szafir making my coronation gown. 'Gold will be perfect.' She gave me a mischievous wink. 'Hopefully this one will stay intact.'

I blushed furiously.

We'd spent half of last night sorting through the aftermath. The castle was largely undamaged, the battle having been confined to the ramparts and queen's turret, which were already being patched up. The courtyard was in tatters though. I'd issued orders for rebuilding until Kaz had pulled me away, demanding that I rest and eat. Only then had I collapsed, half falling into a bath that was like a gift from the gods, soaking away the burn in my muscles after my first dragonride in an age. One which Kaz had joined me in. My blush deepened as scenes from last night played through my head like a favourite song: Kaz pulling me lazily onto his lap. My hands running down his back, holding on as if we could keep each other close forever. Staring up into his eyes to find him already watching me. His dark green vines trailing over his shoulders, down his wet chest as he leaned back in my dragon talon-footed tub, effortlessly lifting me up and onto him. All the while, watching. Forging a connection that distance and time could never weaken. Swearing a silent promise to each other in sighs and kisses and the way he'd sunk his hands into my hair like it was spun silk.

We'd fallen asleep tangled together in my old bed. Awoken to another busy day, organising what was left of the Mazrovian Army and the castle guards and staff – I at least had supporters in the kitchens, judging by the feast they'd sent up for breakfast – telling my story to the governors of the Amber City, and declaring my mother a witch. We began preparing for my coronation, while Kaz sent Mirosław and the rest of the Forest Court home. He had not found Tosia's body, despite Mirosław claiming he had bested her in their duel.

My attention was drawn back to Szafir's mischievous grin.

'What?' Katia asked, her gaze flitting between Szafir and me from the armchair she'd draped herself over before ordering an entire plum cake from the kitchens. Not that I could blame her; she'd been rotting in that dungeon for an entire solstice. 'What happened to the last dress?'

'Nothing,' I said.

At the same time, Szafir theatrically whispered, 'Kazimierz.'

'Ooh,' Katia speared another forkful of plum cake, dipping it in a lavish cloud of cream before devouring it. 'Do tell.'

'There's nothing to tell,' I half squeaked. 'It's . . . it's private.'

Katia paused on her next forkful, scrunching up her nose. 'Wait, you're in love?' I'd forgotten my best friend had the uncanny ability to read my face and every emotion that danced across it.

Szafir snorted. 'Have you not seen the way he looks at her? It's like the moon's shining out of her—'

Kaz strode into my bedroom. Katia promptly choked on her cake and Szafir's mouth clamped shut. 'I thought my ears were burning.' He grinned, looking far too pleased with himself. Reminding me of the huntsman I thought I'd found in the forest, whose charming tongue I knew would land me in all sorts of trouble. He was wearing a dark green suit that hugged all the right places. With his stubble trimmed and his deep golden eyes echoed in the lightning fizzing at his fingers, he made my mouth water. His eyes lingered on me almost indecently, standing there in a simple petticoat as I was fitted for my gown.

'You know what, I do see it,' Katia whispered to Szafir.

I rolled my eyes.

Kaz stopped devouring me with his eyes long enough to pass on a message. 'Pan Jedrick has requested you meet him in the council room.'

I'd never been permitted in the council room before. My mother had only had a council of two; herself and Pan Jedrick, the sole person inside the castle who knew she was a witch. Besides a couple of Angels of Death who couldn't speak her secret, and myself and Katia, who I told all my secrets to, even the ones that hadn't belonged to me. I didn't yet know who I'd appoint to sit at my council. Having Pan Jedrick at my side helped though it still rankled that he'd advised my mother before me, against me. It was the first thing that escaped my lips.

'Ah.' Pan Jedrick's mouth thinned. It looked like disapproval, like when I'd failed to block a simple attack or forgotten my footwork. 'It was never my desire to sit at your mother's council,' he told me. The disapproval belonged to himself, then. I was learning that the people you assumed held all the answers, that you looked to for guidance, didn't know everything. They made mistakes, too. 'I want you to know, prin—' He cleared his throat, shot me a rueful glance. 'Queen Elka—'

'Not yet,' I interrupted.

'Soon enough.' His smile turned bittersweet. 'I never wished to sit on your mother's council until she told me something I couldn't look away from.'

'What did she say?' I asked warily.

Pan Jedrick stood, motioning for me to follow suit. As I did, he strode over to the nearest wall and gave a sharp tug on the oil lamp mounted there. With a click and release, half the wall swung inwards, revealing the top of a staircase, hewn into the honeyed stone of the castle.

'After you.' He gestured.

I offered him a wry smile. 'You taught me better than that.'

Chuckling to himself, Pan Jedrick went first. I closed the wall panel behind us and followed, Pan Jedrick's posture sapling-straight, his joints elastic. Being back in the castle, talking to him, felt right, even as I fretted over what I was about to learn.

The stairs led down to a thick-walled room with no windows. It was stacked high with black stone cannisters. 'Blast,' I whispered, picking one up to examine it. 'What's inside?' The moment I asked I realised I already knew. Pan Jedrick waited for me to draw the same conclusion. 'Magic.' Sucking in a breath, I sat the stone cannister back on top of its pile. 'This is *stored magic.*'

'You are looking at the stolen magic of Mazrovia,' Pan Jedrick said.

'I knew my mother was powerful, but she never seemed to use as much magic as I knew she had.' Because she hadn't, it was all *here*. In storage. She had never been powerful enough to end the battle; it must have been why she'd stayed away before Kaz arrived to distract her. 'But . . . *why?*'

Pan Jedrick's brows dropped. 'I know you remember the day your mother suddenly stopped speaking to you.'

Pain flared in my chest. 'Of course,' I said quietly. Tonight, I would take the throne, become a queen, but deep inside, I was still that hurt little girl whose own mother ignored her, for a reason she'd never learned.

'Your mother was a powerful witch, but she was too curious for her own good.' Pan Jedrick smiled. 'In that way, you're much alike.' His smile faded. 'She dabbled in magic she didn't fully understand, peering through the fabric of time and into the future itself. Until the night before the Purge. That night, when she stared into those deep, dark magics, something stared back at her.'

Dread trickled down my spine. 'What was it?'

'She never told me. As far as I know, she never told a single soul; she didn't wish to burden anyone else with that secret, that knowledge of what fate awaited us all.'

I steadied my breathing. 'She told me that the gods are not who we've always thought they are.'

'Yes.' Pan Jedrick glazed over, deep in consideration. 'That might well be the truth.' His attention trained on me. 'Your mother began the Purge to steal enough magic to arm herself against a threat she believed would crumble our world. She stopped talking to you to distance herself from you. When you grew older and more precocious and daring, she grew more fearful. She cursed you to send you away. To shield you from what was coming, to protect your heart with roots that would forbid anything from killing you. To scare you away enough that everyone would believe that you and she were enemies. She targeted you to stop you from becoming a target for something much worse.'

This information clawed at my lungs, my head. *She'd been telling the truth.*

'I am not defending the way she treated you,' Pan Jedrick's tone gentled. 'Only know that it was never from a lack of love. Quite the opposite in fact.'

'Then why, if she went to all that effort to curse me and drive me away and make everyone believe that she hated me –' I drew a painful breath – 'why would she bother putting up those wanted posters of me? Why did she come to see me in the forest, wearing Katia's face?' My voice trembled.

Pan Jedrick's gaze saddened. 'Her plan was imperfect. She underestimated your instincts for survival. I believe that regret and shame got the better of her. She just wanted to see you again,' he said simply. 'She was so desperate not to lose you, she ended up pushing you even further away. Did you never wonder why she did not kill the forest demon, even when he sat in her dungeon for days? Or your hatchling? She had no real appetite for death, that was all an act. Once she knew you loved them, her resolve not to harm them only solidified. Then you allied yourself with the forest demon and she began sending more curses, trying to alter your path.'

I fought back tears. 'I must tell you something in the strictest confidence. This does not leave this room.'

Curiosity flitted through Pan Jedrick. 'Understood.'

'Before she fled, my mother told me that I have a sister. A twin. I saw her through one of the mirrors. I wondered if she was lying, but their resemblance was unmistakable. She looks just like my mother.'

'Another mystery.' The wrinkles on Pan Jedrick's forehead deepened. 'Queen Serce never mentioned her.'

'She must have been hiding her.' I echoed his frown. 'But why, I don't know. Why not raise us together?'

Pan Jedrick shook his head. 'I have no idea. But whatever reason there was for hiding your sister away, it predated her reason for the Purge and her treatment of you.' He drew a small envelope from his pocket. 'Before the tide of battle turned, before she took to her turret, she requested that I advise you as I once advised her. She also left you this.' He pressed the envelope into my hand, holding it there for a beat as he looked at me. 'You've inherited quite the mess, but you're stronger than even you know. You will make a fine queen.' He patted my hand then exited.

With shaking hands, I opened the envelope. I pulled out a simple note, penned in my mother's elegant hand:

For the coming war.
Sorry I missed your nineteenth birthday.

Frowning, I tipped the envelope upside down. A small piece of amber dropped into my palm. A squirrel. The nineteenth piece in the menagerie she'd been collecting for me every birthday. Dragging in a trembling breath, I held it to my chest, looking at the magic that surrounded me. *Power.* Now that I had it, I didn't know what to do with it. Wasn't sure I wanted it any more if it came with an impending war. A war against a force I knew nothing of and didn't know how to fight.

The throne room was the oldest, grandest part of the castle. Here the stonework was rose-coloured, with red velvet benches, and a ceiling painted in gold.

I strode through its heart, resplendent in gold to match. A glittering gown of my dreams, designed by Szafir to my exact wishes: contoured to follow the lines of my armoured corset before flowing out into a voluminous gauzy skirt, which bore silhouettes of stars and dragons marked out in tiny, hand-sewn crystals. My sleeves were whisper-thin, slinking round my upper arms, trailing entire constellations, forged in crystal. Each time the chandelier overhead caught my dress, I sparkled furiously. Like a living star.

Benches groaned under the people crammed into them, important dignitaries, nobility, and ambassadors and rulers from other countries were squeezed in alongside key figures from the Amber City and across Mazrovia itself. It was also heavily guarded by a retinue of the Forest Court Kaz had ordered to stay behind, alongside the queen's guards I'd inherited. My mother was still alive and I had a secret sister who could challenge my right to rule; just before the trumpeter announced my entrance, Kaz had held my face in his hands and assured me that he would take no chances. Neither of us voiced what we both knew: the time for him to leave was creeping closer.

Ahead of me, on a cushioned pedestal, sat the glass crown. My mother had been wearing hers when she'd escaped through the mirror, but a queen did not wear another queen's crown. Each one was forged anew, as unique as the current queen. Mine had been crafted in a hurry by the best glassblower in the Glass Quarter, who also happened to be Katia's old flame. There were crystal dragons flying through it, to match my gown. When I turned my head and the crown caught the light, they gleamed.

I walked through the silence, my gown rustling over the rose-marbled floor, eyes cut straight ahead. It was time to claim my destiny.

My heart unwavering, I reached out and lifted the crown onto my head.

Kaz's gaze caught mine, that thread between us tightening as I longed for him to stand up here, beside me. I saw in his eyes, swollen with love and pride, how he was torn between wanting to stay and knowing he could not. I wondered if that thread would pull taut or if the distance and time would weigh too heavily on that single connecting thread and it would just . . . snap.

I turned my attention to the glass throne. It sat on a podium at the apex of the throne room, hundreds of years old, dating back to Queen Wanda herself. Drawing in a breath, collecting my courage, I walked up the crimson-carpeted steps that led to it.

I claimed the glass throne for myself.

'I am Queen Elka,' I stated, knowing the words I had to say though I'd never seen a Mazrovian coronation before, never practised for my own; how could I have when it would have meant the death of my own mother? I loved her then I hated her then I tried to kill her and lost her forever. She was gone, but she was everywhere. Haunting me. 'I vow to the old gods that I will serve my life on the glass throne for the good of the Queendom of Mazrovia.'

Applause sounded. A thousand hands praising the new queen, shining in gold and glass, sitting in her glittering throne room. The start of a new era, ripe with promise. *I did it.* The throne was mine. I wanted this. Fought for this, bled for this.

I sat on my throne until the hall emptied.

Until I'd spoken to an endless queue of people, lining up to satisfy their own curiosity, to press their agendas on me, to begin that slow creep of sidling closer, showering me with affection that tasted like lies.

Until I sat on the throne facing the single person left seated in the hall.

He rose to his feet, stalking towards me. 'My queen.' Kaz

bowed. Lifting his head, he appraised me. A smile spread across his face. 'You look good in a crown.'

Standing, I twirled until my gown flared around my knees, sparkling fiercer than dragonfire. 'And my gown?'

'Beautiful.' He halted at the foot of the stairs to my throne. Looking up at me in a way that thickened the air. Reminding me that he was the man, the demon, the demigod who had kneeled before me in his own court. 'But you're even more beautiful without it.'

He surprised a laugh out of me. 'I'm the queen now,' I whispered, scarcely able to believe it.

'You are.' He drank me in.

'I never thanked you.' I gestured to the throne. 'I couldn't have managed all of this without you.'

'Yes, you would have.' His voice was hoarse. 'You, Elka, are exceptional.' Pain shone through his face, making my heart shutter.

'Don't say goodbye to me,' I whispered. 'I can't—' My breath snagged on that hurt. 'I can't say goodbye to you, I just can't. I love you; I can't lose you. I can't lose my heart.'

His eyes unfocused, shimmering with his pain, his love, the inevitability of it all. 'You couldn't lose me if you tried,' he said roughly, half running up the steps to where I stood, in front of my throne. 'I am yours and you are mine.'

I ran my hands up his defined arms, through the moody clouds accumulated there and into his hair. His wild, beautiful hair.

'If I kiss you now, I'll never leave,' he said huskily, drawing a shuddering breath.

'Then don't,' I gasped. 'This hurts too much. I thought we'd have more time.' The suddenness of it winded me.

'I promise I will find a way for us to be together. I would tear the world apart to stay at your side.' He pressed a kiss to my forehead. 'Close your eyes.'

I let my eyes flutter close. Kaz gently kissed each of my eyelids. I scrabbled for his hand, wanting to hold onto him forever. But I couldn't find it. 'Wait,' I whispered, opening my eyes. 'Don't leave—'

The throne room was empty, the doors slowly closing.

CHAPTER FORTY-TWO

I sat at a long table of unfamiliar faces at my coronation banquet. As soon as I could, I slipped away to my bedroom. A shroud of loneliness fell over me. I stared out of the window at the old flag flying high, the one I'd sent the guards searching for to reinstate: red, with a golden dragon soaring across it. The dragon looked like Ogień, giving me another surge of loneliness; I missed Żar more than my heart could comprehend. I was the queen of Mazrovia, but I was alone again.

Staying up late, drinking a flute of sparkling wine by the light of a single lamp, I watched the last guests leave the castle, their carriages pulling away from the destroyed courtyard, their laughter and chatter fading.

I padded through the silent hallways until I reached my mother's old room, the one I'd given to Katia. Raising my hand to knock, I stilled. Whispers and giggles seeped out through the door, two voices I recognised well, twined together in a happiness I didn't care to interrupt. Smiling to myself, I returned to my own room, leaving Katia and Szafir to themselves.

*

Someone was inside my room.

Before I entered, I heard something scrabble along the floor. Drawing my favourite knife, I yanked the door open.

A crimson blur rushed towards me, knocking me off my feet with a delighted squeal.

'Żar?' I gasped, 'Is that really you?' The hatchling pushed his snout into my neck, huffing and sniffing my hair. I wrapped my arms round him, holding him tightly to myself. 'Gods, I missed you,' I cried. He wriggled happily, swinging his tail with contentment. Heaving us both up, I walked over to my window. I'd left it open, the silk curtains fluttering in the breeze. A terrible security risk, but I'd needed to feel the weather in my hair, taste the wind. I used to think that the forest was death. Now I knew it was life. Magic. Terrifying and wonderful all at once. I missed that wildness.

Ogień was hovering outside. 'Thank you,' I said. *'Thank you.'* Those sun-bright yellow eyes, old and wise, blinked in acknowledgement. He swerved to one side, showing me what lay behind him, congregated outside my bedroom window.

Dragons.

Not all that had been trapped in that cave, there were only a handful, but they'd returned. This was why I'd seized the throne, sat that crown on my head. I didn't realise I was smiling until my cheeks hurt.

An idea presented itself to me. I climbed up onto my windowsill. 'May I?'

*

Flying on dragonback through the tapestry of the sky felt like magic. The kind I'd always wanted to have, the fairytale magic of princesses and witches and castles and dragons. It was a star-swollen night, with constellations hanging like jewels. I stretched out my arms as if I were dragging my fingertips through the sky.

The Amber City vanished beneath me, the dawn gates and dragon hangers and castle the last to disappear. Soon, there were fields and country houses and farms. And then there was nothing but trees. Forest, as far as the eye could see. Stary Bór.

I ran my hands down Ogień's back. 'Take me to the forest demon,' I told him. 'Take me to the Forest Court.'

Ogień's leathery wings thumped through the air, carrying me deeper into the forest, to the place where ancient ruins tangled with great oaks and waterfalls. To the very top of the oldest oak, rising above the forest canopy. Where Kaz stood, watching over his territory. Waiting for me.

Ogień glided down, perching on the nearest branch. 'I can never thank you enough,' I told him, stroking behind his wing joint, where Żar loved to be fussed. The hatchling was currently asleep next to the fire in my bedroom, guarded by the rest of the dragons outside my window. Soon, I would return to him. Soon, I would rule over my queendom. Begin to unpick the tangled web of secrets and mysteries and magic my mother had left me. But, tonight, I belonged to the Forest Court.

Running down Ogień's tail, I fell into Kaz's broad arms.

'Home isn't the cottage or the castle,' I told him, searching his eyes. 'Home is wherever you are.' I rose on my toes and kissed him, sinking into his embrace, like I never had to leave.

THE END

ACKNOWLEDGEMENTS

Writing *Forest of Hearts* has been a dream come true for me and though it's been an immensely enjoyable experience, it wouldn't have been half as fun without all these wonderful people.

Thérèse Coen, I appreciate you each and every day! I'm so thankful you're my agent and friend, you're an absolute star.

Thank you to Yasmin Morrissey, who first approached me about *Forest of Hearts* and was an early champion.

Lucy Pearse, my brilliant editor, I'm not only grateful to have worked with you on this book, I also had the time of my life doing so! Your endless support, wisdom, and just the *best* comments left on my manuscripts always put a smile on my face.

Huge thanks to the incredible powerhouse of a team at S&S for supporting me and *Forest of Hearts*, especially Lowri Ribbons, Sophie Storr, Beth Robertson, Ellie Curtis and everyone at sales and international rights. A special shout out to Sean Williams and Alex Forrest for that stunning cover!

I appreciate everyone who has read and recommended my

books, it's because of you that I am here today. Special thanks to all those bookstagrammers, book bloggers, booktokkers, and booksellers, especially all the lovely people at Waterstones Nottingham, and Helen Tamblyn-Saville at Wonderland Bookshop.

Thank you to Jonathan Roberts, I don't know what I would do without you. Here's to all our future adventures. For Amy McCaw for always always being there for me. For Alicja Shellard, it's now weird to imagine a time when we weren't (happily) living in each other's pockets!

For Rory's Favourite Board Game Group (I've put it in writing now so it's canon), Rory Croucher, Ben Humphrey, Aidan Littlehales, Alicja and Jake Shellard, I've had the best time battling Eldritch horror, fighting for the Rebel Alliance, getting evil and stealing cheese from you all.

For Chelsea Harvell, Christine Spoors-Kenny, Jane Kelsey, Sarah Hackmann, Evangelos Palaiologou, Polis and Chris Louizou-Denyer, Vic James, Dandy Smith, Alex McGahan, Kat Dunn, Kate and Angus Weston, Rachel Greenlaw, my Shakespearean Sisters, all the brilliant authors in the Swaggers, and all my friends and family for all your friendship and support. (And little Luca cuddles.)

Forest of Hearts is the first novel I've written that explores my Polish heritage and there are so many childhood memories I've squirrelled within it, like mushroom-picking and terrible attempts at pierogi-making. Thank you to my mum for those, to my dad for encouraging my love of books, and my beloved babcia and dziadzio, who I miss every day.

Thank you to Jane and Chris Brothwood for being my second parents, I appreciate you so much.

For Michael Brothwood, my husband and favourite person, thank you seems too little for everything you do for me. I am endlessly grateful and hopelessly in love with you.

Lastly, I appreciate every one of you that has picked up this book! I hope you enjoy joining Elka's forest adventure and thank you for making this author's dreams come true.

ABOUT THE AUTHOR

M.A. Kuzniar spent six years living in Spain, teaching English and travelling the world which inspired her children's series, *The Ship of Shadows*. Her adult novels *Midnight in Everwood* and *Upon a Frosted Star*, were *Sunday Times* bestsellers. *Forest of Hearts* is her first novel for YA readers. She lives in Nottingham with her husband, where she spends her days reading, writing and playing board games. She can be found on @cosyreads on Instagram, where she makes the best hot chocolates.